THE DORVETHAN CONSPIRACY

THE DORVETHAN CONSPIRACY

BY HARRY F. REY

QueerSpace
New Orleans & New York

Published in the United States of America by
REBEL SATORI PRESS
www.rebelsatoripress.com

Cover image by DeKreator
Cover design by Sven Davisson

ISBN: 978-1-60864-401-8
eISBN: 978-1-60864-402-5

PROLOGUE: THE OTHER D-DAY

27 October, 1948
Tidworth, Wiltshire, United Kingdom
Population: 6,019

"This is the BBC from London."

Marsha dropped the knitting onto her lap as the announcer spoke through the wireless. Her heart skipped faster. It wasn't good. Not at her age. The station had been halfway through *The Marriage of Figaro* and the sitting room felt all too quiet without music. She thought about waking Frank who dozed in his chair in front of the softly crackling fire.

"Stay tuned for a special broadcast from Washington."

"Frank. Frank! Wake up." Both her husband and the basset hound at his feet stirred.

"What is it, woman?" He glanced at the old grandfather clock in the corner, ticking through the silence. "It's not time for tea already, is it?"

"Don't be daft. It's the news. Something's happened."

"About Berlin?"

"They didn't say."

"I wouldn't worry dear." He yawned and the dog followed suit. "Martin says they can keep the airlift going for years. Never mind what the Reds do."

They returned to a pregnant silence waiting for news on the radio, the kind that had occupied each day and every night during the war. They'd never quite known where Martin, their adopted son, was at any given time, only where he had been. North Africa. Sicily. Normandy. Anywhere there had been an Allied victory, a letter soon followed from Martin, from there, several weeks later. After the war, he'd come back to Wiltshire just long enough to get bored and head off to wherever the army sent him. And where they needed him was the most dangerous city on Earth. The pressure cooker, the ruined capital of a defeated empire, the playground of superpowers: Berlin.

Martin had come into their life late. He was sixteen and shaving when Frank found him freezing and huddled in the hold of an ocean liner pulled into the Bristol docks. But they loved him like the two sons they'd lost at the Somme. Back in those days, bad news had come by morning telegram, not broadcast into a sitting room. Every morning that her boys were abroad, she would watch the postman through the window as he made his rounds back and forth across the village square. The old church tower across from their cottage a constant reminder of the Lord's judgment. The old church grave-yard less a symbol of remembrance than a painful memory two of her boys were buried in some corner of a foreign field, not home, here in England. It was a sad thing to admit, but Marsha prayed Martin would find his eternal resting place just across the village green, in the old church graveyard, one day in the far distant future. When men walked on Mars.

The radio crackled and Marsha waited, knitting needles held in stasis while the dog clacked his tongue and the grandfather clock ticked, ticked, ticked down to the next nuclear bomb.

"Good evening. This is the BBC's Leonard Miall reporting from inside the Oval Office of the White House." The reporter spoke in something of a hushed whisper, as if crouched and under fire.

"I'm here surrounded by reporters from across the globe as we await a special presidential statement from Mr. Truman. The broadcasters crowded in this room were handed a sealed folder not thirty minutes ago by Mr. For-restal, the American Defense Secretary. We are barred from reporting the contents until the conclusion of Mr. Truman's speech, but I can tell you the folder is titled Disclosure Day."

More shuffling. Voices from overseas crackling across the wire-less. Marsha's heart was not beating fast but deathly slowly, as when she'd watched the postman mount her garden path in his slow march of death, double telegrams in hand.

"I'm told this is the largest simultaneous radio address ever made. This broadcast is being relayed on every possible wavelength as we await Mr. Truman... and here is the American President now."

A shuffling came. Several clicks and distant voices. A man

cleared his throat.

"*My fellow citizens of the world. What I, Harry S. Truman, am about to say is currently being relayed by Comrade Stalin, General De Gaulle, and President Chiang Kai-Shek in their respective tongues.*"

There was a pause as a man drank water. A glass rattled on the table. Papers rustled.

"*In July of last year, a Messenger came to us from another world. He came in peace. In fact, he came in friendship. His own vessel was damaged from a war beyond the stars, and he was in poor health. During his brief time on Earth, this Messenger shared with us many secrets of technology and science. But he also warned us of the grave dangers that lie beyond our world.*

"*Unfortunately, we were unable to save this heavenly being, his body too strange, and he succumbed to his wounds. But his warning is one we must heed. We are not the only beings in the universe. In fact, there are many, many more species spread across the galaxy. Some may be friendly. Others decidedly not. The Messenger left us with a warning. We must prepare to defend ourselves. If not, we will perish.*

"*The threat we face is far greater than Hitlerism or competition between great powers and our ideologies, as different as they may be. For the things we hold in common will always be greater than our divisions. Our families. Our humanity. And our one world. Today, we forge a new spirit of unity greater and deeper than at any other time, to face a challenge unlike any in our history. Today, we unite to secure our very survival.*

"*All members of the United Nations have agreed to the following resolutions. First, all armed conflict will cease effective immediately. Armies are to remain in their current positions until peaceful settlements have been reached. Second, all nations retain sovereignty over their own people. But for the purposes of planetary defense, we will act as one world through a new agency: United Nations Space Operations Command. Finally, all nations shall share in scientific advancement, which shall be used solely for the betterment, and the defense, of humanity.*

"*We do not yet know what dangers lie ahead of us, but we know one thing. The human race is at our best when we hold out the hand of friendship and cooperation. As we do so now on our own world, so we do to all peoples of all worlds. But we will never waver from our human values, nor from the defense of our ways of life. Now, let us rise to the challenge of our new space age, and may our Gods bless the United Nations of Earth.*"

CHAPTER 1: A WAKE IN THE WILTSHIRE VILLAGE OF TIDWORTH

Tidworth, Wiltshire, United Kingdom
Population: 12,863
Today

Tidworth hadn't seen such a hum of activity since the Reformation. Two dozen black limousines owned by various dignitaries from around the world—and the solar system—parked haphazardly across the village green and in front of the old church tower. It still stood as it had for centuries, always watching over the little cottage that had once been home to the Marlowe family. A steady stream of mourners in expensive black and military beige wade their way through the overgrown graveyard and across the cobbled lane to the thatched-roof cottage, to pay their last respects to the greatest man on earth, or off it.

"So sorry for your loss."

Marlowe shook the heavy man's hand. The fat Russian grabbed Marlowe's thin fingers like he was swinging at a county fair. Marlowe's already-lined brow furrowed deeper. Not so much in pain but from the discomfort of knowing that right beside him, Marlene was quietly smirking.

"Thank you, Ambassador."

Grunting like a steam train, he shuffled towards Marlene, crowding the cottage's narrow hallway and threatening some of the pictures on the wall. Marlene placed her dainty hand into the Ambassador's paw, her sliver of black skin against the Russian's rough hands pockmarked with red and brown.

"*Spasibo, Posol,*" Marlene repeated Marlowe's same words. His wife's Russian had always been flawless, and she never failed to show it off. The Soviet Ambassador nodded to them both and shuffled into the busying front room, where a grandfather clock struck a mid-morning hour.

"Christ," Marlene whispered as a new batch of mourners paraded past security and into the creaking cottage. "Half the Politburo is here." Marlowe studied the gray faces even the most avid news-watcher would barely recognize. Politicking and Kremlinology was yet another field Marlene could beat him in.

"Granddad was a peacemaker."

They smiled and nodded one *spasibo* after another, Marlene curtseying and nodding while Marlowe remained steadfast in his refusal to treat any mourner differently, regardless of their rank and status. As the Russian delegation filed into the sitting room for a very English wake, a boisterous American general in full military regalia came barging down the hall.

"Son, Martin was a helluva guy."

"Thank you, General Richards."

"A helluva guy. I worked under Martin back in the seventies, when Martian terraforming was just getting underway. By God did he know his stuff! There wasn't a space-faring engine he didn't know inside out. Not a single off-worlder he couldn't recognize by sight, back in those days, anyway. Helluva guy." Finally, the hands released. Marlowe slipped them by his side, gently wiping the General's sweat onto his mourning clothes. "Marlene! You've got some big shoes to fill. Martian settlement was his granddaddy's dream. Don't let us down."

"I plan not to." Her smile as fake as the hand that slipped obviously into Marlowe's, if only to avoid her own rough-and-tumble handshake.

"Ah, the UNSOC power couple. Martin and Svetlana were so proud of you two."

"Excuse me, general." That was about all the praise for his failed marriage Marlowe could take. He nodded a firm goodbye and glanced at an imaginary friend within a sea of strangers. Marlene was still attached to his arm and forced to walk away with him. "Can we get a drink?" Marlowe asked her quietly. Her answer wasn't a given, these days.

They stepped into the kitchen Marlowe remembered from the long summers of his childhood, before the dementia had taken hold. The old man—still spritely even in his seventies—buttering bread for chip sandwiches while looking up at the sky, telling the young Marlowe stories of discovering space. Of traversing the very edge of the solar system, powered by Messenger-tech invented by a mad English scientist that no one really understood but Doc Johnson. Raising up sunken battleships from the Pacific and melding them into space stations. Stepping foot on other worlds and gazing back at the blue earth through a telescope.

Now the sandwiches came in pre-made batches, covered in cellophane. A hired helper poured hot water into one of great-grannie Marsha's china tea pots and took it out to refill the mourner's cups. As soon as she left, Marlene cracked open a bottle of vodka, poured it straight into a long tumbler and handed it to Marlowe, the way she used to bring him two pills for his headaches.

"We'll need more than this to entertain the Politburo," Marlowe said, finding some comfort in the burning liquid.

"There's plenty. I told you, I took care of everything." She leaned against the sink, the sky behind her a wide blue. The brightness left her features a little blurry, but there were no ghosts left in this kitchen. The house sold long ago to a now-bankrupt developer to pay for Martin's care. Now it just stood unused, unlived in and uncared for. But Marlowe still had a key.

"I think I prefer your thing, what's it called?"

"Sitting Shiva."

"Yeah, let all those assholes come to me while I wail and cry from a wooden stool and tear my clothes."

"All right, Vladi. People are allowed to show emotion." She poured her own glass of vodka, then refilled his. "It's quite a turn-out. What with everyone so busy these days with the Open Space Treaty."

Marlowe shivered at the very words. He stalked the kitchen for a bitter moment, a fuming inside him that came out of nowhere.

"Oh yes, the thing he fought against all his life. Opening up space to commerce and migration while we put millions of off-worlder's lives at risk. No one cares about defending Earth from alien attack anymore. Half of this lot are a week away from their cushy new jobs. Presidents of Jovian gas farms and CEO's of asteroid mining outfits. Who's left in UNSOC? What's the point of us even existing if nobody gives a shit about the Messenger's warning anymore? Half of them want to make a buck. The other half think Roswell was a hoax, but will cash the checks anyway." He wiped his frothing mouth, hand shaking unexpectedly. Marlene remained steadily unmoved.

"Finished? Good. I'll try not to take that tirade personally. But I can assure you that Mars is not being sold off to anyone under my watch."

"Not yet."

"Why don't we focus on your grandfather today?" An arm patted his shoulder as a grade schoolteacher might comfort a thin-skinned child. "His impact. His legacy."

"It's buried under that church!" Marlowe felt his insides speed up, not slow down. The arm-patting only revved his motor. "He'd spin in his grave if he wasn't just getting used to the soil. You know General Richards took a job consulting for a casino? A casino! The Americans want to build a fucking casino on the Khrushchev-Kennedy Space Station."

Marlene handed him another glass of vodka. It started to help. To blunt the sharp edges of his indignity, of which there never seemed a convenient time to offload.

"At least he never knew about any of this."

"Yeah. At least he regressed to the mental capacity of a seven-year-old long before America and the Soviets sold out space to the highest bidder."

"Seven-year-old?" Marlene's face fell in horror. Marlowe immediately regretted the words. She seethed inside, and he suddenly felt like little more than a fool, clowning around about an immaterial death. Comparing it, even in the smallest way, to the greatest lost a couple could suffer through.

"I'm sorry, Marlene. I'm really, really sorry. It just was the first number I thought of." His words trailed off. They wouldn't be enough. Nothing would. She marched across the kitchen and grabbed her purse. He knew she held back a sea of emotion, applying dark lipstick to darker lips. Investigating the contours of her impossible beauty. Some moments, Marlowe's memory gave way, and he could see his wife in the same way the world did. UNSOC's most powerful Black woman. A force of nature. A rising star of the new generation of space leaders, shepherding the solar system through its greatest change since the Messenger crash-landed in Roswell, New Mexico. Of course, Marlowe had never been good enough for her. The experiment in a classless marriage was ending ignominiously.

"I've got to get back to Perth," Marlene said to her compact mirror.

"Of course." Marlowe poured his third vodka. "Thank you. I mean… thank you for coming."

Her smile came with a momentary delay. "What are UNSOC spouses for?"

"Will you see Charlie before he leaves for Alpha Centauri?"

"I imagine so. There's still some time."

"A week. With you being back in Australia—"

"It's a four-hour flight to New York, Vladi. I'll find the time." The compact and lipstick were returned to her bag. "I imagine you will."

"We were friends since the Academy. Long before I met you."

"Well, I suppose sharing a room with him trumps sharing a womb. So naturally his permanent departure to another star system will be a bigger blow to you than me."

"Okay, Marlene."

She did take one more thing from her bag. A blue UNSOC folder titled 'Decree of Divorce.' She handed it to him as firmly as she'd given him glasses of vodka.

"All we need to do is sign these now together and drop them off at HR." Marlowe snatched the folder. Marlene held out a pen. "Can we just get it over with already?"

"Knowing your lawyer he's added a couple more zeros."

"Can't we just sign now? It's the same basic deal."

"So, you're not denying your side has changed things?" They were down to fighting over kitchen goods and obsolete stereos at this point. The pettiness had engulfed them both and replaced sanity with a steadfast refusal to withdraw from the battlefield while there might be an inch of ground to gain.

"My side? You're the one who refused UNSOC mediation and

made us hire lawyers."

"Good thing I did, or I'd be paying alimony to a woman ten times wealthier than me." He highly doubted anything had changed. Nor would he pay for another round of checks from lawyers which had already drained several savings accounts. But at least Marlowe would not give her the satisfaction of signing the papers on her own terms.

"So we aren't signing today?"

"It's my grandfather's funeral, Marlene. Can I have a fucking day or two?"

Marlene took his snide remarks as cause enough to leave. Purse securely strapped across her shoulder pad, she affixed a vacant stare into the middle distance and marched out of the kitchen.

"Safe flight," Marlowe called after her, but she had already traversed the hallway and the loose Politburo members staggering around therein and left through the front door.

He'd felt supported by her presence at the funeral… for about the first five minutes. But they were several hours past the length of time either one could reasonably stand each other these days. Marlene had far more to risk from a public fracas than he did, even one half-whispered behind a fragile kitchen door. He poured another vodka, tapping his wedding ring against the glass, wondering when it would be time to release himself from so many promises neither one of them had any intention of keeping.

He thumbed newspapers on the kitchen table next to trays of triangle-cut sandwiches. Tuna and sweetcorn, egg cress, wafer-thin ham. That was the height of catering in this sleepy English village that had lost the last of its Marlowes. Yet even in this tiny corner of the English countryside, Charlie Novikov's grinning cheeks had made the front page. Marlene's brother shared her photogenic jaw line, space-black skin and presidential aura. Whether meeting the Politburo or shaking hands on the White House lawn, the Novikov's were a history-making bunch. Marlowe blinked away from the enlightened face of his old friend. He blinked with a flash of the sweaty breaths they'd shared since the dawn of time.

Marlowe had been sixteen when he joined the UNSOC Academy outside Moscow. A little younger than usual, but his illustrious pedigree secured a spot, and a mentor with UNSOC's most promising student, the enigmatic Charlie. They'd first met not in the small, cell-like room they shared, but in the basement shower room. Marlowe and Charlie spied each other deep within the Soviet steam pipes and communal showers of the UN space agency's training camp. Marlowe had just arrived from Luna. Charlie soaping off after a marathon gym session. Wordless glances. Teenage smiles. The quickest of shaking, breathless orgasms rushed out in minutes in case they were disturbed. All before they even knew each other's names. Or families.

Today, the papers heralded Charlie's forthcoming addition to the pantheon of human achievement. He leafed through the national press.

Charlie Novikov: Man's First Interstellar Ambassador.

First Manned Mission to Another Star Readies as Open Space Nears.

Alpha Centauri Settlement: UNSOC's Glorious Last Act.

Only the local rag cared to cover the funeral.

Tidworth Says Goodbye to UNSOC Founder, Father of the Space Age

"Excuse me, Criminal Inspector Marlowe?" Spoke a painfully posh English voice. Marlowe turned to see a slender gentleman dressed in funeral black slip into the kitchen, a leather briefcase by his side. "Vladimir Ilyich Marlowe?"

"Yes?"

"Roger Peterson, the executor of your late grandfather's estate." They briefly clutched hands.

"He had an estate? I thought fifteen years in a care home had bled him dry."

"There were a few... non-liquid assets. I understand you are leaving for Berlin shortly?"

Marlowe blinked. The man had done his homework. Or at the very least, had contacted UNSOC human resources.

"Yes. First thing tomorrow."

Peterson plopped the briefcase on top of Charlie's grinning newsprint face. Snapping it open, he handed Marlowe a thick set of crinkly-yellow papers. He thought for a moment they might be Martin's birth certificate, then vaguely remembered the half-told story that his grandfather had been found abandoned in an ocean steamer at the age of sixteen.

"Perfect time to give you this, then."

"What is it?" Marlowe flicked through the papers, some of which appeared to be legal contracts in typed German.

"What is it?"

"Deeds to a flat Mr. Marlowe took ownership of in the late forties."

"It wasn't sold for the care fund like this house?"

"It's in East Berlin."

"Ah."

"And there's something else. But it's a tad… indelicate, given your position." Peterson anxiously ran his hands on another file, a heavy brown envelope, but seemed unwilling to pass it over.

"Why? Is it a written confession?"

Peterson smiled weakly. He struggled with the decision for another moment but eventually passed Marlowe the hefty envelope.

"It's his diary. His personal diary."

Never knowing his grandfather to be the type, Marlowe tore open the envelope. Inside was a well-used, leather-bound journal. Loose papers poked out of the bindings like a hastily-packed suitcase. It smelled of good whiskey and cheap cigarettes. Without a doubt it had been owned by Martin Reginald Marlowe.

"He instructed this to be passed on to his descendants with the express condition that it must not, in any way, be deposited in the UNSOC archives. Nor should it, in any way, shape or form, be presented or shown to any UNSOC employee."

"That's a bit problematic since I work for—"

"Yes, that was taken into account. The will requires that you don't hand it over to any *other* UNSOC officials."

The intrigue took on another layer. Secrets were another thing Marlowe had never associated with his grandfather. No one had. His tenure at UNSOC, while long and epoch-making, had been marked by a brash openness and honesty about humanity's preparations, or lack thereof, for the coming invasion, as prophesized the Messenger. Everyone, from Marlowe's age and older, vividly remembered the rugged handsomeness and beleaguered, Al Capone-like drawl of Martin on their TV sets. Whether testifying before Congress in a black and white, cigarette in his hand, or sparkling with understated charm in a sit-down interview, the first and foremost UNSOC Director-General was known for his straight shooting. People still cited his quip to a reporter, after returning from the first manned mission to Venus: 'It's damn hot there, son.'

"I understand that your wife is still UNSOC, although once she takes up her new post—"

"Ex-wife." Marlowe continued to examine the diary. He dared to spy a few inside pages. Pages absolutely covered in minuscule handwriting. Notes, arrows, little sketches.

"Oh. I'm sorry."

"Don't be. And the Martian Settlement Authority is still a UNSOC agency. So she's out."

"My duty was to pass the last effects of Martin Reginald Marlowe on to his last living descendant. I... I know your family has suffered terrible tragedies, and you have my deepest sympathies."

Marlowe continued to study the diary, somewhat obnoxiously. He'd learned to filter out meaningless words of sympathy from perfect strangers. The writing on many of the pages was incredibly erratic. Sometimes small and delicate, with single entries running for several pages, back and front. Other entries were simply dates, places and populations. Roswell, New Mexico. New York. Moscow.

"Your grandfather was truly a great man. I am sorry for your loss."

"Yeah, thanks."

Peterson collected his things, nodded a curt goodbye, and left. Marlowe put away the diary and deeds. He'd worry about that later. Knocking back yet another shot of vodka, he prepared to slip back into mourner's duty, readying to introduce himself over and over again and his own grandfather's wake.

CHAPTER 2: PLEASE TURN OFF ALL DEVICES WHEN ENTERING EAST BERLIN

Checkpoint C, The East-West German Border, Berlin
Population (combined): 3,650,000
Today

Marlowe waited to pass through Checkpoint Charlie under a corrugated iron shack. Shuffling forward, stopping, shuffling forward. Rain on the roof provided an incessant, untuned clanging. An awful symphony of snare drums played by rabid monkeys. Enough to drive the sanest man mad. The border guards weren't in East German uniforms but Russian. Soviet soldiers inspecting bags and biometrics at the great fissure between East and West. One of the very few Earth-bound gaps in the Iron Curtain where things could slip in, or out.

"*Sleduyushchiy,*" the Soviet guard called out, beckoning the next one forward to a cold metal table, next to a cold metal officer. He would not let a soul pass into East Berlin without two thumb prints and an iris scan. Marlowe lifted his bag onto the table. He took out keys from his trench coat pocket; not for his own place but for his grandfather's house in East Berlin, the same keys the solicitor had given him yesterday in London. Beside them he placed his vape pen, and his cell phone. Turned off, as was the protocol when UNSOC staff entered any Soviet zone of control. On Earth or off it. The Russians could confiscate his equipment, and had, but they'd never turn on without Marlowe's biometrics. They could steal all the fingerprint data they wanted. His phone was encrypted with Messenger-tech.

"Papers, please," said the Russian, spitting out *please*. A heavy accent lingered, along with the stench of too much cheap aftershave. He must meet a thousand people a day, Marlowe thought, sliding a hand into the pouch of his bag. The soldier's eyes dropped down to his passport, but Marlowe focused on the soldier's crotch. Close. One hand away. Where other men dropped to their knees at the sight of a bottle, or cash, or coke, Marlowe would do it for a man. Any man. He didn't care. Not anymore. He flicked the gold band around his wedding finger and handed the Russian the pale blue UNSOC passport. Their eyes met. As eyes across a locker room. The guard knew where Marlowe had been looking.

"That won't be necessary," Marlowe said to the superior officer holding the biometric scanner in anticipation of another set of fingerprints stolen for Moscow. "Diplomatic immunity."

The officer grunted but lowered the biometric scanner. Instead, he took a cursory glance at the photograph page of the passport held open by the soldier.

He was called Vladimir Ilyich Marlowe in that international co-operative style popular at the height of *perestroika*, when every Reagan Democrat drank vodka and called their kid Sasha or Anastasia. The trend had been popular on the other side of the Wall, too. Marlowe had met plenty of Russians of his generation named Dick Abramovich or Nancy Medvedev. Another meaningless token to the *one-world*-ism that these days was a mocking point of derision; no longer seen as a necessity to save humanity. No one was getting into space without a working knowledge of English and Russian anyway, along with six weeks of gravity training, a foundation course in software engineering and a certificate in Galactic Marxism. The spirit of Disclosure Day still just about alive, but hooked up to life support. The pumps and monitors all plugged into a single electrical strip wrapped in tape and sparking dangerously.

The officer glanced at Marlowe's unzipped bag. Marlowe held it open for him, showing the switched off pad, the blue UNSOC folders marked *Confidential* and the thin manilla envelope containing the last will and testament of his grandfather, divorce papers served by his wife, the deeds to an unknown address in East Berlin, and the leatherbound diary. Perhaps holding some clue as to what Martin Reginald Marlowe had left for his grandson across the Wall in East Berlin.

"*Sleduyushchiy,*" the Soviet soldier shouted, snapping the world back to life. He was satisfied Marlowe wasn't smuggling illegal pads or sim cards in his bag. The soldier beckoned the next one forward. A woman in a raincoat slapped her damp umbrella onto the cold metal table before Marlowe had even lifted off his vape. The young guard gave him a precious moment to collect his things before beginning the inspection of the woman, and for that Marlowe was grateful. In the few bare inches between them, hot breath mingled inside the drafty guard hut. A switch of scents. Marlowe's and the guards. Unseen by anyone but them. The guard's skin under his stiff collar flushed as red as the badges on his lapel. *Why so nervous?* Marlowe might have asked. His eyes stayed on Marlowe. Round and brown and bursting, but his thin lips remained firmly shut, sealed, prickled with blueish stubble Marlowe could imagine rubbing against his own skin. He transmitted those exact thoughts to the guard with a simple, casual smile.

"*Dosvidaniya,*" said Marlowe, lifting his bag from the table as the annoyed woman hurled her wet things down. "*Uvidimsya snova,*" he added with a bare whisper. *See you again,* then he walked straight toward the sign by the door on the left. Written in English, Russian, and French, with a small line of German at the bottom.

You are leaving the American Sector.

"Willkommen in der DDR, mein Herr," the barman said, grinning widely at the only customer in the glass-fronted lobby of the Clara Zetkein People's Hotel. The empty, refurbished building with the Wall at its back wasn't so much a hotel but a co-working space for the world's intelligence services, fully serviced and monitored by the Stasi. Spies tipped, and the barman offered his welcome. But Marlowe wasn't a spy.

"UNSOC discount?" Marlowe asked, flashing his pale blue passport to the waistcoated man who suddenly lost his smile.

"I can give you Rondo coffee," he said, ripping open a cheap paper packet of the East German staple. "There are no buns for you today."

Marlowe shrugged, elbows resting on the polished brass bar. If he was CIA, MI6, even BND, there would be no end of coffee roasts from Havana or Caracas or Ganymede on offer. But he would be whisked away to HVA headquarters soon enough for their review of the latest space-based miscreants due to be deported back to Earth. The East German intelligence service was not just the most effective in the Communist world after the KGB, but had the best coffee of any spy agency, collectively farmed in hydroponic pods on Jupiter's moon Io.

Marlowe stared at life on the street as he sipped bitter brown. It was disorientating after a few months in the West. There were no luminous billboards. No flashing taxicabs splashing adverts for shows or clubs or cell phones. The only thing close to a commercial was a sign in a GSM-SIM store window across the street. The German was a bit hard to understand, but it seemed to offer 100 minutes free per month to any phone number in the Warsaw Pact. Ordinary men in long coats and women with their hair in plastic wrapping ventured quickly through the break in the rain. They walked with simple black umbrellas or netted grocery bags stuffed with potatoes. Men in hats waited patiently for the little green traffic light man to cross the street with rolled up newspapers under their arms. No one zipped by on e-scooters or had headphones bolted to their ears while flicking through a smartphone. Not in the East. Marlowe's vape pen had more tech in it than most ordinary East Germans would see in a lifetime.

With the Wall at his back, Marlowe looked east. From here he could travel straight to Moscow and the city's own UNSOC campus, second only to HQ in New York in size and importance. Moscow hosted the Academy where cosmonauts and generations of space officials were trained. Two poles on a spinning planet, with Berlin the bridge between them. Perhaps in the early 50s, when the foundations of the first off-Earth city were being laid under the Lunar surface and cosmonauts were still exploring the limits of Messenger technology, Berlin had been at the center of things. Today, it was more like an overgrown fence between two plots of land, when both families had long since moved on from a forgotten feud.

Just before the 1993 coup that removed Gorbachev as party leader, he'd given a speech on newly terraformed Mars. The image seared into a young Marlowe's memory, the Soviet premier standing next to Clinton on a grassy knoll under a Martian sky which back then still had a strong tinge of red. They were celebrating forty years of the Mars Treaty; painstaking work building a breathable atmosphere, planting an ecosystem, injecting life into a long-dead world. The two leaders removed their oxygen masks, breathing natural air, gazing across the sparkling green vista beginning to sprout plant life all on its own. The two men laughed with each other as Martian-born flies went wild over new visitors to their environment, these two sweaty politicians and the cadre of officials and journalists following. Marlowe had watched it laying on his grandfather's carpet, sucking dry a carton of chocolate milk. The words Gorbachev spoke were not the usual propaganda Soviet leaders used to talk about the solar system. Absent were the standard lines about the space-faring proletariat inevitably overthrowing the capitalist-industrial complex exploiting their labor. A lecture on Galactic Marxism wasn't on Gorbachev's mind as he and the youthful Clinton wandered around the new Eden humanity had nurtured with the help of Messenger-tech. Gorbachev simply said: *"In space, in the stars, in these other worlds, we have no need for walls."*

In that moment, the world had never been closer to forging ahead in the spirit of combined human endeavor that had once birthed UNSOC, so the young Marlowe remembered the newscasters saying. Families crowded at the border gates of East Berlin, desperate to be reunited with their loved ones in the West. Not since Roswell and The Messenger's warning had the endless battle between communist and capitalist systems seemed as pointless as now. Marlowe had not been the only one to believe that back then, they stood on the precipice of a future very different to the one they lived in now.

But the order to open the Wall never came. By the time Gorbachev returned to the Kremlin, the Politburo had voted to put a bullet in his brain.

The barman silently refilled Marlowe's cup with the bitter, East German coffee. The sun was sliding away again. A dirty green Trabant burned unnecessary diesel outside the hotel. Someone so careless had no need for fuel rations. There was a man in the driver's seat. His silhouette read a newspaper while wearing a hat that obscured his face. This man was most likely Marlowe's Stasi tail. The HVA weren't due to pick him up for another twenty minutes. Marlowe snorted tasteless vapor from his nostrils as he realized the Stasi man was more likely there to tail the HVA agents. Behind him, the hotel lobby chairs remained undisturbed. Free of both dust and life. Hermetically sealed, disinfected, yet highly monitored for the lab rats dumb enough to find themselves inside the Clara Zetkein People's Hotel. A sign on the wall beside bookshelves full of Marxist theory said, in hand-written letters: *Wi-Fi. Free!* An unsophisticated attempt to invade the devices of anyone naive enough to turn their phone on in East Berlin.

Whether in a UNSOC locker room after midnight or any number of public toilets on Earth or off it, Marlowe could easily spot hungry eyes on him. Here, the feeling was the same, but with no eyes visible. Perhaps they came from the other side of the long mirror on the back wall, or a hundred tiny cameras placed on every bottle cap behind the bar. Marlowe sensed every breath exhaled from his body was being scanned, analyzed, and reported on to a gruff commander in a military cap. With the Stasi outside and the HVA on their way, this morning's brunch was missing only one more guest.

Martin Reginald Marlowe. He slipped his grandfather's leather-bound diary from the bag and began to flick through the handwritten scrawl. It began in a bombed-out Berlin in 1947, before there was an east or west. Before even Roswell had been made public. Marlowe both grinned and grimaced at his grandfather's legendary first encounter with his grandmother; two spies, from east and west, duking it out in a post-war, pre-Roswell world. *'The broad stared at me from across the bombed-out bar... a gun nestled between them tight thighs. She flicked aside red hair—'*

"Mind if I join you?" A red-haired woman slipped into the seat beside Marlowe. He slammed the diary shut, wondering for a moment if the woman was real or had been conjured from his grandfather's past. Her lips were painted a dark purple, almost black, in the manner of a vampire attempting to hide their blood-stained mouth. Her accent was international chic, her perfume of the same vintage. She draped a silky beige suit jacket across the bar stool on the other side while her shimmery blouse danced in the faint strings of sunlight breaking through the cloudy sky. Marlowe didn't react to the question. She'd already sat down. The barman brought her a cup of hot water, and a teabag sealed in the packet. Of course, the barman knew what she drank. This place was little more than a KGB canteen. She made sure Marlowe was watching before she ripped the packet open with as much delicacy as a condom package in a dirty restroom.

"Can I borrow a light?" She slipped an extra-long from a pewter holder and toyed with it.

Marlowe lifted his stubby black vape, shrugged and took a puff.

"Sorry," he said, enjoying her ruffled reaction to his disinterest. "Cigarettes are bad for you."

"You westerners." She flicked open her matching silver lighter and took a long puff. The purple lipstick was less a fashion choice than a crude attempt to disguise a mouth deeply lined and worn out from a lifetime of service to Mother Russia.

"UNSOC, ma'am. Not a westerner. Not an easterner."

"So, your imperialism extends beyond Earth's orbit." She blew out cloudy blue smoke that Marlowe did not miss the scent of at all. She glanced at the Stasi agent in the Trabant just as he had, but didn't seem bothered. Every jungle has its hierarchy.

"We operate under the auspices of the United Nations Planetary Security Council. Our mission is to protect humanity—"

"Free from Earthly conflict, to ascribe to higher ideals of yada yada yada. Have you ever seen a student loan snuffed out like that?" She snapped her fingers. "Medical debt?" Marlowe did nothing but suck on his vape. "We don't have such things east of the Wall, and we're always happy to extend the benefits of socialism to those in financial difficulty."

"My, you don't even know my name." They smoked with two half grins. She watched him. He drank the awful coffee, but she did not touch her tea. Stunningly beautiful women often reacted this way to Marlowe's disinterest. She stared at the golden band around his wedding finger.

"Darla Foster." She held out her hand.

"I'm sure you are." He shook it, but not before checking for a sharp needle on her rings.

"Criminal Inspector Marlowe."

"A pleasure, Herr *Kriminaldirector*."

He bristled at the subtle association Foster made between his job and that of the Gestapo. Soviets loved to question any authority that wasn't their own.

"Have the UNSOC budget cuts hit your department yet? I hear there's talk of a revolt by workers in the Jupiter sector if they don't settle the pay dispute soon. And another wave of strikes on the Khrushchev-Kennedy Space Station next week. Don't tell me you aren't also looking for other employ?" She tapped her cigarette into a heavy ashtray, enjoying every word she said.

"What a way to flirt with a man." Marlowe tired of this game. "If you're looking for someone to bribe, might I suggest hanging out at *La Belle* across the Wall?"

She lifted her skirt above the knee to show the place where her stocking should be, but she wasn't wearing any.

"You're still a man, aren't you? Even if you are soon to be out of a job. I have a room upstairs. Women on this side of Berlin care for Western morals as much as UNSOC cares for your pension." She looked at his wedding ring in a more obvious way and stubbed out the cigarette in anticipation.

"Another coffee please, bar keep." That message spat in her face. He'd rather drink East German coffee than take up her offer of casual sex. She sighed, not personally offended but professionally. From her coat pocket she slipped out a crisp white card and scratched words down before sliding it across the bar. She'd written her *nom de jure* above a printed phone number and an email address in typical Russian style. A string of numbers @*space.su*

"HVA will be along to pick you up in three minutes," Foster said, speaking in a whisper and repeatedly clicking her spoon against the teacup for some basic audio interference. Of course she knew exactly who he was. No one crossed into East Berlin unknown. "I'm setting up a special operations bureau." She gave the barman a death glare until he found cause to go and clean the sparkling tables in the lobby. "And I need your help."

"I assume the People's Commissariat for Space Affairs can send a request to the Politburo who can instruct the ambassador—"

"Cut the shit." The poor barman had deigned to return to take his cloth but stopped dead. Foster snatched her cup and flung it across the carpet.

"I'll just go fetch the wetvac."

They waited in suspended animation until he returned with the contraption grunting loudly on the floor.

"There's things going on out there," she said quietly as the machine whirred. She watched the door for Marlowe's escort. "Things you don't understand and things I don't either. And believe me. I'm the best."

"I have no doubt."

"Call me if you come across any suspicious activity. I'll be waiting."

"What kind of suspicious?" He fingered the card but was distracted by three burly men in leather jackets entering the hotel lobby. They spotted their escort in a second. Marlowe turned as if they might be looking for someone behind him, but Darla Foster was already gone.

The silent car whisked him toward Tempelhof. They'd already breezed through the checkpoint thanks to UNSOC plates. He'd be on the plane in an hour. In New York in three. Another full day lay ahead. The nighttime thrill of New York City still too long away. He sucked on the vape, but the scent of Darla Foster's cigarette lingered on his clothes. And her words on his mind. What constituted suspicious in a world coming apart at the seams? A cigarette would do him good right about now. He suddenly regretted that his wife had made him give up the real thing. Many real things.

He checked the meager contents of his bag: HVA's prisoner repatriation forms, the diary, the lease, and the most precious thing in there. Divorce papers. They only needed Marlene's signature, to be dropped off at UNSOC HR, and both their biometrics would be updated. Married to divorced. He'd no longer have that damn morality clause hanging over his head, the subtle threat UNSOC used to keep their married employees in line. His life would change, or at least the pressure would be lifted with something as simple as the checking of a box on an HR form.

At least the Lufthansa flight wasn't busy. Few people but spies, Deejay's and UNSOC employees flew out of West Berlin. Marlowe flicked through English *Pravda* headlines on his pad as they soared through the blackness of the upper atmosphere.

Four Politburo members to attend Alpha Centauri launch next week.

Tensions rise in Armstrong as Open Space Treaty offers promise of Lunan independence.

Karla Landers launches GOP primary bid with promise to abolish UN-SOC.

CNN had a rather different take.

Karla's pledge to Make Earth Great Again and open space for even more mining

Since it was CNN, Marlowe barely finished scanning the headline before ads swarmed the page.

Is there oil on Mars? Invest today and find out! Limited drilling permits selling fast.

Current events were about as depressing as being a landlord in a communist economy. Marlowe flicked the image closed of Karla Landers, the smiling blonde and would-be autocrat in a red cap, and stared out the Lufthansa window instead. Up above, the lunar city of Armstrong twinkled on the moon's face while the hulk of space junk known as the Khrushchev-Kennedy Station sank beneath the western horizon. The stewardess brought coffee. She asked with a wink if he wanted sugar. *It makes life sweeter, honey.* Then she got annoyed as he waved her way, not once looking up from the Russian language *Journal of Lunarology* article he was now trying to decipher. Marlene's language skills had always been far superior to his own. She was an exolinguist by training, after all. It made sense a woman who spent her life studying the alien language of The Messenger could so easily master Russian as to make Dostoevsky read like an *Asterix* comic.

"Now landing at Robert F. Kennedy Interplanetary Airport. Please remember to take all your belongings. We wish you a pleasant onward journey."

"Goodbye now, Goodbye." The stewardesses smiled and nodded as the passengers filed out. The *sugar, honey* one lingered a little longer on Marlowe. She shimmied her shoulders, hoisted up her skirt and bit her bottom lip in a signal as clear as a red-hot phone ringing in the Pentagon.

"Goodbye, sir. Have a wonderful day."

Marlowe nodded, rebuffing her advances one last time. He'd had enough spies coming onto him for one day. Then he was into the cold air of a New York morning.

He carried no luggage but waited at the conveyor belt anyway. He liked to see who had come off the plane. An old bit of anti-espionage protocol most UNSOC staff had long forgotten. Back from the days when the KGB and CIA played UNSOC staff like slot machines, not the four-dimensional chess Darla Foster had inflicted with her white cards and *special investigation bureau*. But still Marlowe waited in arrivals, noting the faces who'd been on his flight.

Another man alone also waited. Their paths had briefly crossed when Marlowe had walked to the back of the plane for the bathroom. The man was young and handsome and wore a slightly disheveled checkered shirt and a knitted tie. He'd been reading a paper magazine held up to eye line and drinking a Diet Coke; one Western treat Russians who travelled were obsessed with. The man read a French magazine. Blue eyes, but dark hair. Sallow, unshaven skin. Perhaps an ethnic Kazakh or a Baltic with a long nose. His eyebrows thick and bushy, suggesting a furry chest Marlowe was more than partial to on a man. A slight bulge in the crotch, but perhaps from his long legs tight against the economy class seat. Marlowe had thought about that crotch in the plane bathroom as he took a leak and stared up at Armstrong blinking from the yellow and white Lunar surface. Great patches of sunflower farms carved Earth's satellite like continents. He'd had the best sex of his life in the hidden tunnels of the lunar city. In its dark corridors. Public restrooms with bulbs unchanged since the seventies. As soon as the divorce was entered into the UNSOC HR system, he would go back for one last hurrah before Luna changed forever. Then he wouldn't care who caught him.

Now here the man from the plane was again, waiting patiently for his luggage. A fresh Diet Coke in his hands. A candy bar too. Or at least the wrapper. Quickly finished and dropped into a clear plastic trash can with the end of the Coke can. An academic, Marlowe considered as he leaned against a barrier under a no-smoking sign. He took a quick puff from the vape, watching the man slide hands into his pockets. Heavy boots painfully mismatched to his jacket. Some regional professor quietly enamored with the decadent West. What other dalliances might he be game for?

Marlowe made an approach. He strode forward, right up to the conveyor belt and a frilly patterned suitcase doing the rounds. He walked with the moving belt while making a show of checking the tag. *Clearly not mine* he indicated with a shrug to the Russian academic with the French magazine rolled under his arm. The Russian nodded back with a polite grin and an empathetic shrug as one would when confronted by a stranger in an airport.

Marlowe seized the space next to the man to continue waiting close beside him. Marlowe rolled back on his heels and drew a long, low whistle with his lips. He spun the switched off phone in his fingers, just to demonstrate he *wasn't* from the Communist world. The suitcases were dwindling, the people leaving to the exit and New York City beyond. Marlowe saw the man's eyes flick to a coming black suitcase. More of a large carry-on. This was his. The man's muscles flexed as he was about to move, but Marlowe beat him to the punch. He snatched the name on the tag. Sergei Moscowitz.

"Excuse me," the man said in such neutral, international English Marlowe suddenly questioned everything he thought he knew about the stranger. "But I think that's mine."

"Oh hell, you're right. So sorry, pal. Here. Let me help." Marlowe lifted it from the belt and stood it upright, hoisting the handle too. "Here you go."

"Thanks."

"Want me to watch it while you use the restroom?"

Sergei blinked. It was an odd question, but Marlowe retained a sincere smile. Eager, broad.

"That's all right."

"Have a good trip," Marlowe said, immediately striding to the bathroom. He didn't turn to look back. The quest for his own bag clearly abandoned. That's what the man would be wondering right about now. Why all the fuss, the shrug, the eye contact with a stranger, and march off to the bathroom without a case? Without a worry.

Marlowe stared at himself in the bathroom mirror, lips stretched wide over his teeth, tongue playing with an imaginary seed. All three stalls were empty. Marlowe had already checked. His heart skipped when the door swung open. Sergei. Wheeling his suitcase, seeing Marlowe standing over the sink, bag over his shoulder, batting away at an imaginary nothing in his teeth. They locked eyes through the mirror. Marlowe abandoned the seed as quick as he had the suitcase. He walked straight to the last cubicle, opened the door, and cast a firm look straight back at Sergei. No smile. Plain, straightforward. He let the door slam on its own. Then bang open, but it didn't fall closed. The stranger called Sergei was standing there. No smile either, but breathless expectation. He wheeled his case in first, then himself and locked the door. Marlowe was already crouched. The man unzipped.

Marlowe peeled down the waistband of the man's underwear through his zipper. Russian letters stitched inside. Marlowe glanced up. The man was already leaning back, eyes closed. Expectation became a choking reality that Marlowe sucked down with glee, as if it was his last night before blasting off to settle Alpha Centauri with no way home.

It was all over in a gargled minute. Marlowe bounced back up, kneecaps crackling as he unzipped his own trousers in reciprocal expectation. A hand inside, Marlowe solicited his mouth toward Sergei's rough lips, but the Russian swerved away. He zipped himself up and offered the slightest smile in awkward thanks. The cubicle door banged closed. Marlowe, alone, wiped useless saliva from his lips, then removed his hand from his now shrinking crotch and fumbled for his vape and sucked in a soothing lungful. Secret stalls were not the place to find closeness, he reminded himself. He fingered his wedding ring, sucked on the vape, and waited the requisite minute to let the strange, international-accented Russian named Sergei slip into airport obscurity.

CHAPTER 3: MAY OUR GODS BLESS THE UNITED NATIONS OF EARTH

Marlowe's cab pulled up outside of the UN building on the Lower East Side. He'd passed the journey deciphering some of Martin's handwritten scrawl. Entries from the strange days when he and Marlow's future grandmother Svetlana had been whisked from Berlin to New Mexico, and confronted with the Earth-shattering sight of the dying Messenger and its damaged craft, and the strange symbols all the scientists in the world had been brought to Roswell to decipher. To read the first-hand account of the early days of a new world which was now withering away before his eyes filled Marlowe with more sadness than the funeral. With Darla Foster's card, he marked the diary at an entry from '48 when Doc Johnson started experimenting with Messenger-tech, and stepped back into reality.

The sky wore a gray face and blew with a brisk chill. Clouds moved quickly across the East River, obscuring Brooklyn and a jet soaring into the stratosphere on its way to the moon. Earthly flags flapped pointlessly in the wind. Ensigns of the USSR, Imperial India, the Republic of China. Marlowe had never understood why people still clung to countries and colors. When the alien empires launched their inevitable attack on the Earth as The Messenger had prophesized, those nightmarish creatures would not stop at invisible lines drawn in the sand.

The entryway to the United Nations was through a prefab annex building, the kind that should have been temporary but had fallen into permanence. Strip lights flickered overhead, and a noisy aircon blew chilled air despite the edges of winter seeping in through temporary walls. The signs written in the languages of the great powers who'd defeated the Nazis and declared an international peace when

The Messenger arrived. It had held this long, the post-Messenger consensus, but decay was everywhere. Marlowe splashed through a patch of water on the ground. Origin unknown.

There was life in these corridors, though. Like the kind that proliferated in the underground tunnels snaking out from Penn Station or Armstrong or a mine in The Maelstrom. Dropped coins, chipped tiles, coffee stalls and disused crates for benches; whole days could be lived outside of the sun. UNSOCers were used to that life. The native Lunans were practically more vole than human. When on Earth, they got anxious when the wind blew, or a bug buzzed nearby. Kids born on Khrushchev-Kennedy simply withered under natural light. God knows which UNSOCers they expected to thrive on Mars with its terraformed meadows, crystal-clear rivers and undiluted air. Everyone qualified to be in space feared nature more than the alien invasion.

Three women in UNSOC-blue jumpsuits marched past him discussing data on their pads. Two Soviet officers in brown uniforms and red star hats laughed with an Algerian wearing French Fourth Republic gray next to a coffee stand. A Lunan sitting cross-legged on a chair behind a divider inspected his biometrics. Native Lunans were easy to spot. Polished skin untouched by natural sun, and always crunching on sunflower seeds. Short blue hair, naturally, and a little pin on their chest stating pronouns in English and Russian: *They/Them/они.*

"Welcome home, Inspector Marlowe," they said, handing back his passport with a cursory smile.

Marlowe shook off the sunflower seed dust. *Home.* What a concept. His step quickened as the linoleum of the annex hall gave way to marble of the main building. He held his bag like a briefcase and sucked on the vape, blowing scentless smoke into the air as he took in the grand entranceway of the main building. Ambassadors, commissars, and their staff clicked booted heels across green marble. A group of eager-faced, blue-suited cosmonauts in training gathered by the entrance, shown the bedazzled star-map on the ceiling by a guide. New recruits. Marlowe had stood in their place once. Gazing up in wonderment at the infinite stars of the galaxy map painted on the ceiling. Another gift from The Messenger. Marlene had stood in this very spot beside him once. Two raw rookies on their way to great things across the frontiers of the solar system. Their eyes had met as they stared at the biggest thing in the UN foyer. The gigantic, silver statue of The Messenger. Big beady black eyes gazing up from an elongated forehead, the crashed ship behind him. One thin finger carved in gold touching the hand of a twice-as-tall human (modelled after Martin), leaning down to offer humanity's hand of friendship. *Roswell, New Mexico, July 7, 1947* was etched around the epic statue's base. Above the scene of interstellar friendship were silver spirals and orbs, half-moons and ringed planets, the grandness of space carved in silver and gold. Ringing that, forty feet above the ground, the immortal words of Harry S. Truman carved in the many languages of the one world: *May Our Gods Bless the United Nations of Earth.*

He tried as much as could to stand in this space and be inspired, as he once had been. To recall the fresh scent of wonderment, before the stench of reality of life in space. Sweat and oil and recycled air. But that had been a long time ago. Now remained only the foul tang of corruption. Planets sold off for politics. The Open Space treaty nothing more than an armed assault on the foundations of this building, the undoing of seventy years of international cooperation from here to the heliopause. Marlowe felt sick.

The current US Administration had brought capitalism and democracy to space, apparently. The Soviets received interplanetary trade unions and a solar proletariat to organize in return. The East and West bringing their century-old conflict to the stars through smiles and handshakes. The rights to settle the new Eden that was Mars thrown to the highest bidder like so much red meat to a pack of starving dogs. The Soviets rubbed their hands with glee over the prospect of sparking a revolution among the proletarian kennels. Raucous and stinking.

Yet UNSOC went about its business as if its reason for being wasn't days away from death. Marlowe watched groupings of hatted heads gather on the marble floor, another statue in the mausoleum of a life now ending. *Adapt* and *change* were the watchwords of UNSOC after Open Space. Yet Marlowe hadn't seen a lick of contrition in the eyes of the men and women at his grandfather's funeral. They didn't appreciate the obviousness of the irony. Burying the first director-general of UNSOC as the institution itself was

[28]

poised to be entombed under an open, democratized solar system. UNSOC was far too pompous to read the writing on the wall and either adapt or change.

Marlowe blew out a puff of vape smoke and twisted his face in disgust at the bitter taste. Or he needed a new vape filter. If he'd been a touch nicer to Darla Foster, he could have taken one of her real cigarettes and stubbed the butt on the marble floor with a new job in his back pocket too. No doubt those who spent more time in this building than he had already lined up new jobs with the new Lunar transitional government, Martian Settlement Authority or the boards of American asteroid mining operations. He was the only fri-er still collecting one paycheck. He passed a woman with a beehive hairdo puffing on an extra-long and holding a paper cup of coffee. He could ask her for a cigarette. Light it up, stub it out across the way. Then his boss would smell it. Cigarette stains stayed on clothes the way other vices slid down throats, swallowed away like noth-ing. One debauched habit was enough, he decided, as he marched straight across the marble floor to his office in the Commissariat for Criminal Investigations.

"CCI, freeze," Marlowe said, bursting through the thin door so hard it shook the glass panel and barely covered blinds. The old, yellowed man behind a desk of old, yellowed papers wheezed in shocked surprise, before falling into a full-chested laugh that only came from forty years of smoking unfiltereds.

"Marlowe, you son-of-a-bitch." Commissar Jack Donahue rose to his feet. He chewed on nothing and spat into a trashcan like the New York cop he'd been since birth. Lower East Side Irish blood ran through his veins despite the brass nameplate written in Russian and English. "How the fuck is East Berlin these days, huh?"

"I owe a couple years' salary in repairs and fees on a secret apart-ment Martin had that I can't sell or rent." Marlowe sat opposite on a hard wooden chair, staring blankly at the files stacked high.

"At least she didn't take that."

"Wish she had."

From his bag, Marlowe pulled out the folder of repatriation pa-pers he'd signed at the HVA meeting and flung them onto the pile stacking up in Donahue's in-tray. "Anyway, we have a problem.

HVA doesn't want them."

"Who?"

"This round of detainees."

"Huh? Not any of them?"

"Nope, not a one." Marlowe sucked on the vape to hold the flutter of nerves at bay. "Schaub went on some rant about *the illegitimacy of the imperialist…* something or other. You know their crap."

"What the hell does he want us to do with them?" Donahue opened the folder to the single sheet Marlowe had hastily drafted on the flight; tracing signatures scrawled on practically see-through paper.

"Dunno," Marlowe vaped. "Says we can transfer them to the new Lunan government for all he cares. Guess Moscow told him to fill up as many Armstrong holding cells as he could. That's sixteen less spaces to hold Soviet-backed insurrectionists when the Lunan Collective of Workers and Scientists starts shooting everything in sight in a couple of days."

"The slimy bastard. And why in the hell did they decide to give every fucking rock and asteroid independence at the same God-damn time? We're stretched as thin as it is. Agents Johnson and Gennadievich found a stash of *projectile* weapons on Khrushchev-Kennedy. *Projectiles.* Bullets. Those Commie bastards. Do they think a space station the size of fucking Long Island *won't* hit Russia if it falls to Earth?" Marlowe sat back in the stiff chair while Donahue riled himself into a predictable lather. "I mean, fucking hell, Marlowe. What kinda chump does Schaub take me for? The KGB are sending grenades to the Juno gas fields. *Grenades*, Marlowe. On fucking Jupiter. They'll light the whole God-damn planet up like the Fourth of July. Morons! What have they told Schaub to do, drill holes in Armstrong's oxygen tanks?"

"Guess the DDR isn't too bothered if Earth has no tide. Not got much of a coastline, do they?"

"Too fucking right." Donahue slid a cigarette from the carousel on his desk between his lips, but didn't light it. "I ain't got the asshole for this anymore, kid."

"I can liaise with S-Nine if you want?" Marlowe offered a hand to take the folder — and burden — from Donahue. "We'll tell them due to the sovereignty transition, it's against protocol to detain those individuals without a valid Earth-bound extradition request. Tell them just to give each detainee with an off-world travel token to anywhere in the system. Let them go work in The Maelstrom mines or a hydroponic farm on some moon."

"Good thinking. Best to just let them all go. Get them off our back." Donahue returned the forged paper to its folder and handed it back to Marlowe, who immediately slid it back into his bag between the scrunched up genuine orders he was desperate to shred and incinerate already. "Thanks for dealing with this one, kid. I tell ya."

"Anytime, sir." Marlowe vaped, which reminded Donahue to light his cigarette. It seemed to calm him. "Any update on my request?" Marlowe remained as still as he could. He knew the question could light a raging fire quicker than a box of grenades on Jupiter.

"Which one?" Donahue said with a slight grin that made it clear he'd heard more than enough screaming about either topic.

"The one you can do something about. Unless you've suddenly taken charge of UNSOC pensions, too."

"Whadya want from me, Marlowe? Huh?" Donahue rubbed his chin as the creaky chair under him strained from the vibrations of a hacking cough. He spat into the ashtray. "If you wanna be on the Martian Settlement Authority, you gotta get on your wife's good side, not mine. She's running the show up there."

They sat in smoky silence. Marlowe chewed his lip. He knew Donahue would struggle to get him high up in the new MSA. Gardener of a new Eden was a highly coveted job. But he also knew Donahue had accumulated enough capital in his long UN career to spend some of it where he chose. Getting Martin Reginald's grandson a job at the MSA wouldn't have cost him more than pocket change. At least Marlowe now knew Donahue wasn't even willing to spend that on his supposed *star inspector*. Or, someone else had spent their own capital to keep Marlowe *away* from Mars. Now his head was spinning into a vat of thick conspiracy. He needed fresh air and a good fuck. Fortunately, his leave week was one sunset away.

"Listen, kid. In your shoes, I'd take that *Genesis* flight to Alpha Centauri before I'd even want to breathe the same atmosphere as my ex-wife. I'm two years from my pension. I'd say sit tight and

I'll help shoehorn you into this chair when I'm off shooting geese upstate, but you're smart enough to know this chair ain't gonna be here when I'm gone."

"Jack, c'mon. I didn't ask for much. I'd do anything for an MSA transfer. Stamp landing cards, count fucking ears of corn, I don't care." Marlowe's heart was thundering. This felt like his last chance. A door was about to slam shut. He had to jam his thumb in, and quick.

"So go get a job as a speculator or with an oil company if you wanna get to Mars so bad. Why you tugging my tits so hard for an MSA job? Huh?" Annoyance frothed at Donahue's mouth. He took a last draw of his cigarette and stubbed it out among the ash where Marlowe's career waited. "Cuz it ain't to protect your God-damn pittance of a pension."

"I just…" Marlowe tried to gulp away his dry throat. "I don't want to be on Earth any more."

"Son…" Donahue's tone melted. "You ain't gonna win her back by getting your balls in the way of her job. She's got more than enough on her plate. What with fucking Karla Landers shipping in dynamite to start mining for oil and Marxist agitators running around trying to unionize the Martian farmers before they've even blasted off from Earth, it's a miracle there's even a Mars to settle. You know they found a hundred and fifty acres of opium up there? Just planted in a fucking field. The Black Moon gang had jammed themselves so far down the throat of the Terraforming Union we still can't clear off the drugs. There we go. First unspoiled planet in a million years and criminal gangs are growing drugs. What's wrong with us, Marlowe? It's a Wild West up there. Worse."

"It's not about winning her back," Marlowe said. "It's my job to protect her. At least… at least until she has someone else."

"She left you, son. She don't want your protection."

"Real loyalty doesn't end because one party betrays the other."

"Whatever, kid. Your life." Donahue finished his cigarette, then lit another from the burning embers. "Tell you what. I'll make you a deal. I've got this cold case. The Russians are busting my ass about it, and now the God-damn Department of Justice is as well 'cause the Soviet Ambassador has a bee in her bonnet about it."

"What case?"

"Beneath your pay grade. But everyone else is working flat out to prevent a system-wide revolution. So hey, if you wanna piss away your career counting cattle on Mars, who am I to stop you? You ever been as far out as Neptune?"

"Neptune? Maybe once or twice. In the early days."

Donahue held the lit cigarette between his teeth while scouring the creaking in-tray for a folder. It was near the bottom. Marlowe reached out to keep the pile steady.

"Well this case is from even farther out. A murder-suicide back in 2016." Marlowe flicked through the pressed sheets inside the blue folder as Donahue puffed, smoke obscuring the distant view of Brooklyn across the river. "On an orbital ship called the *Pegusus* monitoring the heliopause. Farthest manned ship there was. Until it was decommissioned."

"What happened?"

"There was so much blood and guts jammed into the instruments they had to scrap the whole pod from the ship. Even the impact-resistant casing was shredded to pieces. Spooky shit if you ask me."

Marlowe nodded as he flicked through the personnel profiles of the two dead cosmonauts. Alexei Zhukov, a Russian exoclimatologist, and Okechukwu Lammy, a British engineer.

Funny thing, Neptune," Donahue said as he leaned back in his chair and smoked. "Fucken' far. Pissing distance from the heliopause. I remember in the old days—" Marlowe's senses glazed over at another of Donahue's *old days* stories— "some of the guys, they used to say we shouldn't be running around the rest of the system. Certainly not that fucken' far. Wanted to wrap the Earth in some kinda Messenger-tech barrier. Block us all off from space. They thought that was the only way to protect us from whatever's out there. Ha! You shoulda asked your grandaddy about that one."

"Yeah, I shoulda... Jesus Christ." Marlowe winced as he flicked through the file, assaulted by brutal images from the aftermath of the crime scene.

"Yeah, it ain't pretty." Donahue rubbed his temples. Murders did happen in space. People pushed out of airlocks, shoved down a mine shaft, sliced in two with a pneumatic pickax or incinerated in an engine shaft. But for something to happen on a UNSOC vessel, and to two cosmonauts as well, that was rare. Most of the victims, those that got reported, anyway, were hand-boys or shop-girls. Those poor kids from the Indian Viceroyalty or South Vietnam who'd won their national exit visa lottery for the dream of manual labor in space. Two cosmonauts dying, each by other's hands no less, was certainly strange. If not highly suspicious.

"No one else was in the pod at the time," Marlowe said, scanning the case notes. "So why do the Russians have a problem with all this now?"

"Dunno. Maybe they don't like that their guy was pinned as the murderer. All I know is they're demanding the death-in-service report be reopened, and they're giving the DOJ and the Director-General hell about it."

"And the Brits?" Donahue shrugged in response. "Huh. This Lammy kid was on Charlie's AC settlement program." Marlowe stared at Okechukwu's picture. The young man wore a handsome, slight smirk on his full lips. Marlowe would've certainly looked twice at him had they ever passed each other in the Academy or a UNSOC gym.

"So maybe the Russian guy was jealous of that, maybe he owed him money and suddenly was acting like a dick because all his debts got cleared, who the fuck knows. Listen, just do the rounds, okay? Go interview everyone, review the evidence, repeat the findings."

"Where's this Zvezda pod?"

"The what?" Donahue peered across the table at the files.

"The crime scene? It says the *Pegasus* was decommissioned and repurposed into a sunflower farm on Luna, but the Zvezda pod where this murder-suicide took place, there's nothing about it."

"Huh. Weird. So track that down, too."

"So, you want me to do another report about what happened to the decommissioned equipment?"

"Look, Marlowe. I'm just trying to keep the wolves at the gate here, all right? Do me a favor and get this headache off my desk. Let me tell them I've got my best man on the job."

"And that's it?" Marlowe closed the file. "You'll make sure I get my MSA transfer after that?"

"Subtle you ain't, kid." Donahue held the burning cigarette between his lips and offered a hand. Marlowe stood and shook it.

"But, you know, don't make it into a thing. Get me a report that'll keep the DOJ and Cosmonaut Commissary happy, and you'll be shoveling cow shit on Olympus Mons before you can say 'spousal maintenance.'"

"Thanks, boss."

A few minutes after their firm handshake, Marlowe walked straight into the Department for Unidentified Substances further down the corridor from Donahue's office.

"Hey Viktor," he called out into the deserted yet cramped lab. "You ate?"

Marlowe slipped out of his coat in the unlit, dingy room. Overstuffed with every kind of instrument, vial and measure ever invented since Roswell. And a few of Viktor's own imaginative creations, some bordering on maniacal. A fluorescent light flickered above. He heard his friend moving things around in the closet, then several clashes and collisions. That was about the only way to get more office space in HQ, be a kleptomaniac. Marlowe shifted dust-covered beakers to carve a space for his satchel, and hoisted himself onto the only stool unused as a storage unit.

"Vladimir Ilyich!" Viktor said. The bespeckled scientist emerged in the doorway in his typical lab coat and turtleneck.

"How you doing, bud?" They embraced in a back-slapping hug.

"I'm lecturing in half an hour. But come. Sit and have some coffee. Any luck with Donahue?" Viktor asked with his Minnesota twang, unpacking utensils from a box he'd brought out of storage.

"Same old shit." Marlowe filled a travel kettle from a chipped sink then set up two paper cups. Coffee rings and cloistered sugar littered the counter. The only visible spoon was welded to the workbench, and took both hands to snap it off. Marlowe remembered his old roommates' hygiene habits all too well. "Still trying to talk me out of the MSA job. But at least he promised if I... Viktor, the coffee's empty."

"Oh shit. Check under the sink."

"Ronda! Fuck, Viktor. Why do you only have East German coffee?"

"I know, right? New supplier, they say. It's either that or I have to buy it myself."

A full day spent across several time zones was catching up to Marlowe. The amount of sugar he added hurt his back teeth, but it did the job. The old friends caught up. The UNSOC budget cuts concerned Viktor to a point. His long-time girlfriend Helga was also a scientist. They spent their days testing Plutonian soil samples and Neptunian gasses. Investigating and categorizing everything in the solar system. They'd always have work, whether in UNSOC or any number of the shiny new and suspiciously well-funded mining and exploration companies. And as the years went by, the problems two old friends once shared became ever more unrelatable.

"... so we refinanced. Decent rate, not great, but you know how the economy is. Helga wanted the new kitchen, so what can I do. Should be done in a month. You should come over and see it."

"Yeah, I'll get right on that." Marlowe sipped the tepid coffee. There was an invitation that would never be honored. Helga was firmly on Marlene's side of the divorce. Marlowe offered nothing else. Homeowning was the last thing he wanted to talk about. He still had half a mind to ask Marlene to cover the repair bill which clung to his mind like undissolved sugar on his back teeth. Or else throw in a late application to the Alpha Centauri Settlement Program and have his debts wiped out in an instant. The worst part of being born a UNSOCer was the debt relief that usually accompanied an exit visa didn't apply. No wonder so many space folks had rushed to gamble their lives to live on Alpha Centauri.

"It's gotta be tough, I know. We really are sorry for your guys," Viktor said, but quietly. As if straying too far from the official party line could see him exiled.

"*We*? I thought Helga is team Marlene all the way."

"*We* are officially neutral."

"I can't do more politics today."

"Why? How much have you done already?"

"Donahue and his quid pro quos."

"He gave you something on Mars?" Viktor asked the question a little too keenly. Not that Marlowe was fishing for a reason to stay on Earth, but it would've been nice if someone—anyone—suggested they might miss him.

"If I rubber stamp this old cold case he has." Marlowe handed over the *Pegasus* files.

"I remember this one." Viktor flicked through the pages.

"Really?"

"Oh yeah. It was the strangest thing. They had me test all these samples from the crime scene."

"Like what?"

"Usual stuff. Space moss. Some blood, body parts I think. Wanted to see if there was a gas leak or maybe drugs in their system, something to explain the behavior. Murder-suicide in a sealed and airlocked pod is a bit unusual. See here, it says *behavioral abnormalities caused by carbon monoxide leak*."

"Some behavioral abnormalities for the Russian cosmonaut to rip off the other guy's torso and shred it into a million pieces." Viktor shrugged and handed back the file. "So what did the samples tell you? Were they poisoned by a carbon monoxide leak?"

"Dunno."

"Okay, but the tests you ran, it didn't tell you anything?"

"No idea. They closed the case before I got a chance to have a good poke around. I bet you there's nothing written in there that they sent samples out for testing to the Department for Unidentified Substances." Marlowe flicked through the half-dozen typed pages. Viktor was right. "See? Happens all the time. Files come across my desk, samples and such, then walk out the door before I get a chance to look. Sometimes I think they prefer to keep things unidentified. Usually when they've figured out it's worth something."

"But deaths? Murders?"

"Yeah, sometimes. Suspected, at least. Then the files just... disappear. I remember asking if I could go and test the crime scene. Investigate the pod itself. But they said it went missing after the ship was decommissioned. Weird."

"So you just... never know what happened? Or why?"

Viktor was already on his feet, plugging in his webcam and turning on an ancient, boxy monitor.

"Maybe it's best not to know."

Viktor logged into his virtual classroom. Marlowe held his coat by the door but had a hundred more questions.

"Best not to know why two fully trained cosmonauts, one of whom had been accepted for the AC Settlement program, and the other apparently about to publish a groundbreaking paper on Neptunian tidal systems, died in such a violent and bloody way in a sealed pod that just disappeared into what... a black hole? A slip-stream?"

The words hit Viktor, but he was an island in the ocean. It moved him not an inch. He had kitchen decorations and mortgage refinancing to think about. The clock ticked toward the top of the hour, and he fiddled with a wired lapel mic.

"You know the old saying, Marlowe. When you study at the Joseph Stalin Academy for Solar Sciences, you can question everything but the wisdom of socialism." Viktor grinned into the webcam. "Good afternoon. Today we're continuing our eight-part breakdown of the molecular nature of–"

Marlowe left; the door creaked closed by itself. He walked to the elevator slowly, sucking on the vape and feeling the whirring battery of his investigator's brain heat up. It made a nice change from existential ennui. But as he waited an age for the ancient elevator, he quickly realized there were too many questions to answer on an empty stomach.

CHAPTER 4:
HUMANITY'S GREATEST
EVER LEAP TO OUR
NEAREST STAR

Marlowe sat alone in a window seat of the Plaza diner on the corner of Second Avenue and East 45th Street, the favorite haunt of UN-SOC staff, located in a squat building permanently shaded by the monstrous UN HQ one block away. 'The Office,' they called it. The Plaza diner was large but never full. Open all hours of the day with wipe-clean menus in Russian first, English second. And they happily accepted UN canteen tokens as payment.

He studied the *Pegasus* file; the diary and divorce papers ignored in his bag. The case notes didn't add up, that was for sure. Okechukwu wasn't the only one with everything to live for. Alexei had been making breakthroughs in studying Neptune's climate. He pulled up several of the Russian exoclimatologist's published papers on his pad. A murder-suicide needed a motive, and a powerful one at that. They had to be hiding a secret so terrible that the only route out was death. And what was an engine officer like Okechukwu even doing in a scientific pod anyway?

"Here we are, darlin'," said the waitress. The same woman Marlowe remembered from his days as a child sitting here for hours, all but forgotten about by his father having meetings inside The Office. "Cappuccino and a club sandwich. Extra fries, no mayo."

"Thanks, Brenda. God, this coffee is the best I've ever drank. I started the day with a cup of East Germany's finest brown dust.""

"Oh, you poor baby."

"It's been a long day."

"You know your grandaddy had the exact same order." Marlowe glanced up at her, foam on his lip. "I'm so awfully sorry to hear about his passing. They don't make them like him anymore."

"They sure don't."

Marlowe ate as he skimmed Alexei's articles and the *Pegasus'* specs. Donahue was right. There was no information about the Zvezda pod's whereabouts. Strange for something that had cost over a billion dollars to build and was less than five years old at the time of the incident. It just seemed to have disappeared from the official record. One day it was an integral part of the *Pegasus* mission to monitor the heliopause and surrounding planetary atmospheres, then two deaths later and the pod was gone. Like someone thought it haunted and had cast it off into space. Even then it should show up on a scan or two. The only feasible explanation was that Black Moon mafia or some of the lower-grade gangs in The Maelstrom asteroid belt had got their hands on it and stripped the pod for parts. If they'd become so sophisticated they could requisition and repurpose a modern, billion-dollar pod, and a crime scene at that, then it wouldn't be long before those gangs were running the entirety of space themselves. It almost made Marlowe want to call up Darla and ask what the KGB knew about missing pods and dead cosmonauts.

He chewed the last bite of his sandwich, watching the footfall outside as scattered as autumn rain. The diner busied up as the sky darkened. Six o'clock. He flicked through his satchel and looked again at the divorce papers. Perhaps finishing with Marlene here and now would be a good thing. Sign the papers, make the change in their personnel files, and dive into this case. Take a last whirl around the system before 'bumping' back into her on Mars. Marlowe had always been the worrier in their marriage. She'd been born without a healthy fear of danger and hadn't evolved an appreciation of it for when someone who knew better offered a warning. The Martian Settlement Authority has been tasked with getting as many bodies to Mars as quickly as possible. They advertised oil drilling opportunities and land speculation to investors in the pages of the *New York Times* and *Pravda*. They promoted one-way, debt-free tickets to an unsettled planet on gambling websites and the back of bus tickets. That's who Marlene had to contend with now. Criminals and vagabonds from both ends of the spectrum. There was no way Marlowe could leave her alone. Not after what he'd already put her through.

The street outside was busy with UN staff. UNSOCers and soldiers alike. A crowd of recruits clutched notebooks. The diner door's bell chimed like a slot machine. Suddenly and without warning, he saw Sergei. The Russian with the French magazine from the plane, from the airport bathroom; he was on the street, walking through the crowd. Waiting on the sidewalk. Scratching his rough stubble, staring through the windows of the diner as if he'd been told *you'll find him in here.* Marlowe watched him and wondered if it was worth another approach. Their encounter in the bathroom had been one-sided, but memorable. Marlowe could live with that. He always had. He wouldn't do it here, though. Not in the sacred place of the Plaza Diner; on the table his father had once sat at. His grandfather, too. In the place he and Marlene had enjoyed a celebratory dinner with friends and colleagues after the necessary paperwork had been filed with HR twelve years ago now.

Those memories might mean nothing to some people, but they meant something to him. He would make contact with Sergei, still outside, searching for bearings. Offer himself as a traveling service, to slip into his hotel room at the darkest hour, to be used and ignored. Marlowe could live with that. He always had.

Quickly he stuffed the case file in his bag and left cash for Brenda. Something sharp and eager bloomed low in his stomach; an excitement he couldn't quite digest. Perhaps Sergei could even replace Charlie, soon to depart—

The explosion shattered every possible piece of glass, all at once, and Marlowe's ears pounded with a ringing silence. Everything shook. The universe folded in on itself. Flashing white, spinning, stinging. He fell to the tiled floor, on his hands and knees. Smoke burned the back of this throat as the screams and shouts and roar of fire tumbled into reality.

A woman was near the counter. Her face blackened by smoke. Blood covered her hands. Smoke poured from the kitchen, from the windows and the ceiling. Shrapnel and sharp dust hung heavy in the air and coated everything with a dangerous fog that blinded screaming survivors fumbling through. Blood-strewn hands clutching burst eyes. Heads gashed open. Charred heaps of rumpled, steaming clothes smoldering on the floor.

"Come with me," Marlowe shouted to Brenda, the poor woman in a total state of shock. He could stand. He would be fine. She was shaking, bleeding from the face as smoke came like a waterfall from the diner's kitchen, he took her arms doused in copper ash. "Come on, come outside."

The street was screaming chaos. Glass littered the sidewalk and the road. Whatever blew up had exploded into the crowd who'd been gathering outside in the moments before. Dozens of injured sat on the sidewalk, clutching faces, helped by those not or less so. People climbed out of windows, or into them to help those inside. A dozen screaming voices barked orders at everyone.

"Get the injured across the street."

"Find the kitchen staff.

"Bring extinguishers, now!"

"Call The Office. Get the medics."

"Where is she? Where is she?"

"Medic! Call the medics!"

Marlowe led Brenda's shaken body in spattered, ruined clothes toward the bodega across 45th Street, where staff and customers were running out, encouraging the injured to come forward. A man poured water on another's cut arm. He yelled back into the store in Spanish, demanding bandages and water.

"How is she? Is she alive?" The Spanish man asked Marlowe.

"She's alive. I don't know how she is. Her hands… this is Brenda. Her name is Brenda."

"I got her, boss. I got her. Come on, Brenda. Let's get you away from this."

The man took Brenda, who only now acknowledged where she was and what had happened. She nodded thanks to Marlowe as the Spanish man passed her water.. Sirens wailed in the yawning distance. People ran toward them from all sides. Medical people. Help was coming. Marlowe's jaw ached. He could taste only ash and fire. The Plaza was now fully aflame. Red hot tongues licked out of windows. People were moving away. Cars had screeched to a halt farther up 2nd Avenue. The metal frame of the doorway on the corner of the diner was melting. The neon sign hanging by a single wire. He was too close; they were all too close. The air tasted ripe for another explosion. The cooking gas spurring a cauldron of flames. Brenda. The cooks. The folks in the other booths or by the bar or in the bathroom. He tried to see if there was a way to run back in, but it was impossible. A wall of flame roared out of the diner, melting plastic and shattering glass which screamed like the hounds of hell.

"Hey buddy, get back. Get way back."

"There's more inside!" Marlowe yelled.

"We know!"

Marlowe complied to the unseen orders, walking backwards into the middle of the road with everyone else. And Sergei? Where was he? Marlowe quickened his pace but was running in circles. Looking around with all due horror. It was impossible to see a thing. Smoke and darkness. Blown-out streetlamps. The sparkling glass scattered in chunks and the siren of first responders coming closer but now sucked up by a roar of motorbikes. Dirty bikes. They screamed louder than the flames. Deafening. Two or three. Marlowe spun around as several bikes came speeding at them from up Second Avenue. Roaring. People on the back. And flags. Red flags flapping.

"Get down!" Marlowe shouted. His mouth spoke before his brain fully processed the terror that was coming towards them. "Everybody. Get down! Get down now!"

The bikers laughed louder than their bullets. The bike engines crackled and spat as they slowed and began spraying automatic bullets into the crowd. Marlowe saw from the ground up, but dozens and dozens were still standing. Three bikes. Two riders on each. No helmets. Just wild mullets and filthy leathers. Automatic weapons fired everywhere as screams of agony and louder ones of fear swallowed reality. The bikers passed, then turned, coming around for another attack. Shots were fired back, the survivors of the blast were shooting back. It was a street fight. Yelling and screaming. One of the attackers was hit. He fell off the bike as the driver spun and sped away, but the two others returned, standing up on their bikes, not sitting down. Guns in hand, flag in the other.

"Free the Earth!" One shouted. Red flag waving high as the bike revved up. The other bike came next.

"Make Earth great again!" He threw the flag into the chaos. The red banner shimmered across Marlowe's vision. A snake coiled around planet Earth with 'MEGA' written in bold letters across it. More bullets sprayed into the injured and hurt. Shots fired back in an ongoing frenzy. Another shooter was hit and fell from the bike.

The rider was struck as well as the bike skidded into sparks. Shots followed the last one riding away. It swerved. Maybe a hit, maybe not. Those who could dived on the felled shooters as the flames from the Plaza soared ever higher.

Marlowe tasted only smoke and gravel and death. Bodies littered around him. Some would never rise again. Siren after siren after siren. Trucks and vans and the thumping feet of heavily armored NYPD deploying from the backs of vans. Marlowe covered his head with his arms to protect from the stomping chaos of a world gone mad.

"My God," Charlie said, opening up the door to his park-view penthouse. He wore only running shorts and a skin-tight tank top. He'd been working out again, obviously. Charlie's Black skin smooth and shining underneath, studded with the slightest dew of sweat. He sucked on a sports drink while blue and green shadows of the live action news rapidly reflected against darkened New York windows. "Are you all right?"

"Yeah," Marlowe said, dropping his ash-covered bag in the spotless hallway.

"Are you sure?" Charlie's sneakers followed Marlowe as he balled up his coat and threw it on the wide corner sofa surrounding the oversized television in the duplex suite Marlowe had wasted so many nights in. He loosened his sweat-and-blood-stained shirt as he yanked the stainless-steel fridge—a bodega's selection of sports drinks and protein powders. At least Charlie still kept his fridge stocked with beer for when Marlowe came by. He didn't have a toothbrush here, but he had that. Marlowe twisted open the bottle, watching the news report from the scene. "I mean, didn't they want to keep you in overnight?" Charlie slid onto a stool by the breakfast island.

"I told you, I'm fine."

"Yes, but—"

"Charlie," Marlowe sucked down the beer. "I've been poked and prodded and scanned from top to bottom. I am fine."

Their attention turned to the wailing sirens on the news. Helicopter images of snarling traffic and diversions set up across the city. SWAT teams guarding the UN building and soldiers swarming across bridges.

"At least sixteen confirmed dead in this latest of a series of attacks against the UN's Space Operations Command, but the deadliest incident of this type on Earth for months. A night of carnage began with a pipe bomb in the Plaza—"

"Do they know who?"

"Who do you think, Charlie?"

"Them? Are you sure?"

"I was there."

"My God. Those people."

"... comes amid a historic change in space policy with the Open Space Treaty coming into force later this week. The former president spoke just moments ago at a rally for his preferred Republican successor, Karla Landers."

"And now they're blaming us! No one wants to see deaths. Deaths on any side are bad. Really bad. But they've got no evidence. No evidence at all, but they blame us. Look at the Lunans. They hate the UN more than us. Look at these Communist guerillas in all these weird moons. Blame them. People are sick of the UN dictating their lives. A lot of people want to see UN people dead. Not only us."

"Can we turn that shit off, please?" Marlowe finished the beer and took another. "I'm going upstairs to have a shower."

The water ran hot and strong in the glass-paneled en-suite bathroom. New York glittered in the bright night through the shower's double-glazed fourth wall. Home this place would never be. Not New York City, and certainly not Charlie's expensive apartment, provided to those who had signed up to leave Earth permanently. Marlowe was almost jealous.

The stench of a long day surrounded by death drained beneath the tiles, but far from gone from the pores of his skin, no matter how hard he scrubbed. When he came back into the bedroom, Charlie was already naked on wine-red satin sheets, gay porn playing at low volume on the flatscreen.

"What's all this?" Marlowe said, glancing at the screen and toweling dry on the rich carpet softer than Martian fields. "Not shipping your extensive collection to Alpha Centauri?" Charlie ignored him and unpeeled a swab from a sterile pack on the nightstand and held it out. "Are you serious Charlie? Wouldn't it be easier to just not cheat on your Eden partner? Want to take a blood sample from me as well?"

"No no, this will catch everything. Back of the nose and throat."

"Aren't you doing one?"

"I only have sex with clean people."

"Eugh. You're a dick."

Only when five minutes had passed and everything came up negative did Charlie let Marlowe embrace him. The contours of Charlie's body had not changed since those sub-zero nights at the UNSOC Academy in Moscow. An extra round of vigor to mark what could be their last night for eternity. An old habit about to die screaming.

"I'll only be 4.37 light years away," Charlie whispered later, arms twisted around Marlowe's sweaty chest. Marlowe turned and kissed him, stroking his dark, clean-shaven face.

"Maybe less if they prove the slipstreams exist."

"Not that old conspiracy theory. Four and a bit years is not a lot in stasis."

"I'm good." Laying this side on the pillow, he was forced to confront the picture on the other nightstand. Charlie smiling beside a beautiful, regal looking Black woman in their formal UNSOC uniforms. "This is her, then?"

"Yup. Perfect genetic match." Charlie said it with a note of pride, as if he'd mounted the peak of human greatness fathering the most perfect zygotes possible while setting off to settle an unspoiled world with a thousand other self-important specimens of physical prowess.

"How many kids did you end up with?"

"Three are gestating. Two were aborted. So weird, they'll be four years old when we meet them."

"How will they learn to walk and talk if they're in stasis all that time?"

"So you didn't watch the documentary." It wasn't a question.

"No, Charlie. I didn't."

"They use cerebral programing and semi-conscious–"

"Okay, okay. Enough detail."

"Sorry. You and Marlene. I know it's been tough."

"It's… whatever. The divorce papers are still in my bag. I can't

[46]

quite bring myself to... you know."

Once clean sheets crinkled, crunched. Hot breath mingled with the humid air from the bathroom, door open and light on.

"You need to do it and move the fuck on." Charlie offered an arm for Marlowe to lay into, but he wasn't going to fall for that trap again. Feelings for Charlie was the last thing he needed back in his life.

"Well, we need to sign together at the same time and deposit them with HR, so one more meeting is on the cards." Marlowe whacked his pillow and flicked off the bedside lamp, drowning the picture of Charlie and his *perfect genetic match* into darkness. "I wish you luck with your artificially inseminated spawn raised in stasis. All I'll say is those kids are going to have some serious attachment issues. Good luck with raising them while you're chopping wood on... what's it called?"

"Man, you really haven't seen a single one of our TV specials? It's called New Plymouth Rock."

"I'm going to sleep."

The next morning, Marlowe came downstairs to a violent rain drenching the city, the park billowing in the wind far below. He was glad to be dressed in a fresh suit from the few spares he kept in Charlie's wardrobe. But he dusted off ash from his trench coat. The smell of a burning diner and angry bullets lingered still. And Darla Foster's card. He imagined for a moment what he would say were he to call the KGB agent. Where would he begin with the 'suspicious activity' he'd encountered in the last twenty-four hours?

Charlie was in the kitchen wearing only shorts, spooning fruit and non-fat yogurt into a bowl. Work-out equipment and a yoga mat lay out by the floor-to-ceiling windows.

"Want some?"

"God no." Marlowe sat on the stool.

"I can make you coffee? But it's decaf. And I've only got oat milk."

"I'll pass. I'll get a bagel downstairs. I'm headed to the airport soon."

"Oh yeah?"

"Thought I'd take your advice. I'm going to Perth." Charlie

dropped the spoon.

"Are you?"

Marlowe thwacked all the contents of his bag onto the countertop, wiping off the grime and dust they'd accumulated. "She's had a few days to stew. I'll fly down, we'll sign, I'll drop it off at HR, and that's it. I have a funny feeling it's costing me more money every minute I don't do it."

"I'm glad to hear you've come to a decision." Charlie quickly returned to eating. He'd long lost interest in the fourteen-month odyssey of Marlowe's divorce. "So what's after that?" He asked with more cheer.

"I'll catch a transport to Khrushchev-Kennedy, and…" The *Pegasus* file stared up from the open satchel. "Oh. I do have something you could help me with."

"Shoot."

"Did you know this guy?" Marlowe slid across Okechukwu's file.

"Why? Because we're both Black?"

"No. Because he was on the AC settlement program. Back in 2016."

"Nope." Charlie chewed. "Never seen him. And there's no one called Okechukwu in the group."

"I know. He's dead." Charlie glanced up from the file, mildly annoyed Marlowe had brought anything real or depressing into his bubble. He flicked through a few more pages, stopping at the gruesome pictures from the Zvezda pod.

"Fuck, Marlowe. I didn't need to see that."

"Don't you want to know how he died?"

"Fell into a scrapheap shredder by the looks of it."

"Murdered by a Soviet exoclimatologist."

"Huh."

"Who then killed himself." Charlie stopped eating.

"Why?"

"Dunno. But look." Marlowe slid across the photographs he'd been holding onto detailing the state Alexei's hollowed-out shell of body had been found in.

"What the fuck is this? Did he carve off his own skin or something?"

Pieced together, the scene was brutal. All that remained of Oke-chukwu was a torso stump attached to legs. His entire upper body had exploded outward, with bits of jaw and ear spattered across the cramped room, from the bunkbeds to the bathroom. Alexei on the other hand was neatly folded on the bottom bunk. His skin at least. The insides sucked out, gone.

"Donahue says the Russians are making noise about it. They don't like the fact their guy was pinned as the murderer. They want the death-in-service report reopened."

"I'll say." Charlie turned to the printed pages, covering up the disturbing images. "Carbon monoxide poisoning? Did anyone buy that?"

"They did. I guess it's plausible enough."

"Hardly. Look here," Charlie spun the folder back to Marlowe, bare skin leaning across the kitchen island. "The Zvezda is a Kiev-class pod. State-of-the-art. There's no carbon monoxide. What, did they think this is the fifties and the cosmonauts were digging for coal on Hyperion?"

Marlowe chewed his lip, then sucked on his vape, still with a dusty, burnt taste. He blew out much to Charlie's displeasure, who wafted away the harmless vapor. Marlowe had been working on the assumption the carbon monoxide leak had been proved by some missing piece of evidence, hence why Viktor's samples had been taken away. They'd likely discovered some operational flaw in the pod, so junked the whole thing and conveniently 'forgot' to add any detail but the summary to the file. Marlowe vaped again. It was why the Russians were forcing the issue now, he'd thought. The Americans were covering up a 'capitalist' malfunction—wouldn't be the first time—and the Russians were pushing for the embarrassing truth to come out.

"You're saying there's no way one of them went crazy due to carbon monoxide poisoning?"

"How?" Charlie was indignant. And with good reason to be. He'd been born in space. He knew how these things worked. "It looks more like a space-leak."

"Wouldn't they just freeze?"

"No. The vacuum of space doesn't have a temperature." Mar-lowe grimaced as Charlie's know-it-all flaws spilled into the kitchen. "The cosmic microwave background leftover from the Big Bang is 2.7 Kelvin. That's minus 445 Fahrenheit."

"I know the Kelvin scale."

"All right. So you know heat radiation can't occur as rapidly by radiation exposure alone. So when someone is exposed to the vacuum of space, the liquid in the body actually boils from the lack of pressure. And it's not pretty."

"At least I'm only called in to investigate afterward." Marlowe blew out vapor, having rather had this talk when he wasn't about to spend weeks off-Earth.

"I'd say this Okechukwu could've tried to plug a space leak with his upper body, but then–"

"Why would all his insides be… inside the pod?"

"Well exactly. And the Russian's skin suit doesn't make much sense either."

"All right, well let's say they ripped each other apart in some kind of death match, *not* caused by carbon monoxide or whatever. Donahue has my balls to the wall on this one–"

"Lovely image."

"Uh huh, so I need a motive, something. Okechukwu was a fucking Alpha Centauri settler when he died. Someone must've known him. Can you ask around?"

"Oh wow. I don't know, you know? We're recording this Good Morning America thing today and then all stuff at the White House. I don't want to upset anyone."

"Of course, of course." Marlowe put everything away. "Better two gruesome deaths stay unresolved than you *upset anyone.*"

"Marlowe, come on. That's not fair. Wait a second." But Marlowe was already at the door, trench coat back on, bag zipped up. Charlie stood in the hallway in his skin-tight shorts, beyond him flashing suggestions of the gray cityscape.

"I forgot to ask; does it rain on Alpha Centauri? I know you hate the rain."

"Marlowe…" Charlie stepped forward. Smooth muscles bristling under skin so perfect it had been chosen to found a new civilization. Their lips touched, but Marlowe pulled back. "I only have six more days under this sun," he whispered. Marlowe bit the lip which still tasted of Charlie. Involuntarily, his head shook.

"I have a soon-to-be ex-wife, a boss who's got my future in a vice, and two dead cosmonauts. Oh, and an apartment in East Berlin that's about to cost me more to get up to code than the divorce." Now his head was shaking, it wouldn't stop. "And I have a flight to catch." He opened the door.

"Wait." He waited. Charlie skipped to the hallway table and pulled an old brown envelope from a drawer. The only thing inside. "I can't hold onto this anymore." Charlie held it out, his eyes looking on kindly. But Marlowe only stared back, his words stolen. "Anything I leave here will go to storage. They need the place for the next round of settlers."

Marlowe swallowed a painful lump.

"What do you want me to do with that?"

"Maybe you can give it to Marlene." He snatched the envelope and stuffed it in the bag. "Marlowe, I'm really sorry." But Marlowe was already marching down the carpeted corridor toward the elevator. "Vladi! Come on. Don't leave it like this."

But Charlie didn't cross the threshold of his door. Not in his shorts. Not with neighbors and cameras and *Good Morning America*.

Marlowe could lie to Donahue all he wanted. But he couldn't lie to himself any longer. Going to Mars wasn't for Marlene. He needed to be off-Earth. Not in a covered dome on Luna or underground on an asteroid. But under a new sky. Breathing fresh air as he planted seeds or rode horses, slept under the stars on a world with no cell reception, no airport bathrooms, no distractions.

The elevator doors closed, and the descent began. Only then did Marlowe turn to the mirrored doors. He wiped away a tear. He didn't wait for a taxi in the lobby, but out in the rain where he could vape.

CHAPTER 5: FLECKS OF DINOSAUR BONE DISCOVERED ON THE MOON

Marlowe waited at the gate, watching the stewards fret. The storm pounded the window and the runway beyond. The plane invisible through bombastic fog. The inevitable just moments away. He'd said as much to the woman at check in.

"This is an announcement for passengers awaiting Qantas flight four six nine to Perth. This flight has been delayed due to poor weather conditions. We apologize for the inconvenience."

Marlowe's UNSOC tickets granted him access to the business class lounge, but he parked himself in a bar looking out at the terminal, racking up what could be his last few weeks of expenses if Donahue kept his promise. The envelope Charlie had forced him to take weighed him down. An anchor of memory around his neck when all he wanted to do was fly.

Four drinks later, he did nothing but stare at the case notes, holding Alexei and Okechukwu's pictures side-by-side. According to the testimony of the *Pegasus* Station Commander, Okechukwu had volunteered to relieve the Russian after his shift. But Alexei hadn't gone back into Pegasus for his break. He stayed in the pod. Stayed while Okechukwu used his shower. Thirty minutes after his two-hour break started, Alexei was still in the pod. Why? Was he on the verge of some discovery? Why would Okechukwu take a shower in the pod, when he had the same in his own, private quarters? The *Pegasus* crew didn't suffer from the same cramped conditions or crumbling communal washrooms as the vast majority of other ships and stations. It was a state-of-the-art vessel with capacity for fifty. The crew's isolation rewarded with more space than they knew what to do with. Yet Okechukwu, in the middle of his own shift, took a shower while Viktor remained in the *Pegasus'* most cramped, undersupplied spot, in the same place he'd been for sixteen hours. Waiting while Okechukwu took a shower.

Marlowe wouldn't turn up at Viktor's house and take a shower, but he would at Charlie's. Back at the Academy, he and Charlie's eyes would meet across the gym. Marlowe would head down to the showers; Charlie would do one more rep, then wander down as well. The last shower room, the showers at the very back, the ones with the mold and piss-poor water pressure. The ones where no one came. That's where Charlie fucked Marlowe.

Marlowe stared into the busy terminal, this new theory spinning in his mind. Those two were fucking. It was suddenly so obvious. Another complication to add to the file. Another theory no side would like. Hardly Donahue's rubber stamp. What would be worse for the Russians? That their cosmonaut was painted as a murderer, or gay? Marlowe watched the terminal. People waiting and walking, clasping luggage and children, tired and annoyed at the weather delays. In his corner by the window looking out towards the terminal, few could see him staring, counting up the single men waiting alone, betting with himself if he had the energy for a hook-up before a four-hour flight to see his soon-to-be ex-wife. He scanned the terminal for a victim whom he could suck the life from.

"Fuck me," Marlowe said out loud. The Russian appeared just beyond the bar, looking vaguely lost among the moving people. Sergei Moscowitz, or there abouts, was here in the terminal. A chin of stubble gazing up at the notice board flapping delay after delay. A gauze patch above his eyebrow from the explosion yesterday. He was lucky to come away with only that. There was nowhere for Marlowe to hide. Not that he wanted to, but he remained decidedly unsure whether or not he should start following the man who may very well be following him. Then the decision was made for him. Sergei came into the bar.

The Russian found a seat at the bar, facing away from Marlowe's table. He'd likely not seen him. But in the list of suspicious things he'd been keeping track of in his head since meeting Darla Foster in East Berlin, seeing Sergei for the third time in barely twenty-four hours was top of that list. His investigator's training clicked up a gear. There were questions to be asked.

"Leaving so soon?" Marlowe asked, taking a stool next to him. Sergei gulped with shock, as if he'd just summoned Marlowe from the depths of his thoughts.

"I'm always traveling," he offered neutrally, in that international accent with only flecks of 'beyond the Wall.' His stubble was more pronounced than the day before, and in addition to the gauze, there was a nasty bruise under his left eye.

"How are you feeling? You know, after yesterday."

"I was lucky. A scrape. And you? You look well."

"Lucky as well." They shared a smile which quickly felt uncomfortable. Sergei's glass was empty. "Whiskey or vodka?"

"Gin and tonic, actually."

"Interesting choice." This Russian had Western tastes. "Another round please, barman. On me."

They drank and talked only around things, not of them. Not what they did, not who they were or where they were going. Two men firmly in the shadows, not daring to venture into the sun. Like those awkward conversations with a one-time hookup one bumped into at a free clinic.

"Going back to Berlin?" Marlowe asked when the delayed flight to Tempelhof finally announced boarding.

"No. And you?"

"Nope. I still have some time." Marlowe didn't say to where he was waiting to go, nor did Sergei ask. A spy was, by nature, an interrogating sort. They laid out a map of questions which anyone could get lost in. All this might rely on coincidence, or disinterest, or pleasantries exchanged with a stranger; slices from an unmeaningful life. Sergei offered no hint of interest in his life. His body though, that kept Marlowe drinking.

"The next space flight to Khrushchev-Kennedy will commence boarding shortly. Please have exit visas and travel documents ready for inspection."

"Another drink?" Sergei asked as the announcement subsided. In other words, Sergei might have asked if Khrushchev-Kennedy was Marlowe's destination. Marlowe confirmed it was not with an agreement for another round. They drank again in sips of silence, the alcohol dripping towards its due effect. "UNSOC?" Sergei finally asked.

[54]

Marlowe was a little shocked by the breach of their unspoken pact. He immediately checked the inside pocket of his long coat, wondering if the pale blue passport was poking out.

"Why do you ask?"

"Just that... it must be difficult." Sergei was staring at Marlowe's wedding ring, spotted with gin-soaked condensation.

Marlowe didn't react. The ancient counter-espionage training kicked in. At the slightest hint of a threat, one should close down. Do nothing but look for the quickest way out. That was the correct way to react.

"What makes you say that?"

"You know. The morality clause. Can't be easy."

At least he knew now the threat was real. Sergei wasn't raising archaic UNSOC employment rules without good reason. Technically, UNSOC employees could be dismissed for 'immoral conduct.' Infamously, adultery was on that list. A former director-general and several commissars had been felled by the morality clause in recent years. At least on a simple reading of the facts as reported in the press. But UNSOC had three million personnel employed from here to Neptune, with internal politics more complex than many Earthbound nations. Being dismissed from UNSOC was a trauma in line with being stripped of one's citizenship and deported into a stateless existence, so it came with all the payoffs and pensions to make it a last resort most would only begrudgingly accept when the alternative was far worse.

The question remained yawning between their two stools. What did Sergei want?

"I should probably go and wait at my gate." Marlowe drank up. "You never know." Sergei drained his glass too, readying himself as if Marlowe had requested an escort. The flight board behind the bar began to change. Less *delayed* and more *new times*. The storm was clearing. But escaping a tail in a departure's hall would inevitably give away one's destination.

"Wait." Sergei snatched his arm. Marlowe held his things, suspended. The Russian's gaze possessed him. Marlowe would like to think he sucked a cock so good men would chase him across the system for another shot, but he sensed there was more behind Sergei's desperate grip.

"Do you think…" Sergei offered a gin-soaked whisper. "Do you think you have a few minutes?" His stubbly beard revealed desperation. The scent of his skin covered the deep-fried air for a moment.

Perhaps Marlowe was wrong, and Sergei had only been trying to sympathize. It couldn't be easy for him to live under a regime where up until the mid-nineties their bathroom activities could lead to his own arrest and hard labor as a counter-revolutionary.

Marlowe thought about it. A thousand seconds flashed through his mind. A locked bathroom stall, Sergei filling the space Charlie had left. The Russian was angsty, but his eyes bore deep into Marlowe's soul. This was the sort of hookup that could leave him breathless, or without his wallet and passport. His gut begged for one thing, for the rough embrace of a hurried nothing. But in a minute, it would be flushed away, and he'd be one more man removed from Charlie.

"I best be going," Marlowe said, looking out onto the busy concourse, and not at Sergei's wishful eyes. The subtle threat's he'd made still echoed in Marlowe's mind. He might be falling into a self-destructive shame-spiral, but he didn't need to plunge completely into the void. Not with his pension still hanging in the balance. "*Uvidimsya snova*," Marlowe whispered close to Sergei's ear as he gathered up his coat at satchel. The Russian smirked and sipped from the ice of his free drink.

"Sure, see you on Mars."

Marlowe landed in a dark, deserted Perth at close to three in the morning. He'd hoped to have everything signed by Marlene and be on the midnight shuttle to Khrushchev-Kennedy, but the consolation prize would have to be the best, and certainly most problematic, fuck of his life in an RFK bathroom. He'd thought about it the entire flight. The anger, the roughness, the power struggle happening right there in the disabled restroom. Such was the fucked-up psychology Marlowe lived with, that he desperately wanted it again.

Although this southern slice of Earth was still hours from dawn, the heat outside the airport was oppressive. It riveted up from the ground, escaping high in the star-studded sky, bright with the slashed center of the galaxy, always there, threatening to fall and smother them all.

"Where to, mate?" asked the taxi driver, too chirp to be finishing his shift. Marlowe silently passed an address forward. The driver whistled. "That's a good hour and a half south of here. It'll cost ya."

Marlowe stretched a yawn and passed his UNSOC credit card forward.

"Start a tab if you like."

"Ha, got ya, mate. A life on expenses, not bad."

If his flight had landed on time, he might have used up the extra energy to counter the taxi driver's misconception. Civilians in these minor little 'company towns' always thought the same. UNSOCers flew in and out, or up and down, pumping dollars and rubles into hotels and restaurants, always asking for a receipt. But try asking for a cost of living raise when the department's budget is set by fraught negotiations between the US and Soviets, dependent on being passed by Act of Congress, and these days, too often held up by those elected on a platform of dismantling said employer.

At least the wind through the back window offered a soothing breeze in the depths of a close, sticky night. Smooth, empty highways sprawled in wide, orange-hued angles. Perth had been a UNSOC town since his grandfather's days. Here, the sights of the southern sky were more powerful than the lights of this city clinging to the frayed edge of a thousand-mile desert.

"Found them aliens yet, mate?" The driver lit a cigarette with the car's lighter as he knocked eighty miles an hour easily on the violently empty highway. "I know a guy you should talk to."

"Uh huh." Marlowe studied the stars to see which ones blinked and moved. One such pattern looked like a Slovakian cross. The *OS Karl Liebknecht*, if he wasn't mistaken. He'd sucked off a Soviet cosmonaut with a bald head and hefty beard in a shower block on that orbital ship.

"If it had been anyone else, mate, I'd have said nah, you're pulling my leg. But Holden's a bloke you can trust, y'know? Not some bogan drongo. You look into that kinda stuff, do you mate?"

"What kind of stuff, sorry?"

"Sightings. Abductions. Mysteries. The unexplained." The diver turned around, hands giving a spooky shake and not on the wheel.

"I'm with Criminal Investigations." Marlowe could've worked for payroll, it wouldn't have made a difference to the driver.

"My old man was in the navy. You want to talk to him, mate. Phewee, the shit he's seen. Weird crafts flying in a way that doesn't make sense. Even with all this Messenger-tech, zipping and zapping. Whole boats disappearing into thin air, mate. Guys being snatched from the dessert and turning up months later, can't remember a thing. You ever hear of that? Holden's never been the same since, mate. Poor fella. 'Course he could've been sucked into spending all his dough on the pokies in Kalgoorlie. Wouldn't be the first time. But he's got some story about aliens. He won't go back to the mines, 'cause of it. I'd be drinking on the job too, if I'd seen what he'd seen."

"You're not drinking now, are you?"

"Nah mate, not me. Holden. My mate."

"Ah." Marlowe felt it safe to close his eyes, the driver a one-man talk radio show powered by pure conspiracy. The leaps of dissonance it must take to so confidently espouse Roswell and everything that came after is nothing but a hoax, while simultaneously claiming the UN is training legions of alien shock troops on Luna, so of course they don't want ordinary people to go up there.

"My lad Scotty wanted to go take one of those Martian mining jobs. They were paying a fortune mate, a fortune. I said, son, you've got another think coming. He gets a damn good salary mining out in the Kimberley, so he does. Not UNSOC money, mind you, but far better being down here than up there. Christ knows what you lot are doing on Mars. Wild west, mate."

For the first time in years, Marlowe was relieved to turn up at his wife's house—or more accurately her collection of caravans. Marlowe had frequently told her she only needed a rusted-out pickup truck and Confederate flag to complete the aesthetic. The taxi sped away into the desert night, leaving Marlowe in front of a clutch of grimy caravans and plastic lawn chairs. Crickets chirped a splendid song. It was better to tune in to them than the wind screaming between the ocean of radio scopes beyond the blanket of darkness. A thousand ghostly windchimes the size of city blocks. That truly was a haunting sound.

A caravan door slammed open, dislodging an empty beer bottle which spun and smashed on a loose stone. The scream of the crickets silenced, and in its place came the ungodly hum of vibrations beyond sound. It went through him, striking chords within his body like a ghostly bass player. Dizzying his balance, pinging his ears as if he'd woken up under an ocean of pressure. The sensation suddenly sucked from Marlowe every molecule of air. He spun with the Earth, sea-sick on dry land.

"Ah, there he is." Came the cool, unsparkled voice from the darkness beyond. Sweat stung his eyes. "Beware of Greeks bringing gifts of divorce papers."

"I'm not feeling so… good."

"It's the 'scopes. They're turned on tonight. Lucky them."

Gravity seemed to slip from his grasp. As if he'd wandered into those corners of a ship or orbital station where the grav-pumps don't quite reach, and the spit in your mouth floats up your nose.

"Get your ass inside then, I've got padding in here."

They always said Marlowe and Marlene were two sides of the same person. Raised, like most, in the UNSOC system. Parents too busy doing something incoherently fascinating on Venus or asteroids in The Maelstrom to teach affection. They spoke with the same blended accent of their UNSOC schools and UNSOC Academy. They even dressed during their marriage in that same utilitarian style, ordering from opposite ends of the same, standard-issue catalog. Those who had known the couple well enough might even venture Vladimir Ilych Marlowe and Olga Marlene Novikov-Marlowe turned their grimaces into sarcastic disinterest with that same turn of the upper lip. For all their personality similarities, and style of dress and speech, Marlene resembled most of all her brother Charlie. In affection as well as looks. Yet another fucked-up layer for Marlowe's future psychologist to charge a fortune to untangle.

Despite everything that had passed between them. The tragedies, the betrayals, the words and deeds and actions which could never be unsaid nor unheard, Marlene led a helpless Marlowe through the desert.

Marlowe woke to dirty amber light through the prism of dusty blinds. The caravan was artificially cool while a strong wind ruffled the metal casing. The cramped room had a desk and kitchenette, but was covered in stacks of paper files. The floor a parade of star maps and coffee cups holding their beveled edges down. The only clear surface was a fold-down table where he'd placed the steel cup of water Marlene had given him last night, studded by an array of what looked like fossilized teeth from saber-tooth tigers.

In the narrow bathroom, more odd relics of teeth covered the chemical toilet. But a shower head hung from a hook, and he happily used every last cubic inch of water Marlene might have left. At least to wash off any lingering scent of her brother back in New York.

She'd left out loose shorts and an oversized t-shirt which proudly declared *I dig dino-chicks.* He dressed and followed soft voices outside, squinting in the western sunset.

"Sleeping beauty," Marlene said. She sat on a plastic chair, a beer between her thighs and her feet resting on a tough-looking woman with the pale skin and dry, curly hair of a Lunan. They were under a flimsy veranda to protect from the rapidly setting sun.

"What time is it?"

"About time we get these babies turned back on. There's a flight up to K-K at midnight, although you might want to leave before. The vibrations are worse just after sunset."

Marlowe glanced behind him. An endless forest of mountain-sized radio 'scopes rose from the terractotta flatlands. Their spindles pointed eagerly toward the purple sky, begging to kiss the looming darkness and soak up the secrets. He could have been an ant standing at a Normandy grave site. Marlene's creatures were endless. An army she could turn against him with a flick of a button.

"Come have a beer with us."

Marlowe padded barefoot into the sandy shade where they sat, realizing the clothes he wore likely belonged to the strange woman his wife seemed awfully familiar with. "This is Paulina." Paulina only nodded with her beer. Marlene threw him one from a cool box by her side. "That's her office you were snoring in."

"Uh huh." Marlowe snapped the beer open. "What do you do, Paulina? Saber-toothed dentist?"

"Exo-archeologist."

"So, those are your teeth and bones in there? I think one of them is stuck in the couch because my back is killing me."

"Fossils from Luna," Marlene said, sipping her beer. Marlowe gave an unimpressed shrug. It was his standard operating procedure to never give Marlene the reaction she wanted. "The meteor that wiped out the dinosaurs was so powerful, flecks of tyrannosaurus bones landed on the moon."

"Uh huh, fascinating. Well, I've got our divorce papers. But Charlie, he…" he nodded in Paulina's direction, but given how far up Paulina's thigh Marlene's foot had found itself, Marlene was saying in so many words her new 'friend' knew everything. "Charlie gave me back the stuff. He can't keep it anymore, obviously."

"I know. I already went through everything in your bag."

"And you opened it? Without me?" Marlowe flushed with sudden anger. Anger that he had to live this most awkward moment at all, let alone with an audience.

"It's hospital records and two death certificates. Calm down, Vladi." Marlowe shook his head.

"You're going to Mars next week?"

"Starting my job as deputy director of the MSA, yes I am. Paulina is head of Martian archeology. She's got the power to shut down any business development she likes if there's even the hint of a fossil."

"The whole planet is going to become one big dig site, trust me," Paulina added with an insider's grin.

"Uh huh, neat." He turned straight back to Marlene. "So you're taking their bodies up there, then?"

"For the billionth time, yes."

"You understand it makes it harder for me to visit their… graves. I mean, can't you even get a headstone? Something?"

"From next week you can book a trip to Mars like any other citizen, Vladi. In fact, I hear some places will pay you a one-way ticket if you fancy being a builder or a farmer."

"Marlene, please. Those were our children."

"And they wanted to be the first people to be buried on Mars."

"They were seven! It was a joke!"

Marlowe bit his tongue to save himself from another word. The desert had no echo, thankfully. Like space, the wilderness south of Perth was noisy. Crickets and bugs and flies snapping into zappers.

"Just… don't do it without me, please?"

Marlene looked offended by the very accusation. Which told Marlowe she'd been planning on exactly that.

"Fine," she said, throwing cold water on their conversation.

It would do no one good to reignite old flames. At least Paulina looked painfully uncomfortable. Marlene threw on a fake smile. "How's work?"

"Fine."

"I see Charlie's dream of being a celebrity is coming true."

"Are you going to the mission launch?"

Marlene chuckled.

"It's hardly a launch. They're leaving Earth and going straight to the Engels base on Phobos for a month. I'll pop over and say hi then."

"I... never knew they were leaving from Engels? Or staying there for a month?"

"What are you talking about? They have to go meet the Eden fleet beyond the heliopause. Did... did you think they can launch light-speed travel *inside* the solar system?" The women shared a laugh at his expense. "And they're not going into stasis for another, what, three more months at least. Didn't you watch the documentary?"

The winds of sunset faded to the heat of the evening. Pauline disappeared into the control caravan, readying for the procedure to switch on nearly a thousand radio telescopes to sweep the skies for signs of an alien invasion, as the Earth had done every night for seventy-odd years. Marlene took Marlowe into the caravan the women apparently lived in while they waited for his taxi to the airport. One bed in the back. The good bottle opener Marlowe once gave her sitting between them on the table, scattered among corks.

"And signed." Marlene slid across the files and dropped her pen on the table. Marlowe quickly scratched his own name underneath hers. He hadn't even read the agreement again.

"I'll put them into HR on Khrushchev-Kennedy. Saves trying to fax stuff with your internet."

"Good idea. About the funeral... I'm sorry with how we left things. And I am really sorry about your grandfather."

"Thank you."

"He was a great man."

"So they say."

"Do you want me to pay for half of the repairs to the Berlin apartment?"

"You are thorough, aren't you?"

"It's a lot of money, Vladi. You can't afford it."

"And exo-linguists are rolling in it these days, are they?"

"I'm about to move to Mars. The MSA job has a significant signing bonus."

"You're eligible?"

"I think there's a one-year minimum service, but yeah. You think we're going to run the place with untrained knuckleheads from Earth? We're pulling in talent in from across the system. A lot of people are pretty happy to leave a life mining underground asteroids for some newly terraformed Martian beaches."

"And destabilize the rest of the solar system in the process."

Marlene just shrugged.

"My responsibility is to settle Mars."

Marlowe nodded. Another reason to get this *Pegasus* case squared away and the transfer to the MSA put through. And be closer to Charlie. At least for a week or two. Perhaps he could squirrel a secret visit to their facility on Phobos, then punch him in the throat for not telling him there was months to go before he went into stasis. Or perhaps that's exactly how Charlie wanted it.

"I suppose UNSOCers aren't the farming and digging sort, are we?"

"Seems like the White House is right after all," Marlene said, knowing it would annoy him. Then she broke into a grin. "We're all a bunch of soft-boiled liberal eggheads. We need to send some blue-collar workers up there to 'win at space.'"

"And for the Soviets to exploit."

"Now who's being a conspiracy theorist?"

"The Russians have been running guns to the Lunans through the Black Moon gang for months now. They're just waiting for Treaty Day to—"

"Did you think I started to care about space gangs and Lunan politics?" Marlene cut him off with one of her insightfully brutal comments.

Marlowe sighed, then stared out the plastic window in the wistful hope to see some headlights to take him away from all this.

"I would say some things never change, Marlene. But then again..."

He glanced around at the remnants of the women's shared lives. All the way to the *hers* and *hers* mugs drying by the sink.

"But what? You're not the only one who gets to be pansexual."

Marlowe prickled at how breezily she turned a UNSOC norm into a barbed accusation.

"Can we not discuss our private lives?"

"We should've put that in on the divorce agreement."

"Marlene, please."

"Fine. We'll sit here in silence."

They listened to the ground-shaking vibrations of radio 'scopes turning on, disturbed only by the buzz of Marlene's cell letting them know the taxi was a few minutes away. Marlowe's suit was packed in his bag, but he wrapped his trench coat around Pauline's dino t-shirt. He could pick up a jumpsuit and sleeping kit on the overnight UNSOC flight to Khrushchev-Kennedy. The headlights blasted through the plastic window as the goodbye crept closer. He didn't know if she expected a hug, but a half-remembered thought he'd had on the plane overtook the awkward silence.

"Oh I wanted to ask you. I was reading through Martin's diary, and I found something. I thought you might know about it." He stepped out the caravan door and waved at the driver, who kept the engine running. Marlowe pulled out his grandfather's diary, the page that had been puzzling him bookmarked with Darla Foster's card. "These symbols he wrote down. I couldn't find them on the database. Do you know what they mean?"

"Of course," Marlene said, barely giving it a look. "That means Dorvethan."

CHAPTER 6: A STUDY ON THE MANY INTERPRETATIONS OF 'DORVETHAN'

Khrushchev–Kennedy International Space Station,
Near Earth Orbit
Population: 695,507

Sleeping on a dinosaur bone in a metal caravan left Marlowe painfully unable to catch a wink on the flight to Khrushchev-Kennedy. All the pajama bags, reclining beds and starry lights painted into the vessel's roof didn't help either. The news on every other passenger's screen was full of Charlie grinning next to his *Eden Partner* on the White House lawn, so he read through Marlene's old doctoral dissertation instead. It singularly failed to send him to sleep, while also failing to stick in his mind. Except for one phrase in the conclusion he distinctly remembered proofreading many years ago.

The mystery remains in the syntax of Dorvethan being utterly unique, sitting outside the decoded Alpha, Gamma and Omicron variants of The Messenger's language. With the 'Earth' based interpretations falling out of favor since the mid-seventies, no tendency, either absolute or implicational, still adequately explains Dorvethan. In the author's opinion, the semantics and context points to the 'danger' or 'warning' hypothesis of the word and its oddly arranged symbols, but that remains speculation.

'Speculative,' Marlowe remembered telling her, then asking if writing a doctoral dissertation on an untranslatable word meant academia was truly broken. But rehashing old fights with his *ex*-wife in his head was a sure-fire way to get lost on Khrushchev-Kennedy. The place was a demented maze. Designed by four mad architects who famously refused to speak to each other by the final phase of construction. That the flagship of joint Soviet-American engineering had remained in orbit since 1964 was a miracle in itself.

Marlowe vaped and cursed as he ran down a silent staircase that inexplicably skipped the floor he needed on the southern side of the giant 'pit,' a four hundred level deep chasm created when a new section was bolted on in the late seventies. He'd now have to double back through a dimly lit corridor spiked by shuttered store-fronts, their Punjabi lettering reflected in neon puddles of unknown substances.

A clutch of hand-boys surrounded the rusty, single-person elevator Marlowe needed to enter. The six of them stiffened at the waft of Marlowe's trench coat. In a burst of steam-grate air, all but one disappeared.

"Help you with your bags, sir?" The last remaining hand-boy asked in his thick Delhi accent. Although he was surely in his late twenties. Five pairs of quick feet dinged against the corrugated floor a few twists away. This one had been too slow off the mark. "Help you with anything, sir?"

Sweat crusted on his thin brown face. Filmy black hair danced over thick eyebrows. He was handsome, Marlowe thought. A spark of indentured beauty trapped on an island he could never earn enough to leave.

"The Open Space Treaty," Marlowe said, unsure of what else to say in this encounter that didn't seem to go anywhere. "You'll be able to go home now. You won't need to give up your exit visa anymore."

"Thank you, sir. But this is my home." He offered a grin. Perhaps out of politeness.

"The elevator goes down to the ninth district?"

"Yes sir, ninth district. The United Nations district. A very good district."

They both grinned and nodded as strangers do while the clanking infrastructure grumbled from the depths of the space station. Marlowe watched the Indian man tuft his hair away from heavy eyelashes. A suggestion of deep black fur sat beneath the slits of his untidy shirt.

"Listen." Marlowe held the heavy elevator door open and was close enough to the man to be instantly turned on by his natural scent. "I have a room down there, Gagarin Village, twelfth circle, room–" Marlowe checked the landing card in his pocket "sixteen B. Come see me, I'll be there in an hour." He added a wink and flicked his eyes to the man's crotch, so nothing could be misconstrued. The hand-boy's face started to turn, probably working out what he thought he could get away with charging. In Marlowe's experience, there was little that hand-boys *wouldn't* do for the right number of rubles.

"Oh, sir." His head started to shake, ever more violently. He looked disturbed, like he was about to vomit. "No sir. No."

"I'll pay," Marlowe quickly offered, as if it made the situation any better. The hand-boy's durable smile long gone. He backed away, then turned and ran, Marlowe was left alone, rejected even after he'd offered to pay. Marlowe slammed the elevator door closed with all his might, wishing a wire might cut loose and throw him a hundred thousand miles down to Earth.

The shame of the discrete interaction followed Marlowe all the way to the UNSOC human resources department. What had gone wrong in his life that he was propositioning hand-boys in the forgotten districts of Khrushchev-Kennedy? What had gone wrong that they turned him down?

"What's eating you?" asked a woman in a rainbow lanyard with a *she/her/она* badge. She clacked on a computer boxed in beige, with several fax machines chattering away on the desk behind.

"I need to register a divorce." Marlowe offered her the envelope. She made no move to take it.

"There's only one of you."

"So? Everything's signed. I just need my personnel file updated."

"And I need you and your spouse to come in here with you before I can update the system."

"But everything's signed!" He waved the paperwork in the face of bureaucratic immobility. "Do you know how much I spent on lawyers for this?"

She folded her arms. Marlowe took a breath and stared around the office. It should have sat half a dozen people, but they were alone. Boxes of paperwork piled high in the back. What did this woman care? UNSOC were packing up.

"Place of marriage?" She asked with a sigh.

"The Academy."

"Bandar Abbas, Inverness, Gauteng, or Moscow?"

"Since when are there *other* academies? Moscow!"

"Very well." She typed away, then leafed through the papers for their names. "Marlowe." A bolt of recognition slivered through the woman's eyes. It offered Marlowe a glimmer of hope that a clerical error might for once work in his favor. "I am sorry about your loss. Your grandfather was a great man. And I've gone ahead and added a note to your personnel files that you and your spouse will be coming in to register a divorce."

"A note? I have the signed agreement right here!"

"Please take a step back, sir. I cannot process your divorce in the system without both of you here."

"But she's transferring to the MSA next week. Will you have an office on Mars?"

"These are our new office hours." She handed Marlowe a sheet of printed paper. Two dozen places scored out, redacted from existence. Only New York remained, with new hours written out in pen and photocopied beyond recognition.

"Two afternoons a week?"

"We're downsizing. I suggest you call to make an appointment in advance. Have a nice day."

Marlowe turned, knowing fine well *have a nice day* was UNSOC-speak for *I have a stun gun under my desk and I'm not afraid to use it.* He wondered how long it would take Marlene to notice they were still married, and how much more this was going to cost him.

"Wait," the woman said. "Inspector Marlowe, right? Commissariat for Criminal Investigations?"

"Yes," Marlowe nodded, annoyed that while refusing to help, the woman had still read through the divorce papers and knew his name, rank and department.

"This fax came in for you on the secure line."

The wave of disappointment reached its crescendo. Donahue. His heart pounded at the scale of so much on the cusp of going wrong. Fucked over on the MSA transfer, or the pension, or maybe they they'd discovered the East German prisoners he'd ordered released. Commissar Donahue could yell across a secure fax just as well as he could in person.

Marlowe. Soviets still grinding my nutsack on the Pegasus case. Demanding one of their own join investigation. He's meeting you on K-K.

Great. A Communist Party political liaison poking his nose into every minutia of his work.

"Oh, and there's another one, too." The woman handed it over then collapsed back into her chair.

Play nice, Marlowe. It won't just be the cushy MSA job that disappears if you fuck this up. This is one dick-sucking contest you can't afford to lose.

The HR woman smirked like she'd enjoyed reading faxes several times already. Marlowe narrowed his eyes, flicking his coat as if he still wore a gun.

"Have a nice day," he told her.

The bar in the Gagarin Village sat in a squalid quarter of brothels and drinking dens. Shuttered storefronts were watched by impotent security cameras limp from neglect. The place boasted all the fittings of a seventies dive with none of the charm. Exposed pipes leaked into slop buckets in the corner of the bar. Booths around the back of the brass-rimmed island faded into musty darkness, a permanent December in a place beyond months.

Two quiet patrons sat on guard, nursing slow drinks over yesterday's *Pravda*. Marlowe thumbed the useless divorce papers as he waited for the absent barman, his coins ready to trade for the drowning of endless sorrows.

Their marriage had actually ended the day their twins died. A split-second decision. Frozen burgers from a Jersey-side gas station. A robber, passing Marlowe between sliding doors. The flair of angry eyes askew, a hastily stolen sixty-five dollars, the autopsy said. But Marlowe turned away. He knew something was wrong with every blink since that day five years before. But he still walked inside the gas station.

A car alarm blaring, a hot-wired engine revving, tires skidding. Then the almighty crash as the getaway car slammed into the back of his parked SUV. A hot shot from a passing officer. The thief dead, and two young lives strapped into the back seat snuffed out as well. The years since passed like a junk-ship ride through The Maelstrom. Slow and agonizing as each day ticked into a new well of agony, but

[69]

to look back on it now, one might wonder if any time had passed at all. Now, with each blink in every public space, he watched for men. For their bodies. For ones on the prowl. He and Charlie had behaved themselves through the vast majority of his marriage. In fact, they'd barely talked. Since the day they'd updated their marital status at a UNSOC HR office, Marlowe had been a dutiful husband, loyal to a fault. Perhaps it was years of pent-up repression pouring out now, in the dwindling twilight of his marriage. But Marlow knew the deeper reason he hunted men. It was the only distraction from constantly looking out for the twins. The only way to forget he'd once had it all.

With a barman still AWOL, Marlowe gave up waiting for a drink descended back into his grandfather's ramblings in the diary. The minutiae of institutionalization was taking over. The early days of UNSOC following Disclosure Day. Martin's shock appointment as the first Director-General, and his own cowboy cabinet led by the mad scientist and godfather of Messenger-tech, Doc Johnson. How odd the solicitor had demanded this diary be kept secret from UNSOC, and even his wife, since back in the late forties, the UNSOC founders were hashing out the same debate about the meaning of 'Dorvethan.'

'Doc Johnson's convinced it's the little grey guy's name. Scalzi thinks it's us. Svetlana's convinced it's a borrowed word from some other alien language, maybe the ones the Messenger says are coming to kill us all. Man, I wish that little guy could still communicate. We hooked him up to every medical machine in the world, but Doc Johnson says he has two, three days tops. The engine and anti-grav prototypes are showing promise, but there's still so much we need to ask him. Will we see the invasion coming? Will they 'slipstream' right into…'

"Something to drink." The barman said it as a statement of fact. He wiped oily hands on a rag, then spit-cleaned a glass.

"Just a beer."

"Eighteen dollars."

"Jesus Christ."

"New here, son? Think we brew this stuff in space? The bar's for drinking. Don't like it, there's a water fountain round the corner."

Marlowe glowered and dropped his UNSOC credit card onto

the bar.

"Two whiskies then. Single malts." The barman slid the card into his shirt pocket. "And a receipt." If Donahue wanted him to *play nice* with the Soviet liaison, this is what nice would cost. Marlowe soured over the whiskey, flicking carelessly through news stories on his pad, struggling to care about the world and its solar system edging apart at the seams.

UNSOC had sucked the pungent notion of conspiracy theory from all those who passed through the Academy. Students studied the once secret wires between Truman and Stalin after Roswell, learning why the great powers so quickly agreed to Disclosure Day. A post-war spirit emboldened by the simple truth state secrets such as those can never be kept under wraps for too long.

From the late summer of '47, newspaper clippings told stories of a massive military build-up around New Mexico, the very one Martin Reginald Marlowe's diary had detailed. Even some early articles tied it back to reports of a UFO crash outside the town of Roswell. Disclosure Day was as inevitable as bringing the Soviets inside from day one. When the planet faced a threat as existential as demons potentially raining from the heavens, only united would they have a chance at survival, just as they'd united to defeat Hitler.

UNSOC was the antithesis to conspiracy theories. One shimmering reason the alt-right Make Earth Great Again crowd were today frothing at the mouth to tear it all down. Politicians like Karla Landers railed against UNSOC still, even though years of the MEGA lobby's UNSOC budget cuts had crippled its sole purpose through a still-beating chest. With Open Space, they'd effectively taken away commanding space from Space Operations Command, what more did they want?

Marlowe shook his head at the conspiracy of liars who claim the world is built on falsehoods because they're too stupid to accept a reality they cannot understand. He shook his head at the brazenness of their theft. They'd stolen space. He flicked away advert after advert for soon-to-start jobs on the asteroid mines and synthetic THC farms around Saturn's moons. Now open to all. Exploiting above as they'd done below. Maybe those socialists had a point. Because who on Earth was writing about this sea-change coming to the skies? They accepted it as a fait accompli. At most commentators criticized slashing unemployment benefits for those who refused to take an off-world job. They never questioned the wisdom of exploiting space itself. Of turning the heavens into an unrestrained Wild West where one side wanted to extract only profit, and the other side to ferment only revolution. Both the capitalists and communists framed it as a change long overdue. Space was full of resources. It could be rich and prosperous if it was independent, rather than subsidized and run by Earth. And those living in space could decide for themselves how to organize and distribute that wealth.

No wonder UNSOC had moved up the launch of the mission to colonize Earth's nearest habitable neighbor to the very day the Open Space Treaty came into effect. Pivoting, they called it. A desperate attempt to stay relevant, others said. *The solar system secured, UNSOC readies for the next great leap.* Secured. Marlowe scoffed into his hundred-dollar whiskey. The *New York Times* piece he'd opened was a barely disguised UNSOC press release.

Who is Charlie Novikov, man's first interstellar ambassador?

A *Magazine* tie-in with Charlie grinning from his hundredth-floor mansion, taking a stroll in the park with his genetically perfect *Eden Partner,* and leading the thousand other colonists in a shelter-building workshop. *Charlie Novikov represents the pinnacle of man's first century of space exploration. Born to a typical UNSOC family, his Russian mother was a translator and his father served as Nigeria's ambassador to Armstrong, Novikov has done it all. From building uranium mines in the Asteroid Belt to leading the atmospheric enclosure of Saturn's satellite Phoebe, soon to be a major ethanol plantation championed by the former Secretary of Space. The leader of the Alpha Centauri mission's sister is no stranger to the spotlight either. Marlene Novikov-Marlowe was recently appointed deputy director of the Martian Settlement Authority. Novikov-Marlowe married into the family of UNSOC's inaugural director-general, Martin Reginald Marlowe, an icon of the space-faring community.*

"Is one of those for me?" Asked an unseen woman by his side. Marlowe didn't bother to look up. She'd clearly wandered into the wrong bar.

"It's worth more than you charge."

"Who says I have any interest in money?"

Marlowe's throat tightened, the voice shades of familiar. An international accent colored by Eastern Europe he'd last heard in an

East Berlin spy den. The Russian who called herself Darla Foster was leaning on the bar, red hair falling over congealed-blood lipstick. She snatched the second whiskey glass in a second, tapping short, practical nails against the glass as she took a sip.

"Blended." She offered the glass to a man behind her.

Sergei. The Russian. A man Marlowe could recognize by taste.

Any confidence Marlowe might enjoy leaked like coolant dripping down his back. Sergei too. He danced on his heels, a puppy needing to piddle. Ghost-white skin the color of fear the exact opposite to the way Marlowe had left him last, red-cheeked and postcoital. The gauze from his face was gone. A faint red scar sat there instead, prickled with sweat. Marlowe fought quickly to dismiss the many signals of shock.

"He's your agent?" Marlowe asked Darla. Her face didn't move. Spy-speak for surprise.

"This is Sergei Moscowitz, the USSR's liaison to the *Pegasus* investigation."

"I hope he's a better investigator than he is a spy." Darla continued not to react. "I caught him three times following me around New York." Sergei sucked in his cheeks. Marlowe offered only an unkind grin. Did he think there was a sense of solidarity between them?

"You never called me," Darla said, sipping the whiskey.

"I've yet to come across anything suspicious." Marlowe stared at Sergei across Darla's shoulder. Then removed the card she'd given him with her *space.su* email address from its placeholder in the diary.

"I find that hard to believe, Marlowe."

"Who do you work for?"

"I already told you."

"You're not KGB?" She'd counted spies outside the window and ran from HVA agents. But then again, Sergei had followed a strange man into the bathroom. He answered his own question. The KGB would never.

Darla laughed, throwing back her hair. Even Sergei grinned. The barman growled and lumbered over.

"You folks drinking?"

"A round for all of us," Darla drained the glass and slid it across

[73]

the bar. "He's buying."

They sat in a dimly lit booth, Darla and Sergei squeezed opposite Marlowe, whiskey on their breaths and a growing fear in the Russians' eyes. Sergei kept watch on the entrance. Marlowe ran one finger around his glass; they were all his as he'd paid for every drink. His eyes only on Sergei, who offered not even a flicker in return. Darla opened the inside of the Russian version of the *Pegasus* file, stamped *state secret* in heavy Cyrillic.

"Neptune. January 2016." She drew a circle on the blank inside page of the folder. "Two cosmonauts found dead in a sealed pod." She drew a line straight up, free-handing a smaller circle. "Two weeks later, an unmanned radio 'scope on the Neptunian Trojans goes offline."

"Not unusual," Marlowe responded. Darla glared at him under a wave of hair.

"The deaths or the radio 'scope?" Darla said. Marlowe just shrugged in reply.

Sergei was looking increasingly nervous, tearing a napkin to shreds between his fingers. Like somehow Darla was about to find out what they'd done in the bathroom at RFK. What did it say about Marlowe that he wished they could do it again.

"A hydroponic farmstead on Ariel." Darla drew inwards, adding a few shapes to represent the moons of Uranus. "A worker is found dead, the agro-covers ripped to shreds. Not unusual?" Marlowe shrugged. "All that remains of her body is a bag of skin. All the insides have been sucked out. Sound familiar?" Darla let the question hang, but didn't stop drawing. She ran the pen inwards again, scoring the paper file. "Hyperion, Saturn. November 2016. Four workers go missing in a suspected mine collapse. Only in January are their bodies recovered. Or what's left of them. Torsos ripped from the spine. Exploded against the walls of the mine, splattered, frozen." Sergei looked queasy and quickly inspected his fingernails, as if iced gore might still be stuck underneath. Marlowe knew the look of someone scarred by a crime scene. Darla was only getting started.

"March 2017. Launch of the Open Space negotiations. Two deaths on Calypso."

"I didn't hear about any of these cases."

"Of course you didn't." She held her pen like a knife, scarring the wood of the table as she hit circle after circle, across the map of the solar system. "Three deaths on Prometheus, Ganymede, Ceres in the Asteroid Belt, and a murder-suicide in a sealed pod on the *OS Karl Liebknecht*. See a pattern?"

He saw the map she was drawing. It pointed straight to Earth. But that wasn't what bothered him.

"You're claiming there's been… what, dozens of unexplained deaths under UNSOC jurisdiction? And I've seen evidence of none of this?" She began to speak, but Marlowe continued over her. "The Commissary for Criminal Investigations has seen none of this. We have a dual review system. You have to sign off on every death in service, and so do the Americans. If one party is not satisfied, we re-open the investigation. Which is exactly what we're doing now with the *Pegasus*."

Now Sergei spoke up: "Unless both sides cover it up."

Marlowe scoffed.

"Ridiculous. This is… MEGA-style conspiracy."

He leveled the accusation at Darla. She didn't respond, but elbowed Sergei in the side. With enough anxiety to fill an epic, he reached under the table, looked twice at the door, then from his own bag dropped a pile of folders on the table in front of Marlowe. Each one with the same *state secret* stamped in Russian.

They both watched intently as Marlowe peeled a file from the top, mouthing the Russian sounds. The preliminary report of a death on Ariel. A brief description, a farmer called Anastasia Breslev; a bag of her skin found on a farm, just as Darla had said. Marlowe lifted another file. The Hyperion incident. Nothing left of three bodies from the waist up but what was scraped from frozen rock. Even the words poorly translated in Marlowe's head were stomach-churning.

Now Darla glanced at the entrance with nervous worry while Sergei's focus remained on Marlowe, anticipating the counterargument.

"I can't handle stolen state files. And UNSOC has no jurisdiction over what member states choose to disclose or not." Marlowe placed them back on the pile. Darla sat back, visibly annoyed. The files sat as an immovable mountain between them. Protocol dictated Marlowe should get up and leave right then and file a report he'd been shown classified information. Leave Sergei and Darla to their fates as Soviet whistleblowers. But instead, he leaned forward. "If you're telling me the USSR and United States governments have conspired to cover up dozens of suspicious deaths to protect Open Space, or whatever it is you think they're up to, then I don't know how you want me, specifically me, to help. I don't know what you expect me to do."

"Investigate *Pegasus*," she fired back, cheeks aflame and breath hot. "I'm throwing everything I have at keeping the airlock door open an inch, Marlowe. I've put everything on the line. One case. UNSOC can investigate this. You can tell the truth about this one case that came across your desk before they shut it all down."

"Darla, no one is shutting down my investigation. I'll get to the bottom of what happened on the *Pegasus*. Rest assured."

Darla sucked in a deep breath, calming, reasserting her presence. She flicked back hair and indicated she wanted to get up in the politest possible manner. Sergei fumbled over himself to move as Darla stood, purse slung over her shoulder.

"I would like to believe you, Marlowe, but your confidence is not why I am concerned." Darla glared down at both he and Sergei, a mother disappointed by two useless sons.

"What then, ma'am, is the nature of your concern?"

"In quite literally a few days' time, it's not going to matter what you find out about the *Pegasus*." She lifted a glass from the table, empty but for the melted dregs of an ice cube turned amber from the last drops of hundred-dollar whiskey. She snarled it down. "Nobody's going to care, and there will hardly be a UNSOC left to do anything about it."

CHAPTER 7: THE MAELSTROM: LOCATION OF LAST KNOWN SUSPICIOUS SIGHTING

Marlowe closed the diary on his lap and pretended to sleep. Reading notes of Martin's meetings with Catholic cardinals trying to reconcile Disclosure with doctrine and discussing times of the Sabbath on Mars with rabbis was far less interesting after the multitude of images of violent deaths Darla had shown him. Or the lingering feeling that she might very well be right about her allegations of a US-Soviet coverup. So he kept quiet, eyes shut as Sergei flew the rickety ship toward the asteroid belt: a squat, boxy Soviet vessel. Essentially a converted truck with an engine bolted to the back and double layers of duct tape to keep the windows sealed.

Darla had at least kept up her part of the charade. Donahue had faxed him that morning after a glowing report from the Soviet liaison. She couldn't be happier Marlowe was now on the case, and couldn't wait to see what this pair of investigators would find out, chasing down an eyewitness from the *Pegasus*, working somewhere in the Belt. The only positives Marlowe found from the whole situation was Darla's own words. That in three days' time, nobody would give a damn.

"We tracked down a Corporal Bradley Gomez to a mine somewhere in the Belt," Sergei said, unprompted. They hadn't shared a word in over fifty million miles. Marlowe had no reason to start now. "He's the best lead we have. I think this is the best place to begin, no?"

"Which?" Marlowe kept his eyes closed, head resting against cold vibrations, the shaking of his skull adding to the grumbling hum of the vessel that had been vintage since Regan. Space was never quiet.

"Which what?"

"Which mine!" Marlowe sat up, suddenly annoyed by Sergei's very presence. "There's two million 'roids floating around The Maelstrom. Which one is Corporal Gomez supposed to be on?"

"Our source didn't say."

"Your source?"

"The US Defense Department Personnel system."

"Jesus, Sergei. Don't tell me that. So, where the fuck are we going?"

"The Bakunin Collective."

"Damn. I didn't pack my open toe sandals or bring my own bong water."

"I have a—"

"Source. Yeah, I get the picture. How you people won a war, I'll never know."

They flew in protracted silence. More annoying was the half-breaths Sergei kept taking. As if desperate to say something that couldn't quite come out. Marlowe returned to shut eyes and folded arms.

"About the first time we met at the airport…" Sergei said after Marlowe had heard his lips practice the phrase a half dozen times. "It was… out of character for me. I am sorry if you felt used."

"Used? No, it's fine," Marlowe said, more out of instinct than anything else. What, did he expect to find the love of his life, to replace the hole Charlie was making in his heart in some airport bathroom?

"Marlowe, I—"

"I told you, it's fine. I sucked you off, then you left. I wasn't expecting anything more."

"That's why you rejected me at RFK?"

"Can we talk about something else?"

Sergei coughed at the uncomfortableness of the thing being named and reviewed the instruments for no reason. Marlowe watched him through the crack of his eyelids. The scruffy stubble now edging into a beard. The dark hair and sallow eyes that said so much that Marlowe couldn't translate. The not-very-effective spy revealing himself to be something else entirely.

"So," Marlowe said, changing the subject even if Sergei wouldn't.

"What are you?"

"An astrobiologist."

"No. I mean, you know, are you gay? Bisexual? Married?"

"I'm a Soviet astrobiologist."

Marlowe sucked in a breath of recycled air at the heavily layered answer. It said so much, leaving Marlowe staring into a valley of mild annoyance, while on the other side was a field of sorrow. It didn't have to be this way. UNSOC's diversity policy had been a decades-long process of endless sub-committees and working groups that many living in the shadows had preferred not to happen. The process had begun in the early nineties, Marlowe remembered watching it on television as a young boy. Clinton's doomed attempts to allow gays and lesbians to serve in the U.S. military prompted the inevitable question; what about space? The millions of men and women in uniform beyond Earth were subject to UNSOC jurisdiction, not Earth laws. Clinton bringing the debate to the forefront upended the unwritten rule of 'what happens in space, stays in space,' as long as it stays sealed behind an airlock door.

Cases could still be brought, investigations started and UNSOC employment terminated if 'behavior' crossed the undrawn lines of the morality clause. At the Academy, Marlowe had studied a case from the seventies of two men who'd requested the same living quarters on Luna. They had taken their case right up to the UNSOC judicial review panel, before ultimately being dismissed from employment and deported back to Earth. One half of the couple became a progressive state legislator in California, the other half disappeared into a Siberian gulag.

Others felt Clinton's push to come to a single policy for US personnel on Earth and off it had actually prompted the decriminalization of same-sex relationships across the Warsaw Pact countries. Academic debates on Marxist theories of gender and sexuality were tested and stretched. Theorists and activists East of the Iron Curtain faced the might of changing Communist dogma, and won. Change rumbled out from Berlin. The USSR repealed their sodomy laws in 1993, cresting with the Thirtieth Congress of the Communist Party of the Soviet Union officially declaring gays and lesbians as a 'minority group oppressed and exploited by capitalism and deserving of liberation.'

But who wanted to be declared as a member of an 'oppressed minority group?' Tartars and Cossacks had been deported under Stalin. The number of ethnic Turks, Georgians, Mongols, Koreans, Chechens and others making it northward in the Soviet bureaucracy or winning an exit visa to serve in UNSOC was less than the dribble of oxygen leaking out of their vessel at acceptable levels. Sergei already had the dark eyes and square jaw of something non-Russian. Caucus or Balkan or a mix, Marlowe realized how long he'd been staring at the sallow skin pock-marked by stubble. Red at the neck, beads of sweat from sitting in the captain's chair as the dials and nav-screen pointed towards the haunted forest of the Asteroid Belt.

"Planning to take advantage of Open Space?" Marlowe asked, the nav-screen bleeping as Mars passed by on their left. "Perhaps you could find some more freedom with a job out here." Sergei scoffed. Marlowe was so taken by the response he quickly scanned the dials and instruments, as if the visceral reaction had come from a ship reading or a passing transport sending out a distress signal their own ship was poorly equipped to deal with. Marlowe broached the subject again, just to be sure. "There's going to be a lot of demand for astrobiologists. Someone with your experience could easily make a good living."

"You Americans." Sergei tutted and shook his head.

"I'm not—"

"Fine, not an American then. UNSOC born and bred, so you say. But you bourgeoise. People cry out for freedom on Earth, off Earth, and all they get is capitalism."

"Capitalism is a form of freedom."

"No!" Sergei struck the control panel with such force the ship gave a little shudder. "Capitalism is nothing more than capitalism. It serves no other purpose but the exploitation of mankind for profit. Capitalism is slavery. It is a demon that sucks in bodies and devours them because that is its nature. And the demon keepers stand around the mouth of the cave, pointing to the terrifying darkness inside and they say: 'here, here is freedom.'"

"How melodramatic. A Maxim Gorky quote?"

"At least some good will come of this Open Space. Free elections. Free speech. Freedom to organize the revolution."

"If communism is so effective, why does it always need a revolution? Why not let the people decide?"

"Because there is no decency the exploiting class will not shred to overthrow democracy and found their capitalist oligarchy. A handful of elections. That is the only time there is."

"So that's why the Soviets are smuggling weapons up to Luna and across the colonies? To let the 'people' decide?"

"I don't know about these things."

"Of course you don't, Sergei. You're only an astrobiologist."

Marlowe cursed the fact an ejector seat was not fitted to space vehicles. Their ship was too small to have an escape pod, either. And the business of their investigation was still to unfold. The supposed 'evidence' Darla expected to find. The clarification of a theory a million spacefarers and two superpowers could not confirm.

"I assume we're not being bugged." Marlowe made a show of running fingers along the crevices of the window. "Do you believe Darla?"

"What is belief? There are hypotheses. There is data. And there is logical inquiry."

"And what hypothesis about these space murders has your *logical inquiry* led you to believe?"

"That's what we're about to find out."

Marlowe flicked through Darla's secret file once again, as if the Cyrillic could be decrypted a level further and reveal the secrets to the supposed murder-suicide.

"This source of yours," Marlowe said, closing the folder yet again in growing frustration. Both from Sergei's uncompromising attitude and being cooped up in a junk-yard ship. "You trust him?"

"Ah, what a question. Do I trust Abraxes." Sergei laughed for private reasons Marlowe was afraid to probe.

"So he has a name."

"He has a name. And… he's an informer, not *the* source."

Marlowe felt the overwhelming urge to grab the controls and turn the ship around, even if they would risk running out of fuel halfway between the Belt and Khrushchev-Kennedy. Being marooned seemed like a risk worth taking than a wild goose chase through the lawless asteroids.

"So why couldn't your informer just tell you where Bradley Gomez is?"

"I told you. He's not the source. But he can lead us there."

Marlowe stared out the portholes. A billion stars glittered, hiding a billion more secrets. The Belt was getting closer, though. The navigation system bleeped with increasing regularity. Marlowe could almost smell the metallic grind of burning rock mixed with the sweat of a certain type of man. A man who would gladly leave Earth behind and take up permanent residence living under the surface of uninhabitable rocks. The miners were not UNSOC employees, carefully screened and trained, or raised by off-world parents. No, the miners were those who had voluntarily given up their right to breathe clean air. Debt and crime; that's why men left Earth. Certainly not to create a better society.

"Let's just hope your informer leads us to your source who leads us to Bradley Gomez before we end up as the next two victims on Darla's list of unsolved murders."

To that, Sergei had nothing to say.

Only the violet haze of The Maelstrom illuminated the interior of the Seawatch Bar. The warning lights among the scattered asteroids making up for the lack of sunlight this side of the Belt. Here it was always night, and on this part of the chunky, Kyrgyzstan-sized rock known as The Bakunin Collective, it was always damp.

Sergei had sent Marlowe by himself to track down Abraxes, the informer who may lead them to the source who knew on which of the two million rocks of the Belt they might find one Bradley Gomez. Sergei's excuse to 'check the ship' screamed a private update with Darla. So, he'd left Sergei alone at the docking bay, knowing there was little else but the faith of a spy to keep him from flying off and abandoning Marlowe on this rock.

Marlowe wasn't convinced it wouldn't be quicker to skip 'roid to 'roid, starting with the largest which hosted ten thousand miners or more, then filtering down to the mile-sized ones mined by a two-man team. But with three hundred thousand souls in the Belt, it might take some time to find Bradley Gomez.

Of all the damned places in the solar system, The Maelstrom was the perfect place to hide. The amount of cases Marlowe had closed with a *last known location: The Belt* had necessitated the manufacture of a specialist stamp. Those who wanted to get lost among the Maelstrom likely began their journey right here, beneath the dripping pipes and unlit stools of the Seawatch Bar.

A man in heavy coats to keep out damp and cold leaned against the port-hole window, beyond the frayed edges of his dreadlocked beard drifted passing rocks. They left rainbow trails through the dust mites of Belt-space, nothing more than oily residue smeared across space. Marlowe took a stool two down from the man he'd been told by three separate people would be Abraxes. *"He don't got a flying license,"* one passing miner helpfully said. *"But he'll try to charge you like he does."*

"What's good here?" Marlowe said, breaking the rumbling silence interrupted by the scurrying of 'roid mites along dark corners of the floor. Marlowe leaned down to check the bottoms of his trousers were securely wrapped into his socks and boots, feet wrapped around the bar stool to save from an infestation of the hybrid creatures which scurried across the floors here. He was surprised to see Abraxes' leg resting so nonchalantly on the floor. Until a blinking light from a passing 'roid revealed his leg to be a metallic peg.

"Wantin' tae drink?" The man who was supposed to be Abraxes coughed out. Every breath seemed to be an effort. He didn't bother to turn and look at Marlowe but leaned across the bar and lifted up an iron goblet. He rolled it sideways to Marlowe and nodded to the unmanned taps. Marlowe squirted a cup full of piss-colored beer. A heavy magnet on the goblet's underside stuck it to the bar to protect from the frequent 'roid quakes.

Marlowe readied an opening gambit in his head, wanting to make clear he came with authority, but not too much so Abraxes got spooked. A figure approached from the depths of the darkness behind the bar. A woman in dirty overalls who glared at both patrons like she resented their very presence. Marlowe nervously sipped the carbonated crap in the iron goblet, bracing for a harsh attack that he'd filled his own cup. Before the barmaid unleashed her fury on Abraxes, he cut her off at the opening gate.

"This is what you're giving me?" He snapped the magnetic goblet from the bar and flung the fizz-less juice to the ground. He couldn't be asked to pay for something he didn't drink.

"There ain't nothing wrong with the Nogah ale pumps." The barmaid screeched back, arguing like an old married couple.

"You ain't putting it on my tab."

"Gimme your MVT code if you got a complaint, Abraxes. Or are you too chicken-shit
to—"

"It's on me," Marlowe said, defusing the tensions that seemed seconds from turning violent. Marlowe was careful not to show the UNSOC colors of his credit card, but the barmaid took it all the same. "Got anything with more of a kick?"

"Vodka. Home brewed."

"Sounds, um, lovely. One for yourself as well, ma'am. Abraxes?" Marlowe glanced over. "Can I tempt you?"

He shrugged from the depths of his moldy overcoat, the peg leg clanging against the metal bar. He was smart enough at least to know when he was being bought. Their vodkas arrived, tinged with the oily rainbow run-off endemic to the Maelstrom. Marlowe watched the legs of his breath linger in the coldness, the shine of the multicolor tinge before it disappeared from the waft of Abraxes' coat. He reached over and snatched the iron shot glass from the magnetic bar.

"Lookin' to disappear?" Abraxes asked. The barmaid raised a suspicious eye but knew when she wasn't wanted. She flung Marlowe's credit card back at him and slunk away into the darkness. But the UNSOC card was stuck to the magnetic bar. "Or you lookin' to get someone disappeared?"

"Neither," Marlowe said, finally prying the card free. Not before Abraxes noted the UNSOC logo and slighted back against the porthole window, as if he was readying to make a run for it. Marlowe swallowed away a smirk at the thought of the peg-legged bootlegger dashing out of the bar. Although the complex maze of corridors and walkways dug through this 'roid made him think twice about spooking the only one around who knew his way out of here. "I'm, uh, looking to find someone in the Maelstrom. A colleague said you could help."

"This colleague KGB?"

"Close enough. Why? Does it matter?"

Abraxes heaved himself from the bar stool, snatching Marlowe's vodka too before he'd had a chance to so much as sniff it. The peg leg speared a scurrying creature, squealing into death as Abraxes drained the vodka and let the metallic cup snap back to the bar.

"KGB are the only ones what pay their debts."

"So you'll help? My colleague has a ship waiting at the—"

"Meital," Abraxes called his colleague through a bulky contraption strapped to his wrist. "Does that hunk o' junk crowding up my docking bay have a price tag?"

The device crackled like an old HAM radio. Marlowe listened intently for any sign of Sergei or a struggle, but a robotic-like woman's voice cut through the static.

"*Enough to cover a debt, that's for sure.*" Abraxes offered a wide, toothy grin. Not so much toothy but rotten black stumps sticking out of raw gums. His wiry hair and dreadlocked beard over the heaviest of long coats that could easily conceal a ship-killer gave Abraxes the air of a creature from the deep. As if the feared Krakens of old had slithered out of the depths of the ocean and made a home on the rotating asteroids of The Maelstrom. A heavy hand fell on Marlowe's shoulder.

"You def-netly gon' need *my* help, son."

Sergei had seemed relatively unbothered at being held up by a woman with a shaved head and mechanically altered body suit. As if he'd known all along this is how Abraxes operated and had stayed with the ship to stop it just being stolen. When Marlowe and Abraxes had returned to the docking bay, only then did Meital lower the taser. Sergei handed a black credit card to Abraxes, who tapped it on his wrist to check the promised fifty thousand rubles were loaded onto it. Sergei assured them another fifty would be loaded once they found the target, and that was enough to convince the odd couple to board the ship, but in the captain's and first officer's chairs. Marlowe and Sergei had to kneel behind the seats, holding onto rickety handles as their backsides crashed into each other, and hoping wherever their destination was, it wouldn't take long.

"He's at The Lighthouse," Meital said as they darted through the busy Maelstrom space crowded with rocks. Legs of broken drilling machines floated through zero-gravity too, threatening to rip their hull in half at any given second. Abraxes had no eyes for space, though, only to tell Meital she was wrong.

"Bullshit. Muffy Dilinger would pickle his cock 'afore he'd show his face back there. The kid's at Seawatch."

"You peg-legged moon brain. Trenchfall's where we need to go. He's performing a twice-per-shift set at The Lighthouse!" Meital lunged for the wheel.

"Ger'off me!" Abraxes fought back, leaving the wheel unguarded in a constellation of sharp-edged rocks. Only Sergei's quick intervention—diving headlong towards the controls—prevented a collision with a vivacious 'roid careering across the bow. He maneuvered the ship clear with only a slight scratch on the paintwork.

"All right," Marlowe said, aiming to calm himself before anyone else. "Abraxes, move. I'll pilot this thing."

"The hell you will!" The tiny cabin erupted again as Abraxes fought off Sergei from the wheel. Meital's mechanically enhanced body suit finally showed its worth. She held Abraxes flat against the chair while keeping the wheel steady.

"I'll drive," she said.

"Sorry, boys," Abraxes' shout echoed around the cramped space. "Looks like we'll be dead within the minute." He unleashed a laugh as oily as the rainbow residue across the window, but they clambered over each other to swap places, nonetheless. Sergei rubbed his wrist, red and swollen from where Abraxes had smacked him away. Marlowe stopped himself asking Sergei if he was okay. The natural reaction bubbled up in his throat, but he swallowed it away, staring out at the chaotic Maelstrom instead of Sergei nursing his arm.

Despite Abraxes' prediction, Meital kept them alive for longer than a minute. Although she spun the ship in a different direction, taking a cavalier attitude to the floating rocks, leaving Marlowe to instinctively duck as they flew under 'roids.

"So…" Marlowe said, if no one else would ask the obvious. "Where are we going?"

"The Lighthouse," Meital said firmly. "On Trenchfall. A couple hundred miles deep."

"And we're going to see…?"

"The one person in the system Abraxes should be kept far, far away from." Meital said it, but Abraxes smirked in the mirror. "A Delving Prime scrap-heap lad named Franx. He knows the location—and measurements—of every man in the Asteroid Belt."

"How does he—"

Abraxes cut him off with a chuckle. "He's a boy of many talents, our Franx. Queen of The Maelstrom, some might say. And hellofa cute." Abraxes offered a toothless grin to Marlowe and Sergei. This time Marlowe did look Sergei's way. Wandering eyes wondering just what he'd got them into. Meital seemed to be in on the joke, too.

"Let's hope your Franx is one to forgive and forget," she said, steering them away from a loose digger caught orbiting a mined-out 'roid.

"It wasnae my fault, woman! I was abducted."

"And how many brain cells did them aliens leave you with, Abraxes?"

Marlowe glared at Sergei with a *are you hearing this?* vibe, but the Russian remained cross-legged, rubbing his sore wrists. Marlowe leaned between the seats.

"Who abducted you, Abraxes?"

"Here we go," Meital said to herself, yet loud enough for them all to hear.

"Now this is a story worth telling," Abraxes said, twirling loose strands of his beard. Meital leaned into Marlowe, adding:

"Worth listening to is another matter. But this piece of junk ain't got a radio."

"It all started," began Abraxes, "when I took a job running a vat of opium from Armstrong to Hyperion back in '16. At least, I *thought* it was was opium."

CHAPTER 8: THE DECADENT BEHAVIORS OF A MAELSTROM DRAG SHOW

"I wouldn't pay Abraxes much attention," Meital whispered in Marlowe's ear as they waited for the tiny, two-person elevator to return and take them into the belly of Trenchfall. Fifth largest asteroid in The Maelstrom, so Abraxes had declared as they landed. Second only in population to Ceres, the Belt's dwarf planet. Anything had been better than the rambling, ranting story that was less alien abduction, more voyeuristic witness to a brutal mass murder.

Abraxes had been fleeing a bad feeling when he landed on Hyperion, a moon of Saturn, in the days after an American election the anti-UNSOC 'Make Earth Great Again' crowd had surprisingly won. Marlowe distinctly remembered that night, consoling a sobbing Marlene at what was supposed to be a victory party. Abraxes had claimed he'd been paid to cart off ballot boxes of postal votes to Hyperion and bury them in the moon's frozen mine shafts. The shaft had been rigged to explode, though, trapping Abraxes and four miners in a tunnel. Abraxes wasn't meant to be there. He hid in a vent while the miners calmly went about their standard escape procedures.

That was until a creature, a beast, an alien, Abraxes called it, murdered each of the four miners. He hadn't *seen* the alien but watched how the four men acted, and died. Professional miners, easily able to work their way out of a collapsed system with a radio map and some well-placed charges. There was no reason for them to turn on each other, Abraxes had sworn to Marlowe. They only needed to clear one cave wall to get through to the southern hemisphere of Hyperion's tunnel network. An hour of work, if not less. One of the group wandered away to take a dump as the others calmly brewed black coffee before they began the effort. He returned… changed. Abraxes hadn't known how to describe it. From the vent he watched this *changed* man viciously feast on the flesh of his friends, eating their torsos and leaving behind three bloody stumps of legs, then a limp sack of skin of the body that had been 'occupied.'

When Marlowe had whispered to Sergei, voice starting to shake, this was the exact case Darla had described, Sergei responded with: *did you think we were lying?* Marlowe had seen a lot in his time, but this—he tried to swallow away a dry mouth—was starting to get strange.

"I really, really wouldn't worry," Metial said again, as if measuring the depth of despair which had opened in Marlowe's stomach. They squeezed into the elevator together, and she slammed the grate door shut. "Abraxes also thinks UNSOC is covering up an alien attack on the *Pegasus*."

"The *Pegasus*?" The elevator began its freefall through varying levels of gravity. Sometimes it felt like they were falling up, then down, then weightless. Meital's mechanical body suit kept her anchored, while Marlowe had to hold onto the walls for dear life.

"I just think it's haunted. No wonder the heliopause monitors all stay on base at Triton these days."

"You mean there's no one out there anymore where the *Pegasus* should be? Our first line of defense is… unmanned?"

Meital gave a mechanical shrug.

It was a strange relief for Marlowe to slide out of the gravity-defying elevator onto terra firma. His head was spinning more than enough for his body to catch up. But the relief didn't last for long. Abraxes was waiting and snatched Meital's arm with a grasp of fear.

"We gotta move."

Abraxes led them swiftly through Trenchfall's arrivals hall. The cavernous space filled with workers between jobs. Some leaving, some arriving, others just hanging around, waiting for their next paycheck. They loitered on stairways to nowhere, making camp under dripping ceilings or near exhaust pipes for heat. They carried their own tools on their backs; heavy electro-hammers or magno-sickles. Dirt and exhaustion swirled among the men—the few women were indistinguishable from their comrades—and the whole scene left Marlowe in mind of those huge digital paintings in Leningrad. Billboards brighter than Times Square which littered Nevsky Prospekt, showing triumphs named things like *Workers and Soldiers Take to the Streets.*

"What's the rush?" Meital asked. Abraxes couldn't stop looking over his shoulder. The peg-leg dinging against the concrete floor and the fact they were clearly not miners in a crowd was a sure-fire way to be seen when Abraxes wanted to disappear. Marlowe tried to shoulder up to Sergei several times, but the Russian was willing to be of no help.

The rough dregs of The Maelstrom grunted mean looks as their odd foursome rushed by. The miners took more notice of them than the couple of other outliers dotted around the arrivals hall. Fresh-faced young folk handing out *Socialist* Worker newspapers and Styrofoam cups of coffee. Given the amount of balled up newspapers that stank as if they'd been used as toilet paper, it seemed the workers were not too keen on reading. But it was all kindling to a powder keg. Marlowe knew The Maelstrom-division UNSOC headquarters well. A perennially under-staffed four-floor office back on Khrushchev-Kennedy. They all preferred their comfortable office jobs pushing paper to actually making the trip to this sweltering, sweat-stained dumping ground of the dregs of humanity. Marlowe didn't blame them.

It was a known fact that the Belt remained under-inspected by UNSOC administrators. What the miners lost in occupational health and safety protections, they made up for in the lack of identification checks and the chance to make a few extra bucks after quotas were reached. Marlowe hoped the kids sprouting revolutionary zeal would be on the same side as the workers when lawlessness truly hit The Maelstrom two-and-a-half days from now. If people worried about the transition to Open Space getting ugly, this is where the ugliness would happen. Sergei doubtless had the same thought. He finally slid up to Marlowe while Abraxes fretted over three different corridors.

"A beautiful sight, no?" Sergei asked with a smirk. He sipped a Styrofoam coffee; a *Pravda* folded under his arm. "The early days of the Worker's Republic of Trenchfall."

"Lost?" Meital interrupted Abraxes, who was flipping a paper map forwards and backwards. Marlowe was growing nervous at their conspicuousness. Miners seemed to be coalescing closer, and not to line up for free coffee, either.

"I could ask?" Marlowe offered.

"No!" Both Meital and Abraxes responded.

"And I'm not lost, I just haven't been down here in a long time."

A pounding clank from the distance of the arrivals hall gave little respite, although it seemed to distract the miners.

"Um, Abraxes," Meital mechanically yanked his heavy overcoat. "I know you ain't lost, but maybe you wanna get found pretty soon."

They all looked where Meital was staring. The thumping was coming from a group of too many mine workers heaped into an aircar, so it kept smacking into the ground as it skidded through the crowd. The half-dozen workers on board the two-man vessel waved their weapons—hammers and sickles—as they sped straight for them.

"Oh, shit."

"Abraxes!" A screeching voice raised alarm in the arrival's hall. Men parted as the aircar swerved and scurried and careered towards them. It wasn't going straight, but it showed no sign of slowing down either.

"Huh," Meital offered with a strange calmness. "That looks like Sali."

"Abraxes!" The screeching voice screamed again. A large mine worker was driving the aircar. More likely woman than man, but it was hard to tell. "I'll fucking kill you!"

"This way!" Abraxes commanded, shoving Meital then Marlowe into a corridor seemingly at random. He flung Sergei, too, and a Styrofoam cup of coffee splattered across the floor as the four rushed down a narrow hallway, their reflections shattering in dirty puddles of rainbow liquid.

"Can the aircar fit through here?" Marlowe asked, panting as they ran, although Abraxes moved more like a one-legged crab. They couldn't go quicker, as he was the one who supposedly knew where they were going.

"Nope! That's why this way is the right way."

"Grab that skin bag!" Screamed the one called Sali. The aircar smacked straight into the corridor entranceway, barely fifty feet behind. But the crash had disrupted Sali's gang.

"You wrecked my vehicle!" One shouted.

"With the rubles that slimy bastard owes me, I'll buy you a dozen. Now after him!"

The corridor was endless. Nothing but pipes and flickering lights. Pangs in Marlowe's chest made him wonder whether to give up now. Maybe selling Abraxes to Sali would get them to their source quicker.

A whipping magno-sickle interrupted Marlowe's thoughts. It flew just shy of his ear, then landed with a ricocheting thud into a pipe above. The hissing was immediate. A shower of steam cascaded down, obscuring sight and sound.

"In here!" It was Meital. Marlowe spun around, unable to see anything until a mechanical hand gripped around his arm and dragged him through a side door into darkness. They all powered through under the cover of steam as Meital slammed the door firmly shut.

"All safe and sound," Abraxes told them with confidence. He smacked on a flickering torch, illuminating the metal ledge they were on, next to a staircase descending into an endless shaft as deep as the corridor out there was long. Meital used her enhanced strength to wind the hatch wheel shut. Marlowe could be confident no one was getting in, but neither were they getting out. Only Sergei appeared unbothered, gazing down into the endless depths cut through the 'roid.

"I know this place," the Russian said. "The Lighthouse bar is down there."

"Exactly!" Abraxes chuckled and smacked him casually on the back. "We're right where we need to be."

With the other three quite content with how things had panned out, Marlowe had no choice but to follow them down the unending stairwell.

"So, are you going to tell us what happened between you and this Sali?" Marlowe asked.

"Oh, you know the story. I held her husband for ransom. He fell in love with me."

"With you?" He shot back, crueler than he'd intended it to be. Abraxes who was leading the way halted his descent, turning on his peg-leg to stare up at Marlowe. The wiry beard and messy hair obscuring what were once handsome eyes.

"Yes, with me. Of course, I was much younger then."

Meital had no interest in stopping. She pushed past Abraxes and beckoned the others to follow.

"And here I was thinking you'd *improved* with age."

"I'm looking for someone," Abraxes told the serving woman. She glowered at him under a tight and colorful head wrap, her bare arms jiggling as she cleaned a magnetic goblet with a filthy rag, replacing it in the rack above her dirtier than before. The bar was busy and getting rowdier as more miners, skin and clothes sparkling with star dust, crowded the place. At least their attention was expectantly trained on the stage at the far end of the bar, complete with a pole for dancing.

Marlowe stayed several men back from Abraxes. Close enough to hear everything, though, and chase after the man should he try to disappear which, Marlowe believed, was increasingly likely. He glanced back and nodded to Sergei by the bar entrance. He stood there like a bouncer, despite every laughing miner who came in being twice his size and could snap Sergei in half with one hand while chugging a beer with the other.

"I said I'm looking for someone," Abraxes shouted louder to the woman who kept a suspicious eye on their group. Marlowe didn't blame her.

"I heard yeh. You gonna buy a drink first?" But it was hardly a question. Abraxes nodded, and she pulled down the same filthy cup she'd just put away. After spitting inside, she wiped it with the same rag slung over her shoulder, then filled it with ale. It didn't look much more appetizing than the piss water back at the Bakunin Collective. But the miners seemed to be enjoying gallons of the stuff. Abraxes offered a couple of crumpled U.S. dollars as opposed to the tokens the miners paid with. She slid the notes straight into her bosom.

"So who's you lookin' for?"

"Scrawny little kid. Goes by the name Franx, sometimes. Maybe he's in the back cleaning dishes. Or more likely turning tricks in the stairwell."

The woman's lips widened into a gap-toothed grin. Marlowe started to panic, wondering how this might all be a set up. The crowd was getting rowdier. Elbows shoved into him as sweaty, oil-stenched men shuffled toward the makeshift stage.

"He's about to go on," the woman said, then turned to other customers. Abraxes caught Marlowe's eyes and offered only a shrug. Pissed, Marlowe started to fight through the swarm of stained armpits to find out exactly what Abraxes expected to do now. But the light in the bar lowered as the crowd *oohed* in excitement. A strange silence suspended across them all, interrupted only by long burps and sloshing ale. The light deadened to the point Marlowe swallowed a dry retch of anxiety, until a spotlight shone onto the stage, illuminating two long, dark legs in diamond-heeled shoes. Slowly, the light moved up the figure's body as the whooping grew louder from a hundred hungry beasts.

"Hello, boys." A voice like a man's said to the chomping crowd. Dazzled in the spotlight, the figure approached the pole, strategically wrapped in strips of rigging, the kind workers wore when lowered into the mines. The figure flipped a long silver wig across their bare back, skin the color of a sunset, as they mounted the pole to the cheering crowd. Marlowe was struck more by the ecstatic crowd than the thin-framed drag act swinging from the pole.

"What Franx ever saw in Abraxes…" said Meital, having appeared next to Marlowe. A golden whiskey held in her clawed hand. She shook her head as six-inch heels on stage pointed to the ceiling.

"That's Franx?"

"Come on, boys," the figure—Franx—shouted as he dangled upside down from the pole, held on only by his high heels. "Who wants to love me now?" A pounding dance track pulsed through the bar as Franx owned the pole, flipping and twisting while the audience went wild, pelting him with tokens and rubles.

"The one and only," Meital sighed. The crowd had left them all behind. They were close to rushing the stage. Grabbing and waving as Franx spun on the pole, offering high fives and a perky ass to be squeezed by a lucky few. "I was gonna say he never got over being dumped by Abraxes, but seems like I stand corrected."

The only one who wasn't watching the performance was Abraxes. He sat hunched on a bar stool, and glugging down the entire pint.

"Now boys," Franx shouted from the stage. "Which one of you knows how to drill a hole?"

The whooping and cheering from the crowd intensified with the firm possibility any one of them could drill it with enough rubles.

Marlowe had been driven to drink by the tension. Their motley crew sat in a booth a half-staircase up from the stage. The men danced below to tracks of Franx's own mixing, so he'd said, while the star himself sat across from them wrapped in Chinese silk. Two of the biggest, brutish men Marlowe had ever seen stood behind his chair, a Praetorian guard of sorts. Abraxes sat across the table, nervously tapping his peg leg while Meital, Sergei and Marlowe backed up behind him, yet the giant two miners outnumbered them all.

"That's him, boys," Franx said, dabbing mock tears with a stitched handkerchief. "That's the man who broke my heart."

"Could we talk in private?" Abraxes asked. Franx sipped a blood-red cocktail from an unmagnetized crystal glass, then clasped the delicate silk gap where a bosom should be. The men behind him rolled back on their feet. Only then did Marlowe notice the pipes stuck into the back of their belts. Unmagnetized. Untraceable.

"No," Franx said, after considering the request. "I don't trust myself around you." He did bat long, black eyelashes, though at Marlowe, not Abraxes. His tongue flicked out, lapping up the cocktail like a kitten.

"Trust me," Abraxes said, nudging Marlowe in the side. "That's a black hole you don't want to go down."

"Then what in Lenin's name are we doing here? I have an encore to perform."

"I need your help." Abraxes was laying out his cards on the table. But Marlowe shook his head as Franx rioted in a shrieking laugh. He wanted to play poker, Marlowe could see. Folding at the first ante was not the way to keep someone like Franx entertained.

"You? Want help from me?" The miner guards joined in Franx's forced laughter. Until he snapped his fingers and they both fell into silence. "I'd rather pay my taxes than help you. After what you did. That you'd even show your face here." The men with pipes clasped their hands behind their backs. Metal clipped against elastic waistbands, "No apology. No gold. What kind of woman do you take me for?"

"Franx… you're not a woman."

"You bastard."

The gloopy red drink splattered across Abraxes' face, but it wetted them all. Marlowe's fingers lacquered with the sticky stench of aniseed.

"Bring me another, Hank darling." Franx handed one of the miners the empty glass. He left to the bar, but not without a nasty grunt at the soaked group. Abraxes sat in the wetness, dripping from the knotted braids of his beard. "Well, I do thank you all for coming to my show, but I rather think we're done here." He made no effort to move. "You can show yourselves out."

Abraxes stared up at Marlowe with a shrug. Like he'd tried his best, failed, but was taking the payment nonetheless.

"All right," Marlowe said, pulling out the only other chair around the table and sitting between the two men. Franx clutched his chest as Marlowe drew close, anxious to get the words out.

"It's not Abraxes who needs your help, it's us. Sergei and I." The Russian at least nodded in agreement. "We're UNSOC investigators—"

"UNSOC?" Franx drew back in fearful shock, the miner brought his pipe into the foreground.

"No, no." Marlowe raised innocent hands. "We're investigating an incident that happened on the *Pegasus*. It's an orbital vessel around Neptune. There was a murder-suicide back in 2016."

"I know the *Pegasus* incident." Franx said with a quiet nod. "You're investigating the Kraken."

"Excuse me?"

"That's what Abraxes always called it." Abraxes nodded. "It's what we all call it."

"The… Kraken?"

"You got a better name for the thing that keeps sliding into sealed pods and killing us?"

"You know about these cases?"

"'Of course we know. It's been terrifying us all for years. Typical that you Earthlings don't give a shit. Never have, never will." Franx lost interest as the miner returned with a full cocktail. The writing was plain for Marlowe to see. Franx might know the detail of every murder in the system, but he was loathe to help. Sergei stepped forward.

"There's been cover-ups," Sergei said, pulling in all the attention. "UNSOC, the Americans. Even my government. We know that."

"And we're here to stop it," Marlowe added, at least keeping Franx listening. "We're here to get to the bottom of all this, I promise you. But to do that, we need your help. We need to find someone who was on the *Pegasus* back in 2016. His name is Bradley Gomez. If you know where he is, we'd be glad to know. We have to speak with him as soon as possible."

Franx thought on it for a moment. He sipped the cocktail, touching up the fine silks draped over his thin frame. Only in that moment did Marlowe let himself imagine Franx and Abraxes together, in whatever strange relationship a hairy, bearded smuggler and a clean-shaven twink had enjoyed. Space made strange bedfellows, but Franx and Abraxes might just be the oddest of all. When Franx did speak, it was unexpected.

"I told you, Abraxes, Communism doesn't work."

"Not this shit again."

"The Earthlings are only interested in helping us out when their capital is at risk. Open Space is bringing investors to the stars, so of course they send their… *handsomest* investigators to hunt down the Kraken who's terrorized us so."

Marlowe didn't know how to react. He looked to Sergei for support, but the Russian was as stumped as anyone. Only Abraxes was finished with the games.

"Can we go?" Abraxes asked. "*She's* not going to help us."

"Are you going to help us?" Marlowe demanded of Franx. He sipped the cocktail again but replaced it on the table with a determined hand.

"'Of course I'm going to help you. I own thirty-five percent of Belt Industries. We're a newly formed commodities conglomerate me and a few of the boys slapped together. We're planning an IPO on the Nasdaq next year, as it happens. The last thing I want is the damn Kraken spooking my prospective shareholders."

"Is that so?" Abraxes shot back. "You must have been working quite hard to pull this operation together. Sorry… your *holes* must've been working hard."

"Overtime, as it happens. 'Course you don't need reminding, Abraxes. You're well aware of my multiple talents." Franx turned back to Marlowe, eyelashes fluttering overtime, too. "But I'd give it all up for my one true love."

"Shall we find Bradley Gomez first?"

"Yes, good idea." Franx shot up, draining the cocktail in several gulps. "Boys, prepare my travel chest. The Queen of The Maelstrom stands ready to help our Earthling allies."

"Wait," Marlowe said, not completely understanding what he was about to purchase, if anything. "So, you know Bradley Gomez?"

"'Course, darling. What do you want to know about him? Shoe size? Cock size? If he's a top or a bottom? Well, I can't speak to that. He's one of the *straight* ones. Eugh, just imagine. Spending all one's time among the company of the hunkiest fellas in the system but sticking it in a thing that bleeds for four days a month yet doesn't die." Marlowe didn't know what to say, but the group was preparing to leave. "We'll take my ship."

"We came in our own." Meital finally spoke. Franx seemed offended by the very act.

"You can follow," Marlowe said, afraid to shatter their agreement.

"Good idea," Franx agreed. He began to shuffle toward the stairs, flanked by his men. "I converted the ladies' lavatory on my ship to a dark room." He winked at Marlowe, but stopped in his tracks when Abraxes got up. As quick as a flash, Franx slapped Abraxes across the face. "Betray me again, and you can add every 'roid in The Maelstrom to the list of places where you're worth more dead than alive, you beast."

Then Franx shuffled from the booth with his bodyguards, leaving the four alone.

"Maybe I'll fly with you, Meital." Abraxes rubbed his cheek.

"I think that's wise," Marlowe said, glancing over his bruised face which appeared to have been cut slightly by one of Franx's rings. He offered Abraxes a gin-soaked napkin.

"Don't. I deserved it."

CHAPTER 9: THE MANY PURPOSES OF A LIVESTOCK TRANSPORT VESSEL

Franx's ship hummed through The Maelstrom. Rainbow dusted 'roids swarmed in the blackness of space, with no light but flashing red dots warning passing vessels not to come too close. Bradley Gomez was out there, Franx assured them, but he would not say exactly where.

Franx's ship was far larger than Marlowe had expected. A converted *Quayle*-class livestock transporter from the days when UNSOC had tried to farm cows on Europa. Franx had turned the multi-level ship into something of a floating boudoir. He called it the *Cleopatra*. Dozens of rooms quickly constructed with cheap plywood and vinyl circled out from the central space which hosted a collection of low couches warmed by a deep red light. A view of The Maelstrom swarmed on either side, just behind the locked door of the cramped cockpit.

Hank, the cocktail fetcher, was piloting the ship and didn't want to be disturbed. But their slow, steady pace a few miles above the raging belly of the Belt pointed to an auto pilot, with Hank likely asleep at the wheel. A certainty if Fyodor, the other one of Franx's bodyguards, was anything to go by. He was asleep on the next couch over, snoring louder than the rumbling ship.

Franx himself had led Sergei into the bowels of the *Cleopatra* some time ago. Sergei had expressed interest in seeing the old-style engine the ship still used. *Quayle*-class transports were fitted with a methane-based propulsion systems, literally turning bull shit into power. Franx boasted that when he was running low on standard diesel, he'd dock at Ceres or Ida and throw an all-you-can-eat curry night.

Despite Fyodor's snoring, Marlowe was quietly grateful with an hour of peace. He'd been left with a profound disturbance in the depths of his soul by Franx. An uncomfortableness he could only compare to needing his appendix removed. Marlowe located the disquiet somewhere among the frivolity with which Franx seemed to approach life. And he knew it to be jealousy.

One of the supposed benefits of growing up UNSOC was being unburdened by Earth-based conventions. Racism, misogyny, class prejudice and, since the mid-90s, homophobia, were officially banned in all UNSOC jurisdictions. Those born on Earth but who left it later in life were expected to be burdened by the baggage of the class-based societies they grew up in, which is where the space-natives came in to teach them the values of utopia. But little thought was ever given to someone like Marlowe. Or Charlie, for that matter. Born into supposed utopias, Marlowe's place of birth was the Svetlana Kozenko Maternity Ward on Khrushchev-Kennedy—named for his grandmother—but he had been raised in the strict social conventions of Earth. Caught between superpower expectations. Trained to be a pioneering adventurer who willingly sacrificed himself for the good of the state. Either state, it didn't really matter. UNSOC was beyond states. Beyond too, the human weaknesses of *feelings.* Their sole purpose was the defense of humanity itself. Fighting a noble war that less and less people cared about. Swearing oaths of loyalty, patriotism, courage and selflessness when it seemed everyone else had tossed out their integrity and embraced capitalistic self-enrichment. Only no one had bothered to tell Marlowe.

But Franx, he lived with no hint of shame. He knew exactly who he was: a space-born kid whose home was most people's place of last resort. To those born from hand-boys or shop-girls or without a UNSOC parent willing to acknowledge them, Earth was nothing more than a glowing orb in the night sky they could no more visit than the center of the galaxy. Citizens of nowhere. Not just undocumented, they were the Uncounted. Human beings whose home had never been Earth.

Footsteps disturbed Marlowe, but not Fyodor who continued to snore like a broken engine. Low voices. A tinkling laughter and a parting whisper. Sergei and Franx returned from the depths of the ship with wide smiles on their faces. Marlowe had never seen Sergei smile. Nor his hair tousled, nor the quickness with which he re-buttoned his trousers when they spotted Marlowe watching.

"There you are," Franx greeted him with a distracted smirk. He'd changed out of his silks, too. Now he only wore a loose pair of overalls strapped across one bare shoulder, with nothing underneath. The smiles between him and Sergei couldn't be missed. Like flying towards Jupiter, the biggest thing in the night sky was painfully obvious. Sergei had never thrown a sheepish smile Marlowe's way, yet for Franx, he was nothing but boyish grins.

"Are you serious, Sergei?" Marlowe said in his angriest Russian. "Fucking the source in the middle of an investigation?"

"Excuse me," Franx cut in, speaking English but clearly having understood. "You may address me as Queen of The Maelstrom."

At least the smirk was wiped from Sergei's face. He shunted closer to the cockpit, waking up Fyodor in the process.

"I'll go see how far we are," Sergei said, knocking on the door and being let in. Fyodor, seeing Franx, pretended to never have been sleeping in the first place and followed Sergei. The door slammed closed, locked, and Marlowe was left alone with Franx.

"Oh, don't pout!" Marlowe sucked deeply on his vape instead. "And don't smoke, either." Marlowe kept his gaze low, annoyed by the sight of Franx's sunset flesh disappearing beneath the overalls. "Let me fix us a drink, hmm?"

Space might be noisy, but neither Franx nor Marlowe emitted a sound. They sat in stark contrast to the guffaws of Russian laughter coming from the cockpit; Sergei making friends with more Maelstrom ruffians, no doubt. Franx's drinks were sickly and strong; home-brewed moonshine flavored with citrus rinds. The sort that would put a weaker, Earth-born stomach into intensive care.

"Since we're sitting here," Marlowe said eventually, sipping on the second drink, tongue loosened by the first, "let me ask you about these mysterious deaths you seem to know so much about."

"Don't you wish to be regaled of my exploits from lowly space whore to Queen of The Maelstrom? Born in a Lunan brothel, so was I. My ma a lowly shop-girl, all of seventeen when she had me."

Marlowe sighed and sipped his drink. Another round of poker. If he wanted Franx to open up to a greater degree, he'd have to play a hand.

"I listen better when I can vape."

"Oh, go ahead then. Poison your lungs." Marlowe breathed out a whirl of vapor that misted the far window. "When one's lived their whole life never having taken a breath of natural oxygen, one thinks a bit deeper about the miracle of breathing."

"You were telling me about your mother. Is she still on Luna?"

"Beats me," Franx shrugged. "The cunt sold me off to an ore transport captain the minute I could stand on my hind legs. 'Course, life hadn't been easy for her, neither. She was born in a brothel too, but on Khrushchev-Kennedy."

"You're... second generation space-born?" Marlowe's mouth hung open in genuine surprise. He hadn't considered the Uncounted having their own children, and those being old enough to sit across from him with a drink in their hand. His scope of space expanded exponentially. There could be hundreds of thousands of them. Millions. "Maybe with Open Space, you could go home?"

"Home to where? Spend all my pennies on a one-way ticket to Saigon and beg for a passport because I heard a whisper my grandma came up from that way? In five minutes, I'd be begging for an exit visa."

Marlowe nodded, but didn't bother to correct him that Open Space was doing away with exit visas as well; Franx's point was well taken.

"Life... must not have been easy for you. I'm sorry."

"Is this an official apology on behalf of UNSOC?"

Marlowe didn't bother to correct himself now, either.

"I can only hope Open Space makes life better for you. It's a big change, you know."

"Yes, rather like the decline and fall of the Roman Empire."

"Is that how you see it?"

"You Earthlings have always seen me as something of a Visigoth, so why not?"

"Maybe things will get better."

"Do you think they will, Marlowe?"

Marlowe didn't have to think, but he took a drink and vaped anyway. The suspense wasted on the certainty of his answer.

"No." They drank in a rumbling silence. Perhaps a wall had

come down, perhaps not. But Marlowe was sitting knee to knee with someone who knew the hidden corners of the system likely better than anyone alive in UNSOC. He was still building the case in his mind. Despite the revelations from Abraxes and Franx, the conjecture of deaths they took as fact, hearsay from a smuggler and an Uncounted was hardly the stuff death-in-service reports were written on.

"I've got something to show you," Marlowe said. He reached for his forgotten bag and pulled out the state secrets handed over by Darla. The Russian files sat on the couch between them. "Have a flick through. See if anything here rings a bell."

Franx did so as Marlowe drank and vaped but blew the scentless smoke away from Franx. His thinly-plucked brow furrowed as he flicked through the files. The deaths on the frozen moons of Prometheus, Ganymede, Calypso. Franx paid more attention to the case closest to home on Ceres, the most populous part of the Maelstrom at fifty-thousand strong. Marlowe realized the true number may be much higher if he was to add the Uncounted.

All the cases were strange, but Ceres was particularly challenging. Three body stumps found in an underground water extraction facility. Their torsos exploded, like all the others. The bag of skin normally found next to one of these murder sites hadn't been discovered anywhere nearby but discarded behind the back of a loading dock on the other side of the dwarf planet. Having read quite enough stomach-churning details, Franx closed the files.

"This is all you have?"

"All?"

"It's a tenth, if that."

"You're serious?"

"Oh yes, Marlowe. Plus the details are all wrong. This one from the *Karl Liebknecht*, Laurent Navoir, I knew him. And it wasn't a murder-suicide."

Marlowe opened that file, reading over a detail he'd skimmed the last time. The deaths had taken place in a sealed pod, just like on the *Pegasus*, but a hole had been blown through the side. The body of Tobias Albeck, a Yugoslavian engineer, had never been recovered. Presumed lost in space. The body, or at least the skin, of Laurent Navoir remained inside the pod after automatic emergency procedures sealed up the space breach. The report ended with a similar hypothesis to the *Pegasus* deaths. An attempt to seal the hull had led one of the bodies being sucked into space from the inside out. At least on the *Karl Liebknecht* there was some modicum of evidence. Or causality.

"How do you know it wasn't a murder-suicide?"

"Because…" Franx sipped his own drink, eyes staring deeply into Marlowe's, an eastern queen hypnotizing Mark Antony, just as she'd done to Caesar. "I was there. I was Tobias Albeck."

Marlowe whacked his own cocktail glass from the table in a burst of violent energy. He'd not felt such a bolt come to the surface in many years. The fury broke like a wave, dissipating while the shattered glass still tinkled against the far wall. Franx simply crossed his legs.

"Don't fuck with me, Franx. I'm serious."

"I had no, and have no, intention of *fucking* with you, Marlowe." Franx leaned forward, close enough for Marlowe to smell his own hot breath reflecting against Franx's smooth skin. "I've lived in space for thirty-one of your Earth years. I've been burned on Venus and frozen at the heliopause. And I've known a damn fine number of people who've died in space. Some from a gravity malfunction, some from falling equipment. Some starve to death, marooned on a broken ship. Some are killed in a gang fight, some die by suicide. But over the last few years, while all you Earthlings fret over space politics and Galactic Marxism, I've noticed a strange uptick in the unexplained. You wouldn't know since most of the deaths are among us Uncounted. We don't have a UNSOC passport or an exit visa or a home nation to be deported to. When we die, we die. They didn't count us in life, so why would they bother in death? But I've seen it, Marlowe. I've been cheek to cheek with death. Call it the Kraken, call it an angel, call it an alien. Most of us have only heard the legends, but I've seen it all."

Franx finished his own cocktail and placed the glass carefully down, still in breathing distance with Marlowe. He took the vape pen from Marlowe's unfurled hand and sucked down a deep drag. Franx blew vapor from his nostrils, burning like a dragon, then placed the vape back in Marlowe's hand.

"The real Tobias Albeck died of Aids several years ago, in my arms. I smuggled what treatment I could for him, but there was no long-term solution but to return to Earth. Of course, he wouldn't dare. He'd be court-martialed the second he returned to the East. Do you know how they treat people with HIV in Yugoslavia?"

"Not well, I imagine."

"No, not well at all. Tobias offered me the use of his identity on the condition I give him a good death. Something that would mean his mother could receive his pension. So, I found myself masquerading on the OS *Karl Liebknecht*, stealing odds and ends. That's when I met Laurent. By Lenin, he was handsome. A sweep of black hair, a thin little mustache, cock like a diamond-tipped drill. His job was to monitor the developing Martian atmosphere. We would lay for hours in the sealed pod beyond the reaches of the ship, gazing down at the perfect white clouds just starting to form in the Martian sky. the rolling hills sprouting green grass, the crystal-clear seas learning how to deal with dual-moon tides. We were like a couple of gods watching our newly made world spring to life.

"I was asleep, but the clanging woke me up. The pod was in total darkness. We were around the dark side of Mars. I couldn't see a thing, but I heard his breathing. Something had changed. Labored, sweaty. We came into sunlight, and I'll never forget what I saw. Laurent was naked, pressed against the wall, body drenched, skin… crawling. Like something awful had burrowed into his body and was aching to burst out. He beckoned me closer. I thought he was sick; had eaten something from the molecular re-processor that wasn't quite reprocessed.

"He touched my face, and this grin came across it. Sick and… wet. A million little teeth. Sharp points and a tongue that slathered out, licked my neck…" Tears stained Franx's cheeks. The most terrifying part of the story was that it made someone like him cry, although he did it all without a sound. Like he'd never known another way to cry but silently. Marlowe offered a hand on his knee, but Franx didn't need it. Or didn't notice.

"But you got out. You escaped?"

"Only because there was a gravity malfunction. It used to happen from time to time, and it happened right then. A stroke of dumb luck. We started floating away from each other. He roped out his arms and tried to swim toward me, but I launched from the wall straight to the airlock, and just before I escaped from the pod back to the ship, I shot him."

"You shot him?"

"I think I hit his leg, foot maybe. It's hard to aim in no gravity while trying to zip on a space suit and helmet. And I blew a hole in the pod as well." The tears had dried up. A look of determination returned to Franx. The momentary lapse had left them both quiet, both cold.

"I'm glad you made it out."

"He said something. Shouted it more like, in this weird voice. Laurent had always talked with this cute French accent, but when he shouted at me, screamed at me as I was trying to escape, he sounded different."

"How so?"

"You ever heard an Englishman talk? Not like now, but in the old days. One of those very proper, BBC type voices you'd hear talking about the war or Roswell. He sounded like that."

Marlowe could hear the exact voice. His own father had a distant inflection of proper *English* English, diluted in the international sea of being brought up in UNSOC. Although his grandfather, Martin Reginald Marlowe, had always talked like a wise guy who'd been dragged up in the Bronx before a nice couple from Wiltshire found him in a shipyard and took him in.

"What... what did this Laurent say?"

"Weird stuff. I didn't understand it. Like, he wanted to taste me or something. It was all such a blur."

"That's okay. I can't begin to imagine how traumatic it was."

"Thanks. I haven't told many people about that. The few that I have don't really believe me."

"Not even Abraxes?"

"He believed me, but he's always got a better story. I came face to face with the Kraken, so he lost a leg to it."

"Well, we're going to get to the bottom of it, I promise you that." Marlowe sucked in a worried breath, feeling like he was lying to Franx, and wondering why he felt guilty about doing so. Getting to the bottom of it and writing up the report Donahue wanted to read were sounding more and more like very different things. And there was no evidence, none that would stand up to objective scrutiny.

Franx had seen what he'd seen with a stolen identity. Even an Uncounted just being on the *Karl Liebknecht* was a crime in itself. Marlowe's investigatory mind took over. He'd heard a lot of sob stories in his life, but what could he do but take down notes, filter out the irrelevant details, and write up a report that could be shared with the Department of Justice and Commissary of People's Laws?

Marlowe glanced at the smashed cocktail glass. He felt bad for making a mess, and worse because ultimately, he was going to let Franx down. The kid was cute. He could see why Abraxes was enamored with him. Marlowe slapped his legs and readied to stand, the conversation having petered out. He wanted to check in on Sergei in the cockpit. The laughs coming from there had been less, and Marlowe didn't like the idea all three had fallen asleep as they flew through The Maelstrom.

"Oh, can I ask you something?" Franx said. The casualness with which he spoke didn't hold Marlowe back from knocking on the cockpit door. "What's Dor-than?"

It took a moment to process the sounds, but then Marlowe thought for a harsh second the gravity had failed. But no, he was still standing on two legs. He swallowed hard.

"Do you mean Dor-*veth*-an?"

"Yeah. That was it. What's it mean?"

"Um... why do you ask?"

"Laurent, well, *the Kraken* that took over Laurent's body, said that was his name."

"His name?" Marlowe's heart was pounding. "What do you mean his name? How do you know that?" He needed Sergei to open the door and turn this ship straight to Perth and grab Marlene. To sit her down with Franx, then dial Donahue in. Hell, dial in the Director-General as well. If not the goddamn president of the United States and chairman of the Politburo.

"Yeah, he kept saying Dorvethan. *Dorvethan, Dorvethan, I'm going to eat you...* blah blah blah. 'Course, I'm calling it a Kraken and he was calling himself Dorvethan. It's probably just untreated syphilis that's driving us all insane. I mean, what other explanation could there be?"

Franx laughed. His brown cheeks cut into a broad grin that could launch ships and break hearts. The cockpit door creaked open. Sergei stood on the other side with a bored nod. Hank and Fyodor were playing chess; two hulking great men hunched over a tiny magnetic board perched upon sensitive instruments designed to protect the ship from the streaking rainbow dust trails of the violent Maelstrom swirling ever closer.

"Can we talk?" Marlowe said, wondering if from Sergei's point of view, it looked as if Marlowe was ready to burst out of his skin as well.

Sergei's room stank of sex. A small, repurposed cow shed with a soft bed, red-light lamp, and homoerotic charcoal paintings adorning the walls. The rooms on the *Cleopatra* were hardly designed for sleeping. They were still six hours still from the undisclosed location Franx had promised Bradley Gomez would be, but Marlowe couldn't sleep in his own boudoir; the floor spotty and stained with the remnants of whomever the room's last occupants had been. Now, he couldn't talk either with the stench of what Sergei and Franx had done in this room. How often and how vigorous had it been that the smell of sweat, spit and cum still lingered.

Sergei lounged on the bed in only trousers, flicking through *Pravda* and decidedly uninterested in Marlowe's freak-out over Franx's *Dorvethan* revelations. The burning in his throat had abated, but still, he wanted the Russian to take interest, not just lay back and shrug his shoulders.

"I told you," Sergei said, turning the pages of Cyrillic ink and pointedly ignoring Marlowe's red-faced rant. "There's something funny going on. Suspicious. Covered up." Sergei said it with all the interest of a flight attendant explaining the evacuation procedures.

"But what is it? A creature that can slide through walls, survive in space, inhabit bodies then leave them nothing but bags of skin? That's been… covered up. All this time!"

"You don't need to yell in my ear. This is a small room, Marlowe. I can hear fine."

"Sergei, you just told me we have to report what we found and give the honest conclusions that we come to. Do you really want me to write that aliens, Sergei, *aliens*, were responsible for the *Pegasus*, if not hundreds more unexplained deaths, and what's more than that, we think it's called the same thing that The Messenger might have been fleeing from in 1947?"

Sergei glanced up from the newspaper, the shrug now in his eyes, as if he and Darla had already come to the same conclusion a long time ago. So much so he was almost bored of alien talk.

"Somebody must tell the truth. Why not UNSOC?"

"You mean, why not me?"

"You are the criminal inspector. There's been crimes. Many, apparently. So why not write it down, tell the world?"

"Why not the Soviet Union? Your citizens have died. Warsaw Pact citizens. Why are you not willing to state it if it's so obvious?"

"Ah ha," Sergei lowered the paper to reveal a grin Marlowe did not like. "But that is why we fund the United Nations. To say things our politburo does not want to have come from their mouths."

"They'll believe me?"

"Unlikely. They'll probably think it's more of a desperate attempt for UNSOC to stay relevant in the new era of Open Space."

"Yes," Marlowe nodded, agreeing with multiple sentiments.

Marlowe had never cared for chess. It had been an elective class at the Academy, one Charlie had reveled in. Marlowe did sometimes swing by the chess hall to watch his secret lover engaged in a battle of wills over wooden pieces. Getting boxed in then angling for plays to get out. Charlie was a good chess player right up to the end game. That's what everyone said about him. He lost interest after the initial thrust and parry, the exchange of pieces, the battle of wills. Charlie's lovemaking was hardly different. The rush of the opening set pieces; in the locker room, behind the auditorium, up against a closet door. He was good at the smooth middle, the lingering kisses and gentle poundings. But when it was all over for Charlie, he was finished playing. The pieces were to be put away, un-thought of until the next time he had an urge for a two-person game.

Marlowe was no longer in the small room of the *Cleopatra*. The smell of sweaty men took him back to the dark, cloggy dormitories of the Academy. To sitting in a chair in a high-ceilinged hall, across the table from a serious Russian in Trotsky-glasses staring at pieces scattered across a board. The chess clock ticking, ticking, ticking. The people watching. Marlowe, watching, from the sidelines. And Marlene, too. Standing shoulder to shoulder. The sister and the secret lover.

[109]

Marlowe's hands were no longer his but Charlie's. Black fingers hovering over black pieces. Boxed in. Trapped in a game he didn't know how to play. Every permutation of the report Donahue expected led to a checkmate. Tell the world what the evidence said, and he'd be laughed out of UNSOC. Fired, if he was lucky, if not charged with some form of incitement. Do nothing but regurgitate a cover-up, and Sergei would report to Darla who'd spin every wheel of her influence to deliver on Marlowe the retribution she'd so subtly promised. *Failure to undertake a satisfactory investigation*, Donahue could stamp on his file. *Jeopardizing international cooperation.* The promised Martian Settlement Authority job long gone. Fired from UNSOC, if he was lucky.

There'd been a scramble, a race out of the pits and bear traps of life, but no one told him. Marlene had divorced him. Charlie had abandoned him. His children were dead, and no cause could stir even an inch of his soul. He was not Sergei laying cross-legged on the bed, satisfied that he and Darla were midwifing the footnote inside an early history of the first space-based revolution. The footnote that would become a chapter, then entitle the sequel detailing the second, greater revolt. If only they'd seen it coming, the histories would say. If only they'd believed that crazy grandson of Martin Reginald Marlowe when he warned the world The Messenger's warning had come true.

But history is full of the tune of tragedies. Such are the fates the unlucky will play. An endless darkness crept in from the corners of Marlowe's vision. His eyes narrowing to the smug guy sitting on the bed. Charlie. Sergei. Charlie. The metallic taste of vomit laced with powdered caffeine rose in his throat. Then a fuzziness, like the static on an old TV, broadcasting Truman's message to the universe. These days it was a new message. 'Come and get us, aliens! Our defenses are down!' Marlowe reached out to grab the wall, the spinning did not stop. The gravity stabilizers stopped working, but just for him. His world went black.

Marlowe walked through a desert. Hot wind obscured his vision. Paper cups whirled around the sudden entrance to a hangar. Roswell. In the yellowed emptiness, a white-coated crazed scientist fiddled with bits and bobs. Some were stuck on the ceiling, others floated in a weightless state. Marlowe got closer, hearing the scientist mumble to himself in a cut-glass English accent. Things were moving under the man's skin. Bugs and worms and evil. *I warned them... the engines will lose stability beyond the heliopause... no one listens to me. No one cares about crazy old Doc Johnson. Oh, it's you, Marlowe. Marlowe...*

"Marlowe." Hands shook his shoulders. He was slumped against the door, his back aching from what felt like a kick, or a bruise from the handle. Sergei hadn't even dragged his body to the bed. "Wake up."

"I'm up. I'm here. I must've... fainted." He was back in the tiny cabin on the *Cleopatra*, wiping sweat from his forehead. Sergei's vodka-breath was almost a relief. What part of his grandfather's diary had instigated *that* nightmare. Old Doc Johnson, possessed by Dorvethan. The first man to touch the Messenger, the last man to see the creature alive.

"Don't faint. You're the investigator."

"Yeah," Marlowe said, getting to his feet by himself and shaking out all lingering thoughts of Roswell. They still had nothing concrete. No evidence, no statements, and had trusted their travels to a questionable twink and his bodyguards. "Yeah, Sergei, I *am* the investigator. And you're the liaison who isn't supposed to get in the way. So, if you fuck a witness again, I'll have no choice to put that in my report."

Sergei scowled. Marlowe scrambled for the door handle, sliding it open. He might not know how to play chess, but at least he'd felt like he'd flipped the board.

CHAPTER 10: AN ASSESSMENT OF WORKING CONDITIONS IN THE CIRCUMSTELLAR DISC

Mars was rising beyond the Belt. An unspoiled swirling green-and-blue orb, dashed with fluffy clouds circling the fat equator and capped with pure white snow of an unspoiled polar region. It looked like a planet a child would draw. Using crayons of bright green and deep blue, coloring in the jagged lines of the great southern land-mass; the protruding legs of rocky peninsulas and the scattering of dotted islands straying beyond the undefined lines. It looked like the pictures the twins had once drawn, stuck to the fridge the day Marlene came home and told him about the plans to establish a Martian Settlement Authority, and she wanted in. Now those children's drawings contained all the places it would soon be Marlene's job to name, to manage, to settle. The untouched Eden felt as distant to Marlowe as Earth must feel to Franx.

"Off you pop now," Franx declared, clapping his hands as the *Cleopatra* maneuvered into the asteroid's docking pod. "I've got back-to-back shows in Midway and a sure thing waiting for me on Ceres. So, it's time for you folks to dis-the-fuck-embark."

The ship shuddered to a jolting halt as they docked. Not on a 'roid itself, but a space-based waystation circling a cluster of six hamlet-sized rocks. Like much of The Maelstrom, these asteroids were too small and unstable to host a ship, so were serviced by a floating pontoon instead. An orbiting bridge that would point and shoot at the 'roid they wanted. The trick was to get across before the bridge was crushed by a passing pile of rocks and everyone inside was incinerated in a flameless fire.

"Are you sure Bradley Gomez is here?" Marlowe asked for the sixth time, while Franx seized him by the shoulders and marched him toward the airlock door.

"Yes. On Delving Prime." A depressurizing hiss announced only one way forward, into the darkness of an airlock. Beyond lay the wilderness. UNSOC health and safety regulations required these death-traps be serviced twice a year. Even in the vacuum of space, Marlowe was sure he'd be able to wipe dust from the surface. He'd be lucky to find an antique fire extinguisher.

"Wait!" Marlowe said, just as Franx was wiping his hands of them both. Sergei was already inside the airlock, tapping his foot with folded arms. "When will Abraxes and Meital be along with our ship? Interviewing Bradley Gomez won't take more than an hour or two, and there hasn't been any word from them. Has there?"

Hank and Fyodor remained like boulders blocking any way out, while Franx fiddled with the controls. But didn't answer his question. The bodyguards were quite clearly indicating Marlowe could either be inside the airlock when it depressurized or caught between space-proof doors.

"Not to worry," Franx shouted over the heavy hiss of a sliding airlock. "I'm sure they'll be along any minute now."

Marlowe swore he could see the little shit grin as the doors slammed shut, sealing him and Sergei into pressurized silence. Marlowe stared at his own reflection in the swirling glass, as the *Cleopatra* broke off its connection from the waystation and abandoned them.

"Abraxes and Meital aren't coming, are they?" Marlowe said, intent on his reflection.

Sergei sighed, as if all this was already known to him, and he was bothered Marlowe wasn't keeping up.

"I think not."

The waystation opened up like a waiting room in an asylum; nothing more than broken tiles on the floor and a filthy coffee machine in the corner. The lights flickered on as they entered and kept flickering over the greenish painted walls also growing space moss. Sergei blew hard on the dusted terminal—Marlowe was right about that—and wiped off moss with his sleeve. Marlowe consulted the paper chart pinned to a corkboard.

The names of all the people who inhabited the mines were supposed to be written down. A register of sorts, health and safety precautions so nobody would go unaccounted for in the event of a disaster. Or more realistically, so the Office of Circumstellar Mining back on Khrushchev-Kennedy could quickly stamp a death-in-service approval before anyone at the Commissariat for Criminal Investigations had a chance to ask questions.

The only thing that was properly recorded on the cork board were the names of junior CCI agents who had passed through these parts. Marlowe, like most CCI agents, had to do a stint investigating crimes in The Maelstrom. Those who survived a year of outdated equipment, roving gangs and blatant bribery were rewarded with the benefit of never having to return.

"I guess it's true," Marlowe said, only realizing after that he said it out loud,

"What is?" Sergei asked from the control panel he'd managed to make beep angrily.

"Nothing..." Marlowe flicked through the wilted sheets of paper, scuffed down with the names of agents vaguely familiar to him.

"Okay." Sergei was not interested, but Marlowe was well beyond the point of caring.

"I heard rumors they never lifted the hiring freeze from a few years back, you know, after they brought S-Nine in to deal with space-based security."

"Oh...kay."

"You can see here, there's been no new agents come through here in three, nearly four years. Crazy."

"Don't worry," Sergei hissed through strained breath as he heaved the rail door open, "I did it myself."

"Good job."

"So, your UNSOC doesn't keep track of who is here anymore? We're going in blindly?"

"We're trusting your source. Franx assured us Bradley Gomez is on Delving Prime, so to Delving Prime we shall go."

Marlowe shoved past Sergei to slide into the rail car. A four-person vehicle that always reminded Marlowe of a pump trolley on an old railroad. Complete as it was with handles in case of a malfunction and one literally needed to hand-power the cart from Delving Prime back to Kalamazoo.

"Oh look." Marlowe wiped a layer of green moss from the carts' scratched handles. "B.G. was here," Marlowe read from the litany of English and Cyrillic initials, dates, and assorted graffiti. "There's a cock drawn next to it, but I don't think it's connected."

Marlowe pretended to investigate the etchings and let Sergei struggle with the rail door, until it heaved into place. Only then did the tunnel in front of them flicker into life. Hydraulic hissing stopped and started every few seconds while Sergei's hand hovered over the big red 'go' button.

"Wait," Marlowe said, as the hissing and clicking continued. "If we go too soon, we'll be shot into space in only this cart, or fly smack into a rock wall."

"How do you know when it's connected to Delving Prime? The control panel says it's ready to go."

"Wait for it." Marlowe listened for the vaguely familiar *clink, clink, clink* of a distant key trying to find a lock. What he hadn't said was that the receiving end, whoever was sitting in Delving Prime, had to allow the rail bridge to lock on. If Bradley Gomez didn't want to be found, the clinking simply would not cease, despite what the control panel had said, or the blinking green light bolted between them.

Then it stopped.

"Let's go," Marlowe said, and the cart shot into the flickering darkness of a tunnel with an unknown end.

Marlowe came-to tied to a chair in a filthy cavern carved from pure rock. The only source of light was a naked bulb swinging from an exposed wire as the asteroid spun in the chill of space. Sergei was beside him; hands also tied behind a folding chair, but he was still unconscious. Oily liquid smelling of sulfur dripped onto Sergei's cheek, failing to wake him even as the run-off dribbled dangerously close to his mouth.

Marlowe desperately wanted to rub his pounding head. It was hard to fully open one eye. They must have smacked him in the face after whacking the back of his skull. It all happened in a rapid blur he now painfully re-lived. They slammed through the airlock into a scene more reminiscent of the drug busts of Donahue's past. Four men had been hulked over a complex array of vials and tubes, cooking up methamphetamine in the chill of an asteroid. The artificial gravity on this side of the rock turned way down to aid the chemical processes, so their flagrant misuse of the mine's grav-boots was the first violation Marlowe noticed. He'd barely had a chance to reach for his badge, or whisper the words *UNSOC,* nor mention he wasn't interested in documenting the litany of crimes being committed, from grav-boots indoors to controlled substances being improperly manufactured on UNSOC property, if they only identified Bradley Gomez.

It had been a lot to say in the short space of time it took for one of them, Bradley Gomez in fact, to launch up from the ground and leap through the air with barely a tenth of the newtons per kilogram required on Earth. "I'm Bradley," he'd said in reply, "who the fuck's asking?" But the metal boot struck Marlowe first in the back of the knee, then the back of the head, as the same fate befell Sergei half a second later from someone else.

Wherever they were now, tied up to chairs in the dripping, freezing, carved-out edge of an asteroid, at least the gravity was turned up to a comfortably Earth-like 9.8 newtons per kilogram.

There was no door, but a figure emerged from the darkness. Bradley Gomez. In rubber shoes now. And a pair of overalls open from the navel up, revealing an oily vest clinging to a chest sculpted by years of artificial gravity-assisted manual handling. He played with something unseen in his hand. Marlowe's heart thudded at the worry it was a weapon. Maybe a blade coming to slit their throats. It shone bright against the hanging bulb.

"In two days," Bradley said, folding the object between his fingers. "UNSOC won't have any jurisdiction out here." It was Marlowe's badge. The only thing that had likely stopped them being killed on sight. "Maybe I'll wait and kill you both then. Keep things nice and legal."

Bradley's wink made Marlowe realize he was far from joking. He struggled against the rope, but it wasn't coming loose. Nor was Sergei showing any signs of waking up.

"Listen," Marlowe said, sweating despite the temperature being a smidge above absolute zero. "I'm not here about the drugs. I'm investigating the *Pegasus.*"

Bradley strode forward, furious sweat flying from the coils of his chest hair and splattering against Marlowe's face.

"Well I didn't fucken' kill 'em!"

"I never said you did." Bradley scowled and rocked around the room like a suspect about to be arrested; clearly triggered by mere mention of the orbital ship. "I'm just trying to find out what happened, that's all. Do you know what happened to Alexei Zhukov and Okechukwu Lammy? You served with them on that ship in 2016, didn't you?"

"I remember those faggots."

The word hung aggressively in the air. Sergei's heavy breathing and the *drip, drip, drip* of probably toxic run-off funneling along the scraggy hairs of the Russian's cheek. Marlowe wondered what side Sergei would take, if he'd been awake. The path of least resistance, no doubt. Perhaps he was right.

"Are you saying they were in some kind of relationship?" Now Marlowe's breath caught up with the situation. What did it mean, if they were lovers? Did it make a murder-suicide more likely, or less? The synapses of Marlowe's investigatory mind tunneled a way out of this predicament while the reality of what his subconscious wanted to say made him sick. It made logical sense in UNSOC's world. A hidden couple. A lover's tiff. Degenerate behavior. Okechukwu could have had his participation in the Alpha Centauri Settlement Program revoked. Alexei could have had his discoveries about Neptunian tides dismissed under a cloud of scandal. The exoclimatologist was still state property of the Soviet Union. Sleeping with a Black British engineer was hardly the thing stellar careers were made of. Did one want to break it off? Had another been cheating? Okechukwu would be leaving, just as Charlie was. Permanently. The thought gnawed at his throat as he followed Bradley storming around the room.

"'Cause of those faggots, I gotta live out here? How the fuck's that fair, huh?"

"Why don't you untie me and let's talk about it," Marlowe responded.

The smack across the face flashed like flickers of lightning. Bolts of electricity shattered behind Marlowe's eyes as he waited for the crack of thunder.

"It's 'cause of you fuckers I'm stuck here." Bradley readied to swing again, but when Marlowe spat out blood he pulled back. The worry being Bradley preferred a clean body to shoot through the exit tube.

"Listen," Marlowe ran his tongue over bloodied lips. "I'm not responsible for what's happened to you. I'm just trying to find out what happened on that Zvezda pod."

"I told you. Some*thing* broke in and killed them both, then the pod got junked on Luna."

"Luna? Why?" The surprise from Marlowe that a billion-dollar pod would be dumped outside of Armstrong and likely be stripped and sold for parts *more* than the revelation a *thing* had murdered two UNSOC employees reflected in Bradley's gaze "Were Alexei and Okechukwu involved with the Black Moon gang?" Marlowe let the logic of the questioning fall over Bradley. "Was Black Moon responsible for their deaths so they could steal UNSOC property? Was anyone else from the *Pegasus* involved?"

"Black Moon? Nah. No way. And how the fuck would I know?" But Bradley said it quick and anxious enough it was clear he knew *someone* in the supply chain had been involved in selling the pod off to Black Moon. "I told you everything I knew about all that shit. It was a creature. A beast. An alien for fuck's sake. I told you and I got sent here. My career, my life fucken'... revoked. I was a corporal in the US Space Force before I was seconded to UNSOC, and the deep state took it all away. You know what's going on out there, don't you. Our president did, and y'all silenced him 'cause of it. Secret fucken' aliens and shit. Not my fault one snuck into a sealed pod and murdered two fags, is it?"

"But didn't the president deny the existence of aliens? I mean... wasn't that the whole point of making Earth great again? That there's no risk, so no reason space can't be privatized and developed?"

"That's what the deep state wants you to think."

Marlowe nodded, although he was pretty certain from years of politicians' speeches leading to underfunded UNSOC budgets and sheer disinterest from the American partners, that the former president who'd championed 'Make Earth Great Again' was an avowed Roswell-denier. But with Bradley still pacing the room, Marlowe wasn't too keen on belaboring the point.

"So, are you saying that some unidentified force was responsible for the deaths of Okechukwu Lammy and Alexei Zhukov?"

"No fucken' doubt. I told you people about it, and what do I get? Stripped of my rank and exiled to this shit hole."

"Well, I'm sorry about that, Bradley. Truly." He nodded, noting the increasingly unhinged pattern of Bradley's steps. The unanchored breathing as craggy as a Martian coastline. "I'm just trying to find out what happened, that's all." Marlowe attempted his most reassuring voice. "Maybe if the truth comes out, you could... be reinstated?"

The maniacal grin returned. But the body still wanted to pace, tap, flicker. It looked like one of Viktor's science experiments, like mercury being chased around a petri dish, except the lab equipment was poised to leap out and suck Marlowe's insides out.

"There's a hundred thousand metric tons of gold on this rock. In two days' time, we become the Republic of The Maelstrom. Or I can call myself King of Delving Prime. Why not, eh? Nothin' but carnage out there. Carnage and chaos. But I'm sittin' on a fucken' gold mine. A literal gold mine."

"And a meth lab."

The smack came hard again.

"See how I know you're full of shit? You UNSOC cunts are all the same. The hell with waiting two days. You're in my kingdom, why can't I kill you now?"

The UNSOC badge fell to the ground and out came a real knife. Rusted and blunted from the over-oxidized air.

"Listen, I can help."

"The fuck you can. Where was your help all the years I've frozen my balls off in this dump? Huh?" The coppered blade glinted as Bradley held it high. One flick from his arm and it would come down in an agonizing slice. Marlowe winced, but Bradley only laughed at the fear. "You'll be the last UNSOC fucker in my kingdom."

It wasn't Marlowe's first near-death experience, but his brain seemed to think it would be the last. The only faces that came to mind were the two he'd spent so many years trying to forget. What had once been the fullness of love replaced with the very opposite; scouring the solar system for the cheapest thrill of a basest desire, all so he'd never have to think about the holes those two had left in his heart.

[119]

The names Marsha and Frank had been his grandfather's suggestion. Although slowly losing his mind back then, the old man still managed some good days. Visiting his newborn great-grand-children—twins at that—was not something the old battle-ax was going to miss, dementia or not. Marlene's father had pushed for Nigerian names, but her mother wanted Jewish ones. Neither Marlene nor Marlowe were particularly keen on commonly accepted Russian names, so Martin's suggestion of honoring his adoptive parents sat well with the couple.

Warm memories washed over him, obscuring the cold. Marsha and Frank playing in the sand of a Caribbean beach. Marsha and Frank chasing after Yuri, their German Shepherd, in the back garden of their Brooklyn brownstone. Marsha and Frank playing with toy rockets in the bath. Marsha and Frank peering out a transport ship window at the pristine blues and greens of Mars. Marsha and Frank listening intently as their mom described in wide-eyed detail how one day they would live on Mars. Marsha and Frank imagining life in a pristine wilderness. Marsha and Frank listing the animals and foods which would be allowed on Mars. Dogs, cats, foxes and werewolves, yes. Llamas and tigers, no. Ice cream, pizza, schnitzel and beans, yes. Borscht and plantain, no.

"I'm not UNSOC," came a rough voice. It coughed, spluttering out a horrible taste, no doubt, and the surprise of waking up tied to a chair while a lunatic with a knife readied for murder. "I'm not UNSOC," Sergei said again. It seemed to annoy Bradley more than stop him.

"The fuck do I care? You came through the rail together, didn't you?"

"Yes, but I don't work for UNSOC."

"So?" But the calmness, or simply lethargy of Sergei's revelation, had spiked Bradley's plan. "Who do you work for, then? Huh?" He lunged forward with the rusty blade, but Sergei didn't flinch. "S-Nine? Some other bunch of fucking fascist internationalist liberals who're gonna steal my gold?"

"I'm the Soviet liaison to the investigation of the *Pegasus* being conducted by Comrade Marlowe." Sergei nodded to him, acknowledging Marlowe's presence at least. Whatever the Russian's plan was, at least it seemed to include them both. "My location is constantly tracked by the GRU. I must report to my superiors in Soviet military intelligence every six hours. I do not know for how long we have been illegally tied up for, but I know that when we left Trench-fall, the Earth-link was out of service, so I did not file my report."

"You think it's my job to maintain this shitty equipment?"

Marlowe wondered if Bradley had failed to grasp the key part of Sergei's tale or was simply stalling for time.

"I don't know," Sergei continued with characteristic calmness. "But what I can tell you is a joint GRU-KGB committee is currently discussing why one of their agents on Delving Prime has been out of contact beyond protocol. Comrade Marlowe, where are we closer to; Ida, Ceres, or Phobos?"

"Out this way? Phobos, probably."

"Then the Fifteenth Red Army Space Division will be scrambled. Their commander is Belorussian. Ruthless people. If I have missed my second check-in, a cruiser with nine hundred fully armed Red Army space commandos will be on their way." The rusty knife clanged to the ground. "Comrade Marlowe, has it been over six hours since we landed at Delving Prime?"

Marlowe didn't know, but didn't get a chance to answer.

"Stay right there," Bradley yelled, flinging Marlowe's badge back at him. He disappeared into darkness. No door slammed or airlock hissed. They were likely deep in a mine shaft, where it was all too easy to turn up dead.

"Nice of you to wake up," Marlowe said. Sergei was busy trying to untie himself. "Don't bother, it's reinforced nylon—" But Sergei was already free. He kicked back the chair wandered over to investigate the way Bradley had left before paying Marlowe any attention. "How did you do that?"

"KGB train us." Sergei shrugged, before returning to untie Marlowe, although it felt like a partial afterthought.

"Fuck that's sore." He rubbed his wrists. Being free gave him nothing. In the moments when he thought he was about to die, the greatest comfort was the wonder he might get to live forever in the memory of his children. Just a soul wandering through space, re-playing those seven perfect years ad infinitum.

"The American wasn't any help?"

"Your witness…" Marlowe trailed off, unable to raise the anger the other part of his brain wanted to throw at Bradley, or Sergei, or both. Only the anger at the whole universe and life itself had been unlocked. What Marlowe had kept hidden away for too many years, knowing it would never leave. It would never leave. "Your witness was for my benefit?"

Sergei could play cool as a European cucumber all he wanted but he was not a better actor than he was a spy. A nervousness greater than the one driven by Bradley's knife gripped his suddenly thin-looking frame. Gaunt cheeks sucked inwards, the rushed stubble and bare light etched a picture of Sergei looking like a young Joseph Vissarionovich Stalin.

Marlowe came closer, and Sergei stepped back. There was little space for this dance. The cold had infected both their chests so only constant movement held back shivers. The haggardness, the exhaustion like a dream where one's legs are too heavy to walk, yet there is no choice but to push forwards, onwards, deeper into the drawing chaos.

"You brought me here," Marlowe shouted, sick of Sergei's aloof-ness, and it clearly scared the shit out of the Russian, "just so I would *believe* an alien killed Okechukwu Lammy and Alexei Zhukov?"

"There was no other way." Sergei swallowed not once but several times. The shivers contained to his throat now closing up. The rock wall beckoned. Sergei reached out both hands as he backed into it but snatched them back as the cold burned. "Nothing else convinced you people at UNSOC. Nobody cares that this is it! The Messenger warned us, and now the monster is here. The Politburo doesn't care. The White House doesn't care. You must, Marlowe. You *must* believe."

Marlowe stopped. He'd wanted to punch Sergei in the face. He was readying his freezing hand in a fist to get in the one good, hard smack he was due, but it dissipated in the verisimilitude of Sergei's simplistic deception. It was pure KGB. He imagined Darla writing it down on a paper file, each step of the process, then shredding it and burning the paper trail.

"Why would I believe a conspiracy theorist?"

"You heard him." Sergei's shaking voice was barely a whisper. A frightened response to Marlowe's cold dead tone. "MEGA, deep state, those obvious lies. He has dissonance from what he saw with his own eyes, to what he thinks in his twisted mind. A man who does not believe in aliens. No, a man who does not believe in aliens so much that he was dishonorably discharged from the US Space Force for demanding soldiers to vote against UNSOC, the only explanation he gives you for their deaths is—"

"Dorvethan."

"What did you say?" Marlowe pulled back, letting the shivers overtake his body. If Franx had gotten him halfway there, then Bradley had plunged him over the edge. It was only unfortunate that there was no way back. They started at each other for far longer than was necessary. There were many truths about himself Marlowe could not admit out loud. He would now add Dorvethan to that list.

"How long," Marlowe said, blowing out a breath that became a stutter, "until the Fifteenth Division gets here from Phobos? Because I think we need to get the fuck out of here, and fast."

"Ah."

"What 'ah'?"

"That was a lie."

"The KGB don't come after their agents who go missing?"

"No, they do. But I'm not KGB. I'm an astrobiologist. I don't think they'll even open the airlock if I come knocking."

"So, we're fucking trapped?"

He shouted louder than he'd intended. The anger vibrated around the rock, the fear and loathing in his voice almost giving the asteroid energy, twisting it just enough to demonstrate effect like jumping hard in an elevator. Swinging it just that much to prove not all physics can be defied forever.

But there was little time to worry about that. Through the mine shaft, a sharp breeze snatched their attention to the place Bradley had disappeared into. A noise was coming from the shifting blackness. Not steps but scraping. Bradley had returned. The rusty blade now sparkling from unknown light. The oil-rag skin drenched in sweat despite the cold. The dim light seemed to stick to Bradley, illuminating the dirty overalls cut to the navel. A stench had entered the cave, for that's where they were. Not the smell of brutal cold from an environment devoid of temperature. Not the taste of metallic rust from mining equipment and shards of cut rock. Not even the caked-in sweat of working men. Something more. Something worse.

Something long dead. but forced back to life.

"Well well well," a cut-glass English accent poured from Bradley's mouth. He smiled so widely it showed in the sinews running down his neck. But under the skin, the thing forced back to life struggled to find freedom. Swirling like a sunspot, readying to lash out and lick whatever was in its way with a fiery tongue. A tongue from a mouth of a million spiky teeth. Bradley's mouth unhinged like a python. Wider than any human jaw should be able to do. A snake ready to eat. A beast ready to feast. Skin splintering like broken leather. As if the creature inside Bradley was bursting at the seams but still had that perfect BBC pronunciation. "Finally, we meet, Mr. Marlowe."

He was blocking the only exit. The figure. The beast. Inflating. The cold hand of terror twisted Marlowe's stomach. The spattering of his soon-to-be exploded torso he could almost see against the rock wall.

Then the far-off explosion came. At first a slow, distant rumbling, but increasingly louder and nearer, as if Delving Prime was being pressed against one of its rocky neighbors. It surprised them all. Bradley, or the creature inhabiting his skin, twisted the human neck farther than it should go to look. The last thing Marlowe saw was Bradley's jugular straining so hard it could snap like a twig.

Then the lightbulb shattered, and complete darkness enveloped their rapidly contracting world.

CHAPTER 11: WHAT HAPPENS ON DELVING PRIME, STAYS ON DELVING PRIME

"Run."

Marlowe said what they were both thinking. As the lightbulb exploded, Sergei's hand gripped his arm. They ran, but not before Marlowe had smacked face first into 'Bradley's' body. The creature stumbled, surprised by the sudden darkness and whatever had exploded in the distant parts of the mine. An irregular drilling that sounded more like bullets echoed from the distance.

Spindly teeth had scratched his forehead. He'd felt the twisting of whatever horrors lived under the skin. They rushed to the surface the instant their bodies touched, Marlowe a living, breathing magnet. The creature alive beneath Bradley's shell strained to suck him in.

But Sergei did not let Marlowe go, even as Marlowe stumbled. While the creature lashed out an ice-cold scream at unheard decibels, they ran. They ran towards the shriek of bullets and the smell of sulfuric fire.

Twisting rockways with scratches of light etched into cragged edges outlined their path forward. Yet the creature was after them. Sergei and Marlowe slipped and sprinted through the weaving tunnels cut through the asteroid, arms running along freezing rock to find the gaps and twisting corners before they could be seen.

Whatever was inside Bradley kept tumbling down. It panted and roared, incompetent at managing two legs and two arms, yet gaining on them, nonetheless. Just before they took a sharp turn, Marlowe glanced back. Bradley skidded into view a dozen feet away. Blood and scratches pock-marked his body, the overalls had been discarded. The filthy vest he wore torn to shreds, the human body naked and ready to burst. What should have been Bradley's muscled thighs looked like a maggot-infested carcass—something trapped, furious and flailing just under the surface, desperate to get out.

Sergei snatched Marlowe into a hard left, then quickly along a straight path, then left and left again at a crossroads. They kept towards the ricochet of bullets ringing against stone and the screams and shouts of those being hunted and shot. But that plan crumbled in a deafening hail of gunfire just around the corner. A groan of death silenced by a point-blank shot, and the shadow of a fallen body illuminated large on the cave wall. Figures wrapped in rounded helmets danced across veiled reality. Undoubtedly soldiers of a certain stripe.

"In here," Marlowe whispered, jamming his fingers into a sharpened grate that—thankfully—opened when he yanked it. Marlowe stuffed Sergei into a gash between the rocks, then climbed in and whacked the grate closed. They would not suffocate in the air tunnel, but the chilled breath of oxygen pumping from behind might freeze them to death. Or ignite from a stray bullet.

Guns continued firing. Marlowe edged back, knocking against Sergei's shivering body crushed between the rock, holding himself up like a spider. Marlowe just waited for something to crawl along his neck. These dark crevices at the convex of air and moisture were a haven for things not wanted near skin. Perhaps that's all that had happened to Bradley. He'd fallen asleep on a chair near an oxygen pump and 'roid bugs had burrowed into his body and laid thousands eggs.

"Shh!" Sergei hissed and snatched Marlowe's mouth as if his thoughts were making too much noise. Marlowe's breath steamed from his nostrils across Sergei's hand. Through the grates, three, four, five armed and black helmeted soldiers rushed around the corner.

"Where is he?" One soldier yelled. Clad only in Velcro black, a sharp yellow 'S-9' was stitched into the arms of his uniform. Same with each of the other soldiers. Their weapons held high, fingers on the trigger. S-Nine shot first and asked questions later. Never mind the trail of dead bodies they'd already left behind.

"Blue team," another said into his wrist. "What's happening on the north side?"

"Two hostiles neutralized. We're dismantling the meth labs now."

"Tag and load any finished products onto the ship. No sign of him?"

"North side secure. No sign of the target."

"Franx wouldn't lie about their location, he wants the UNSOCer arrested," the soldier said. The familiar name cut deep through both Marlowe and Sergei. His fingers slipped from Marlowe's mouth, but Marlowe put them back in place. He needed someone to keep him quiet. "The target must be somewhere here. Find him, now. And neutralize the Soviet."

That settled Marlowe's worry Sergei's next move would be to turn him in. S-Nine wanted Marlowe alive, and Sergei dead. Their chests moved in quiet unison while weapons scoured the hallways a few feet away.

The S-Nine soldiers moved out, heavy armor and primed weapons shaking loudly, boots pounding the ground. Sergei finally released his grip to slap away a bug that squealed on being crushed. The footsteps of the S-Niners faded back into the network of tunnels they'd come from.

"Let's find the escape pod," Marlowe whispered, readying to move away the grate. But Sergei knocked his hand away, while nearly collapsing onto Marlowe's back in the process.

"And if we don't?"

Marlowe was ready to take his chances, after all, he was wanted alive. Plus, the cramped chasm had sent his feet to sleep, a less-than-ideal situation when unlimited numbers of 'roid bugs could have already burrowed up through his pant legs. But the sudden return of shouts and gunshots held him back.

It was loud, but not close. The words indistinguishable, but the sound of fury channeled through the winding rockways. The bounce of bullets; whole clips being sprayed from multiple weapons. S-Niners might be little more than thugs with guns, but they knew how to shoot. Unleashing unending streams of bullets was not the sign of a mission going well. As uncomfortable as it was, Marlowe strained his neck round to glance at Sergei, at least to check he was hearing the same thing. The whiteness on his face said it all.

One by one, the guns fell silent. Out of bullets, or the soldiers out of time. A subtle sound took over. A humming or a buzz. It came in waves, cresting beneath their beating hearts. It came closer, married to thudding footsteps, swaying like a drunk.

A shadow danced across the rock. It was hard to see through the grate. Marlowe leaned forward far enough for Sergei to snatch his shoulders, then whipped his legs around Marlowe to stay steady, and keep them both backed into the crevice. But Marlowe couldn't peel his eyes from the shadow dance. His brain rushed to make sense of the long limbs and twisting shapes. A man. A head. Shadows dancing beneath the skin, a lava lamp set to demented. Bradley. But he was crouched over something, and causing the strange hum, the gnaw and buzz that ended with damp squelches.

The shadow twisted. Enlarging then disappearing. From behind the bend, the object itself was flung into their line of sight. His mind stretched to process, then wished it never had. A pair of legs. That was all. Torso gone. A horrendous stump where hips should be. Only the yellow 'S-9' stitched into the thigh. Bradley had struck. No, not Bradley. He'd end up as nothing but a sack of skin soon enough.

"Dorvethan," Marlowe whispered involuntarily. And wished he hadn't. The shadow stopped. The creature that had been moving away, the creature whose cut-glass English accent *knew his name* was returning. The shadow enlarged. Sergei was shaking. His legs unable to hold the position, Marlowe himself struggling under the growing weight of the Russian on his back.

The grate crashed into the ground. Marlowe tumbled out, hands outstretched to save his head smacking off rock, twisting to avoid Sergei falling on top of him. He landed on his feet, but Marlowe's weren't working. He tried to stand, but both were out cold.

"Get up!" Sergei screamed. He yanked Marlowe up, but not before he caught sight of the creature coming out of the shadows. A body that had a million maggots writhing inside it, a chest soaked in blood, and a million little teeth ripped open in another grin. The lips smacked in the incongruous English.

"There you are, Mr. Marlowe."

A bright sparking flame shot straight to Bradley's chest, then hands yanked Marlowe to his feet and a flare gun scattered on the ground. The miner's body S-Nine had dropped before now lay on the ground with an outstretched hand, the crude weapon Sergei had pried from dead fingers. But there was little time to offer a firm handshake. Sergei lifted the grate Marlowe had collapsed onto and flung it straight at the flaming, screaming creature now staggering back into the shadows.

"Move!"

The feeling had returned to Marlowe's legs, but he wished it hadn't. Pins and needles screamed from thighs to toes as the blood rushed back, but Sergei wasn't planning on waiting around for Marlowe to feel better. His arm spun under Marlowe's and yanked with all the force he could muster as they began to run. Sergei ran. Marlowe twisted and shuffled after him, every step a screaming agony. Surely less than being eaten from the torso down, so Marlowe chomped on his tongue with every screaming step.

They ran under strip lights and bundles of cables crisscrossing the ground. They were in more lively parts of the mine. The kitchen they'd careered into was perhaps ahead, but returning to the way-station was not a good idea with S-Nine and a nightmarish creature who feasted on humans on the loose. Nor was there any ship waiting for them up there. The best they could do would be to switch from Delving Prime to another mine.

"Look," Marlowe said, stealing the briefest second to shake out his painful leg. "The red wire. It's the exhaust pipe."

"So?"

"It'll take us to the escape pod."

"Are you sure?"

"You want to wait here and find out?"

Now it was Marlowe's turn to lead the way. His legs burned with a dull but excruciating ache of five marathons. But the bright red tube bundled with black and blue cables above gave him hope. It twisted through the corridors left and right and straight ahead. Marlowe followed only that. Sergei had to yank Marlowe back from colliding face-first into sheer walls at various points. Sergei kept focused on whether or not the creature was giving chase, but Marlowe only looked up. Each turn through the maze of tunnels sliced into Delving Prime offering a brighter beacon of hope they would get off this rock.

"Careful!" Sergei cried out, yanking Marlowe's shirt to save him trampling a body splayed across the ground. Overalls ripped down to his waist, blood pooling from his trampled face. A miner, but at least one whose torso remained intact. Shot by S-Nine, not mauled by an alien being. Sergei unfurled the cold fingers clamped around a flare gun, still loaded and ready to shoot. Marlowe spied a butcher knife partially hidden under his collapsed body and kicked the corpse over before snatching it up.

"They were unarmed," Sergei said. A note of regret washing over him.

"Of course they were unarmed. This was a mining colony. They decided to cook meth, not smuggle weapons."

"S-Nine aren't after drugs."

Marlowe gripped his new knife tighter. If Sergei wanted to untangle the knot of blame, he could start with the bright idea to drag them across The Maelstrom to Delving Prime to interview a fanatic who would've killed them both if it wasn't for the bloodthirsty beast he'd been consumed by. Panting, Marlowe examined the wire that had now oddly split into two, left and right.

"Should we not go?" Sergei said, anxiously looking back, flare gun primed to shoot at every rumble. Marlowe pointed his knife up at the split red wire.

"Any ideas?"

Sergei examined the options. Marlowe attempted to evaluate the other wires and cables, but none offered a clue. He knew red meant emergency, and that was it. On moons and orbital ships across the system, one could follow a red wire to an escape pod. He'd just assumed it would be the same on an eight-man asteroid.

"Left," Sergei finally said.

"Any particular reason?"

"When in doubt, always left."

"Good enough."

They ran left, the corridor twisting before quickly turning straighter and wider. Big enough for equipment to be wheeled along, or carts of minerals taken to the drop-off point. Bloody handprints caked the stone walls, already frozen in the icy environs. Panic returned to Marlowe that the creature would have left them another bloody stump of legs to find. But the deadly trail led them to the battery of escape pods, where at least one injured person had managed to use, given the smear of frozen red across one of the terminals in front of the half-dozen tubes.

"There's only one left!" Sergei investigated each tube again and again. "How can there only be one?"

The more reasonable question was how could even one person fit into one tube. The escape pods were as snug as a coffin, designed to be a temporary escape route for a collapsing mine. But more likely used to fire manufactured drugs out of The Maelstrom, waiting to be picked up in the quiet void of space around the Asteroid Belt.

"We can't fit," Sergei said, sweating despite the cold. A roar from further down the corridor chilled their spines. Blood-curling and hideous. Human vocal cords stretched to their very limit. A glut of tension passed between them. Sergei stood a half-foot closer to the escape pod, its door sprung open and waiting for one slim figure. The creature was after Marlowe, that's what he could say. It would be true. Just as S-Nine were after him and wanted to kill Sergei.

"We can both fit, but let's do it now." The threat of leaving one of them here dissipated as Marlowe kicked off his boots and began to remove the torn trousers too. These flimsy pods were no guarantee of survival, either, fired off into the Asteroid Belt with barely twenty-four hours of oxygen. Another scream of million-toothed terror from Bradley, closer now than before, caused Sergei to throw his bulky clothes off, too.

"I'm in," Marlowe said as he slotted his bare skin against the cold steel and glass of the escape pod. His white vest riding up his back and underwear sticking to his legs. But there was little time to get comfortable. Sergei, now stripped to those familiar boxers with Cyrillic lettering stitched into the waistband, whacked the 'on' button on the control panel and the tube whirred into life. "Come on," Marlowe held out his hands in a bizarre hug, welcoming the body he knew by taste into an intimate form of survival.

Sergei's extra few inches of height mattered. They pressed together, stomach to stomach, as Marlowe found a nook in Sergei's neck and their legs weaved together in the only way that was remotely comfortable. Marlowe reached out blindly to slam closed the hatch door, holding onto the handle as it seared into place instead of wrapping his arms around Sergei as comfort dictated. For his part, the Russian stayed at an angle, so his hip poked into Marlowe's crotch, instead of his own.

"Push the button," Sergei said.

"You armed it."

"You have to launch it from inside."

"It's not automatic?"

The riotous scream they'd dismissed for being far away was now here, crying out in an agony worth decades. Cackling in a hacking crunch for the one thing it wanted to feast on.

"Marlowe!" The creature inhabiting Bradley roared. He saw the beast through the clouded glass steamed up from their roasting breath. The scent of Sergei's salty sallow skin as intoxicatingly taut as it had been back in the airport bathroom. He scrambled for a button, any button, as the twisting creature bounded towards the escape pod like a freed gorilla ready to overthrow its brutal masters.

"Marlowe! The button!" He found two. Smooth and square and needing a good ounce of energy to depress. One was surely go, the other surely abort. "Marlowe, push it!" Only Sergei's skin and shoulder blade filled his vision. And the memory of those boxers rubbing against him. Pulling them down in the stolen minute of a briefest encounter in an airport bathroom. Adding up those minutes of stolen pleasure throughout his life could bring him to an hour or two. A few hours from life; not even enough for anything interesting to flash before his eyes.

"Marlowe!" Bradley screeched out, raising his blood-soaked fists and skin nearly black from the inside beast almost done with its host's body. There were only two options in the Soviet-made escape pod. Neither was labelled. So why not left?

Horror-soaked hands smacked on the glass and steel. Black, dead fingers flayed off from Bradley's fists like soaked rubber gloves. What had once been a not unhandsome face now barely a skull, a million spiked teeth screaming out into the nightmare of Delving Prime. At least if the button was wrong, Marlowe thought, the hatch door might smack into the creature now gnawing at the glass and pounding it with his fists. The terrifying sound of a slight crack in the escape pod casing sent Sergei's arms tight around Marlowe, his semi-naked body shaking in fear at literal death an inch and a half away.

Bradley's attacks on their coffin had obscured the rumbling rush of power which now sparked into a crescendo. The escape pod shook, but whatever relief of pressing the right button was constrained by the last smack Bradley managed to let loose, leaving behind the tiniest spider web of a crack in the top corner of the glass.

And then it was over. The escape pod launched with missile speed, spinning in a dizzying rotunda which ceased the moment the outside turned black, and they were cast into the absent gravity of space. There was no place to move in the coffin, so the impact of weightlessness was confined to gently smacking against the glass and steel and knocking into each other's sweaty bodies as they left the blinking lights and swirling rocks and a screaming creature baying for blood far below.

A casual dream of silence overtook them both. A weightless hug; forced upon them, unseen by none but the blinking red of Jupiter two hundred million miles away. Marooned on wreck of wood that would sink soon enough. They could search all they liked in the great black ocean, both men knew the chances of death were far greater than zero.

"Nothing on the horizon?" Marlowe asked. Sergei spun them gently clockwise, his arms above Marlowe's neck to tap at the rudimentary computer. Marlowe resisted resting his head back into the shoulder nook, it seemed unprofessional in the circumstances. The hairs on their stomachs tickled and tangled with each other in the gravity-less tube; about the only intimacy either could tolerate.

"There's no scanner, only a distress signal."

"But it will tell you if someone answers the call, no?"

"It should."

"Someone at the Office of Circumstellar Mining will register an escape pod was launched," Marlowe said, reassuring himself out loud. "And all those S-Niners who died. I mean, there's no way they can ignore it. Their patrol vessel must be nearby." He heard Sergei gulp. And felt it, as well, the crux of his prickly neck tight against Marlowe's shoulder.

"I hope someone other than S-Nine will find us."

"They've got no authority to arrest either of us, that's for certain. Whatever those guys were saying on Delving Prime… it's not right. Just imagine S-Nine arresting me. It's not going to happen."

"You have a lot of conviction for someone who's authority is ticking away."

"Open Space or not, Sergei. S-Nine cannot interfere with a UN-SOC investigation. That's a fact. And you're part of this. I'm not letting anything happen to you."

"That's nice of you, but I fear the facts here in space are changing."

"Listen to me." Marlowe gripped Sergei's bare back. Sergei stared straight at him, nose to nose. "We're going to get picked up, get our asses to Luna where Bradley said this Zvezda pod was junked, and prove with whatever blood spatters from a ripped-off torso come from this creature we both saw with our own eyes match the deaths from every file you showed me."

"The files are on Delving Prime." Fuck, Marlowe thought. So was everything else he needed. From his grandfather's diary to his vape pen and the unfiled divorce papers. The thought of telling Marlene she was welcome to go picking through the bloody wreckage of Delving Prime and file them with UNSOC herself made him smile, if only for a moment.

"Sergei, with what we both witnessed—"

"*Warning. Eighteen hours of oxygen remaining. Please conserve use.*"

"What the fuck?" Marlowe said as the message repeated itself in Russian. "Escape pod life support systems are meant to be loaded with twenty-four hours at least by regulation. Thirty-six if fully charged." He spun their bodies ever so slightly to investigate the crack Bradley had made on the glass. It seemed only internal. A tiny ribbon from the top corner. This thing was designed to withstand a medium-sized object collision. If it should bounce relatively harmlessly off an asteroid, it sure as hell should survive a hard fist bashing, even if from an alien.

"There's two of us," Sergei said, without emotion. But the words unspoken were that this thing was built for one. "Try to sleep. We can only wait now."

Sergei stretched out his arms and legs, touching both the top and bottom of the tube and pressing himself against the curve. With nothing to anchor him, Marlowe started to float around, facing outward into the void. Charlie had never spooned him. Not even in their later years when there was no one to stop their sleepovers. Staying overnight in a stranger's hotel room or inviting someone into his for longer than fifteen to thirty minutes was hardly Marlowe's style either, so he could not recall any time someone had hugged him from the back, arms folding around his chest and stomach, while warm breath gently fell on the back of his neck.

Green hills tumbled onwards under a reddish-gray sky. The tinges of millions of years of rust and dust were hard to completely expunge from the Martian atmosphere. The rain fell brown and the rivers ran burgundy, but the iron and magnesium that irrigated the land grew forests a hundred feet tall and grasses an adult human could get lost in.

Marlowe stood upon a stony hill, the great northern hemispheric ocean just about visible, but he was more interested in an inscribed rock that came to his waist. 'Here stood the first two humans to breathe air on Mars, William Jefferson Clinton and Mikhail Sergeyevich Gorbachev, on the third day of March, 1993.'

But Marlowe knew the rock to be false. Martin Reginald Marlowe had been the first man on Mars. He knew it from the stories his grandfather told as he sucked on cartons of chocolate milk and watched TV.

'Bullshit!' The old man shouted from his armchair. 'In 1951 me and your grandma took a stroll up Olympus Mons. 'Course it was all red back then. And without the oxygen. We had on two of them ol' space suits. Looked like a couple of nineteenth-century divers, so we did. The lighter gravity helped. Used to be a third lighter on Mars, you know. Your grandma didn't mind that!'

The old man yelling at the TV faded from reality, the green valleys of tree-sized leafy plants blew in the western wind.

"Frank!" Marlowe shouted into the wild. "Marsha? Come back here!"

"Oh, they shan't hear you." The cut-glass English voice spooked Marlowe. He spun around and saw Bradley, jumpsuit open to his waist, skin crawling like a back massager stuck on violent. "Coniferous Martius, we call it. First plant native to another world." Bradley sucked on an unlit pipe while his torso rippled from pec to navel.

"Marsha, Frank, get back here now!"

"I told you, they won't hear you." The posh English voice as incongruous as the sea of green plants growing in a Martian valley. "Those leaves are the size of a bedsheet and thick as a pavement slab. Wonderful natural tents, mind you. Keeps the heat in and noise out. You could sleep soundly under there for a fortnight. And likely sustain yourself by nibbling around

the edges for just as long. Full of potassium and calcium, those leaves are. I tell you, we've created quite the sustainable Eden, here."

"Marsha. Frank... where are my kids?" He wanted to grab Bradley by his bare neck and strangle him until he offered some answers, but the million spiky teeth in his grin and the swirling nightmare under his skin held him back.

"I told you, Martin. They're Martians, now. Gone to the soil. Worm food. We have worms on Mars, you know. The size of snakes. First organic life native to another world. Wonderful source of protein, if you don't mind the slithery-ness. They're feasting on the first humans buried on Mars, Martin."

"I'm not Martin. I'm Vladimir."

"A Ruskie? My my, Martin. They'll be the death of us. Never trust a Ruskie. Stalin will be out riling up the proletariat faster than you can say Galactic Marxism. I appreciate what you're trying to achieve with UN-SOC, Martin, I must say, but it'll never last. Soon enough we'll forget all about our little Messenger friend and the Yanks and the Reds will be at each other's throats. Think the Cold War is bad on Earth, Martin? Don't you know in space, all war is cold."

"Marsha! Frank!" Marlowe ran down the hill, rocks scattering at his feet and the great waving sails of the endless green valley ready to welcome him in, to be lost forever in its maroon horizon.

"Food, shelter and sustenance, Martin!" Bradley called out, his accent echoing in the sky rusting over for the coming rains. "Mars provides humanity with everything it could ever need. But how long does Eden last? Eh? About two hours remaining!"

"What?"

"Marlowe!" Sergei said, straight into his face. "There's less than—"

"Two hours of oxygen remaining. Please conserve use."

Marlowe dripped with sweat. But in zero gravity it didn't so much drip down his spine but float, showering Sergei with little droplets.

"It was four hours twenty minutes ago." Sergei's face was a picture of fear. It was either no emotion whatsoever from him, or far too much. "We're going to die out here."

"How'd you know it was twenty minutes?"

"What kind of question is that?"

"You don't have a watch, there's no clock." Marlowe studied the redness in the corner of Sergei's eyes. "You could've been asleep too."

"It's going down quickly."

"Someone will be along to pick us up soon."

"What makes you so sure?"

Marlowe had no reason to be sure. In fact, all signs pointed to no. No flashing lights across the black horizon. No bleeps from the emergency radio system. Nothing but cold silence. But with Sergei sweating and fretting, Marlowe wasn't going to spend however many hours or minutes he had left whining about it.

"I can't believe this is how I die." Sergei had turned to full-on depression. Heavy red eyelids were all Marlowe could see. Freckles flushed his cheeks, ones he'd never noticed before. Or never cared to. The brushy hairs of his untrimmed mustache quivered, arms gently shaking as he squeezed against the narrow edges of their tube.

"Sergei…"

"No. It's all so wrong." His voice a whisper. A sad testament delivered at the unexpected climax of a series of unfortunate mistakes. "I'm sorry for bringing us into this mess, Comrade Marlowe."

"You can drop the formalities, Sergei. You can call me Vlad, for all the time we have left."

Sergei cracked into a suggestive smile.

"You asked me once what I am." Marlowe's immediate response was a disinterested shrug, but uncalled for meanness when suffocation was mere hours away was tasteless. He'd long forgiven Sergei for the bathroom incident. In fact, Marlowe wasn't sure he'd ever really been upset about it.

"Who are you, Sergei?"

"Someone I don't wish to be." Sergei looked away, but in their coffin, the equilibrium was upset, and Marlowe had to slide an arm around Sergei's waist to keep from floating smack into their emergency response system. A single salty tear floated from Sergei and landed on the dry edge of Marlowe's lip. "There's a big research facility outside of Baku."

"I know it."

"That's where we met, Eteri and me. He's an engineer, Georgian." Sergei smiled, but back towards the Earth. "Was an engineer. And a radical."

"That seems like a dangerous combination."

"It was. I think… that's why we worked. I kept his secrets. And he kept mine." Tears were threatening the systems, but Sergei kept smiling. "He always wanted us to run away together. To Berlin, or Mongolia, or space. Maybe if we had…"

"You don't know these things." Marlowe hugged him, held his shaking skin tightly against his own. Delving into his sour taste, but one that was oh so captivating. "I'm sure there's nothing you could have done."

"I could have come out here sooner. He was exiled to The Maelstrom."

"Maybe he's still out here?" Marlowe immediately realized how stupid he sounded, excited as if Sergei would, or could, get in touch with his long-lost lover to save them. He shook his head, nonetheless.

"Remember the disaster at Magenta Terminus?" Marlowe shivered at the memory, silently nodding. "He died there." Marlowe nodded again. There was nothing more to say on it, nor to ask. A thousand miners, and likely countless more hand-boys and Uncounted, gone in an explosion that took out three neighboring asteroids too. If Eteri hadn't perished in the fire or been suffocated by toxic smoke, he would've died by space exposure. Bodies had been found floating with their limbs eaten by toxic sludge, their skin melted from fire, then entombed by the absolute zero of space. Marlowe remembered the limbs bouncing off the ship's screen as they made their way through to investigate.

There was nothing to say. Marlowe hugged him. The smallest gesture with someone he'd shared more than teardrops with strangely felt greater than all the intimacy he'd ever had with Charlie, or anyone. The idea of intimacy made him nearly laugh. What was closeness in the frozen infinite blackness, when even on Earth, everyone's neck was constantly craned to the sky, waiting for the inevitable return. No wonder it had been so easy for millions to vote for someone who told them to stop worrying what was going on 'up there.'

Sergei hugged back.

[138]

"Seventy-five minutes of oxygen remaining. Please conserve use, or dock."

"Nice of them," Marlowe said, blinking away his own tears suddenly floating through the thinning air, "to remind us to dock."

Sergei looked him in the eye, holding Marlowe's face by cheek, stroking the edges like it was all about to disappear.

"I have question."

"Now seems about the best time to ask it, Sergei. Shoot."

"What made you approach me at the airport, when I was waiting for my luggage?"

The memory hit hard. A handsome man, traveling alone. Not Western, but familiar enough with the West to not seem lost. Was it the rumple he'd spotted in Sergei's crotch as he walked to the back of the Lufthansa flight? Was it the blinking glance they'd shared? Or how firmly he'd stood alone in the arrivals hall, awaiting luggage, no rush to be met by anyone. He was a man, and he was there, that's what Marlowe should have said. Hundreds, thousands had stood in his place before. In locker room showers, on train station platforms; in Lunan corridors and space-station elevators.

"What made you follow?"

The question at least elicited a smile from Sergei, and it made his face bubble. The hard-edged nose and prickly hair softer from it, the edges of a face a man could love. Or at least spend a lifetime wondering if he would ever love him back.

"Less than one hour of oxygen remaining. Please dock immediately."

They kissed first with their hips; stomachs pressed together, dicks suddenly hard with the realization this time might be the last time. Grizzled chests and sweaty underwear. Sergei yanked Marlowe's down as strong lips muscled from a lifetime of speaking Russian smacked into Marlowe's.

There was no space for anyone to go up or down, only deeper into each other. The kiss both a brutal and tender act. The best of intentions meeting one last hurrah. As they broke, they panted, hearts shuddering while a red light flashed their location to absolutely no one.

Sergei sucked on Marlowe's neck, biting so hard it made Marlowe pant more. Firm hands tugged his shoulders. In the zero-gravity of their soon-to-be grave, Marlowe twisted quickly. Sergei spat into his fingers then wiped them directly into Marlowe. Three hands fell flat against the pod's glass, Sergei's remaining one directing the firmness of his dick up and into Marlowe.

Gasping would only suck up more air. And Marlowe didn't need to gasp. Sergei fit inside him perfectly. The heat suddenly on inside the pod as they fucked and twisted in a floating rainfall of sweat and spit.

"Less than thirty minutes of oxygen remaining."

Sergei's hands scoured Marlowe, fingering every part of him and intermittently grasping at his own cock, spending some precious moments of air. Marlowe swung one arm around the back of Sergei's neck. With every thrust, they had to pull each other back together against the desires of zero gravity.

It was just as well the end was coming, Marlowe thought while Sergei grunted towards climax and jerked Marlowe closer, too. Because nothing, not a dozen men at a time or all at once, would be better than this.

"Attention. Oxygen store has been depleted. Please refill before next use."

Teeth bit into skin, into lips, gasps ejected into the soundless air, the oxygen-less environment. As ecstasy overtook them, Marlowe wondered which inspector from his department would happen across their entwined bodies. Would they have the courage to write down the truth in their report, or would the inspector think of the wife Marlowe still technically had. The family Sergei was attached to. The pension pots and death-in-service benefits that needed to be paid, the laying to rest of Martin Reginald Marlowe's grandson best done without the cloud of scandal.

No, Marlowe thought as he refused to let Sergei stop thrusting inside him despite being all spent, not one element of the truth, of them, or of Dorvethan, would ever see the light of a natural sun.

"Oxygen store depleted. Securely attach nozzle to refill. Keep away from open flame."

"You're still hard," Marlowe whispered.

"I can still breathe."

"So don't stop."

He didn't. Unlike every other encounter in his life, this one was not over the moment the giving party decided. Whether that was

Marlene, Charlie, or any number of nameless bodies. It was as if with every further thrust, another moment of life was bought.

"Oxygen store replenished. Securely detach the nozzle. Keep away from open flame."

The first note that gravity had returned was the spray of bodily fluids splashing against Marlowe's feet. Then they started to slowly slide down the tube. Sergei's bare ass squelching against glass.

"This is the OS Karl Liebknecht." A live voice, a human one, said through the comms. *"You are safely aboard. Our medical team is coming to assist. Please remain in the escape pod."*

It took all of a rushed breath for Sergei to push Marlowe hard against the pod, while his elbows and knees knocked him about as Sergei fought to untwist his soaked underwear and get them back on, all with his jizz-covered feet.

"I think the jig's up, Sergei."

"Shut up and give me your vest."

Marlowe sighed, and wondered only if he'd need the promise of certain death to cum so hard again.

CHAPTER 12: A FULL MOBILIZATION OF RESOURCES IN REGARDS TO AN ONGOING INVESTIGATION

The medical room of the *OS Karl Liebknecht* was cold and old and stank of disinfectant. The ceiling was so low Marlowe feared to stand up from the gurney bolted to the floor. Three other rusted beds lay empty in the sick bay. Their crumpled straps frayed from holding down bodies, no doubt. Either from the sudden loss of gravity… or being held down against their will.

"Am I free to go?" Marlowe asked, swinging his legs in his smocks as the grizzled doctor slid over on the squeaky wheels of his chair, consulting a paper chart.

"Not quite yet." His accent was Spanish, perhaps Cuban or Venezuelan. But he wasn't like those handsome young Hispanic doctors the Communists stuffed their health services with. Doctor Alejandro Babakov had a mean gray streak running from his hair to his thin mustache. "I've examined your comrade." Babakov flicked through the chart and said nothing else, as if waiting to coax a confession from Marlowe.

"How is he?"

"He has elevated liver enzymes."

"I guess he drinks a lot."

Babakov raised an eyebrow from the chart.

"I'd like to run some more tests. On both of you."

"I'm perfectly fine, doc. A bit spooked and dehydrated, but otherwise fighting fit, thanks very much."

With a bloodthirsty alien loose in the solar system, Marlowe was ready to leap from the bed and let the gown swing open as it may, but Babakov wheeled even closer. Grasping his pen like a knife in a hold up, he flicked to the back of the clipboard.

"When were you last treated for venereal disease?"

The question was delivered flatly. Army doctors might not be known for their bedside manner, but at least they got to the point. When Sergei and Marlowe had tumbled out of the escape pod, the rescue crew had been kind enough to focus on giving them rehydration packs and wrapping their bodies in reflective blankets. The condition of the escape pod was ignored as they were rushed out of the docking bay. But Babakov had also been part of the welcome crew, and he hung back to no doubt peek into how two men had survived for nearly fourteen hours with a one-person oxygen supply. Marlowe swung his legs.

"I was prescribed a course of penicillin a couple of years ago."

"Routine checkup?"

"No," Marlowe said, also flatly. Babakov glanced up from his checklist. "I had symptoms."

"Which were?"

"Is this really necessary? I need to meet with the captain. I need to eat. To shower. To get to Luna." Marlowe didn't add: before the literal end of humanity comes. You know, doc, that thing we've all been worrying about since 1947.

"Simply protocol in these… *circumstances*, Inspector Marlowe."

Babakov said it like a parent who'd caught their child jerking off onto the good china. Marlowe sighed. He used to be embarrassed by all this. Not so much embarrassed but ashamed. Like the secrets he'd been able to keep locked behind bathroom doors and gym shower curtains had to be yanked into the open. Inviting a doctor into a cramped cubicle, asking them to pass judgment as Marlowe fell to his knees, or bent over. Now, he wanted to laugh. Whatever he'd had, or *might* have now, was a damned sight more curable or treatable than whatever had infected and no doubt killed Bradley.

"Itching. Trouble passing stools. Rectal—"

"I beg your pardon?"

"I had rectal syphilis."

Babakov gave that same type of sigh which kept Marlowe spending all day waiting at the drop-in clinic in Kreuzberg and paying out of pocket when a prescription or vaccination was required. Anything was better than UNSOC-soaked judgment. Babakov flipped to a different page.

"Are you now, or have you ever been, a practicing homosexual?"

"That's it." Marlowe jumped from the bed, hitting his head on the low ceiling in the process, but it was worth it. Babakov slid back in his chair.

"Inspector Marlowe, I have not discharged you yet." But Marlowe was already stuffing his legs into the dark blue UNSOC sweatsuit left out for him in the corner.

"Like I said, doc, I've got places to go and people to arrest. Well, not so much people but—"

"Inspector! You're not cleared to—"

"I know all the boys say this doc, but I really was tested a few days ago." He was almost grateful for Charlie's insistence. "Since then, I've only practiced homosexuality with Sergei Moscowtiz. You can let me know if he's harboring anything, all right? Now, I'm going." Marlowe slid open the medical room door to a narrow but long corridor busy with men and women squeezing past each other, eyes on Marlowe joining them in his blue sweatsuit, as opposed to their well-pressed uniforms and Russian whispers.

"Inspector Marlowe—"

"No time, doc. Practice makes perfect."

Marlowe squeezed through the submarine-like corridors of the ship to the captain's broom cupboard. After the confined spaces of the *Cleopatra*, Delving Prime, the escape pod and now the *Karl Liebknecht*, the claustrophobia could quite easily leave Marlowe unhinged. Quite easily indeed.

He yanked back the door to the captain's office and slid into the squished, six-sided room, covered in open wires and crackling monitors. Sergei was jammed into a chair against one corner in the same post-Babakov blue sweatsuit as Marlowe, with Captain Wilkes glowering over and working himself into a lather berating Sergei.

"Tell your buddy," Wilkes said to Sergei, but glancing at Marlowe as he squeezed into a seat one removed from Sergei, "ain't no sonofabitch takin' this ship to Armstrong."

"But Captain Wilkes," Sergei was red in the cheek from pleading, "we must get to Luna, ASAP. And it's too dangerous to travel through normal means. I told you that S-Nine—"

"I fail to see how any of this shit is my goddamn problem."

Wilkes grinned the same way Donahue did when playfully trapping a subordinate from some other department to do his dirty work. Wilkes and Donahue shared the same Boroughs accent; an unreconstructed drawl dripping down the generations of native New Yorkers who'd found themselves as numerous as the entire Soviet Empire in the upper echelons of UNSOC. If it wasn't for their gold-plated pensions shipping them off to the golf club at fifty-eight, there'd be nothing but foul-mouthed old Irish and Italian men running the solar system.

"That's not really your call, captain." Marlowe said it calmly. The only way to take these guys on was to undercut them. Spear their spinning energy with a simple stick through the spoke.

"I beg your fucking pardon?"

"Comrade Sergei and I are in the midst of an active criminal investigation. You are familiar with chapter nine of the UNSOC operational code, I assume?"

"I'm familiar with section twenty-eight that says fags are not fit to serve."

"That section of the code was expunged in 1998. Chapter nine allows for requisition and mobilization of any and all UNSOC property and resources in regards to an ongoing investigation."

"You've got to be kidding me."

"Shall we check the handbook?"

"I know the fucken' handbook!" Wilkes roared in fury, his face a red Irish lather, his fists a couple of mallets he only wished to swing. That's the other thing claustrophobia does. Makes a simple man think he's king of his castle. An easy pattern to fall into when there's no one else around to tell him no. Bradley thought he was king of Delving Prime. Open Space might be about to make every two-bit Bradley across the solar system think himself king of his own rock, but this vessel was very much UNSOC. And in UNSOC, they worshiped Byzantine layers of tedious bureaucracy.

"We need to get to Armstrong straight away," Marlowe said, once again keeping the quiet part in his head, the bit where he wanted to scream: there's a fucking alien on the loose! But he feared the slightest drop in his professional shield would see him storm the cockpit with the rusty leg of a chair, and drag this ship back to Delving Prime with every gun and bomb triggered to blow up that Godforsaken asteroid. Wilkes stood tall with his arms folded, coming to terms with the fact there was no way out. "It's hardly more than an eight-hour detour."

"Fifteen. I'm not wasting my good engines."

"Well, perhaps you can vacate some private quarters for us to rest up, then." Wilkes' face dropped. Marlowe had the sense the *OS Karl Liebknecht* would be soaring across the Lunar landscape in a little more than six.

"Separate, or together?" Wilkes trained his ire on Sergei, who started to wilt under the vicious gaze.

"Whatever you can find us." Marlowe glanced noticeably at the door. He'd save Wilkes from the indignity of being asked to vacate his own office, and the captain stormed out of his own accord, slamming the door shut with such force the ship shuddered a little.

"Did you check in with Darla?"

"Yes, but…" Sergei nodded to the red corded telephone bolted to the wall. Every call made to or from it would be transcribed, translated and archived. Perhaps Darla and Sergei had their own secret code, but Sergei and Marlowe did not. Given the cramped corridors on the ship, this was likely the only place they would be alone for quite a while. The overcrowded subterranean city of Armstrong was hardly a place for private conversations either.

"Were you able to update her?"

"I confirmed what we already knew, that the suspect is at large."

"Jesus. That's one way of putting it." The idea of *suspect* conjured in Marlowe everything but the last images of Bradley. "What did she say?"

"They are very busy. Worker uprisings on Titan, Dione and Hyperion. The Americans sent in the Marines to put down a meeting of a soldier-scientist provisional Soviet on Phobos and now the Politburo is threatening to suspend cooperation with the UNSOC treaty."

"Fucken' hell. Wait, on Phobos?" A stab of hope sliced through his stomach. Maybe they'd call off the Alpha Centauri launch if Phobos was caught up in an armed rebellion. Or maybe they'd skip their month-long sojourn and head straight for the next star.

"I saw it on news when I passed by the mess."

"God, it's all falling apart, isn't it." Sergei offered little more than a cold stare. Marlowe could hear the words he wanted to say. The smugness that only came when a Russian had predicted something would go wrong, and it came out much worse than expected. "Did you tell her we narrowly escaped death?"

"I told her we are now safe and en route to Armstrong."

"Sergei!" Everything that Marlowe had pent up exploded in a shout that no doubt stopped people outside the door. Sergei returned a look of surprise, then anger, then culpability. "S-Nine are after me and want to kill you, and you sent them a telegram saying we're heading to Luna?"

"M-maybe... maybe... maybe they'll think—"

"Jesus. Just... just fuck off for a while, okay? Let me deal with this."

Sergei didn't argue. In a harrumph of annoyance, he squeezed out of his chair, elbowed past Marlowe, and slammed the door shut on his way out. It might cost them their lives, but having one mistake to dangle over the smug Russian might be worth it.

After several minutes of temple-rubbing that did little but make his head sorer, Marlowe picked up the red receiver.

"Operator."

"HQ please. CCI. Commissar Jack Donahue."

"One moment." Marlowe listened to the hum of the ship shuddering in between the bitten down edges of his fingernails. On Armstrong he always felt watched. Although that might be because he was always watching. But among the screeds of soldiers and scientists, workers and hand-boys, staring over his shoulder for S-Nine too was not something he relished. "Whom may I say is calling?"

Marlowe sniffed at the operator's question. It was unlike Jack to screen a call. He usually relished any excuse to jump up from the task at hand, light up a smoke and either yell or be yelled at through the phone. The din of the far away communications room carried on beyond her neutral voice. AUX cables clicked in and out of departments as they'd done since the forties. Only a creature as bastardized as the United Nations could run a solar system through telegrams and telephone exchanges.

"Tell him it's Inspector Marlowe. And I have a code red."

"Of course."

The operator executed her job perfectly. The simplest yet most magical words Marlowe uttered splashed into a wave of protocol. A little red bulb would now be flicking on her monitor. Donahue was a Commissar, so no higher authority had to be patched in, but whatever other call he'd been on would now be placed on hold as the operator cut short his conversation. Every second was of the essence, so Marlowe hadn't even been placed on hold.

"Code red, Mr. Donahue. Yes, Inspector Marlowe for you." Clicks and whines and distant voices patchworked from New York to the space between Mars and the Maelstrom. *"Can you confirm? Sir, it's a code... uh huh. Okay, I'll tell him.* Inspector Marlowe?"

"Yes?"

"Mr. Donahue is unavailable. Can I take a message?"

Marlowe blinked. And kept blinking until the sanity returned to his dried-out eyes. He knew the code red protocol would involve a print-out of this conversation landing straight onto Donahue's desk. It would be marked UNSOC classified, a sure-fire way to get this memo in front of every intelligence agency in existence. This was it. The defining moment of his career. He wondered for a moment if this was how his grandfather felt. When first confronted with the Messenger, or some other choice in an unknown chain of events, when he could have leaned in or tapped out, and things would never be the same again

"Yeah. Tell him..." Marlowe sucked in a mouthful of recycled air, then breathed out his obituary. "Tell him the Soviet Liaison and I were attacked on Delving Prime by the same extra... extra-terrestrial that murdered Okechukwu Lammy and Alexei Zhukov on the *Pegasus* in 2016. Tell him this ET inhabited the body of our only witness Bradley Gomez who confirmed that the *Pegasus* was an alien attack, before he was seemingly possessed by the same kind of alien and ripped through the torsos of half a dozen S-Niners who jumped down to snatch me and shoot Sergei for some reason. You'll find the evidence plastering the hallways of Delving Prime. We've commandeered the *Karl Liebknecht* to take us to Luna as Black Moon supposedly bought the murder pod from the *Pegasus* and stripped it for parts. Oh, and I'm under the growing suspicion that the untranslatable word *Dorvethan* from the Messenger's ship is actually the name of this alien or aliens that are not only responsible for the murders on the *Pegasus,* but dozens if not hundreds more that have been covered up by the USSR and USA to avoid damaging their precious Open Space Treaty, and quite likely covered up by more than a few folk in UNSOC as well. So, if Sergei and I can get some serious back up sent to Armstrong, several divisions of the Space Force and Solar Red Army at least, and put the entire solar system on red alert for this murderous creature, we'd be very grateful."

There was a second without words, but not without sound. The clicking AUX's and distant voices of the communications center carried on in the background, as they always had, stuccoed with Marlowe's heavy, shaken breathing.

"I'll see that he gets the message."

"Thank you."

That was the problem with things that seemed like they'd always been. People assumed they always would be. He hung up the receiver and the rotary numbers made a mangled ding. He patted down his jumpsuit, instinctively searching for the vape he no longer had. "Fuck." Marlowe settled for a paper cup and rusty water tap in the corner as the ship's engines growled a different tune. The normal hum that faded into the background shifted up an octave, pulsing in glorious beats as engines powered by Messenger-tech announced the plotting of a new course to Armstrong. In the decrescendos, water droplets from the tap broke free of their artificial gravitational pull, and they floated up.

Safely alone, Marlowe's hand shook as he tried to bring the musty-smelling water to his lips. It was so much harder to find motivation to save the world, when there was nothing left in it he wanted to save.

"I need a fucking cigarette."

CHAPTER 13: A VERY DIFFERENT WELCOME TO THE LUNAN PROTECTORATE OF ARMSTRONG

Armstrong hummed among the web of tunnels, burrows, and passageways to nowhere. The Trebizond of the solar system, it was conceived in the early days as a second Babel. A world capital where governments would never have to worry about the people storming the palace again. Not until they figured out a way to climb to the moon. The plan hit a snag in the late fifties when the moon's core proved an unusable geothermal power source. Investment flowed to Khrushchev-Kennedy instead, but a circumference of shafts had already been dug under the Lunar surface. As lengthy and as complex as many of the world's metro systems put together, Lunar Commissar Neil Armstrong pioneered the moon and its endless subterranean world as the natural home for UNSOC's battalions of scientists, engineers and academics. As long as one didn't mind living like a gopher.

A curious culture had emerged on Armstrong, as the sprawling underground city itself had colloquially, then formally, become known as. The main hub of warehouse-size spaces and interconnected passageways was on the solar side of Luna. Studded by greenhouse-style periscopes growing sunflowers where natural light flooded under the surface through intricate mirrors. Life on Luna was particular, both communal and transient. Things worked informally and were governed by strict yet flexible and meritorious hierarchies.

Marlowe didn't have the patience though to fondly remember his time on Luna or speculate on what would become of the most populous off-Earth place once Open Space hit. The *Karl Liebknecht's* four-person transit shuttle juddered towards Lunar orbit, and with less than half an hour until they landed, Marlowe was too busy biting his nails by the window. Distracting himself by trying to remember the location of a vape store inside Armstrong also didn't help take his mind off the fact 'Dorvethan' was on the loose… and looking for him.

Marlowe bit too far, drawing blood on his thumb. He glanced back at Sergei sitting as far away as he could in the small shuttle, flipping through a French magazine as casually as the day they'd met. But their purpose for working together seemed about as useful as the plan itself. What would come next, once they found some concrete evidence that 'Dorvethan,' or whatever this alien could be called, had ripped through the *Pegasus* and sucked on human flesh like a lobster tail. All he could imagine was standing in front of a UNSOC tribunal while Franx corroborated their story with a flamboyant flourish. The mental image of The Maelstrom's queen storming out of the General Assembly after throwing a drink in Donahue's face gave him at least the chance of a morbid chuckle. Sergei glared his way, and Marlowe shifted further towards the porthole, hiding his demented grin while imagining a drunken Abraxes challenging the Commissar to a fist fight as the entirety of Marlowe's career circled around a dirty drain.

Their shuttle weaved through the busy space of satellites and testing equipment orbiting the moon rock gray and sunflower yellow Lunan surface. Craters covered by dazzling greenhouses and excited light leaking out from the world below. From a distance these bright yellow greenhouses looked like giant sunflowers themselves. A hippy-painted world for an alternative lifestyle.

"Do we have a plan?" Sergei asked, interrupting Marlowe's incessant tapping of the porthole glass.

"*We*," Marlowe said with an unkind snigger. "Maybe *we* should never have started this thing in the first place. What are *we* supposed to do with a clock ticking down the hours to Open Space, S-Nine on our tails, superiors who don't care, and a homicidal alien causing mayhem—"

Sergei marched over, spun Marlowe's chair around and shook it so hard he thought it might detach from the floor."

"You are an investigator, are you not?"

"Sergei—"

"Are you not!" Sergei's face also showed signs of wear and tear. His stubble had become wilder, more unkempt, and dark bags had quickly grown under sallow eyes. But the fire behind them, that was raging. "There's no one left. Darla, she's been after this thing for so long. It consumes her. It kills her she can't be here hunting Dorvethan down herself."

"Why doesn't she?" Marlowe asked, a bolt of anger overcoming his depression. Why were they doing all of Darla Foster's dirty work?

"You Americans… it's so easy for you to get up and leave your job. Do you think a senior Soviet space scientist can just walk away from hers?" The flash of frustration melted away. Marlowe conceded the point. Sergei took the closer chair opposite, and they both stared down at Luna. Several deep breaths later, the hum of the ship took over from pounding hearts.

"I always heard life on Luna was like a hippy commune, or San Francisco," Sergei said, slipping a slim metal hip flask from his UN-SOC overalls. He took a swig, then handed it to Marlowe. It felt like the realest moment the two of them had shared. Two soldiers in a fox hole. Or two men waiting for bad news at a free clinic.

"Rum, Jesus. You must have some good friends on the *Karl Liebknecht*. And it's not completely like a commune… mostly. People study galinium refinement, or cosmic geo-spacing, or heliopause studies, or—"

"Anything to avoid an honest day's work." They shared a grin, and the rum. "What did you study then, when you lived on Luna?"

"Nothing serious. My wife. Well, ex-wife, was doing her thesis at the academic collective. I wasn't particularly interested in exolinguistics, but I spent some time with a sociology collective. They were re-conducting the Stanford Prison experiment. Made me think twice about joining the CCI."

"But you joined anyway."

"I did…" Marlowe took a double swig. He hadn't thought about that time of his life for many years. But they weren't far out from Luna, and those ghosts of his past still haunted the moon.

"Your parents wanted you to be a criminal inspector?" Sergei's question cut a sharp line of surprise through Marlowe.

"My folks?" Marlowe trailed off. Heat overcame him all of a sudden. The hip flask started to shake, threatening to spill rum onto his stuttering hands.

"Marlowe? Are you all right?"

He was sweating despite the climate control. He broke a parched throat with another drink, and blinked himself back to reality.

"They died. My folks. Long time ago." Marlowe replaced the flask cap and heaved himself from the chair. He needed to investigate the civvy clothes reluctantly provided by Captain Wilkes. They couldn't walk around Luna looking like a couple of UNSOCers and expect to find anyone willing to share some secrets. Sergei joined Marlowe sorting through the raggedy black sweatshirts and heavy-duty dark jeans. They'd fit right into Armstrong with these clothes, at least.

"You were young?"

"No," Marlowe said, studying the way he measured the size of one sweatshirt against another, holding it at the collar, then tracing the sleeves through his fingers. The same way he'd watched his mother do when picking out clothes from the UNSOC depositories for her growing son. "I'd already left the Academy. I was here. It happened while we were on Luna. Newly married." The sleeves were too short on this one, and the neck was too wide. Marlowe tried another option. Dark green instead of black. He hoped it wouldn't make him stand out. "This one will fit you." Marlowe handed Sergei one of the sweatshirts and kept the green for himself. It was soft inside, unlike the others where the fabric had been laundered out of existence.

"The *Laurel Reef* bombing?"

Sergei didn't ask it unkindly, but with quiet understanding. Marlowe's silence told him everything. At least Sergei didn't make some show of putting his arm on Marlowe's shoulder or turning his face into the worrying look of wonder and pity. Sergei simply lifted a sweatshirt and held it against his own body. Always the wrong way to measure, his mother had told him.

Marlowe worked desperately to seal the gap in the damn holding back the past. By the time he completed his induction to the Commissary for Criminal Investigations, the years-long *Laurel Reef* investigation was wrapping up. Not that they'd have ever let a rookie with a conflict of interest anywhere near that investigation. The explosion on the VIP shuttle between Armstrong and Khrushchev-Kennedy had taken out five ambassadors, two Politburo members, a secretary of the US Space Force, and nearly a hundred assorted members of Congress, the Communist Party of the Soviet Union, and various UNSOC officials. That's where his parents fell, among the last in a long list. That was the problem with a personal tragedy being wrapped up in one of the largest terrorist atrocities of the late nineties, one's grief became institutionalized.

Instead of personal mourning or a family plot to visit, there were vigils at UN HQ, receptions at the White House and the Kremlin. What more could one say in a personal eulogy when it had all been written about with far more eloquence in the obituary section of the *New York Times* and *Pravda*. The black letters of the headline from three weeks later seared into his memory. *Son of UNSOC founder among lesser-known victims of Laurel Reef.*

Lesser-known. What did that make Marlowe?

"Marlowe?"

"Yeah." He snapped back. The past was of no use today. Nor any day. Black Moon was still in its infancy in the nineties. They didn't have the technical capacity or the connections to smuggle C4 onto a VIP ship. The suggestion the Lunan Independence Movement had any terrorist capability was more of a conspiracy theory than the bombing being an inside job, and the Lunan Collective of Workers and Scientists was a Soviet-backed union with no motive for murdering so many high-profile Russians. Dozens of suspects were cycled through. Maelstrom crime gangs, Chechen separatists, renegade West German intelligence officers, African National Congress fighters, Japanese doomsday cultists. All evidence was incinerated in the vicious vacuum of space. The case was closed. *Unexplained* stamped across the file.

"We'll be landing soon," Sergei said. It was the kindest words he'd yet spoken.

"Right."

Sergei offered nothing else but started to change. Marlowe followed suit. He only wondered after they'd changed into the civvy clothes if Sergei was offended Marlowe hadn't taken in his momentarily and obviously naked body. Now dressed like Lunans, they could leave everything else behind.

"Okay, so how do we play this?" Sergei asked, looking more like a prisoner of war than a scruffy scientist. "I think we should split up to track down the Zvezda. Two of us walking around like a couple detectives will bring bad attention."

"That's not a bad idea," Marlowe agreed. "We can pretend to be on the hunt for black market parts. Stuff that could have come from the Zvezda if it's been stripped down and sold off. I can ask around about a fourth-gen gravitational expropriator. It's the most expensive thing on the pod, and who would spend so much on a new one of those? Maybe you can look for... I'm not sure."

"The Russian victim was studying Neptune, so tidal weight optics?"

"Oh, good idea."

The shuttle was slowing, bumping into the thin atmosphere.

"Marlowe..."

"It's all fine, really. We've got bigger problems in the very near future than the ancient past." He slipped into a long, stained trench coat the *Karl Liebknecht* had sent them away with and caught his reflection in the port hole. A long coat over a dark sweatshirt and darker jeans as thick as chain mail. Boots that were surprisingly comfortable for being Soviet issue uniform. It was giving homeless chic with a cryptic touch. Perfect for blending into Armstrong. Add a fedora and he'd be his grandfather.

The vibe was off in Armstrong's central arrival's hall. The warehouse-sized, metal-and-concrete cathedral of social choice theory was supposed to feel like a college quad on a late May afternoon. A timeless place where stress existed only for the select few who lived for the latest drama. Everyone else was supposed to be lazing about in hetero-flexible friend groups. Chatting over a picnic blanket, mildly dodging a frisbee thrown their way with all the pep of a shaggy dog in the midday sun.

The Armstrong Marlowe stepped into was more like a wild house party after the guests knew the police were on their way. Grad student pace had been replaced with the energy of the Grand Central concourse at Christmas eve rush hour. Desperate folks marched, ran even, from one far side to the other. People clambered up emergency staircases to the next level and next level up. Never stopping to gaze over the metal banisters, nor stopping to chat or just watch the slow rotations of people trading in the only currency required on Luna: information.

They'd split up the moment the shuttle emptied them out, doors snapping closed and revving its engines back to the *Karl Liebknecht* with barely enough time to escape the blast zone. The plan of what to do next, if and when the Zvezda pod was found undiscussed. Quietly, Marlowe was pessimistic of Sergei's plan. The solar system was a big place to hid things. Hell, an alien had been murdering in their midst for years.

"How many years?" Marlowe asked himself, standing on the edge of the oddly busy Lunan concourse. He should start with Black Moon. These days, their reach across the inner system was unparalleled; from farming narcotics on empty Martian fields to selling Kalashnikovs on Saturn's moons. Making contact with them was easier said than done, though. Most lives on Luna could be lived without even knowing of their existence.

The discordant sight of so many Lunans going somewhere *quickly* aside, Marlowe weaved through the largely long, gangly and pale folk who'd been born and raised in Armstrong, as he headed toward the Welcome Mat. Like the darkened arches at the far side of a Roman forum, the Welcome Mat was where a new arrival could settle into a beanbag with a Styrofoam cup of filter coffee while tapping into the latest Lunan gossip about which experimental groups were faltering, and what was the up-and-coming one to join, and navigate the complex maze of underground corridors to find the best parties traded like treasure maps.

Marlowe tried to listen to the talk as his boots crunched over sunflower seeds scattered across the main concourse, the ubiquitous Lunar snack.. Sentences were hard to catch, people were moving so quickly, but the tone was clear. Hurried, anxious, edgy.

"Is it today or tomorrow?" One woman said to another. Marlowe slowed his pace to listen. Her friend was rapidly flicking through a *Pravda*. 'Open Space, Red Space' was written in big Cyrillic block letters over a map of the system with an array of solar bodies colored red. Moons of Saturn and Jupiter. Spotted bodies of The Maelstrom. Phobos, where Sergei had mentioned a worker's insurrection had just taken place. All roads led to Luna. The image of the moon had a hammer and sickle superimposed over it. Space was open, and the gloves were off.

"Excuse me," the friend said to Marlowe. He shrunk away from staring at their paper. "Do you know what day it is on Earth?"

Marlowe swallowed a grin. The out-of-touch Lunan stereotype was a hard one to shake.

"Gee, sorry ma'am," Marlowe gave his best 'aw shucks' shtick. "I only came from out Ceres way and—"

"Excuse me, what day is it on Earth?" she stopped another passerby. A tall engineer with their hair in dreadlocks and a *They/Them/ они* badge prominently displayed on their breast. They glowered at Marlowe as if Open Space was his fault entirely.

"It begins at 0230 Lunar Time. Do you have a place to shelter?"

Marlowe slunk away. They were acting as if the Open Space Treaty coming into effect was like a comet hurtling through the system. A transitional government was taking over from UNSOC authority, and its main purpose was to simply draft a constitution and hold elections within a year. Wasn't everyone being a tad too... dramatic?

Although there might be some need for drama. Marlowe turned instantly on his heel when he spied a patrol of five S-Niners. Dressed head to foot in black, visors down, heavy weapons at the ready. Perhaps that's why Lunans were moving so quickly across the concourse. The sight was intimidating, and intentionally so. Marlowe took a longer route round to the Welcome Mat. Slipping into alcove shadows, he spooned Turkish coffee into a tall, dirty glass and added boiling water from the samovar. None of the dozens of people milling about the Welcome Mat were in a rush. Many were also agog at the stressed-out crowds. Laughing, sipping coffee, crunching on sunflower seeds. Not all life on Luna changed so quickly. Marlowe slid into a low bench of peeling paint. The busy concourse was several groups of people away. Here they were safely snuggled into bean bags and perched on bar stools.

"Did you get your VitD shot last time?" Said one elongated older woman to her shorter, younger companion. She was Lunan through and through. Her shining black skin utterly free from having been touched by natural weather.

"I wasn't here for long enough then," the friend said, chewing her way through a handful of sunflower seeds and discarding the shells on the ground.

"Worth getting now. Who knows what the transitional gov's going to do with healthcare."

Marlowe sipped the thick black coffee and appreciated the brief moment of not feeling like everything was falling apart. He only began to enjoy the six months he'd spent here with Marlene when he learned to wander off by himself, sitting alone in canteens and chill zones. Drinking coffee like there was no such thing as night and day. There wasn't. Only tired and not tired. Engaging in passionate debate or sitting quietly; lying about or getting up to no good. For just a second, he could forget himself and the weight of ending worlds, and just sip coffee like a Lunan.

A young man on a beanbag stole his attention. Turkic features with sunset skin. Smooth yet freckled, like he'd been frozen at the cusp of youth. Or brought to Luna when he was a boy. Jet black hair was tied up in a tight ponytail, and his sharp eyes nodded widely as he listened to his friend; a curly-haired, bespeckled man doing his utmost to emulate Trotsky, as so many of them were.

"Well as I said, there's a place for you in our experiment," Trotsky said, with more than a lingering smile to the statuesque young man. Getting a hot guy to join an experiment was a coup in itself.

"But you're in the sixteenth quadrant, no?" Hot guy cocked his head and grinned.

"Closer to the seventeenth."

"Eugh. So, I'd be eating lentils three times a shift?"

Trotsky could see that was a losing argument. He shifted gear and edged closer to Hot Guy's spread-out knee.

"You'd get your own hammock."

"I've got a bunk where I am."

"You and three hundred others."

"So? it's a big experiment."

"We're four. Stick around until data collection is done, and I'll guarantee your name is third on the journal article."

That intrigued Hot Guy. Trotsky let his hand linger on the young man's knee. Nearby, the young woman chewed her last sunflower seed, then was helped up by her lanky friend. Marlowe tucked in his legs as they shuffled past, on her way to get a VitD shot before the transitional government took over, so it seemed.

"Will I get to share a hammock with you?" Hot Guy said, the smirk only growing. Trotsky seemed mightily pleased with himself. Such was the way people conducted business on Armstrong. Marlowe found his admiration of the two slink into something like longing. Perhaps for their ignorance of the terrible things going on, or simply nonchalance. When their waking motivation was not the future of the human race, but simply their own lives. Career, comfort, desire. The taste of envy came as bitter as the black coffee.

"Marlowe!" A vaguely recognizable voice called from behind. Marlowe feared to turn around. "What's the Commissariat for Criminal Investigations doing round these parts, eh?"

Hot Guy and Trotsky snapped their limbs away from each other and stared accusingly at Marlowe. He quickly rose to greet the only man he knew who could be so tactless.

"Jesus, Matt," Marlowe said through gritted teeth to the short and stumpy engineer. "I could be undercover."

"Ha! You sonofabitch." Matt thrust Marlowe into an oil-stained handshake-hug. Matt was an engineer, permanently in filthy overalls with a rag hung through a belt loop like a good luck charm. Engineer was perhaps too generous. He repaired climate control units, just like he'd done in the Bronx. "What's a bastard like you doing up here and not telling your ol' buddy Matt, eh?"

Marlowe shrugged that it wasn't his fault, and left his glass on the sunflower shell covered table, stealing one last, lingering look at Hot Guy.

"Thought I'd drop in for the fun and games."

"Ha! Fun and games. Oh boy, are you in the right place at the right time. C'mon a minute and wander with me." Marlowe followed his old friend. Fortunately, they blended in because Matt, one of the few people on Luna paid a wage for their time, always walked quickly.

They shared friendly outlines of the intervening years on a march across walkways over busy experiment-rooms and down deserted corridors with flickering lights. Sometimes, Matt stopped to fix a bulb with a screwdriver as they chatted. Matt had long known about his separation from Marlene, although Marlowe wasn't quite sure how. Matt said it was through mutual friends, but from Marlowe's memory, his old Armstrong drinking buddy had not played a significant role in Marlene's circle of linguists.

"People really waste their time talking about us?" Marlowe asked, still unable to imagine himself the subject of anyone's gossip.

"For sure. The director's grandson splits with the woman who's gon' be first president of Mars. We live for this shit."

"She's the incoming deputy director of the Mars Settlement Authority. There's no president."

"Well, there will be, and mark my words, she'll be it. That new MSA director-general, Yuri what's-his-name, he'll bow out in a year or two. He's past retirement as it is."

"Jesus, Matt. I hope you're saving some of this gossip for your own retirement."

"Hey, I fix a lot of climate controls, all right? Stuff just... floats my way."

"Is that right?" Marlowe had been planning to broach the subject of the Zvezda pod, in a roundabout way, of course. But Matt seemed to be living through his mouth, and he didn't owe a shred of loyalty to Marlowe. "If you know everything there is to know on Armstrong, then what the hell's going on over here?"

Marlowe pointed to a crowd gathering at the far end of a wide-open common space they'd stumbled into. It was one of the nice ones. With benches and trees. A glass roof bathed them all in a sepia tone from the sea of sunflowers being grown above.

"Dunno," Matt said, hands on hips and staring into the distant crowd. "But they sure are noisy."

It was true. It sounded like a protest or demonstration of some sort and was attracting the attention of other passersby. Joining the mildly interested pedestrians, they wandered over.

The crowd had got themselves worked up over what looked to Marlowe like a shuttered store front. Boarded up windows slathered with graffiti, some signs for the Lunan Independence Movement too, but those were everywhere. Strange that there were 'coming soon' posters plastered on the chipboard of the storefront, but what exactly would come soon had been repeatedly scored out or painted over.

"They're upset about a store opening?" Marlowe asked, giving a slight shake of his head at just how ridiculous Lunans could be. At least a hundred were chanting slogans in unintelligible Russian and pumping their fists in the air. Matt glanced at him sideways.

"When was the last time a store opened on Armstrong?"

"Oh... right." One was opening, or was hours away from doing so as soon as the clock ticked over to Open Space and Luna was no longer the administrative function of UNSOC. "What's supposed to be here?"

"A McDonalds."

Marlowe doubted anyone but him had heard Matt, but at the same moment, the crowd seemed to become wilder. The fist-pumping chants screamed at the shuttered store were doing nothing, why would they? More dangerous than that, their anger had nowhere to go. A fist began pounding on the boarded window, then another, and another. Soon, the entire front line was charging headlong at the soon-to-be first fast-food restaurant on Armstrong.

"*No capitalists in space!*" Some started chanting. A new group had joined in from a corridor to the right. A younger crowd, angrier, with hooded black sweatshirts obscuring much of their face. "*No capitalists in space!*"

"Should I tell them there's a Pizza Hut on Khrushchev-Kennedy?" Marlowe whispered through a half-smile.

"Shh!" Matt yanked him back as the crowd surged forward. If he'd heard, he was not amused. "These kids are bad news."

On that point, Matt was right. The new vanguard wasn't interested in banging on a few bits of fiberboard, they wanted to tear down the entire shop. Nails screeched as they were ripped out of metal, then the shatter of glass separated the crowd like oil from water. Most backed away, scared at the light poking through ripped up barriers, and the movement of what seemed like people inside. Yet the flammable oil rushed forward, boots first, kicking through boards like screen doors and reveling in crunching glass.

What sent a bolt of fear through Marlowe was the glint of metal arrows being loaded into crossbows made from bent pipes. He hadn't seen those weapons in years, once a favorite of the banned hard left gangs that had all but defeated periodic attempts to bring some measure of free market capitalism to the moon. That a new generation had discovered these easily made weapons that were traditionally used to kneecap anyone who threatened the socialist status-quo did not bode well for the transitional government, or fair elections.

"Bosses are fascists! Bosses are fascists!" A loud thump and several prolonged shouts scorched the fluorescent-lit inside. More than a dozen had breached the hole they'd kicked through and seemed to be taking their running amok to a far greater degree inside. Those still watching from the out were treated to a pin camera play of hooded thugs trashing a plastic-coated fast-food joint.

As a high-pitched scream was cut viciously short, pounding steps from a corridor in the far right punched the concrete. It wasn't more rioters, but S-Nine, instead, in typical full tactical gear, weapons at the ready. Dozens of them were marching close, peeling away remaining layers of the onlookers as if they were more afraid of the law enforcement than the law breakers. For the first time in his life, Marlowe was, too.

At first, his years as an officer of the law made him want to run towards the scene. To flash his badge and update the S-Nine unit leader on the number, manner, and demeanor of the youths currently ransacking the restaurant. But Marlowe had no badge. Nor was he very sure the little authority remaining to him as a sober investigator would last beyond the 0230 deadline. Only then, with several shiny S-Nine helmets staring into the remaining throng, did it clock in his brain that S-Nine, or at least some of them, had his name on their list.

"We need to get out of here," Marlowe spewed out, tugging Matt's arm.

"Ya think?"

They ran with the crowd. S-Nine had their hands full with the screams, shouts and sizzle of spilled hot oil aflame inside. As Matt and Marlowe, and tens of others, reached a wide thoroughfare, shots rang out from back there.

Marlowe glanced back. Above the running of sweaty heads, the black-booted private security force had torn the person-sized hole wide open. Folks were being dragged out with their hands zip-tied behind their back to be met with the butt of a rifle smashed into their face.

"*Down!*" Black-helmet hate stood over bloody-faced teens. The stench of burning oil on fresh plastic, sweat and hurt drenched the normally blank metallic taste of Armstrong air. And people ran. On Armstrong, they ran. Something had changed out here. Whether sparked by the opening of a fast-food place, the reaction to it, or the wind that had blown both those things into being. This was no longer the place of sunflower seeds crunching under soft-soled shoes. Now it was smashed glass under steel-capped boots.

"C'mon, Marlowe, let's fucking move it."

CHAPTER 14: GOD DOES NOT DWELL ON THE DARK SIDE OF THE MOON

Marlowe had quickly shooed Matt away. Matt wanted to hunker down in his bunker, like most of Luna, it seemed, as news of the McDonalds riot spread quickly on fearful lips. Despite demanding Marlowe join him in hiding and they could split the several rations of vodka he'd saved up, the riots would make it all the harder to make contact with Black Moon. But with some real evidence on his side, Marlowe could throw it back to Donahue. And Darla. Let the Politburo and the DOJ and the goddamn White House deal with an alien on the loose.

The *Karl Liebknecht* had spared only a couple of basic cellphones for him and Sergei. Most of Luna didn't have much of a signal to make the device useful, but in a bright spot of empty, open warehouse, where the burning sun filtered through a glass domed sunflower pod, finally, there was some signal.

No message from Sergei, but he sent one anyway asking if there was any update. Then he tried to call Donahue, but the direct number just rang out.

"Son of a bitch."

Back up on Luna requested again. The message was delivered, but unread.

Resting against a cold metal wall underneath a sunflower greenhouse, his legs wanted to slide his backside to the ground. But rest was not an option, at least not yet. and certainly not on Luna. The cell gave him his bearings. He was west of the Messier Crater, so the dark side wasn't far away. As unsubtle as it was, the dark side of the moon was where things happened on Luna that shouldn't be seen. Where the maze of mapped tunnels faded into illegal hovels.

Unsanctioned experiments carried out by those who may have been ordered to leave, Uncounted lives lived by those who had no right to be there in the first place.

Marlowe walked for half an hour along a main thoroughfare and saw no one. Freshly chewed sunflower seeds suggested the barren landscape was only recently abandoned. He came to a tram stop on the south-western line that at least had a few grimy faces awaiting the car, and three S-Niners standing guard on the platform. Marlowe kept his eyes down and back turned, but Marlowe only knew how to stick out. The UNSOC badge had never been questioned before. The way he walked through a crowd or a train station was less about blending in, but making himself known to the right people. To law enforcement, that he was one of them. To UNSOCers, that he was one of them. To men he might meet in the bathrooms, that he was one of them. To be afraid of authority, of what they might ask or want or do, he'd never been one of them before.

The tram car thundered into the station with a whoosh of stale air. It sucked the light from the station for a few flickering moments like the New York Subway from Marlowe's childhood. The main difference being this car's graffiti was half in Russian. Fortunately, S-Nine did not climb aboard. Marlowe let go of an anxious breath, sliding halfway down the plastic seat as the tram screeched toward the last stop open to human habitation, Vallis Rheita. Beyond that, Marlowe might find the answers he was looking for.

Life on the dark side of the moon flowed like sewer water in a city-state under siege. Stagnant, rotting remnants of what life had been, or could be, echoed through a hemisphere of endless shadows. On parts of the Lunar surface officially designated as Armstrong, natural light did flow through from sunflower domes, bouncing as far as hidden mirrors could take it. But light was not infinite. There were many parts of the solar system the light would simply never touch.

Another half an hour from the station at Vallis Rheita stood the border. One of many hundreds of gateways, not officially demarcated like in Berlin or split down the middle of the European continent. But, as a stream flows into a flooded field, the stench just rose until it was clear one was wading through shit.

On this borderland, though, the line was somewhat obvious to those who were looking to cross it. The tiled walkway lit with bright, if flickering lights, abruptly ended. The pathway didn't stop, but it narrowed to a rough-edged tunnel cut into bare lunar rock. No one could pretend to wander this way by accident and think they were still in civilization.

Marlowe breathed in dank air; unfiltered and unprocessed. There were stories of people wandering too far into the unmapped parts of the dark side, falling down holes or getting lost in an endless loop of burrows, and suffocating from an oxygen outage, a frequent occurrence so far from an air source.

For six months in his second year in the CCI, Marlowe had worked the Lunar Vice desk. The memory of those incursions across the border of light and dark made him shiver even now. Kids hocked up on space dust, digging eyeballs out of their crusty sockets when the light of a torch burst into their drug-addict hovel. Nests of human remains made by those small furry creatures, not quite a rat, not quite a snake, but with a sting worse than a scorpion who could slither up an untucked pant leg faster than a weasel.

Marlowe immediately tucked his pant legs into his socks then double laced his boots around his shins. He regretted how unprepared he was to go over to the dark side. He'd be lucky to leave without a dozen of those critters' larvae burrowing into his skin. He came with no flame gun, or regular gun. No stab-proof vest, no vials of navroxolene in case of a junkie scratch, and no back up. Neither Donahue nor Sergei had answered. Yet whatever happened to the Zvezda pod, and the last shred of evidence of how Alexei and Okechukwu had died, would be through this darkness. Someone must know. There were far, far worse terrors among the dark side than a simple crime gang like Black Moon, Marlowe reminded himself. Six months in vice had taught him the best way to get a gang member to crack was to leave them alone in an unlit tunnel five miles deeper than they'd ever want to go. They'd crack in twenty minutes. Marlowe could spare twenty minutes to get this case off his back, once and for all.

Not five minutes into the dark side and along the rough-cut rock, a warm light and whispered conversations drifted in from a tunnel to the right. Steel hexagons reinforced the tunnel edges and lightbulbs hung from the bare metal brackets, illuminating a way towards a lost tomb.

A steady chanting drew him forward, like cloistered monks down a Moscow backstreet, quietly singing their frowned-upon devotions. A few more tentative twists later, the tunnel opened into a broad, long alcove transubstantiated into a chapel. A dozen or more figures sat low among scattered chairs, singing different hymns toward a hastily built altar. There stood a priest, not clad in Orthodox silks or the bright greens of St. Patrick, but a woven blanket slung over his shoulders. He held up a Styrofoam cup overflowing with red wine to a crucifix erected above the altar, smelted from discarded metal pipes.

Marlowe stood in quiet awe for a silent moment as the congregation of a God-forsaken place muttered along to their own prayers, not so much guided by the shabby priest, but praying alongside. Those in attendance were clearly of the dark side. Not scientists, not workers. Nor any person who had a right to live in the light. A few aging hand-boys who whispered in Cantonese as they helped each other off their knees. As did some gaunt figures with collapsed cheeks from a lifetime sucking on space dust. Also, gangly Lunans who's heads scraped the rocky roof, and a clutch of clunky, heavily bearded men surrounding one elderly yet refined woman. Marlowe would bet his meager pension that she was Black Moon, and those were her bodyguards.

Presently, the Mass seemed to finish, as the priest turned back to his flock, while greeting Marlowe at the back with wide eyes and a bushy smile.

"The Lord be with you," said the priest, with an accent that betrayed Italian or Spanish origins, but Earthly, nonetheless.

"And with your spirit," the congregation muttered.

"Go in peace and bring light to the darkness."

"Thanks be to God," the congregation finished, and shuffled over to a couple of folding tables at the side of the alcove. There were some loaves of bread and trays of chicken 'liberated' from a nearby canteen, but also bundles of thick socks, candles, torches, an open first aid kit, and what looked like bottles of discarded medication. The congregation was more interested in shaking pills and investigating the small print on the label than the food or clothes, at least at first.

"Peace be upon you, my son," the priest said, having wandered next to Marlowe without him noticing.

"I'm sure it's a noble act of charity to provide food and medicine to the Uncounted," Marlowe said, instinctively reaching for his badge that wasn't there, "but religious services on UNSOC property are illegal."

The priest gave no reaction, but said: "If you're here to arrest me, may it wait until after our Narcotics Anonymous meeting? It starts in half an hour, and these people could really use a friendly ear to listen to them." The priest spoke with calmness, and a voice that was almost melodic.

"I'm not here to arrest you... Father...?" Marlowe was unsure if that was the right title, but assumed the priest would correct him with his name.

"I'm glad to hear it. Would you care for a friendly ear?" Marlowe pulled back at the question, but the priest didn't let up from the soft smile through his beard. "Or you can help me bring down the top table," the priest nodded to the altar, which was in fact only another folding table with a white sheet spread across it. "I can ask one of our friends if you don't want to," the priest nodded to the group now busily eating. "But it's the only real food most will eat all week."

Marlowe gently smiled back. Guilt he understood. The priest carefully removed the metal crucifix, finished the remnant of sacrificial wine in the Styrofoam cup, then carefully folded up the altar sheet. Giving Marlowe gentle directions, they collapsed the rusted table legs, then arranged the collection of stools and chairs into a semi-circle.

"There, all ready. Thank you, my child."

"Vladimir," Marlowe said. S-Nine may have passed out his name already, but it felt strange to lie to a priest about something as simple as his name.

"Vladimir, nice to meet you. I'm Father Michael." The priest held out a hand that was boney and scarred. There were no rings or jewels as Marlowe might have expected. Just a set of wooden rosaries wrapped around his arm. "I have some real coffee in my office. Care for a cup?"

"You have an office?"

Father Michael chuckled and shuffled around the back of the altar, where there was a cramped antechamber sliced into the rock, a thin curtain partitioning the hovel off from the main space. Father Michael lived here. A camp bed was covered in heavy blankets, while books and Bibles smothered a tattered table and chairs. Father Michael grumbled quietly to himself as he lifted a two-ring portable hob and balanced it on a chipped sink, twisting on the gas canister it was attached to and pottering about with packets and cups.

"Tell me, son," he said as the water began to bubble and the alcove filled with the thick scent of Turkish coffee, "what's on your mind?"

"I don't know much about religion," Marlowe looked for a place to shift a pile of damp books from the chair. "But isn't a confessional supposed to be, you know, dark and separated?"

Father Michael took the books from Marlowe and shoved them on the bed. Marlowe sat and the priest filled two blotted glasses and joined Marlowe on the chair opposite.

"I find there's enough darkness in these parts, don't you? So, how can I help you, Vladimir?"

"You invited me here, father."

"You came into my church."

"I didn't know it was a church. I'm looking for something else."

Father Michael smiled. He drank deeply, almost finishing the glass in one gulp, letting the froth dirty his stained beard even more.

"Simply a matter of perspective, son. I'd say you're exactly where you need to be."

"I'm looking for Black Moon, father."

It didn't faze him.

"You can take your pick from my congregation. Although you don't strike me as one who needs their services. No," he answered his own riddle, "you're too intelligent for S-Nine and your face is far too weathered to be Lunan. So… UNSOC?"

"Correct."

"Strange times. UNSOC allying with Black Moon. You not placing me under arrest." Marlowe took an uncomfortable sip of the strong coffee.

"I'm working on a bigger case." Marlowe leaned forward, staring the man down like he was any other witness. Forming the question in his mind that could turn a witness to a suspect. But Father Michael cut him off with a wave of his arms and his own serious look.

"I work on the biggest case, Vladimir."

"Saving souls?" Marlowe said with a dismissive smirk.

But the priest shook his head. "Helping people."

"Do you think I need help?"

"We all need help, son." Father Michael glanced at Marlowe's wedding ring, still stubbornly around his finger. The only personal item that had made it through so much turmoil. He flicked his ring, but not because he missed Marlene, because he was desperate for a nicotine fix. "What does your wife make of all this, then?"

"She's…" Marlowe thought for a moment, twisting the gold band up to his knuckle, then back down again. It made him not think of Marlene, but her brother Charlie, and the endless parade of silent figures who'd filled up the space Charlie's absence had left in Marlowe, since they were barely teenagers. He thought for a moment, whether or not to confess it all to Father Michael. The story coalesced in his mind, forming itself into logical, tragi-comic chapters.

Teenage lovers in the cold, Muscovite hallways of the UNSOC Academy. Marlene the lynchpin that gave their secret relationship an acceptable sheen. But as Charlie drifted into his own orbit, the only way Marlowe could hold onto the closest thing to love he'd ever known was to follow Marlene. Carrying her books to advanced linguistics classes. Taking the same neo-physics courses and bunking up together on Khruschev-Kennedy, meeting up with Charlie for a drink when he had an off night from his fast-track pilot training program. Charlie, flashing smiles across a row of bar stools. Charlie, stripping off his vest in the locker room and throwing Marlowe that look he got in his eye. Charlie, holding himself to the highest standards of a best man, wiping Marlowe's tears, kissing him on the cheek and reminding Marlowe this was all for the best. In fact, there was no other way. Neither of their careers would survive an ethics investigation, not to mention the embarrassment brought to their families, and to Marlene's burgeoning career as the premier Messenger linguist of her age.

"I didn't cheat," Marlowe said, staring at the coffee grains stained against the glass. "Not while we were good. Nine years. From the day we were married till our babies died. I never even thought about it. I was faithful as a husband and as a father. I did everything right. Everything by the book. I did what everyone told me to do... but still, you took it all away." The tears burned as they dripped down Marlowe's cheeks. He wiped them away, fingers stinking of coffee and judgment. "Didn't I do everything right? Didn't I?"

"I don't know your life, Vladimir, but I'm sorry for what happened to you." Father Michael took Marlowe's hand, held it without asking. "You've been through terrible tragedies, and no one can judge you."

"God does, isn't that what you people say? It's all part of God's plan, or if I hadn't had impure thoughts or been that way before my wife, I wouldn't spend every day spending every ounce of energy to block out this agony. My children were taken. My parents were taken. So that's what my wife's dealing with. A husband who's an orphan and who let his children die. A husband with a distance she could never broach, with secrets she never could quite figure out. So go on. You and God can judge me. I'll wait."

Father Michael watched Marlowe for quite some time. Marlowe gave him a show. Shaking from the shoulders down. Getting up, sitting down, picking up books and throwing them back onto the camp bed. Spilling his secrets was not something he'd had in mind. Nor was tearing open the pain of the past going to help one lick in the problems of the future. Of right now, today. Gathering some damn evidence before he was shot by S-Nine, Black Moon, or Donahue himself. Only when Marlowe finally sat back down, one leg shaking, did Father Michael deign to speak.

"Ten years I've been here, Vladimir, running a church on the wrong side of hell." The priest spoke softly, and it helped Marlowe swallow back the vicious beasts of his tortured life. The air itself was quiet. There was a relief that came from being on solid ground, even a moon, more than a ship or a station. Maybe it was that gravity here only had to be enhanced, not made from nothing. Or deep beneath their feet was a magnetic core. Marlowe thought of that as Father Michael drew in a long breath and stroked his coffee-stained beard.

"And there's one thing I've learned above all. God," Father Michael said, "does not exist." Father Michael let the words flutter like

[171]

poisonous scarabs. The cross around his neck glinted in the dim and distant light. The strange hymn ringing in their ears, between coffee cups and soft speech from beyond the alcove curtain. "Not in space, anyway. God the Father, the Son, and the Holy Ghost is real, but God lives down there, on our world, on our planet, where Jesus Christ died for our sins." Father Michael crossed himself and kissed the crucifix. His face seemed to wither, the sinews holding his eyes together under a furrowed brow shriveling like a grape left under an air conditioner.

"Up here, the only one judging you, Vladimir, the only one who's respect you should be concerned of, is yourself. Ask yourself that, son. Are you proud of your own life?"

If Marlowe had wanted to answer or even take a moment to think on the question, the chance was robbed by a cauldron of shouts and crashes from beyond the curtain. Marlowe jumped up, reaching for the gun he did not have, while Father Michael did not move, as if this was a ruckus he'd been expecting.

"Father! They're trashing the place!" Peeking out from behind the curtain showed chaos. Hooded youths, their faces blacked out in balaclavas, were kicking over chairs, trashing the altar and smashing up the food tables. Half the congregation, including the Black Moon members, had disappeared, while the others huddled against a wall, shielding themselves from a coming punch. "Father, don't you want me to do something?" But he was mumbling to himself, holding the cross, eyes flicking up to heaven in desperate prayer. The chair-smashing destruction continued unabated outside. Marlowe quickly scanned the alcove for any type of weapon. It would be less than a moment until they crashed in.

"Under the pillow," the priest said. Marlowe dived across and snatched up a stubby six-shooter.

"There's only one!"

"They came for me, not for you." The calmness unnerved Marlowe more than the near dozen hooligans and their orgy of wanton destruction.

"The hell they did." He cocked the revolver and ripped back the curtain. "Stop! *Hvatit!*"

Neither shouting in English, nor Russian, nor the pointedly aimed gun had a measurable impact on the chaos. The youths continued trashing the makeshift church, throwing legs of chairs and ripped up Bibles dangerously close to the huddled congregants. Marlowe ran over to the scared, shoeless old women who shivered in more fear of him than the youth cracking through the table with a hammer. Marlowe booted the kid right in the face and he stumbled back. A narrow band of shocked eyes glared up at Marlowe, as the kid shouted something quickly in Russian and a few more scurried over.

"Get out of here!" Marlowe demanded, pointing the gun this way and that. But now he was surrounded. Six, eight, ten of the hooded, hammer-holding rioters swarmed around, spinning a web closer. Up against one man with six bullets, they liked their chances. Marlowe knew he could get off two, maybe three at most, before a hammer blow from the periphery would crash through his skull. The frail figures Marlowe thought he was protecting wailed in a flurry of quick-spoken prayers. Or curses. Who knew if they were in danger before Marlowe jumped out with a gun.

"Leave. Them. Be." The strangely booming voice of Father Michael called out from the alcove. He clasped the crucifix from around his neck in both hands, holding it high above the fray, trying to divine light from the darkness. He'd seized their attention. The religious symbol seemed to cause them unbearable anguish. They left Marlowe and his gun and rushed to Father Michael, knocking into each other like blinded dogs sniffing out fresh meat. While Father Michael was surrounded, those congregants cowering behind Marlowe rushed toward the immediate opportunity to flee. The last six scurried into the low-lit corridor Marlowe had first come from, leaving dirty footprints from bare, scabbed feet on the shattered tiles.

Gun by his side, Marlowe had no sense of what to do next. Threaten arrest? With what authority. Shoot them? With what bullets.

"Hey!" Marlowe settled for, stepping closer but lightly on his feet. "Get outta here. Leave him alone."

It made no difference. The collective appeared nervous to make a final move, although they could easily swarm Father Michael in seconds. They surrounded him like hyenas, ready to strike their target but conscious of Marlowe's gun. Father Michael stood like a martyr, holding a cross aloft and muttering psalms so quick or so foreign they could've been incantations.

Only a violent crash from where the escapees had run disturbed their fresco. Marlowe turned before the others as a barrier—perhaps an upturned table—was erected at the cavern entrance and a violent caucus of bald men clamored behind it. They had come to plug a breach, to stop an invasion and mark the makeshift church as a no man's land. Marlowe didn't know which side was trying to invade the other. It didn't seem to matter when the shooting began.

Marlowe dived behind a pyre of tables where the food and socks had been, sticking legs of broken chairs on a floor of torn up tissue Bibles. The bald men behind the barricade had let off a single shot from a repeating rifle. It struck a hooded antagonizer deep in the back. Maroon soaked from his black jumper and pooled in the crevices of the tiled floor. None had noticed like Marlowe had. They still circled, pawed and prodded at the priest, who continued muttering his own last rites. Then another bullet smacked a masked youth in the head, through his hood. A bulge of brain matter splattered against the inside of the closed hood, and the second body dropped dead. Then, all hell broke loose in the church.

The hooded youths were armed with makeshift crossbows. They fired off bolt after bolt in the direction of the blocked tunnel, as the antique rifle kept up a steady stream of shoot, reload, and repeat, punching dusty holes into the far rock wall as opposed to dropping more bodies. Hiding from the low-tech fire fight brought deja fear back to Marlowe. He'd been this scared of a punctured lung or shattered kneecap before, during his days on the Lunar vice squad. The weapon choices revealed familiar actors: Anti-religious and anti-capitalist agitators fought with crossbows. Marlowe had no doubt about it. They loved nothing more than firing off home-made metal arrows salvaged from a scrap heap into the kneecaps of anyone they found undermining Communist orthodoxy. Those Mc-Donald's workers may have suffered the same fate. A coordinated attack on a business and a church was all but a declaration of war by the Soviet-backed Lunar thugs.

On the other side, behind the barricade, an antique rifle was one of the weapons of necessity used by Black Moon. A combination of deadly, cheap, and relatively easy to liberate from a forgotten UN-SOC store.

The two sides traded shots that more often missed and lumped holes in the rock. One hooded youth dodged toward the tunnel entrance to try and retrieve a few scattered bolts, until a rifle bullet shattered his chest, and the kid collapsed in a heap, gurgling blood through their tied-up hood. The youths were down a third of their number already, and their unexpected losses drove attention back to Father Michael. One hoisted up a machete, the type used for cutting down sunflowers and held it to the priest's neck. The firing from Black Moon's rifle halted while a few crossbow bolts were gathered up and they found new hiding places behind the priest or in the corner of his alcove. Only Marlowe remained in no man's land, crouching behind a plastic table that would do nothing to shield him from a bullet or bolt. But he was not the focus of attention.

"This is not your place!" Black Moon shouted. "Unhand him and leave the dark side."

"All Luna is ours!" Yelled back the lanky youth holding the vicious knife to Father Michael's exposed neck. The priest was no longer dressed in the calm clothes of a martyr. His robes had somehow become bloodied. Sweat shimmered down his scalp and his mumbling of prayers had turned into a quivering bout of tears. A nasty beating was no longer on the cards. This standoff would not result in a double kneecap replacement, not while shining metal was held against his neck. His mumbling tears grew louder.

"You... you must all leave this place." Father Michael oddly swallowed away his fear.

"Shut up!" The would-be executioner gripped two hands around the machete. But fear had departed from Father Michael. It settled on everyone else instead. On Black Moon who rose from their barricade, one bolt-action rifle between them. On the Lunans who crowded into the priests' alcove, all but the one holding the machete, and on Marlowe, too, who clambered to his feet and pointed the six shooter straight at the hooded kid.

"Vladimir," Father Michael stared at Marlowe, giving attention he really didn't want when in the middle of an armed standoff. The machete wielder was getting agitated. Several of the Black Moon men had disappeared, presumably running back around to plug the way the kids had come in. Marlowe held the gun steady, but from this angle, hitting anyone but Father Michael would be a miracle.

"None of us belong here, Vladimir."

"Shut your mouth!"

"There is no God beyond Earth! Lead your people home!"

A rifle shot, the machete coming down, or Marlowe's own gun, there was no way to tell what sparked the chaos. But all happened at once. Shimmers of Black Moon men rushed in from the far side beyond the ruined altar throwing heavy rocks and a burning ball of rags at those hiding in the alcove. Smoke quickly filled the church, but not before Marlowe watched the headless body of Father Michael collapse onto the ground, followed by the body of his executioner, that Marlowe had slugged two bullets into. A couple of rifle bolts from Black Moon collapsed the murderer's chest, too. As Marlowe ran toward the priest's decapitated body with hopeless failure, the ground beneath his feet unmoored from its axis like the gravity had gone. It took a moment to realize it couldn't completely go on Luna, so some other force had knocked his head onto the rough ground. But by then it was too late. The darkness had come and swallowed everything.

CHAPTER 15: AN INVITATION TO A PARTY FOR THE DEATH OF THE OLD WORLD

Darkness swirled around a pain that both seemed to be located at the back of Marlowe's head but also yawned out across time and space and the dimensions of the universe. He stretched above it all, dangling over synapses and strings that beat and bounced, rushing as a river over rocks, empty pockets punctured through existence. Places beyond. Things outside.

Marlowe flicked his eyes open and shut, but the darkness remained the same. Something scurried across his leg, and he violently kicked it away.

"Hello?" A match was struck, a flicker of light a body or two away burning his eyes, or a burning ship ten thousand miles away. "I don't mean any harm." He was on his back, elbows against a rocky wall freezing to the touch. He *couldn't* mean any harm. The light from a match flickered closer, leaning down to greet him, and a thousand tiny things slithered away.

"I know you mean no harm," said a woman, her voice smooth and full of age. "That's why you are still alive." She reached out a bony hand which Marlowe took and helped him up. The light lowered and revealed her face, the same one that had been in the church congregation before the attack. Smooth like a Lunan, but long and drawn and tired like someone who forever lived in darkness and deceit.

"I tried to help him. I tried."

"I know. He died a martyr." She walked away, lighting one candle that set in motion the automatic lighting of a hundred more. Ropes of fiery light burning in a crisscross pattern across a gray, rocky cavern. She wore the same tattered blankets woven into a heavy coat that Marlowe had seen her in at the church, and snakes of her hair disappeared under a loose-fitting hood. An endless quest for warmth that was life in the shadows. There were no tall, bald guards around her, but neither did there seem to be any way out of the cave. She sat down at a metal and glass hexagonal table, a re-purposed panel of a sunflower greenhouse. She poured them both a cup of moonshine. Marlowe drank it all immediately, the bitter alcohol burning a welcome hole in his throat. She poured him another.

"Bold of the Lunan Collective to attack over the border," Marlowe said. She nodded.

"One attack out of many. They seek to keep us here while they launch their coup."

"From what I saw, S-Nine had security pretty well covered in Armstrong."

The woman rubbed her stubby, nail-bitten fingers around the metal cup, but did not drink. "S-Nine will not keep a peace for long." Now she drank, smiling gently with certainty of what she said.

"What makes you so sure?"

"S-Nine operates on profit. The transitional government will keep them paid for a time, but Armstrongers will never work for a profit. The red flag of the crescent moon and machete will hang in the city soon enough."

"You seem happy about the prospect."

"I have hope for the future." She lifted her cup around the fire-lit cave. "My half of the moon is soon to become a second West Berlin. With all the American dollars that brings."

"And your gang becomes what, a new state?"

"What's a state but a gang with legitimacy?" She now grinned, this future leader of one half of a divided moon. Her teeth nobbled stumps. But the flash was quick and then gone. Her eyes narrowed back to Marlowe. "I assume you are not a defector to our cause?"

The idea of Black Moon being a cause sent a shiver up Marlowe's spine. He tried to get off the subject of solar politics and back to the point. "I'm in the market for a gravitational expropriator. Fourth generation only."

"You think we have something like that?"

"I think you can get it."

"Why should I do such a thing?"

Marlowe leaned forward, snatching the jug of moonshine and pouring himself another cup. It was weaker than he remembered. "Think of it as your first trade agreement with another state… also one looking for legitimacy."

"I see." She chewed over Marlowe's request, no doubt putting two and two together. A single fourth-gen gravitational expropriator of the sort to be found on the Zvezda pod would be powerful enough to run a warship or stick together a small asteroid the size of Delving Prime. "I'm not sure we have much interest allying with a piss-poor clump of rock. Money and gold are not as valuable commodities as you would think."

"I'm not from The Maelstrom," Marlowe said, telling the truth but readying to lie. He took off his wedding ring, the last part of his old life still left, and held it up to the light for the woman to see the inscription on the inside.

"Marlene and Vladimir Marlowe," she read. "Is Martin Marlowe's grandson offering me his wife?"

"Marlene is deputy director of the Martian Settlement Authority." A vague note of familiarity passed over the Black Moon woman, as if she knew that information, and only now realized why it was important. "A Lunar-Martian alliance is—"

"Please, Mr. Marlowe," she refilled his cup with a tittering smile, "call me Sandra."

"So, Sandra, does a fourth-gen gravitational expropriator seem like something you'd be able to procure?"

"Quicker than you might imagine, Mr. Marlowe."

"It cannot be removed from the original engine casing. Once you've sourced it, I can travel to wherever it might be."

"Oh, I don't think it will be too far of a journey." Sandra stood. "But the independence festivities are less than a solar hour away. Why not join us for the Open Space celebrations, and let me make some enquiries."

Marlowe drained his cup, stood up and shook the hand she offered. "Sounds like a deal."

"Wonderful, may our agreement be the start of a long and fruitful relationship between the future Martian Republic and the Free State of Western Luna."

"Cheers to that."

Lunar techno music pounded to the beat of a violent laser light show. Deep underground, in a cavernous space that had the appearance—and signage—of a Soviet missile silo, the party carried on. People danced in electro light and luminous war paint… and not much else. The dividing line between Armstrong and the rest of Luna might be light and dark, but in the deep underground raves, darkness and light intermingled, and everyone was so off their face, few could tell the difference.

Marlowe sucked down a sunflower-brewed beer. Terrible, but it didn't cost anything. The vile taste ensured there were only so many of these any human could drink in one sitting. His leg restlessly tapped against the bar. The thought of some creature like Bradley Gomez sliding between sweaty bodies, feasting on torsos filled him with terror. How many would the monster get before someone noticed? Who would even have the ability to stop it, if 'Dorvethan' indeed could be stopped? Marlowe touched beneath his coat where his gun should be. He was defenseless, like the Lunans partying beneath giant screens where interplanetary ballistic missile should be, blinking eyes ticking through to a final countdown.

For a moment Marlowe thought he saw Sergei slip through the crowd, but managed to lose sight of the only other person who looked as out of place as he did. It was better to be ignored, he thought, sucking on his fourth bottle of dark brown sunflower beer. At any moment, Black Moon could tap him on the shoulder and take him to the Zvezda pod they had hidden somewhere.

Two figures came to sit on the stools next to Marlowe, and he turned slightly to ignore them, but also listen in. They wore boiler overalls and carried spanners. Not exactly going outfits.

"Soviets went too far," the closest man said to his companion.

"Nothing but provocations these days. Think they'd calm down and wait a minute. Were you there?"

"At Komarov Square? I'd be dead."

"It was that bad?"

"The fire at the McDonalds got so far out of control, S-Nine had to deoxygenize the whole sector."

"Fuck me."

"Yeah, 'cause we need more bodies bouncing around the surface and clogging up the pipes. If S-Nine make us clean up their shit one more time, I'm going to the union, I tell ya."

"Better do it soon. Transitional government's ready to ban the unions."

"Bullshit. Where'd you hear that?"

"You need to come to the meetings once in a while. They're gonna ban the Collective, then they gon' start charging for food, for beer, for sunflower seeds."

"They'll be riots."

"Why d'you think there's so many S-Niners around these days?"

The pessimism made Marlowe signal for yet another beer. It was doing something to him. He took several large swigs from the fresh bottle to dissipate the chrysanthemum tang burning in the back of this throat. But the problem was with the beer, and now the earthy taste of fermented seed juice was enough to make him retch. Who said socialism didn't work, Marlowe thought. When the product is that substandard, then of course there will be enough for everyone.

The large screens bolted around the inner tube of the silo, and also a boxy TV behind the bar, offered live-streamed visions of a solar system on the cusp of complete change. The taste it left was more bitter than the beer. UNSOC was dying before his very eyes. As if every Republic in the USSR, or every State in the USA, was about to declare independence all at once. So, what was the point of Moscow or Washington anymore, when there was nowhere left to govern?

Images flashed of dignitaries on Phobos, on Ceres, on Titan, on Europa and Io and Ganymede and Calisto and Armstrong, even Khrushchev-Kennedy, sitting down at makeshift tables, signing documents, shaking hands. UNSOC was left with junkyards worth of clunking hulls and orbital stations swerving around the sun, now having to pay fees for the privilege of docking and cleaning out their carbon tanks. Reality felt wrong. Like the timeline had been screwed up somewhere along the line. Maybe it was back in 2016 when the unthinkable had happened; Okechukwu and Alexei were murdered and the conspiracy theorists won the nomination and then the presidency and set the whole solar system on course for radical democracy. Or perhaps sometime before; another crash, another explosion, another tragedy that robbed existence of the one person who could have stopped all this. Or maybe it was back in '47, when Marlowe's own grandfather stared at the Messenger in a crashed cradle, and they all went public. Maybe it should have stayed a state secret all along. Maybe Father Michael was right, and neither God nor man belonged beyond the Earth's sky.

"Are you Marlowe?" A finger prodded him in the shoulder. A bald man stood over him, beard a flaming red, bushy and stained with coffee. Skin smooth and unweathered. Black Moon.

"That's me." He tried to stand up from the stool, but gravity was not on his side. The gangster caught him.

"What's the matter with you?"

"Nothing. Beers." Marlowe hiccupped in the man's face. He fingered the cell. "Let me call my friend."

"Be quick about it."

"Sergei!" Marlowe shouted into the phone whether it was still ringing or not. "There's a man here... seems like your type." The two in overalls who'd been sitting beside him offered an odd look, and the bearded Black Moon gang member was nonplussed about it, too. "He's taking me to find the gravity ex... ex..."

"Expropriator."

"Yes, thank you. And I... Oh, fuck. That's Charlie." The phone in his hand fell to his side, as the TV stole his attention. The Black Moon man stared with him, and so did the other two.

"What?" Asked the bearded man, when the strikingly handsome spaceship captain on the TV waved to reporters and TV cameras, a generational ship on its ladder behind, poised to launch from Cape Canaveral.

"That's Charlie! Charlie, you know, Marlene's brother." The bearded man gave him nothing, so Marlowe turned to the two men beside. They stared at him like they would any drunk spilling into their conversation. "He's going to... somewhere. Somewhere far."

"Alpha Centauri." One of the men offered.

"Yes! That's it. As far away as he can get from me, that's where Charlie's going. But they're doing a month on Phobos first. I bet he didn't tell you that, did he? Hm? 'Cause he didn't tell me. Oh no. But dollars to rubles he told Marlene. 'Course she knows. How much to bet she'll see him once more before he's gone forever, huh? How much?" Marlowe held out his hand to shake, but no one took the bet. The bearded man was growing impatient.

[182]

"What the fuck's this all about?"

"Commitment!" Marlowe shot back. "Self-respect. Am I not worth it?" Marlowe was drunk enough to know balance was not his friend, but jabbing his finger into the bearded man's chest helped him stay steady. "Not even a 'here's something to remember me by. Just… woosh. Gone." Charlie was waving through the television as the camera panned across to the thousand, the colonists and their Eden partners, starting to traipse into the gigantic ark ship known as the *Genesis*. "Okechukwu should've been there, you bastards!" Marlowe shouted at the TV. "Don't pretend you didn't know, Charlie."

"Is he with you?" The bearded man demanded to know of the other two. They shrugged away responsibility. "What you're in search of is outside, we have to go through an air lock. And I ain't taking you anywhere in this condition. Sober up and find us again some other time."

Marlowe barely registered the threat. He was squinting at the television, trying to read Charlie's lips, hand in hand with his genetically perfect Eden partner.

"Oh yeah?" Marlowe shouted, shaking glasses as he slammed his fist on the bar. "But will you eat his ass, bitch?"

"Hey hey hey…" hands grabbed Marlowe's shoulders, pulling him back and keeping him steady. He tried to turn around, but the figure squeezed his arms to his body. "He's okay," a Russian accent spoke. "Just… very tired. Very shaken. We can go to the outside. We can go with you. I'm in charge."

"Ah!" Marlowe suddenly figured it out. "It's you, Sergei. I thought a babushka was calling on her bear friend to crush a second babushka who beat her in a borscht eating contest."

"Please," Sergei said to the bearded Black Moon man. "Don't listen to him. I promise you, there won't be any trouble."

"Now the bear is arguing with the babushka and trying to up his price." A fist with a thumb sticking out jabbed into the small of his back. "Ouch! Sergei, you're about six inches too high."

"Quiet, Marlowe. We need this intel. Darla is waiting on it."

"Oh *Darla. Darla. Darla.* Anything for *Darla.* That KGB—" A hand covered his mouth and something sharp and metal prodded into his side, just under the rib cage. The Black Moon man had already reluctantly started to wade through the crowd, and turned back to see why they were not following. "The KGB," Sergei whispered, "are everywhere. They were following me and forced me to help the Collective. I got away only now. We have less than an hour to find this pod, find the evidence and get off Luna before the KGB, S-Nine, the Collective, UNSOC or anyone else on our long list of enemies finds us."

"So it's *us* now, is it?"

"Marlowe!"

The Black Moon man stared back. "Problem?"

Sergei shoved Marlowe forward, he shook his head, and they began the long, slow fight through the partying crowd.

The barren coldness of the Lunar surface sobered Marlowe up to the point of knowing he needed to take a mighty piss, but he was also no longer drunk enough to just do so in his space suit and deal with the consequences after.

"You're hopping, Marlowe," Sergei's voice crackled through the helmet on the direct line.

"Sorry. How much farther to go?"

"Ask him yourself."

"No, you ask him. He thinks I'm a fool."

"Okay."

"Okay what? Are you asking him?"

Sergei didn't respond, focused only on following in the Black Moon man's trail. The man appeared larger outside than in. Standing against the bleak blackness of infinity, he dwarfed them like a walking statue. His footsteps grooved into moon dust and kicked away loose rocks that bounced endlessly across the barren surface, like pebbles on a frozen lake. They were in the narrow strip known as the gray zone. Not quite the light side, not quite the dark. A place where they'd find craters full of junk and shrapnel, not acres of sunflowers growing in their greenhouses.

"Over this ridge," Black Moon said to them both. Marlowe however was weighing up the need to take a piss and wondering how long it would take exposure to the thin lunar atmosphere for his dick to turn black, shrivel up and fall off. Or would it inflate like a blow-up hammer at an ice hockey game, as the oxygen-less outside sucked whatever life was left through his cock. Not a bad way to go, necessarily.

"Help him down," Black Moon commanded Sergei as they approached the crater's edge. It took another moment for Marlowe to get there, but when he did, he realized he'd need all the help either would be willing to give.

The crater spread out like a football field from the vantage of the stadium roof, except it was the size of fifty football fields and stuffed exclusively with junk. There was so much rubbish that it was hard to see where the trash ended, and the crater surface began. Pipes stuck up from mini mountains of shattered greenhouse panes. Spokes of engine parts and wings from vents and air turbines. A forest of the ubiquitous Armstrong metal bunk beds. Long, dented cafeteria tables. Shimmering, shattered solar panels crumbling into the dust. And off to the side, so distant a brief scan would miss it, was the remnants of the 'U' shaped Zvezda pod from the *OS Pegasus*.

"You'll have your answers there." The Black Moon man spoke with a tone that sounded all the more ominous coming through an earpiece in their helmets. He began to jump down the crater's edge, letting the low gravity surface help him down, ledge by ledge.

"Give me your hand," Sergei demanded, seizing Marlowe's arm before he could say anything. "Ahdeen... dvah... tree!" They jumped on three. Their bodies experienced the rush of weightlessness for a brief moment. A normal feeling from the moment when a ship broke through the Earth's upper atmosphere, until the gravitational expropriators powered up, and the Messenger-tech blasted a wave of artificial gravity around them. There was some gravity residue that crept up from the city below the crater, so they did not float as high or as fast as the UNSOC men and women who'd first stepped foot on the lunar surface all those years ago in 1949. Marlowe had the strongest memory that the honor belonged to his grandfather. A line buried away in a UNSOC manual somewhere, that Martin Reginald Marlowe, despite being named Director-General, insisted on testing every new ship, every new space suit, by himself. Putting his own life at risk before he'd ever let one of his employees do the same.

"The spirit of UNSOC," Marlowe said, wrongly thinking the helmet wouldn't pick it up and broadcast what he said to his two companions.

"What he say?" Black Moon demanded, turning around mid-jump, dangerously spinning before gravity snatched him back to the ground.

"He thought he saw a UNSOC ship," Sergei said, pointing up to the twinkling darkness of satellites, docking pods and space stations. And the glowing orb of blue and green still just about visible across the crater's lip.

Since the depth they'd jumped into was at least a mile lower than the surface, the leaks from Armstrong made the gravity in the crater's bowl at least an entire Newton stronger. They could leap across the rubbish pile like gazelles, some more graceful than others. Sergei made it to the Zvezda pod first, sprinting through the airless atmosphere so rapidly Marlowe wondered if he'd trained as a gymnast, or perhaps he needed to take a piss as well. It was the clunking Black Moon man who took the longest, falling in front of them with a crush of radioed curses and grunts.

"It's locked." Marlowe said. A heavy metal bar was bolted to the only hatch door visible amongst the junk, blocking the turning wheel to open the door.

"'Course," Black Moon grunted and shoved him aside. "Valuable shit in here."

"Where did you guys get this?" Marlowe asked, but Sergei nudged him hard in the side. The man unclipped the metal bar, but swung it over his shoulder as they entered into the pod. Inside was eerie, and deathly silent. The slivers of light seeping inside illuminated control panels and bundles of wires that swung down like an untamed jungle. Until what was formerly the air lock door was slammed shut by the Black Moon man, and they fell into total darkness.

"Give me a sec," Black Moon said, tapping on a handheld device that emitted only enough light to shine onto the orb of his helmet. "I can turn the air on."

They waited in silence. Perhaps Sergei was afraid to move, but Marlowe was shifting himself like he had ants in his pants and was sitting at the front of a funeral. At least with oxygen coming in he could unzip his suit and relieve himself. Although pissing over a crime scene was rather undignified.

To get his mind off his bladder, he glanced into the foggy black of the long corridor that he knew eventually snaked around to the monitoring station. It's where Alexei must have sat, watching the tides on Neptune, when Okechukwu came to visit. As Marlowe took a few vague steps forward, the metal floor rang with an echo, the way it must have done in the emptiness of space, when the Londoner approached the man he would die with. Marlowe still could not shake the feeling that these two had been lovers. Conversely, if they had not been, perhaps Okechukwu would have survived. He would be boarding the generational ship to Alpha Centauri right about now. Perhaps glancing over at Charlie, sharing a quiet grin and a knowing nod.

Charlie had never given Marlowe an answer to his eternal question. A question he'd begun to ask when they resumed their sexual relationship, after the nearly ten-year gap between the start and effective end of Marlowe's marriage to his sister. Charlie had that night been accepted to the AC settlement program. He received the email as they drank cold vodka on Viktor's rooftop one November night as the party downstairs in his apartment carried on perfectly fine without them. Only the two of them were upstairs, watching the New York City skyline flicker, skirting around the cold detachment every UNSOC person felt to any of Earth's wondrous sights.

"What're you going to do when you're there?" Marlowe had asked, his vodka hand freezing, but needed to drink.

"What do you mean?"

"You know what I mean, Charlie."

"Can't say I've given it much thought." Charlie had grinned. The way he did when a certain notion came over him. A curling lip of desire that emanated like a radioactive shockwave. Marlowe was just the one closest to the core. It would suck up anyone. "But who knows. Maybe I better get it all out of my system now. What do you say, Marlowe?"

"What do you say, Marlowe?" It was Sergei, tapping on his helmet, not passing him a vodka. "Do you want to take it off?"

A run of electric lights flickered on above them, illuminating the long jungle path through the wires and around the eventual bend. Black Moon had taken his helmet off, and Sergei was in the process. Neither seemed to have asphyxiated yet. Marlowe joined them. The air was stale, but fine. Yet there was an odd note too. A familiar stench that had more in common with the subway entrance at Columbus Circle on a bitter winter evening than a deconsecrated UNSOC pod on a lunar crater.

"Is that… hot dogs?" Marlowe asked, certain he was about to be roundly ignored for being drunk.

"And cheeseburgers," Black Moon agreed, sniffing forward. As they headed around the bend, the stench of fast food became notably stronger. They came to a complex array of blacked-out screens, keyboards and monitoring equipment that had grown a thin film of space moss on it. Not just on the equipment, but a trash can's worth of empty soda cans scattered around the place, alongside crunched up wrappers which had once held molecularly-reconstituted snack food.

"Do you know where the gravitational thing you want is?" He asked like a bored realtor. An entrance to what could be the living quarters, and the scene of the deaths, pricked Marlowe's attention. He prodded Sergei and nodded to it.

"I think in here," Marlowe said. The Black Moon man accepted it without question. Sergei held his cell at the ready to take some pictures. Marlowe sucked in an anxious breath. Everything they'd been through these last few endless days was rushing headlong to a final conclusion. The evidence; for, against, or inconclusive, would be right through this door. Marlowe was already narrating the final section of his report in his head.

After contacting the Lunar-based criminal gang known as 'Black Moon' who were in possession of the crime scene, the Soviet liaison and I entered to survey the situation. Photographs attached in Annex A.

"Jesus," Marlowe said as Sergei rammed the door open with his shoulder. They all held their noses from the virulent fetor of chilled death. Marlowe stepped forwards, into the crime scene. Maybe it was the beers, or maybe a lack of oxygen was slowly asphyxiating them, but he had the strongest sense of what awful events had transpired here.

CHAPTER 16: A JOURNEY THROUGH NO MAN'S LAND

UNSOC Orbital Station Pegasus, Neptune Sector
January 19, 2016
Population: 8

Space is noisy. Always a hum, a buzz, a chirrup of a pressure gauge or a bleet from a monitor no one knows how to shut up. A million sounds to remind the cosmonauts death comes in the silence.

Okechukwu gasped in recycled air. The eruption of what he'd just read for the fiftieth time in the *Pegasus'* living quarters now swarming over him in itchy waves. He was getting off this scrap heap ship at the ass-end of the solar system. Finally. A lump rose in his throat as he flicked through life-ending words on his pad. He now knew the place he was going to die.

Congratulations! After rigorous screening, your application for the Alpha Centauri Settlement Program has been accepted. Launch date is scheduled in 8-12 years. Training will begin this July when you will be matched with your Eden Partner. You must refrain from all sexual contact until then and thereafter. Any infection will be grounds for immediate termination. Please upload your bank details and total liabilities, including any student, medical and personal debt for your AC Settlement debt clearance benefit...

A distant toilet flushed. Bradley re-entered the living quarters, puffing out his cheeks. The red-faced American's blue UNSOC jumpsuit was obnoxiously unzipped to his steroid-sculpted stomach. Okechukwu narrowed his eyes at the unwelcome company, then snapped his pad closed as Bradley fumbled with the television remote. The man scratched his balls with the other hand then sniffed his fingers, before flipping the remote and catching it with his scrotum-stained hand. A one-way ticket to Alpha Centauri couldn't come quick enough for Okechukwu.

The TV crackled like an old set from the 40s when Truman first revealed the Roswell landings and confirmed man is not alone in the Universe. For all the 4K HD screens the Americans insisted on decking out UNSOC vessels with, three billion miles from Earth would screw up any broadcast. *OS Pegasus* was the last manned vessel in the solar system. But the handful of cosmonauts on the orbital station weren't terraforming Mars, mining Triton or doing Tai Chi on Armstrong. No, they were Earth's early warning system against the grave extraterrestrial threat the world had been waiting for. Pegasus might be humanity's first line of defense, but it was also the last place Okechukwu wanted to be.

"Damn lousy piece of shit signal." Bradley smacked the flat screen hanging precariously above the cramped break room like it would make a difference. The television responded by turning off. "Well shit."

"There's no point trying to watch anything live," Okechukwu said, as Bradley openly winced at his calm south London accent. "Watch something from yesterday's data burst."

"Fine, but no soccer, I mean *foot-ball*." Bradley stormed to his end of the table and gulped down a protein shake. The molecularwave in the corner could reconstitute any solid food they wanted, but Bradley insisted on drinking his calories like the meathead bro he'd been born to be. He flicked the set to yesterday's news broadcast.

"Leading in the latest primary polls from New Hampshire and South Carolina, the businessman has stunned the politically correct establishment with his brazen attacks on the space-based elites, and derided wasteful spending by UNSOC. Here's what he had to say at a rally in Iowa last night:

"You know," screamed the red-faced man at a crowd of red hat-wearing fanatics. *"They want all this money for moon bases and space stuff. It's crap. Pure crap. How much have we already wasted making Mars pretty and green, and they won't let anyone build there. We could have big, beautiful towers on Mars, we could have golf courses and casinos, but the liberal elites at the UN don't let us. Who are they to say we can't do what we want? They say we gotta protect Earth from 'aliens'. Woo. Spooky aliens from outer space."* The crowd roared in laughter. *"It's all fake, my friends. It was all a hoax. Believe me. Roswell, alien invasions, spooky*

space monsters. They lied. It's a fraud. But they can't fool me. They can't fool me. I'm a very smart guy. Very smart. We can open up space to business. To profit. It's a wild west up there and you're all cowboys. Who's ever seen an alien?"

"Do you really think he can win?" Okechukwu asked, if only to cut through the head-spinning noise of conservative pundits questioning the basic reality of Messenger-tech on which the *Pegasus* operated.

"Look, he has a point. What's it been, seventy-something years and not a single sign of any alien? I mean, who even knows what happened at Roswell back then."

"But... we know," Okechukwu said, slightly trembling. "It's well documented. There was a crash landing by an extra-terrestrial being. The Messenger warned us Earth is in danger, gave us what tech it could, then died."

"Yeah, but you don't really *know* that, do you? You're relying on what someone told you. It's all second hand."

"But... It's part of UNSOC basic training. It's... it's the reason there's a city on the moon and trees on Mars. I mean, this ship. The artificial gravity keeping our feet on the floor. It's all Messenger-tech." Okechukwu's heart pounded in his ears. Bradley was supposed to be his senior. The man had flown recon missions in the asteroid belt before this. "You're... you're a fucking cosmonaut."

"Hey, I'm just asking the questions," Bradley said, raising his hands as if he bore no responsibility for his own words. Thankfully, the break room door hissed open and the station's captain, Hunter, walked in consulting charts dancing across his translucent, hand-held pad.

"Got the TV working then?" Hunter said, not paying any attention to the simmering tension. Bradley crossed his legs and turned up the volume.

"Just watching nutjobs trying to win elections by questioning the basic tenets of the modern world." Okechukwu said.

"Um, boss," Bradley said with a smug smile. "UNSOC employees are supposed to be politically neutral, right?"

"Uh huh," Hunter nodded like a dad more interested in his tech than squabbling kids.

"See?"

Fuck you. Okechukwu mouthed silently, but not before Hunter caught sight.

"Eh, excuse me." Hunter snapped his fingers. "That kinda language might fly in South London, officer, but not out here." Bradley grinned.

"Sorry for saying that your mother is a pig-fucking hillbilly, Bradley."

He slammed a fist on the table and leapt from his seat.

"You what!"

"Eh, pipe down, Bradley. Okechukwu already apologized. Now if we can return to the management of this billion-dollar vessel? One of you needs to go out to the Zvezda pod and relieve Alexei."

"I'll go," Okechukwu said, standing up without a second thought.

"Just make sure to depressurize the—"

"I know, I know. I'll gladly take the risk of suffocation over another second here." Okechukwu glanced at Bradley, nodding along to yet another deranged, senseless exchange during a primary debate. "Even if I did suffocate, I think I'd have more brain cells than that."

The opportunity to relieve Alexei was all Okechukwu cared about. But having sex with the Russian was like trying to stroke a deer under the chin in a meadow. The conditions had to be absolutely perfect. The slightest noise would spook him away.

Okechukwu floated through the gravity-free narrow tubes that delineated the *Pegasus'* sections like an insect's anatomy, following the markings written in Russian, French and English towards the very end of the "U" shaped station where the Zvezda pod jutted out like a foot not quite covered by a blanket.

Zvezda was supposed to monitor the heliopause: the solar system's invisible frontier which marked the boundary where the solar winds ended, and interstellar space began. Keeping watch was like inspecting a dyke for cracks. An important job, but one that would hopefully never be cause for excitement. Any sort of disturbance in the heliopause might suggest those vicious alien empires fighting unseen wars in the stars were finally on their way to Earth. When Okechukwu lay awake in his bunk to truly think about it, once he'd finished cycling through every memory with Alexei, part of him wished it was all a hoax. What was humanity expected to do with a vague warning from an extraterrestrial visitor who'd died a few weeks after crash-landing? Sit and wait for a war they didn't know if they could win from an enemy they didn't know anything about?

Okechukwu put wandering thoughts to rest with a focus on the practicalities of getting to Zvezda. His stomach twirled at the thought of what he and Alexei could do with an hour or so of passionate isolation. He slipped into a heavy, well-worn space suit marked in neutral blue UNSOC colors but clipped a Soviet helmet into place. The Anglo-American ones had a risk of cracking that, although rare, was said by the manufacturer to be within an acceptable range of potential cosmonaut death ratios. At least when the Soviets trained cosmonauts, they had no budget ceiling on keeping them alive.

Space wasn't natural for Okechukwu. He hadn't grown up with an obsession for the stars, like so many others. He hadn't been born on Armstrong or the Khrushchev-Kennedy Space Station, growing up watching Earth from afar. He'd simply been lucky. Entering the UNSOC employment lottery after his engineering degree and winning a coveted exit visa to leave Earth behind and become a citizen of the solar system. Luck had followed him from that moment, although the stages of it seemed drawn out by years. Solving a propulsion problem of the exact dimensions a professor had once forced their class to figure out. Discovering he was the Gagarin station commander's type and sleeping with the man until he was the most senior engineer in orbit around Jupiter. Meeting Alexei in a Khrushchev-Kennedy men's room before finding themselves stationed together on the *Pegasus*. And now, thanks to a brief tryst in a UNSOC gym with a gorgeous hunk named Charlie, he'd been named one of the lucky thousand colonists who would be the first to depart the solar system to settle a new world orbiting a new sun.

As he exited the airlock for the short hop through the void to Zvezda, Okechukwu needlessly held his breath. Neptune hung below; a glowing blue world seemingly suspended by invisible strings. But the planet was spinning, as they all were, around the sun, as the sun spun around the Milky Way's core. If Okechukwu was to remain stationary; enchanted by the methane blues shining through the infinite blackness, Neptune, the solar system, the galaxy itself, would keep on spinning and leave him behind. If Alexei wasn't on the other side of the airlock, Okechukwu might have stayed. He could have. State-of-the-art oxygen pellets in his suit recharged from solar winds. Water and basic nutrients were produced through infrared photosynthesis. Seventy years of hybrid human-alien tech made him like an explorer standing on the shore of an unsailed sea, but able to dive right in and swim until he reached whatever the other side held. A slight bit of force, less than was needed to kick off from the side of a swimming pool, would send Okechukwu drifting endlessly, farther than any human had yet been. But he would not be alone. Danger drifted somewhere in the ether. Alien civilizations and horrors they could scarcely imagine. This deep in space, this close to the frontlines, Okechukwu couldn't shake the feeling he was being watched across the void of no man's land.

"Alexei?" Okechukwu called out as soon as the airlock depressurized. Zvezda opened into a long corridor swarming with bundles of wires. The monitoring station and living quarters were tucked around the corner. Alexei was usually here to greet him, because it was a long way to walk alone through the darkness. Without another option, Okechukwu followed the vague hint of light in the distance, hearing only his echoing footsteps against the metal floor and the drip drip drip of a leaky cooling system. "Alexei, what are you doing?"

The Russian was hunched over a complex array of screens, lit only by a long fluorescent bulb hanging lopsided from the creaky pipework ceiling. A bottle of vodka—almost empty—sat next to crunched up wrappers from molecularly reconstituted snack food. The stubble on his chin didn't quite reach into his pale white cheeks, and his eyes were burnt red from so long staring at screens.

"Alexei?" He might be angry, or busy, or upset. Drunk was also a distinct possibility but drunk still led to sex. Often better than sober. "Is everything okay?" A moment passed between them. Alexei knew he was there, but the charts swirling on the screen held his attention for just a bit longer.

"Come look," the Russian said in his thick Muscovy accent as he rolled his chair back. Okechukwu nestled into Alexei's lap, as he always did, and the Russian responded with an arm around his middle and a kiss on his shoulder. "Look." Alexei tapped excitedly on the screens which, to one who wasn't an exoclimatologist, showed nothing but numbers and lines. "This has never been observed before."

"W-what?" Okechukwu asked, slightly nervous. He felt the eyes from space on him again and glanced over his shoulder at the curve of the capsule hiding the long corridor, and who knew what else.

"Volcanic booms under Neptune's ocean. Look. When it hits atmosphere. Boom, boom, boom!" All Okechukwu could see were meaningless bumps in a graph.

"Oh nice... Hey, did you find out anything more about that anomaly?"

"Hmm?" Alexei's excitement about Neptune tampered down. They'd argued over it a few shifts ago. Okechukwu wanted Alexei to report it, but Alexei was worried giving that kind of news to UN-SOC would destroy his career—both their careers—in an instant.

"I don't know if it's statistically significant."

"Alexei. You told me the heliopause is in retreat."

"Slowly."

"Does it matter at what speed? The universe is supposed to expand, not contract. If some force is pressing everything closer together so much that our own solar system is shrinking by a mile a minute—"

Alexei's mouth covered his with a wet kiss. Okechukwu tried to pull away, but the kiss kept coming, then a hand drifted up his thigh, and he gave in.

"Well... I guess a mile a minute is not very much in space. I'll just go and have a quick shower."

"Oh, yes. If the universe is going to collapse back to the singularity, it might as well happen when we're making love." Alexei kissed his neck as Okechukwu stood and stretched, trying to put aside the dark Russian humor. But something chirped on the desktop and Alexei's attention returned to Neptune's atmosphere. Okechukwu slunk into the living quarters.

Alexei's clothes littered the floor. The bottom bunk was covered in yet more wrappers and empty soda cans. The Soviet cosmonaut had an obsession with cheap chicken burgers. At least the bathroom steamed itself clean once a shift. Okechukwu dropped his overalls by the bathroom door and slipped into a welcome shower. Heat and water were in endless supply. But sometimes the hydrogen and oxygen molecules forgot about the artificial gravity and scattered droplets floated upwards toward the plastic ceiling.

Okechukwu slipped a soapy finger inside himself, preparing for Alexei's coming girth, when a mighty crash from beyond the bathroom stopped him dead. He turned off the water, body still covered in bubbles. A clanging, dragging sound ricocheted from the ceiling. Like frozen pipes screeching back to life after a long frost.

"Alexei?" Okechukwu yelled, toweling soap out of his eyes. "Did you leave the depressurizer on?" The shattering yelp of creaking metal wasn't going away, but instead rushing around the armored plates of the Zvezda pod like storm winds battering open windows on high seas. Groans louder than heavy footsteps weighed on the structure both near and far, banging like... like someone was trying to get in.

"Alexei?"

The Russian was standing in the bedroom by the door, the terrible noise suddenly over. Okechukwu wrapped the towel tighter around his waist as the Russian's eyes scoured his still-wet body. Alexei licked his lips. Okechukwu had never seen him do that before. He stood with his arms drooping like a Neanderthal, back hunched, UNSOC overalls pulled across his shoulders like a cleavage-enhancing ball gown. The light flickered, illuminating the crevices of Alexei's chest and the smattering of black hair Okechukwu thought he knew so well. But something looked like it was moving beneath his skin, or the light was playing tricks. Alexei's heart beat out of his chest like a cartoon. His face even paler than normal. And his skin had the sweaty sheen of damp plasticine. Suddenly, the hunched over demeanor flipped. Alexei stood straight up and tall as the overalls slid completely to the floor. Okechukwu gasped and jumped back at the sight. Alexei's cock, never on the small side, had engorged to twice its normal size.

"Alexei... wow." Okechukwu salivated at the sight. He loosened the knot of his towel, eager to capture this unique moment before they realized the Zvezda was structurally unstable or whatever the cause of the noise had been. "Are you all right?"

"Why yes, Okechukwu, I am perfectly fine." The cut-glass English accent spurred Okechukwu's attention back to the pale face, now grinning more widely than humans were normally capable of. More surprisingly, the Russian managed to pronounce his name perfectly for the first time ever.

"W-why do you sound like that?"

"Why? How is he supposed to sound?"

"He? You, Alexei. You're meant to sound like... you."

The Russian came quickly forward, moving as if his muscles were in charge and the body was just along for the ride. Okechukwu backed up but hit the bathroom door. The wet, squidgy tip of a cock now inhumanely large poked Okechukwu's stomach, the only thing stopping Alexei's advance. He stank not just of sweat and vodka, but the pungent metallic smell of methane-rusted iron infused with the absolute zero degrees of outer space. Alexei's hand dragged up Okechukwu's trembling body, as if the Russian didn't know how hands worked. Okechukwu's heart rioted, the certainty this was part of the Russian's weird sense of humor dissipating with each crawling globule stretching underneath Alexei's flimsy skin.

"A-a-alexei.... w-what are you—" The lights flickered, but the noise did not return. Whatever had caused it was clearly right here, breathing out frozen air.

"Shh." A bitterly cold hand closed around Okechukwu's neck. Alexei grinned. Mouth unhinging like a python. Wider than any human jaw should be able to do. A snake ready to eat. A beast ready to feast. Saliva as sticky as after-sex stuck to Alexei's lips as they parted. Not saliva. Teeth. A million needle points. As if the creature inside Alexei was bursting at the seams. Okechukwu could barely stay conscious over his shaking and those long, drawn out teeth a breath away. He hardly noticed he could no longer swallow, Alexei's hand gripped so tight around his neck there was no air coming in or out. In those last beating moments, Okechukwu knew this wasn't Alexei. The creature spoke. Dark, crystalized. Cut glass. English but vicious. "I've always wanted to taste one of you people."

A black tongue whipped out from hellish teeth. Okechukwu's screams murdered by the vice grip around his throat. The creature breathed frozen air stinking of sulfur into his ear. Lips parted in a sickening swirl of sticky death. The hand released, leaving him gasping for life. Okechukwu had no more strength to scream. It wasn't tears of fear rolling down his face, but shock. This was it.

"What… are… you?"

"Dorvethan," it whispered. "Dorvethan comes to us all." Then it licked the skin from Okechukwu's neck, leaving a searing pain and burning flesh before a million teeth plunged into his throat, and Okechukwu's luck ran out.

CHAPTER 17: A REASONABLE DELAY INTO THE ASSESSMENT OF TWO DEATH-IN-SERVICE REPORTS

Marlowe and Sergei worked quickly around the crime scene, taking pictures of every square inch of the living quarters. The blood-splattered bunk beds. The blood-splattered floor. The blood-splattered walls and blood-splattered bathroom door. Their Black Moon escort refused to come in. The bodies of Okechukwu and Alexei had at least been removed, but Marlowe checked under the bed and in the sliding door cupboards to make sure.

"They wouldn't clean this up?" Marlowe asked out loud, trying not to retch as he bent down to take pictures of the trail of blood going from the bed to the bathroom door. Or was it the other way? They'd need an expert review.

"They junked the pod, so what would be the point?"

"True, Sergei. True. Any sign of forced entry? I take it whatever killed them didn't come in through the roof?" Marlowe started to investigate the living quarter's ceiling, running the cell phone across it section by section, taking pictures of the blood splatters that had somehow made it so far up, lodged into every creak and crevice.

"No more working on the assumption this was a murder-suicide?" Sergei said. Marlowe was ready to kick Sergei in the back, but saw he was smiling.

"There's that famous Russian humor. Make sure you get copies of all these to Darla. I'll go through the official channels and put everything on Donahue's desk, but I'm less and less convinced he's—"

"Marlowe, what's this?"

Sergei had climbed up the bunk bed to take pictures of the air grates but was now staring in quiet shock at something next to it, illuminating it with the torch for his cell. Marlowe clambered up as well, his back dangerously close to Sergei's front. The heat hummed from Sergei's body, the now familiar sensation of Sergei's hot breath on the back of his neck.

"What am I looking at?"

It was through the grate. Grooves or dents inside the air duct that didn't seem like the usual rivets of metal or bolts.

"Fingernails?"

"Or claws." With some heaving effort, Marlowe tried to dislodge the grate. Sergei held the torch high with one hand, and Marlowe with the other. Even if it turned out to be nothing but the scratchings of a space rat, the strength of Sergei's supportive arm around Marlowe's middle as he unhooked the grate softened the blow of Charlie's departure... just enough to offer a glimmer of hope. He'd move on from Charlie. He'd move on from this case. Life itself would move on, as it always had. As it always would. The grate fell free and landed on the top bunk in a puff of space moss.

"Marlowe? What is it?" Sergei held up the light. Spotlights or the sun itself would be of no more help. It was as clear as it was unspeakable. Marlowe dared to run his fingers over the sharp grooves of the symbols, ripped into the steely cold metal, and just above the scene of the crime. "Marlowe?" Sergei had shuffled closer, a hand around Marlowe's shoulder now. "What language is that? What does it say?"

Marlowe swallowed a painful gulp as he stared at the now familiar markings. Written in his grandfather's diary and confirmed by UNSOC's foremost linguistic expert Marlene Marlowe.

"I don't know about the language, but I know what it says. It says *Dorvethan.*"

It took Marlowe several minutes of walking around in a circle in the cramped living quarters-cum-frozen blood bath to get his thoughts together. His immediate action had been to send the image of the word straight to Marlene for confirmation. Sergei insisted on doing it for Marlowe to let him pace. Sergei was being oddly supportive, Marlowe thought, as his boots crunched over blood frozen to the floor. Strangely kind of Sergei to volunteer to send classified material of an active ongoing UNSOC investigation. The protocol breach far lesser for Sergei than it would be for Marlowe. If he'd thought about it more, and if Sergei hadn't offered, he may have asked him to do so anyway. This case could not get hotter, or more explosive. UNSOC would be hunting for any technicality to fuck him over on as they surely would work double-speed to dismiss the overwhelming evidence. They wouldn't want to answer the question of how symbols recorded from the Messenger's ship in 1947 had ended up on the scene of a murder in the farthest reaches of humanity's reach into space in 2016. They'd haul Marlowe before a tribunal and demand to know how *he* knew of these things before they'd countenance the real question. His grandfather's diaries, Marlene's thesis, even Darla's treason would all come into play, especially when he told Sergei what they would have to do next.

"We have to go visit every site from Darla's dossiers."

"Where the other murders were?"

"Yes. Every one. Go right to where those deaths took place and scour the crime scenes for those symbols. We need overwhelming evidence."

"Evidence of what?"

"Sergei. Those symbols... You know who my grandfather was, right?" Sergei nodded, taken aback by Marlowe's agitation. "He was there when they excavated the Messenger's ship, and they found that word, Dorvethan, written on the ship's screen. Endless academic papers have been written about its meaning. They say it's a loan word to the Messenger's language, or maybe a warning, or something bad, no one knows for sure. But I mean... the evidence is just..."

"Overwhelming."

"Whatever killed Okechukwu and Alexei, whatever killed those other people in Darla's files. Whatever killed all those other Uncounted Franx was talking about, whatever killed Bradley Gomez, whatever tried to kill us, Sergei, its calling card are those symbols. It's Dorvethan."

"Marlene confirmed it," Sergei said, reading from his phone. "She wants to know where you are."

"Don't say anything. We need to get the hell out of Luna first of all. Maybe we don't need every location. One or two at least. And we need to think about how to go public."

A loud bang on the door scared them both.

"Are you two done?" Black Moon shouted through the door.

"Just a second!" Marlowe shouted back. "I… I need to use the bathroom!" Marlowe ached to keep his breath in check, it could all unravel so quickly. "Put the grate back," he said to Sergei. "Give me a second to piss, and let's get the hell out of here."

Marlowe closed the bathroom door. It's white plastic a brief welcome relief from the blood spattered, alien-carved death room. While he relieved himself into the toilet, he looked around the last place Okechukwu had been. The shower still had water particles frozen to the sides and the ceiling. There was a rug outside of the shower door, with vague imprints of two wet feet frozen in time.

Alone inside the tiny bathroom of death and plastic, he could almost smell Okechukwu. See the way he moved and the flutter in his chest as he opened the door in nothing but a towel, ready to greet his lover. How long had the parasite lived in his body before exploding outward and devouring Okechukwu's torso? It would have to be studied. The half-life of infection. Was this one creature going from host to host, or was it exponential? How was a person exposed? What were the symptoms and the incubation time?

Marlowe breathed on the small mirror, holding his breath for some secret message, but none came. Okechukwu had not expected to die that day. And it killed Marlowe he could not yet bring him nor Alexei justice. Or that justice for them meant a wholesale re-think of the organizing principles of the solar system. Of all life off Earth. Right at the time they'd just been reorganized. There were no simple answers, no one to put in handcuffs. Justice often evaded Marlowe's line of work, he knew, but it didn't make the failure of justice any easier to bear. Death came in the silence. Body to body, in the most intimate of acts. Okechukwu must have known it. Charlie knew it, with his drawer full of rapid tests. Sergei probably knew it, if pressed. Marlowe had known it once, too. The day after he found himself engaged to Marlene, he'd taken himself down to the medical department on Khruschev-Kennedy, and suffered the most humiliating round of pokes, prods, needles in the arm and swabs up the urethra. The traumatic memory of a sexual health screening probably had done more than keeping him straight for the next ten years than any sense of fidelity to Marlene. And that was probably by design.

But when he lost his children, he lost his life, too. He should have died that day. He didn't quite know how or why, but in the depths of his desires, Marlowe should have turned and followed the thief as they passed by each other through the automatic doors. He stalked him for one, two, three steps. When the sirens sounded and the police cars drove up and the spooked thief made a run for it, Marlowe had tackled him, throwing their bodies to the ground. The police dived out of their cars, pulling their guns out and pointing them at the thief, not Marlowe who kept him on the ground in position. As a policeman reached for his cuffs, another officer tried to take Marlowe's statement a little too quickly. Marlowe let down his guard. The thief spotted his opportunity. He spun around and shoved a knife straight up, right into Marlowe's abdomen. The officers fired, putting five bullets in the thief as Marlowe collapsed to the concrete, clutching his stabbed side. While Frank and Marsha sat in the back of the car, perhaps watching, the ambulance came, and the paramedics ran desperately toward the scene as lights flashed across the freeway and the cars kept on driving. With a few final gasps, Marlowe told the officers that his children were in the back of his car, and to call his wife Marlene immediately. Tell my kids I love them, he would have said. Tell Marlene I love her too. That's what he would have said, as the paramedics pumped his loosening chest in vain. With his last breath, Marlowe would turn to see a smiling officer open the back of his car and tell his kids not to worry, their mommy was on her way.

That would have been the end of Vladimir Ilyich Marlowe. Dead outside a New Jersey gas station. Survived by his wife, his two children, and his grandfather, Martin Reginald Marlowe. The old man was informed of his grandson's death but was not expected to make the journey from Wiltshire to UNSOC HQ for the funeral, given his dementia. Donahue would give a eulogy, offering a smoky laugh when they remembered the good times, then a warm hug for Marlene. Charlie would have been there, too. Holding his sister's hand, looking blankly down at the grave, remembering those years of their youth when they'd fallen in love with each other, but reality forced them to take another path. Just like so many others. Maybe one day, Charlie would build a better society on Alpha Centauri.

[203]

Maybe one day, Marlene would make better decisions for the people of Mars. Marlowe's death would have accomplished so much more than these grubby years of his life ever had, or ever would.

Wiping away tears he did not need Sergei to see him shed, he slid the bathroom door back open. Sergei held a gun. It wasn't pointed at Marlowe, but at Black Moon. The big, bulky man was on his knees, hands behind his head.

"Sergei! What did he do?"

Whatever he'd done, the evidence of it was running quickly in the pod. Heavy feet, many feet, dinged and danced their way closer. Black Moon must have finally paid attention to the raft of suspicions Marlowe and Sergei… or more likely Marlowe, had left in their wake. Having been through one gun fight with them, Marlowe didn't fancy his chances bluffing his way out of another.

"Sergei, what's going on? What did he do?"

But the bearded gangster did not give anything away either. On his knees, he stared straight forward, at the impressionist art gallery of blood frozen to the floor and up the corner of the wall. The barrage of footsteps was coming closer. It sounded like a small army.

"I warned you, Marlowe," Sergei said, voice flat, gun poised. "I tried to warn you."

"About what?" Marlowe's heart was running an unexpected marathon.

"They got to me after we landed here. Forced me to help the Collective prepare for the revolution."

"Who did?"

"The KGB. Marlowe…" Suddenly his eyes flashed a moment of apology. Quiet and sad, a genuine sorry for everything. But that sorry was not accompanied by any sense of atonement. It was a mere fact. He was sorry, but what could he do?

The gun went off just as the door was ripped open. Marlowe instinctively clambered backwards, right up against the side of the bathroom door. His head brushed against the thickest patch of frozen blood. The Black Moon man's dead body, his bald head pierced with a steaming black hole, fell flat on the ground. The only witness to Sergei's confession dead on the ground. But it wasn't his gangland comrades who stormed in, but Russians. Dozens of them. Red Army soldiers dressed in their space uniforms, helmets on, holding

Kalashnikov's adapted to fight in the vacuum of space. They rushed into the room, not pointing their weapons at Sergei, but straight at Marlowe. He raised his hands but couldn't take his eyes from Sergei. Sergei did not return his stare, but greeted a tall, vicious looking man who stepped into the small room between the soldiers. He was not in uniform but was clearly in charge.

"Comrade director," Sergei said to the man in Russian. "This man is the threat to space security."

"Valensky," the KGB man said, stepping forward and offering a hand for Marlowe to shake, safely surrounded by a dozen guns pointed at Marlowe's head. Staring still at Sergei, who refused to look his way, Marlowe side-stepped over the dead body between them and gently shook Valensky's hand through the shock.

"UNSOC Criminal Inspector Marlowe." Valensky nodded like he already knew everything there was to know about Marlowe. Despite the number of guns outnumbering him, Marlowe found his sanctimonious side. "This is an active investigation under the auspices of the United Nations Planetary Security Council. This is a crime scene." Marlowe glanced sideways and each of the barrels barely a meter from his head. "And… I'm going to have to ask you… and your men… to leave."

Valensky waited a beat before cracking a smile, then gurgled a laugh that went on long enough for Sergei to start grinning as well.

"Herr *Kriminaldirector*, you are amusing."

"I'm glad you think so, Director Valensky, but this operation is sanctioned by UNSOC and has been undertaken specifically at the request of the Soviet government. Sergei here is the liaison. I don't care how many guns you have. You do not have the authority to interfere with this investigation." Marlowe quickly gulped away the sense of ridiculousness he felt even saying those words. Of course Valensky had the authority when he brought with him a small army, and Donahue left his messages unanswered.

Valensky stepped forward, his boots crunching the frozen blood on the floor. New blood from the Black Moon man Sergei had murdered pooling between the ridges of the existing spatters, and quickly formed a red frost. Valensky's boot snapped that, too. He was close enough Marlowe could smell the deceit on his breath. Tobacco and vodka and lies. He smelled like Sergei.

"You might have missed the time, Comrade Marlowe, but it's a little after 0230." He pulled back the sleeve of his space suit to reveal an old-fashioned analogue watch, similar to what his grandfather once had. Several hands moving independently of each other showed the time in Moscow, New York, Luna, Phobos, Khruschev-Kennedy and Mars. "UNSOC's jurisdiction over Luna has come to an end and you, Herr *Kriminaldirector*, are persona non grata."

"I think it's up to the transitional government to decide that." The firing squad cocked their weapons and Valensky's face soured.

"I am the transitional government!" Flecks of frozen fury spattered across Marlowe's face. He kept looking at Sergei, for some remorse, for some logic, for something more than simple resignation. But none came. The coward spoke with silence. "It's time to drop you back home, Comrade Marlowe. I have a ship waiting outside. I can take you straight to New York, or I can drop you off for a three-month detour at a gulag in the Neptunian Trojans. The choice, as they say, is yours."

Marlowe just shrugged, there was no fight left in him, not with Sergei's knife jammed into his back.

"I assume the accommodation is first class?" Marlowe asked, hoping his self-importance would grate on someone. Valensky offered a false grin, then stepped aside to clear his way to the door.

"Let's go."

Marlowe stepped over the dead body. At least the evidence was in his pocket, with a copy already with Marlene.

"He has a phone," Sergei called out. Marlowe stopped dead as a gun was pointed at the back of his head.

"Give it to me," Valensky demanded.

"Sergei!" Marlowe didn't dare turn around. "Did you send the files to Marlene? You said..."

"Do not address my agent," Valensky said without any nicety left. "And give me your mobile telephone." Marlowe slipped it from his pocket and held it back like a baton. All this work, all the evidence, for nothing. Well, not entirely for nothing. He'd learned Sergei was a snake who should have his dick chewed off in a glory hole. Marlowe started to wonder how he could engineer such a scenario.

There was a loud crack of plastic, and the pieces of his phone fell scattered to the floor.

"Destroy the pod," Valensky ordered in Russian. A final indignity to their endeavors. At the door, and with one soldier only on him now, Marlowe turned back. The other men were helping Sergei lay explosives at different corners of the room. They had enough to not only destroy the entire pod, but blow a new crater as well. His and Sergei's eyes met, just for a moment. The anguish on the Russian's face immeasurable. He was torn up, turned out, beaten and broke, and said it all to Marlowe with a low stare that quickly melted away. It made Marlowe feel a little better, to know how badly Sergei felt, at least now. Marlowe wouldn't offer condolence, nor sympathy, but something he hoped would burrow under Sergei's skin, the memory of which would scar him forever.

"Oh well," Marlowe said, "another day at the office. No hard feelings, eh Valensky?"

"I'm happy to hear you say that." They wandered into the corridor as soldiers rushed out after then, layering explosives across the billion-dollar pod who's continued existence caused such an affront to the superpowers' plans for space. Any death and destruction should be caused by them, not an unidentified sentient creature.

"Hey, Valensky?"

"Yes, Marlowe?"

"Got any real smokes on your ship? I'd consider defecting for one."

Marlowe didn't look back, but from the corner of his eye, he knew Sergei was watching.

The KGB ship was a sizable, if clunky vessel. Walls painted vomit gray and cracked tiled floors gave off a Soviet police station aesthetic, which was of course entirely apt. Marlowe sat across from Valensky in a small, windowless debriefing room as they rumbled back towards Earth. A digital rendering of a mean-looking Lenin stared down at them both. An old television set in the corner silently showed images of the countdown to the now imminent launch of the Alpha Centauri settlement ship. The TV graphics ran down a list of key facts about the impending journey while Valensky wrote down meticulous notes from the debrief, now he was dressed in a more typical KGB uniform. A red band around his hat which sat neatly on the desk kept the peace between him and Marlowe.

"I don't know how you expect to 'drop me off,'" Marlowe said, while Valensky continued to scratch notes in a logbook. "I don't have a passport or any money."

"We already faxed New York for authorization to make you a repatriation pack." Valensky did not look up from his scribblings. Cursive Russian was impossible to read the right way up, let alone upside down. "It will be ready by the time we arrive at the Brezhnev-Carter Orbital Station."

"Funny you've got passport making facilities on board."

"The Committee for State Security operates by the book. I would hate for you to feel mistreated."

"Uh huh. Hey, what about that cigarette? I lost my vape while running away from that violent alien I was telling you about." Valensky sighed, having taken down Marlowe's account of the last few days like a doctor meeting a patient at a lunatic asylum. But he whipped open a drawer and tossed an open soft pack of Marlboro Red and a book of matches onto the desk. "No Soviet Laika's here, then?" Valensky gave only a slight look while Marlowe struck a match. The papery softness between his lips was a long-lost change from the hard plastic of the vape. He pursed the damp tip and sucked in a rush of delicious nicotine. Valensky did the same.

In a swirl of thick smoke that lingered like they were making backroom deals; Marlowe watched the silent television. The *Galactic Ship Genesis* was the first of its kind, the news anchors mouthed while the key facts flashed up on the screen. A behemoth of a craft that stood two and a half miles high, and another mile and a half around at its widest point. The ship would be deconstructed once on their new world in Alpha Centauri, to build homes and farms for the thousand colonists. Six months after their arrival, the first children gestated in the onboard labs, now four and a bit years old, would be hatched from their stasis chambers, perfect genetic creations from their perfectly matched Eden partner parents.

By the end of their first Earth year on their new home of Plymouth Rock, the colonists would send a probe back to Earth with footage and data and, crucially, the request to send either another batch of colonists, or a rescue ship. In the four years it would take the probe to arrive, a second Galactic Ship, unnamed as yet, would be readied for launch. The second launch would have space for five thousand colonists, or be sent with only a skeleton crew in order to scoop up the survivors and bring them back to Earth.

But, the muted newsreader said, if all goes to plan, within twenty years Alpha Centauri could have a population of close to three hundred thousand people, including the first humans conceived and born on another world. Marlowe sniffed at how easily they dismissed the Uncounted. The people in this solar system who had already been born and raised outside of Earth. The GS class of ship had been given the moniker *Marlowe*, after the recently departed first director-general of UNSOC. Marx was right that history repeats itself as farce. Charlie being taken away forever on a *Marlowe*-class ship. Just maybe, Marlowe might think about joining him five years from now.

"Something wrong?" Valensky asked, looking up from his notebook.

"No, just enjoying the festivities. Say, can you turn that up?" Valensky raised an eyebrow but wheeled his chair over to the television and did so, just enough for the crackling sound to be heard of the news anchor's excitement about a *"historic day for UNSOC, and for humanity."*

"Funny how quickly they've all forgotten about Open Space." Marlowe shifted in the chair, so his knee rested against the table edge. "I mean it was only what, six hours ago, and the news is going to be showing individual profiles of every single colonist for the next how long. I mean fuck, they're only going to Phobos. What about the Soviet takeover of the Lunar transitional government? News cycles, I tell you."

"Make yourself at home, won't you?"

"I've just been shepherding your agent around for the last week, some pretty difficult days, by the way, and you blew up my evidence so, I think I will, yeah. Tell me, is Darla his handler, or is he her handler?"

"Darla?"

"Yeah, Darla Foster. She said she wasn't KGB. I didn't believe her. Nor Sergei, either, given his sheer incompetence at following me around New York." On the TV, Charlie wrapped up his last ever conversation on Earth with the mission head, ready to board the monstrous ship.

"Sergei followed you around New York?"

"Yeah. On Darla's orders. She cornered me in East Berlin. Jesus, I thought you people were meant to be an intelligence agency. Don't seem to know much." Another thought occurred to Marlowe at exactly that moment. He'd just ratted Darla and Sergei out to someone who could do some serious damage to their careers. If not persons. "Darla Foster," Marlowe repeated. "She gave me a card with an @ space.su email address. Showed me a whole bunch of classified files, too. Unsolved murders from across the solar system. The ones you've been covering up over the last few years. Well, you and the CIA."

Valensky remained steadily calm, giving nothing away, not even a blink out of time. Spy-speak for surprise. Marlowe sat back, enjoying just the modicum of satisfaction that if he was going down, he wasn't going alone.

"Marlowe—"

"Please, call me Criminal Inspector."

"Indeed. Whatever lies our citizens have been espousing will be dealt with, and severely, but you have no evidence—"

"Oh, I don't need any evidence."

"Don't you?"

"Calm down, Valensky, I'm only writing a report. Sure, I'll include conjecture and hearsay, and the fact a KGB strike team interfered into an investigation of the deaths of two cosmonauts, one of whom was supposed to be on this very ship now on the TV if he hadn't been murdered by an alien. Makes the report all the more... what's the word... newsworthy. Don't you think?"

Valensky closed his notebook, firmly but slowly, then pushed back his chair so it scraped the tiled floor.

"If you will excuse me." He walked smartly to the door as Marlowe lifted both feet onto the desk. The door closed and then was locked from the outside.

He knew he shouldn't feel so self-satisfied, but he did, and it was... satisfying. He didn't blame Darla for trying. More for the lack of follow through. As a conspiracy they were running against the Soviet and American governments, it was hardly well-thought out. Get a UNSOC investigator to pull on a string they'd been trying to expose for years, if not dangling it directly over UNSOC for all that time too? Marlowe could draft a report which contained a blow-by-blow account of every *suspicious activity* he'd encountered in the last week. Even if he drew the Dorvethan symbols from memory, or had returned with the cooling system panel where those alien words had been carved, the report would still be quashed. It wasn't only the superpowers who wanted Open Space to succeed. UNSOC had very clearly made peace with its loss of the vast majority of the solar system to newly formed independent solar states. It was the rest of the galaxy they wanted now. And what good would that jurisdiction be if news of a loose alien was taken seriously?

Marlowe listened to the MEGA-appointed UNSOC director-general be interviewed in front of the *Marlowe*-class ship.

"And what's the next frontier for UNSOC?"

"Well, Jan," the director-general stood on the launch tower, inches from the rumbling ship, in a pristine white silk pantsuit. She knew it was against protocol to be anywhere near a launch site without protective equipment like Charlie was wearing, standing right beside her and grinning like a maniac. But of course, for this DG, nothing was more important than image. *"As Captain Novikov's ship reaches 99.99% of lightspeed, it will launch hundreds of probes which will zip to other potentially habitable worlds, and send back vital data to pinpoint the next targets for colonization. Our experiments with molecular asymmetrical singularity transport drives and, of course, the elusive slipstreams could mean we achieve faster than light travel within the next decade, and with that, the entire galaxy will open to us."*

"Are you prepared to encounter extraterrestrial threats? What happens if one of these probes finds a world that's already inhabited?"

"Well, that's an extremely unlikely scenario. Our exo-cartographers have been pouring over the Messenger's star map for decades and found zero signs of even stone-age equivalent societies, let alone spacefaring. In fact, many of the systems we would have expected to contain Kardashev-type civilizations based on the Messenger's data don't even exist. We simply can't detect them. Hundreds of them."

"Many today do question the veracity of the Messenger's claims. Some even wonder if the Roswell landings happened at all. Are you also calling into question those events?"

"No, not at all. But I do think it is important that we ask questions and verify for ourselves what's going on out there. There's no reason to be afraid

of space, and I can assure you that UNSOC, and our brave galactic captains like Charlie Novikov here," she gripped his arm like a demented mother-in-law while he smiled so broadly it seemed as though his cheeks might split, *"he'll be at the forefront of this new era of space exploration beyond the heliopause."*

"Director-general, thank you, we'll let you get over to mission control. We're now just minutes from launch…"

His feet on the desk, Marlowe drew another cigarette from the pack. He held the match, ready to strike, watching his lover prepare to enter the ship; the last one in. Head of the Alpha Centauri mission. Earth's de facto ambassador to a new world. There was an argument, Marlowe thought as he struck the match repeatedly, trying to get it lit, that Charlie leaving might finally allow him to move on, whatever that meant. The thought was distant, somewhere in the periphery, alongside the chance of losing his job or dying in a space accident. A consideration for sure, but one he'd never given such serious thought to. Watching Charlie prepare to board the ship brought the situation into four-dimensional focus, like being sat in front of an employment tribunal with a pile of evidence stacked up against you.

Yet an odd feeling kept Marlowe focused on the television screen, the unlit cigarette hanging from his lip. The camera had zoomed into Charlie, profiling 'Earth's hero' as he mounted a final staircase to the ship's entrance. Marlowe wasn't listening to the voice over or reading the facts of Charlie's life as they flashed on the screen, but he was watching the cheeks he once caressed. The shape of his head he once held to his chest, the thickness of his neck slipping into a well-fitting space suit as the world watched Charlie. Marlowe didn't believe the searing memory facing him on the screen. He blinked, perched on the edge of the chair, he yanked the television set closer, dragging it across the tiles until the static fuzz laid heavy on his eyelashes.

"No…" Marlowe heard himself say, the cigarette stuck to his upper lip. "No, no, no… it can't be." Those bulbous sores on his neck should be smallpox or cancer, that would be better. Through the fuzzy TV screen he could see those lumps in Charlie's neck were… moving. Moving across Charlie's body while he stood at the top of the staircase, the open entrance to the *GS Genesis* waiting to welcome their captain and leader. Charlie turned to face the camera. His face crushed in a grand smile as wide as it was unnatural. An outstretched hand waving, but in a jerking, crotchety fashion. Like Charlie had only been taught to use his limbs in the last few minutes. And then his skin. It wasn't a distortion of the picture beamed from Cape Canaveral into space. It wasn't any sort of steam or hot air making the frames move, although those explanations were perfectly conceivable. Expected, really. Only two people left alive would recognize this image for the infinite danger it contained, and one had already sold his soul.

"Looks like we're having some trouble with the picture here, but we're minutes from launch…" It was Charlie's eyes that convinced Marlowe. Narrowed slits which stared obliquely into nothingness while a limb thrust caustically into the air, even as slithering worms rumbled underneath his black skin. The smile that was… too wide for a human. The cigarette fell from Marlowe's lips.

"Let me out!" Marlowe screamed, banging and rattling the locked door. "Abort the mission! Let me out! Abort it! Tell them to abort it!" His banging rattled the tiles. It interrupted the TV picture, but the answer from the other side remained the same. Silence.

"Now we see Captain Charlie Novikov board the Genesis *as his crew prepare to leave Earth for the very last time."* Marlowe snatched the picture of Lenin from above and flung it at the door. It broke but did nothing to the door. Then he stabbed at the door with shards of the destroyed frame.

"It's an emergency! You need to abort the mission. The *Genesis*, tell them to stop."

"First, the thousand-member crew will spend a month on Phobos as final checks to the engine are made and each crew member prepares for stasis where they'll stay for the next four years. And we see now the ship's door closing, and the final countdown begins."

"Valensky!" Marlowe pounded on the metal door until his hand felt broken. Then he switched hands. "Valensky! Let me out." He flung the chair at the door. It clattered and fell but did nothing. The table was bolted down to the tiles. He spun in circles as if floating in zero gravity, searching for something, anything to motion an escape. He jumped on the table and began punching the ceiling, but the only exit for air were thin slits through a metal grate that wasn't coming out. From the table though, he launched into a shoulder-dive at the door. It would have floored a man. But it did nothing to the prison cell door.

"Ouch, fuck!" Holding his possibly broken shoulder, there was nowhere else to look but the television. "Valensky! Valensky... no..."

"*Captain Novikov there preparing for launch.*" The screen was split in two. One half, the massive, mountain-sized ship starting to rumble hydrogen vapor from the engine. The other half, a shot of Charlie in his space suit, strapped into a chair between three other crew members in the narrow cockpit. His face slim, mean, determined. The hoax was over; the whole world was seeing the truth. Caterpillars rummaging under Charlie's skin. Sweat glistening on his face. Demented hands around the controls. But the camera, it simply panned out to show more fully the three other crew members in the ship's cockpit.

"*Novikov looking rather nervous, isn't he?*"

"*Well, you would be too. Just moments away from the countdown now. Man's first mission to another solar system. Who would have thought back in the forties...*"

"*You know there was a bit of a debate back then, in the early days, about whether humanity should reach out to the solar system at all, or focus only on planetary defense.*"

"*Yes, it's a fascinating history of UNSOC. It's why the first director-general, Martin Marlowe's name is attached to this class of ship. Ultimately it was his view that won out over the misgivings of the first head of research and technology, Dr. Eugene Johnson.*"

"*A tragic figure himself, I believe?*"

"*Yes, he went missing at some point in the fifties after developing much of the Messenger-tech space exploration relies upon today... and it looks like we have a countdown.*"

Blood rushed through Marlowe's mouth. Not from his lips but the hand he'd been sucking on to numb the searing pain from banging at the door. With one finger bit bloody, he switched to another. The ship shook the cameras as it readied to blast off. Nothing could stop it now. Even if Valensky opened the door this second. He gave the door once last shake and shove. No hope.

"Oh God... please Charlie, fight this thing. Whatever you do. Fight it."

"Six… five… four… Oh. Looks like we already have lift off."

One side of the television showed the *GS Genesis* blasting off from Cape Canaveral from the point of view of the mission control tower, dozens of miles away. The other side was showing a scene of growing disquiet. The crew members beside Charlie were desperately touching buttons and instruments. Without sound, only picture, they leaned over to each other in their strapped-in positions as their bodies shook from the blast off. The ship had already cleared the falling launch rigging. It cleared half a mile, then a mile, then chaos broke loose in the second half of the screen.

One crew member unclipped and flung themselves at Charlie. With a hard smack, Charlie pushed them away and they slammed onto the cockpit roof. Another tried to grab the controls, but Charlie turned and bit their neck. In the rustled view of a shaky camera, the whole of humanity must have watched in abject horror as their hero gnawed on another human's throat. He turned back to camera, his face a bloody, grinning mess of esophagus and entrails.

"Oh God! What's happening?"

"Cut the feed! Wait… is it coming toward us?"

The whites of Charlie's maniacal eyes shone through in an infrared hell as a dying crew member clutched their torn apart neck. Then one half of the screen fell to static as Marlowe dropped to his knees, tears rushing down his own bloody face.

"No… Charlie. Please no."

But it wasn't Charlie anymore. No one would ever realize, but Charlie was already gone. The other half of the television stayed with scheduled programing; the view of the launching ship from a camera mounted atop mission control. Through clear blue sky, several miles or more in the air, the ship began to curve. Like a mountain being lifted high, then swinging back towards Earth. The curve was hard to see at first, the *GS Genesis* looked to be changing perspective. It wasn't leaning left nor right, but forward, towards the camera, an arc of hydrogen rocket fuel streaming from the engines displaying the inevitable path. The demon had won.

"Oh God… no!" Rustling of mics and papers revealed a studio that had finally cottoned on to the Armageddon coming their way. Where anchors should have been narrating a triumph of mankind, there came the soundtrack of human tragedy. Banging, screaming,

equipment being knocked over. *"Leave her! Just save yourself!"*

Someone out there in TV land had the good sense to switch cameras. They got rid of the static of the cockpit crime scene and switched from the mission control-mounted view to one from a drone or helicopter hovering high above the scene, and quite far away. Out of the flatlands of Florida, the chemtrails showed the ship's obscene journey. Straight up for the first few dozen miles, until evil had seized control. Then the ship began to barrel back down. A diesel-colored rainbow streaking through the sky. It was too monstrous to turn fully and make the head of the ship point downwards. Instead, it was like a whale coming in for a belly flop. On top of mission control. The ship's enormous shadow covered the clutch of space town buildings. A two-and-a-half mile wide asteroid falling, a sea beast collapsing on delicate coral.

Marlowe lost his breath when impact came. He almost felt it too, up in space, in the bowels of this ship. Shocked voices calling out, disbelieving the truth before their eyes. As the ship imploded, a fireball as big as a mushroom cloud soared above and outwards across central Florida. The shockwave hit the helicopter camera first, before the inevitable ring of fire came next. The last scenes the television showed were from a chaotic nosedive from the chopper, ready to crash into a world on fire.

The screen cut back to the anchors in New York. Two ashen-faced women with blow-dried hair, mascara running, unable to process the unfathomable. There was nothing to say. Marlowe and humanity just watched in quiet shock.

CHAPTER 18: A DECLARATION OF WAR BY THE SPACE-BASED, GLOBALIST ELITE

Marlowe had been stuck at the Brezhnev-Carter Orbital Station for eighteen hours. He arrived just as they locked down the Western Hemisphere and had already purchased a ticket to New York by the time they froze all travel to, from, or on Earth. They would have frozen all travel system-wide, but Open Space had recently robbed UNSOC of that power.

With his emergency UNSOC credit card, Marlowe bought a cheap pad and worked on his report in the departure lounge that became his perpetual home. Under fluorescent lights that never dimmed, starkly drawn against a blackness of space that never lightened, he wrote and wrote. Cross-checked facts still saved on his old cloud drive. Reviewed the *Pegasus* schematics. Knocked away every other theory with brutal logic until there was only one conclusion. Whatever *Dorvethan* was, it was here and causing death and chaos on a now exponential scale.

In between his drafting of an alternate history of nightmare creatures unknown in number, scale or purpose, his eyes flicked up to the quiet news playing from departure lounge TV's. The people he was stuck with, miners and traders and officials waiting for the eventual permission to return to Earth, did not care for their own marooning, only the human tragedy which could be seen with the naked eye from up in orbit every six hours. A burning red blister seared across Florida, a cone of smoke like a thousand Vesuvius' spilling into the Atlantic. Marlowe had watched the same newscast everyone else had. He'd reacted with the same shock, the same horror, but only he blamed himself. Quietly, another unspeakable tragedy was added to his shoulders. The roster of deaths. The sheer scale of the updates read out by the news anchors every fifteen minutes silenced whatever muted conversation might have bubbled up between the stranded passengers in the intervening minutes.

"The confirmed death toll has reached nearly thirteen thousand people, including the UNSOC director-general, the secretaries of space, defense, and several dozen Congresspeople and Politburo members. Another four thousand from the Cape Canaveral area are believed still missing. The thousand colonists on the Genesis *perished instantly, along with thousands more in the immediate impact zone, stretching around a radius of at least nineteen miles. Investigators are working around the clock to piece together the last days and weeks of Charlie Novikov's life. His sister, Marlene Novikov-Marlowe, has pledged total cooperation with the investigation and expressed her shock and outrage at her brother's unconscionable actions."*

On the constant verge of being exposed as an invisible actor in an endless news cycle, it was a welcome moment when Marlowe was finally able to board the Earth-bound shuttle, leaving behind the rolling news. On the way down, he re-read the report he'd drafted. Detailing at least his version of how such a tragedy had come to be.

Arrivals at RFK was deathly silent. Akin to wandering through a graveyard at dusk. It was odd to walk the same route as his last trip to the airport, either a week or a lifetime ago. He did not wait by baggage claim this time, to scour the faces of the few suited men waiting. But it was not because of some moralizing respect for the weight of tragedy. If anything, recent events had severed whatever remaining links to the world of ethical behavior he might have still clung to. Morality was dead, of that Marlowe was sure. The priest on Luna had said as much himself and then died. No, Marlowe did not return to playing with subtle glances to invitations for a toilet-block meeting for the simple fact that he was being followed.

There was no point in trying to lose the tail. Everyone *should* know he was returning to HQ. Anything else would have raised perfectly reasonable suspicions that should be worthy of arrest. In the back of the cab, unspeakable tragedy dressed up as news played out on the small screen.

"The president has placed the state of Florida under martial law, while Republican hopeful Karla Landers is demanding all UNSOC staff be interned, claiming the attacks were carried out by 'rogue elements unhappy

with Open Space.' Meanwhile, riot police on Armstrong have shut down a series of election-related rallies after the Lunar transitional government announced a suspension of all campaigning during the period of mourning in the wake of the Genesis disaster, where the confirmed death toll has risen to sixteen thousand."

As the cab drove along the East River towards the UN, a National Guard roadblock halted their progress. They waited in a short line of vehicles to pass. From the corner of his eye, Marlowe saw red flags waving along the East River Esplanade. It wasn't Soviets though, for why would it be? More people working in Cape Canaveral were native Russian speakers than English. The cleaners, the movers, the loaders, the engineering staff. It was always the complaint. The Russians got the raw end of the UNSOC deal, so they said. Now they paid the price in brawn, while the Americans paid the price in brain.

The protestors were angry. Shouting and rushing against hastily arranged barriers held together by a skeleton staff of NYPD. The red flags they waved Marlowe soon recognized: MEGA. The television in the back of the cab had switched to local news. A helicopter was broadcasting live pictures from outside UN HQ.

"Thousands of anti-UNSOC protestors have gathered where Karla Landers is expected to address the crowd later tonight. Calling the actions of Charlie Novikov 'a declaration of war by the space-based, globalist elite.'"

"Just say Jewish," Marlowe said out loud.

"Papers, please," the National Guardsman called out, tapping on the window. Two of the cars in front had already been sent away, forced to turn around on the highway. Marlowe handed over his freshly minted UNSOC passport. A suspicion in itself. He could be trying to get in and blow the place up. In truth, the building should have been locked down. "Carry on, inspector."

The cab drove through the blockade, but not before a shower of plastic bottles and a few eggs cracked onto the roof, thrown by the MEGA crowd. The driver got frightened and cursed in Hindi, but the armed Guardsmen whacked the bonnet to keep them moving. Before they got close to the off ramp, the driver unlocked the door and screamed for Marlowe to get out.

Against bright pink and purple streaks of a bitter twilight, Marlowe trudged towards the UN building, towering like a gravestone against the evening sky. He was running on less than empty. The adrenaline reserves long depleted, whatever energy he had to keep going driven by a morbid need to pass through the Styx and fully into the Underworld.

After navigating another four roadblocks and security barriers, both outside and inside the building, Marlowe was finally into the chaos of a collapsing, besieged city making its last stand. The walls had somehow been breached. Fear was pouring in, the certainty of a coming massacre seeping through with the screams and shouts beyond the tumbling walls.

Marlowe marched through the prefab annex that was the entrance to the UN, now a triage for the faltering state. The flickering strip lights above made obsolete by spotlights erected for temporary office facilities or rows of camp beds behind medical curtains. For the wounded whom there may be. People in blue UNSOC uniforms, Russian military garb and American Space Force fatigues ran riot along the corridors. They moved quickly in fours and sixes, stopping only briefly to share the latest puzzle piece of rumor in Russian and English.

Broken linoleum of the annex hall gave way to the scuffed marble of the main building. Its green sheen had always maintained a contemplative dullness that now simply elevated the incongruous rush of frightened officials. People ran with perhaps no real idea of where they should be running to. Their boots and heels clipped and slid across the polished floors, all the way to the grand entranceway and its gigantic statue of the Messenger and first contact. Their fingers outstretched to each other, against a star-map ceiling dazzled with diamonds marking out the constellations that Charlie's ship should have launched hundreds of light-speed probes to.

May God Bless the United Nations of Earth, read the immortal words of Harry Truman, melded forty feet above the ground, picked out in silver and gold. Beneath the words, those United Nations were being pulled apart. Gone were eager-faced cosmonauts or dignified ambassadors and their reveries. Now all that ran along the marble floors was fear and chaos. One constant remained, though. An HR woman with puffy hair, smoking an extra-long cigarette.

"Can I bum one?" Marlowe asked.

"Sure, honey," she said, offering up her pack with acrylic nails.

"We're all gonna need one."

Marlowe was still smoking it by the time he got to the CCI office. He stubbed it out in the ashtray in the corridor outside. He didn't want to give an inch of ammunition to Donahue. Marlowe smoking a cigarette was a sign of one of the four horsemen of the apocalypse. He needn't have worried. CCI was empty, including Donahue's office. Marlowe clutched the flash drive the report was stored on, unwilling to leave it unguarded on Commissar Donahue's messy desk. He'd deliver it by hand. Reading it, believing it, was hardly of Marlowe's concern now. He just needed to hand it over. Among the manilla files on the desk were Charlie's personnel files. A lot of them. Psychometric evaluations and stacks of material marked *AC Settlement Program*. Marlowe opened a folder, sliding a thin piece of facsimile paper around, eyes adjusting to the miniscule typeface.

"Marlowe?" A raspy female voice said. Marlowe spun around.

"June, how are you?" Donahue's longtime secretary swerved in with a stack of folders, her glasses on a chain dangling against a smoothed-down bosom.

"He's been waiting for you, hun."

"I was stuck in space."

"Well, he's still waiting for you." She stood where Donahue usually would, piling up folders and placing new ones on top. Adding single sheets of memos and faxes in the order they should be read. "He's over at the crime scene," June said, staring at the folders. "He wants you to meet him there."

"The crime scene? Like… Florida?" God knows how he was expected to get down there. June looked up and narrowed her eyes.

"Charlie Novikov's apartment." She said it like it was blindingly obvious or should have been.

"Right. 'Course."

"Well?" She screeched after a moment. "What are you waiting for? Move your fanny!" She slapped his arm with a folder.

"I'm going, I'm going." It might have been the total exhaustion creeping up Marlowe's neck, but their normal banter felt stilted. Faked for appearances.

Instead of going straight down to find a way to get to Charlie's, now known as Prime Suspect Location A, Marlowe wandered down the hall to find Viktor at the Department for Unidentified Substances.

"Viktor?" Marlowe called out, knocking on the door, then opening it without waiting. The lab was as much a state as it always was, if not more. Takeaway containers stuck to the bench and overflowing from the waist bin designed to hold no more than a few paper cups. "Viktor, you here?" A window was open, drifting in cold evening air and the shouts from the MEGA crowd attempting to surround the UN building. Viktor's office overlooked the East River, and Brooklyn was painted in brilliant streaks of mauve. Upwards, the lilac sky sapphired into royal blue. The lights always moving. Ships, stations, satellites, stars. The human-made indistinguishable from the distant stars that tonight, were just a little bit farther.

Viktor wasn't in his storage cupboard either. It was after five, so he was likely gone for the day. Marlowe powered up his old friend's desktop computer and bashed in the password that had never been changed while the machine whirled into life. He scribbled a quick message on a post-it, stuck it to the monitor, then dragged and dropped the file from his flash drive onto Viktor's desktop. Thankfully, he left a note, because the virtual desktop was messier than the countertop. Just to be sure, he dragged the file to the very top of the screen, then drew an arrow on the real-life post-it and stuck it on the screen directly under where the file would be on start-up. The post-it read: *What happened on* Pegasus.

"Commissary of Criminal Investigations," Marlowe said, flashing his passport at the police guarding the entrance to Charlie's building. They waved him through. The long trench coat he'd been wearing since the *Karl Liebknecht* at least let him fit in with the crowd of federal and UNSOC investigators swarming around the building. On Charlie's floor, the apartment door was wide open, with officers and investigators using the hallway as their own personal meeting space and break room. None looked twice at Marlowe as he recreated the familiar steps to his lover's apartment.

Their once secret abode was now a ripped open wound. Plastic-gloved crime scene investigators carried wrapped-up boxes down the staircase from Charlie's bedroom on the upper level of the duplex. Specialists ran scanners over walls and the chest of drawers where Charlie had kept safe what was left of Marlowe's children's lives.

"In or out, sir?" A woman called out to him. She was stacking plastic boxes of Charlie's clothes under the skeleton staircase. She stood up and fixed her short blonde ponytail without taking off her plastic gloves.

"In." Marlowe closed the apartment door behind him. It gave a sliver of silence into the apartment. The chatter from the hallway dented. Inside were professionals carrying on their investigations in silence. "CCI," Marlowe said to her, peering at the several stacks of packed up clothes. "Why are all his personal effects still here if he'd left for the Cape? None of this was in storage already?"

"I thought everyone knew," she said, as she was handed another box from an investigator further up the spiral stairs. "He sent a memo pulling out of the AC program a few days ago."

Marlowe forced himself to offer no reaction. He swallowed the information like any other fact of a case.

"On what day, exactly? What were the circumstances of the departure?"

"You'd have to ask the lead investigator, sir."

"I'm the lead investigator." She gave him a double-take at that, but eventually nodded. Tempers often ran high after tragedies, particularly in multi-agency jostling. Her uniform was FBI, but this was undoubtedly a UNSOC case. "I was stuck on Luna. So, I need to get caught up on everything, right now please."

"Come upstairs with me." She led the way up, but Marlowe could have found his way to Charlie's bed with his eyes closed.

Charlie's room was little different than he remembered it, the ruffled bed sheets were still a deep burgundy, but now four investigators were dabbing for prints across every possible surface.

"Detective Lovitz?" She said to a young man with a thin mustache and a plain brown suit, taking pictures with a pad. Lovitz turned to them, an FBI badge hanging from his coat pocket. "This is…"

"Criminal Inspector Marlowe," he offered a hand to Lovitz, who shook it gladly. "CCI."

"Good to have you with us." The woman who'd brought him up took another plastic box from the bed, the contents rattling around inside. Out of the corner of his eye he saw through the clear plastic:

DVD cases. Dozens of them. He shuddered inside at the thought of Bureau psychologists getting their hands on Charlie's porn stash. "It's a real shit show up here." Lovitz said it as soon as the woman had walked down the stairs, as if he'd been waiting for her to leave. Marlowe glanced around the familiar bedroom. The door to the en suite was closed, but plastic wrap poked out from the door frame.

"Jesus," Marlowe said when he saw what was laid out on the bedside table. "What's all this?" As if he didn't recognize the swabs and sexual health testing equipment.

"We believe the suspect had engaged in sodomy with the victim. Likely consensual, but we can't yet confirm until the autopsy." Marlowe stared at the test and the open drawer. It had contained several dozen sealed testing packets when Marlowe had last been here less than a week before. Now only one unopened test was left.

"Wait, what did you say? Victim?"

"Y-yes sir. You… haven't been briefed?"

"Let's assume no."

Two of the investigators working in the closet glanced up, dropping swabs into sealed packages and sharing a look with Lovitz. Marlowe didn't quite understand what it meant, but Lovitz suddenly grew nervous.

"Brace yourself, sir." Lovitz headed to the closed bathroom door. Marlowe was getting annoyed. Fifteen thousand people were dead in Florida due to an alien attack, and they wanted to poke through the contents of Charlie's bedroom.

"Listen, son," Marlowe said while Lovitz started to peel back the plastic sheet. "I've been an investigator for nearly… well… shit."

Lovitz was pale looking at the scene in the bathroom. Marlowe almost wanted to do a dance and also vomit. The torso-less body was cramped up against the glass walls of the shower, gazing out into Central Park as the final licks of sun set. Naked, blood-soaked legs splayed out and the rotting stump of hip bone and the end of the spine smeared the window. Like on the Zvezda pod, blood was splattered everywhere. Like a paintbrush had been flicked high and low across the bathroom, dousing the whole place.

"It's been photographed?" Marlowe asked, somewhat surprising Lovitz.

"Of course, sir."

"Good. Photograph it again, and make sure physical copies are printed and widely distributed to the field offices, and to UNSOC. Don't leave them digital."

"Well… all right. But aren't you—"

"Surprised? Is that what you were going to ask me, Lovitz?" Marlowe wanted to wander around the bathroom, but unlike on Luna, the blood was not frozen in place. But he kept the plastic sheet held open, taking in the proof of his thesis that Charlie had become whatever Dorvethan-type creature had been plaguing the system since 2016, or before.

"It's one of the worst things I've ever seen," the young Fed said, feeling comfortable to swallow away an obvious retch. Marlowe nodded, finally letting the plastic cover shielding the bathroom from view fall back into place to Lovtiz's relief. He quickly shut the door as everyone in the bedroom began to suffer from the renewed stench.

"This is nothing, son. I've seen it all before."

Marlowe found Donahue in Charlie's chrome and marble open plan kitchen, drinking coffee from a paper cup, and chewing out a terrified investigator as the New York night twinkled in the floor-to-ceiling windows beyond.

"If you'd sent the fucken' samples when I'd fucken' told ya, they'd have been back by now!"

"Sir, we—"

"I don't wanna hear it. Now fuck off." The investigator gratefully scampered by Marlowe, lowering his eyes as he passed, not daring to wish him any luck. "Jesus," Donahue said to himself, still not noticing Marlowe. He pawed at the windows, an unlit cigarette hanging from his mouth. "Can't this open?"

"You might get sucked out."

"Marlowe! You sonofabitch. Get over here." Swallowing away his fury at being abandoned on Luna without back up, Marlowe stalked over, and Donahue yanked him into a bear hug. "Look who finally got here, huh?"

"Yeah, no thanks to you."

"What the hell are you on about?"

"I called you for back up. I called the switchboard and you ignored me."

"Ah," a flicker of recognition crossed Donahue's eyes, but he then quickly smiled, like figuring out an excuse was the next thing on his to-do list. "Never mind about that now, this fucken' case. Jesus Christ, I'm glad to have my best guy back and on it." Marlowe remained staid. "Listen, let's talk about it all tomorrow, all right? You look like shit. Hey, I got you a room downtown. New phone and computer and a suitcase of clothes waiting for you there, all right?" Donahue slipped a hotel keycard into Marlowe's top pocket.

"Why?"

Donahue threw up his hands in faux despair. "'Cause you're standing here in your brother-in-law's apartment who committed the worst goddamn atrocity in living memory. You're gonna be at his funeral tomorrow, and if you think what's going on at The Office is a circus, you ain't seen nothing yet."

"You abandoned me up there. Sergei betrayed me to the KGB."

"Who?"

"And I found the Zvezda pod but the KGB blew it up!"

"Keep your voice down, all right? None of these assholes have clearance to hear about that shit. And in case you can't fucken' see, we got bigger problems than that."

"Here." Marlowe thrust the flash drive into Donahue's fist.

"What the fuck is this?"

"The answer to everything. To this crime. To the *Pegasus*, and to the countless murders just like the one that happened upstairs that've been covered up for God knows how long. And spoiler alert, it's not fucking Charlie."

Marlowe turned around from Donahue's shocked face looking like a punched duck and marched away from the kitchen he knew so well. His breath ran heavy in his chest, a pain of so many edges it was impossible to count. Past the investigators, the Feds cataloging everything in the apartment, he stormed down the corridor. Police drinking coffee shifted out the way as Marlowe's coat flapped like a bat shrieking into the night.

Marlowe stumbled out of the hotel's shower, kicking away the small plastic bottles of vodka and whiskey he'd drank while inside. Steam whipped around the ultra-modern interior of the hotel room, which had no bathroom door. It steamed the windows, hiding downtown New York from fifty floors up. Wrapping the towel around his aching muscles, he cracked open a beer from the now raided minibar—it was UNSOC's dollar after all—or better yet, Donahue's. His new phone had just about finished being backed up with all his data. He'd been nearly five days out of contact since the incident on Delving Prime, but he didn't expect anyone to be looking for him. He made a bet with himself if Marlene had got in touch. If she had, then he truly didn't know his *still* wife, and would stop drinking and go to bed. If not, if she hadn't sent Marlowe a message with so much as the address of the funeral or shiva house, then he would phone down to reception for several more drinks, download all those apps Charlie had always laughed about, and suck cocks until dawn.

Marlowe threw the damp towel back into the bathroom and sucked the beer bottle dry. Tugging on his balls, he felt a prickle of lawlessness fog over him. The phone turned blue and pinged; the backup was complete.

"All right Marlene. Are you gonna make me track down the MEGA nutcases to find the funeral tomorrow?" Top of the array of five days' worth of messages, alerts and emails was Marlene sending an address for tomorrow, and a warning of heavy security. "Am I counting a group message?" Marlowe asked himself as he scrolled through so much crap he didn't know why he'd bothered restoring all his data in the first place. But then he got close to the end, or more accurately the start. In the hours after Delving Prime it must have been, in the coldness and darkness of the asteroid, tied up to a chair as pre-Dorvethan Bradley stood over him and an unconscious Sergei. Messages from Charlie. A lot of them. And calls. And emails. And voice notes. Marlowe sat his bare ass onto the clear plastic chair, his entire world, his entire life, shrinking down to the six-inch screen.

Marlowe, I can't do this. I can't go to AC.

Marlowe. Can we talk about it?

Marlowe. Answer me please.

I can't go because of you, ok? I fucking love you. I know that makes me a dick for doing this to Marlene, but you're divorcing her. So what the fuck? Why shouldn't we be happy?

I'm not going to AC. I told them. And I'm staying in this apartment, too. I guess you're busy or running around the galaxy like you always are. But I'm here for you, ok? I'll be right here where you left me.

I love you.

CHAPTER 19: A SHIVA HOUSE IN LONG BEACH, NEW YORK, FOR A MONSTER

The next day was a busy news day. One hundred and fifty survivors were pulled from the rubble of Cape Canaveral overnight. Another three hundred were found alive in a collapsed warehouse by the time prayers had finished at the cemetery in Brooklyn. Rituals performed by a mumbling rabbi over an empty coffin. They could thank the stories of hope coming out of Florida for the lack of a full news camera scrum. A couple of bored photographers taking lazy shots from across the street was all the funeral party was subjected to.

The official death toll passed twenty thousand when Marlowe accompanied Marlene into the back of the mourner's car, on their way to the shiva house hosted by Marlene's aunt out in Long Beach. Marlene scrolled through her phone as the car, and the following entourage, rumbled over Atlantic Beach Bridge. A gray Long Island sky threatened rain.

"What the fuck is going on in The Maelstrom?" she asked. "Three mining colonies clubbed together and invaded a fourth asteroid? One half of Ceres declaring independence from the other half? A communist insurrection taking over Trenchfall?"

"You didn't expect things would be chaotic after Open Space?"

"Well, not so quickly."

"I guess it's easier to govern a world where no one lives, isn't it?"

"Don't give me shit about Mars, Vladimir. Anderson is doing fuck all to help. With Cape Canaveral out of action I've had to blow holes in my budget to secure launch space for the horse boxes. Even with a genetically accelerated breeding program, we're still going to be eighteen months behind having enough horses and cattle to sustain the population growth model." Marlene lowered the car window, letting in dashes of spray from the Atlantic Sea. She lit a cigarette. Marlowe had never seen his wife do such a thing. "It's a fucking nightmare."

"Are you..." Marlowe began, about to offer a piece of unhelpful snark. But Marlene knew the tone and with a low growl warned him against it. "Aren't you going to offer me one?" She threw the pack across the middle seat and he lit up, hiding his quiet satisfaction at being able to smoke. "This is new."

"You try playing fucking God."

They smoked for a few minutes in silence as the car joined suburban traffic and rain began to fall from the sky. Marlowe forgot how much he appreciated a cloudy day. It was almost enough to make one forget there was anything up there, or that any of it mattered.

"Why exactly do you need horses on Mars?" The nicotine rush left him emboldened. "Opening a race track up there?"

"We're not going to have pollution?" She threw the butt from the window.

"And those companies drilling for oil, they'll be using pickaxes?"

"For all I care. I'm not allowing so much as an extra particle of crap. No engines. No diesel. Nothing invented after the Industrial Revolution. The atmosphere is fragile enough as it is."

"Jesus Marlene, you're running a planet, not overseeing the renovation of the house on Myrtle Avenue." Marlowe knew he'd hit upon a seam of unfiltered pain. She sucked in a deep breath while Marlowe suckled on the last dregs of the cigarette, and prepared.

"A 'friendly chat' with the contractor will solve all the problems, will it now? The old 'man to man' is it? You need balls to do that, Vladimir. And that's why I stepped in to fix the mess you left in the old house."

"Plenty of balls on Mars for you to order around."

"Oh, don't throw that back in my face. You were never mad the contractor fucked me. You were just mad he didn't fuck you."

"I had no problem with the fucking when it was singular, darling. It was the fucking over of us, in the plural, and costing ten grand more which I had the problem with."

"I think you fucked me over plenty of times after that, don't you?" Marlowe shrugged, trying to let the anger seep out like poison trapped under a fingernail. They could scream at each other until they were blue in the face or people on the street were banging on the windows, but it would get them nowhere. Marlene, however, was not one for backing down. "In fact, I don't think you're done with fucking me over, are you?" Marlowe did not react. "Don't act all surprised."

"I'm not. Just trying not to incriminate myself."

"A strange woman from Armstrong got in touch with me, does that ring a bell?" Marlowe shrugged, much to Marlene's annoyance. "Well, not really Armstrong, the dark side of Luna."

"Got in touch with you?"

"With my office, yes. Repeatedly."

"Oh." Marlowe continued to stare out the window, but Marlene's interest remained.

"Oh indeed. It seems the Black Moon gang are under the impression the Martian Settlement Authority undertook an act of espionage. Akin to a declaration of war, she called it. Pretending to want to buy a fourth gen grav expropriator, then blowing it up once the location was shown to *our* agent."

"It was the KGB who blew it up."

"So you *do* know what I'm talking about. Ah ha." Marlene dripped in sarcasm. "I was under the impression this system-wide gang leader had spent too long on the dark side and had gone completely bonkers. Perhaps she'd heard your name in passing then read an article about Mars and put two and two together and was trying her luck. But you actually made her promises? Ones I was supposed to keep?"

"You don't need to do anything."

"No, just make enemies with the Black Moon gang. Jesus, Vladimir. You're determined to fuck me over till the day I die… or we get divorced. I assume you filed the papers?"

"Well, about that—"

"Don't even bother." She sighed. "Since I'm still technically between jobs, there will be another few months of spousal support to discuss."

"Another few months?"

"Yes, by the time my lawyers have written to your lawyers… then with the holidays coming up."

"Marlene, your lawyer is your cousin. Mine charges three hundred dollars an hour."

"Oh, that reminds me. I better call Sandy about the bagels." Before Marlowe could say another word, Marlene was talking into her cell. "Sandy, hi. We're about twenty minutes away. Listen, did everything arrive? Oh great… no, don't worry. If there's leftover salmon we can keep it for the morning… I'm in the car with him now, actually—" she covered the speaker with her hand and said to Marlowe— "Sandy says hi." He shrugged her away. "No, well I don't think his lawyers have sent the final approval, that's why. Oh, you instructed UNSOC to have a look? Oh good. No no. What's another six weeks or so. Better be sure nothing was filed twice." Marlene offered a wide grin. Marlowe lit another cigarette.

The last time Marlowe had been at this windswept old haunt overlooking the angry Atlantic had also been on a cold winter's day. Then, as now, a brave few souls walked dogs along hail-frosted sand dunes. Then, as now, Marlowe watched from the bay windows of the front room, wishing for the sea to break the palisades and swallow him whole. Marlene had sat shiva for their children here, too. The ghosts of the Long Beach front room rattled their chains with every tinkling of a glass or ding of the front door opening. Back then, their own home had just entered the thrall of a projected six-week renovation, of which they would never enjoy the eighteen-month fruits of. Bickering about the mess on Myrtle Avenue was a proxy for unpicking the long, untied ends of their marriage. The thing that fizzled like a thread burnt with a lighter. The cut is not smooth nor perfect, and all that's left is the smell of smoky fabric and burnt fingers. But fighting about Myrtle Avenue was a ritual Marlowe did understand, unlike the ones going on behind him.

Marlene sat on a low wooden chair in the center of the living room; the only one to do so. Orthodox Jewish women in wigs and black skirts, from her Aunt Vivienne's side of the family, flittered from the kitchen to Marlene, offering a full plate of food once every eight to ten minutes. Each time she would politely refuse, and they would take the food through frosted glass doors to the dining room, where it would be placed on the buffet table for the Orthodox men, with beards and black hats, to pick through as they milled around.

They were waiting for another set of prayers to start, but it wasn't clear from the overheard conversations exactly when that would be, or how anyone would know. People arrived through the unlocked front door at their own convenience. Mainly neighbors whom Marlowe had never seen in his life before, let alone Marlene. But she greeted them all with courtesy, sometimes clasping their hand as they leaned down to talk to her in the quiet voice of tragedy. When they parted, they'd always share the same sentiment: *I wish you long life.*

"There's seven days of this?" Marlowe asked, pouring them both a whiskey. She sipped it gladly.

"Not for me. I'm flying to Phobos the day after tomorrow. Pass me my phone." Marlowe rummaged in her handbag by the fireplace and found it. But his hands trembled as the screen lit up with a barrage of incoming messages. What was he meant to do about Charlie's last words? Or Donahue's silence? Donahue had studiously avoided him at the funeral, keeping his eyes forward or low. Saying nothing as the Hebrew prayers hid the enormity of a tragedy no one understood. No one but Marlowe. He'd wrestled with telling Marlene, but couldn't answer the question of 'now what?' What did he want her to do about it? Join the crusade to 'clear Charlie's name?' The entire system had watched as he bit through the throat of a cosmonaut, then crashed the ship into the world's largest spaceport. His sister and brother-in-law were supposed to do what, exactly? Go around the morning shows with a theory of a concerted Soviet-American conspiracy to hide the truth of a murderous alien creature on the loose? That could infect anybody and any time and would leave ripped-out torsos in its wake?

"Vladimir, my phone?"

"Oh, sorry."

An Orthodox woman was plodding over with several types of fish and pickles scooped onto a glass plate.

"Fucking Christ Almighty!" Marlene shouted. The woman detoured straight to the dining room. "There's been an attack on Phobos."

"What happened?" Marlowe started searching through the details himself.

"An attack on our loading base."

"No casualties reported," Marlowe read from the news report he pulled up, breathing the slightest sigh of relief.

"As yet."

"Who was it?" Marlowe asked. She was reading emails and live updates. He was stuck with the news. "Communists?"

"They… butchered a thousand horses. Fucking hell. Stole the carcasses. Left the heads." She was up from the chair, collecting her bag and looking around for who she needed to say bye to before making an immediate exit. Before Marlowe could say a word about it, she offered the lowest glare he'd perhaps ever seen on her. "Tell your Black Moon friend if she wanted a cold war with Mars, she's fucking got it. The cunt."

Marlowe gulped down whiskey as Marlene rushed into the dining room to begin the fight to try and leave behind her shiva-sitting duties. The women flocked into the dining room from all parts of the house, displacing the half dozen Orthodox men who migrated from there to the living room, wandering dangerously close to Marlowe. They offered only cold glances and whispers in another language that Marlowe knew perfectly well were directed at him. He didn't even bother with a polite nod. He just walked away.

The kitchen repeated the washed out-wood aesthetic of the rest of the house. As if the Atlantic had flooded the place so many times they'd simply accepted their fate as an extension of the frozen, snow-frosted beach. Like at a family barbecue they'd never had, every counter under every cabinet was covered in large plastic catering trays of pre-made sandwiches and crates of off-brand sodas. Donahue was here hiding out, leaning against a fake-wood countertop. Contently shoveling herring into his mouth and biting into a salt bagel like it was a donut.

"You've kept yourself quiet," Marlowe said, tearing apart a dry bagel but doing nothing but crumbling the dough between his fingers. He wasn't hungry, but his hands needed to do something. Donahue kept eating. "I thought… you'd have something to say about the report. You know, since it has implications for the *Genesis* investigation. And, for like, all of the world and the entire solar system

and, you know, the future of humanity and stuff." The awkwardness of his words echoed back, and he swallowed dryly, as if sitting
on an airplane when the engines had just cut out. The oddness of
the silence struck him. The only sound was Donahue chewing, lips
smacking as only a man left temporarily alone in a catered kitchen
can. There was a limited stretch of time Donahue could eat without
anyone around him counting plates, and Marlowe was cutting into
that time.

"Pass me a soda," was all he said, swallowing away indigestion.
Marlowe reached over and stretched a can toward him. Donahue
cracked it open with one hand and drank deeply, silencing a burp,
and returning to forking fish around his plate. "How long were you
fucking Charlie?"

The accusation was leveled without salience. With no inflection
of judgment. Just a question to establish fact. No, not fact. That was
already a given in Donahue's mind. This was simply a question of
timeline. A question which left Marlowe quietly unable to breathe.

"Ah, there you are." Marlene hooked her bag over her shoulder.
She nodded to Donahue. Marlowe's heart whirred like a propeller
about to rip out its screws. "Want a lift to The Office, Jack? I need
to go back now. The car will be here in a minute." Marlowe quietly
hyperventilated, his nails digging into the false wood workbench.
"I've got to figure out a way to get to fucking Phobos." Marlene
flicked through her phone with annoyed grunts. "Don't know of
any flights going straight there, do you? Going via Khruschev-Kennedy will take forever."

"Did you know?" Was all Donahue asked Marlene. Marlowe's
legs lost their muscle mass. He hung on, staying upright, only because his fingertips burrowed into the underside of the MDF counter. She returned a slightly shaken head; a jerk from the neck up
which failed to disturb a single tightly wound braid on her head.

"Did I know what?" Donahue could have been asking if she
knew the herring was off. Or the soda was flat. Or the salt bagels
had run out. Or her husband had been fucking her brother.

"Donahue... please, I—" The paper plate was flung at his head.
He dodged, but it splattered against the kitchen cabinet anyway.
Flecks of white fish covered the floor and the counter. Marlene
clutched her neck, protecting the one part of her body vulnerable to

flying white fish.

"Your DNA's all over that apartment." Marlowe retreated into himself, his spine convexing between the countertop and the upper cabinet. Wishing to be sucked away through the garbage disposal. "The sheets. The bathroom. The kind of stuff that doesn't belong at a murder scene unless someone was very, very familiar with the place." He didn't look at Marlene, nor Donahue, but could see them both, at opposite ends of the kitchen, blocking the way out to the living room and the back door too. "You're the last one he spoke to before he went to Cape Canaveral. In fact, apart from that poor bastard in his bathroom missing the upper half of his body, and yes, the bottom half was sodomized, you're the last person alive to have visited a crime scene where a mass murderer lived."

He didn't see Marlene nor Donahue anymore. Mentally, he was covering his ears and rocking backwards and forwards on the floor. He was chewing flesh from his arm in the hope to eat himself alive. All of that came out in an excruciating blink, and a stinging tear.

"What exactly is the hypothesis here, Jack?" Trust Marlene to attempt to rationalize the situation.

Donahue snickered. He drained the rest of his soda can. "You're not a fucking moron, Marlene. Your brother and your husband weren't exactly sharing some local skirt they'd picked up at a bar, were they? No, your husband was fucking your brother. Funny how these things hide in plain sight. I dug up a citation they got back at the Academy. For being drunk and out of uniform. Ha! I bet they fucken' were."

Marlowe couldn't see anything. Not Marlene and not Donahue. Blurry shapes moving like planets around a distant sun. But human beings cannot close their ears.

"You're wrong about one thing, Jack," Marlene said firmly. Not showing any more reaction than a hoisted bag over her shoulder.

"Yeah, you're right. A co-conspirator to mass murder was fucking the prime suspect."

"Oh no," she said, "I know my brother. Maybe he's a mass murderer, who knows what really happened up there. But he'd never subject himself to getting fucked by *that*."

On that point, Marlowe found himself nodding. Charlie never had let himself get fucked by Marlowe. Perhaps he was a dogmatic top, or Marlowe really was as low and pathetic as the two people closest to him in life firmly believed.

"Marlene…" The word stretched out his lips. He didn't bother with Donahue, only the woman he wished knew he'd once loved. "Charlie did nothing. Nothing. You saw the footage. It wasn't him. That word, *Dorvethan*, that's a creature from—"

"You shut your mouth!" Donahue roared.

"From another world, Marlene. It's an alien. It's here. Maybe it's always been. But it's here and it's killing people. I saw it. You have to believe me, Marlene." A soda can narrowly missed his head.

"That's classified!"

"You have to believe me. Charlie didn't do this. He was… he was already gone. Dorvethan took him over."

Marlene shook her head. She kept shaking it. Swinging from side to side like following the last ditch attempts to win an endless Grand Slam. She wouldn't cry, not until she was alone in the back of a car, the partition sealed.

"The one thing I hate about space," she said, head shifting from uncontrollable shaking to uncontrollable nodding. "Is that I know hell's not real. Because I wish… I wish to the God no one can see… that you had a place there to burn."

She turned and left. Marlowe took three steps to run after her. but Donahue's voice lassoed him back.

"Don't fucken' move."

"She needs to know the truth!"

"There's no fucking truth!" Donahue marched forward. Now they were alone, he slammed Marlowe against the cabinets and held tightly to his collar. The angry, pig-nosed face groaned with red and fury. "No one gives a fuck about your fairytales. You've got nothing but an alien fantasy to cover your ass. Whatever you got up to in Delving Prime, no one's buying it. Least of all the people whose job it is to clean up your mess." Marlowe pushed him off, harder than he'd wanted. Donahue took it in shock, like a punch.

"You've done nothing!" The roar was enough to shake the house. "How long have you known, huh? How long have you known about all this shit and you've sat on your fat Irish ass—"

"That's classified!" Donahue's scream brought herring from his lips and faces to the door.

"Ten billion people watched it on the fucking TV! You know it's here, and you know it's coming for us. Admit it, Donahue. Admit—"

"Shut the fuck up!"

"Admit it!"

"Shut the fuck up!"

"Admit it!"

They screamed until their foreheads ached and their faces had turned soda-pop red. Bodies were at the door. Several men in black hats, a few concerned women in wigs murmuring behind. Here were two associates of the woman who'd already left. Screaming at each other in the kitchen. Breathless and hot. Fury and sweat dripped from Marlowe's nose, and he saw the same coming down Donahue's forehead. The man dabbed himself dry with a paper napkin, then folded the thing into his jacket like a brightly colored pocket square.

"Once again, so sorry for your loss," Donahue said, giving the egregious bow he always used on the 'ethnics.' "We're just leaving. I promise you that."

The onlookers nodded in their annoyance, slipping away to give them both a clean exit.

"Donahue, listen." But his boss turned away. "Listen to me." He grabbed Donahue's arm before jumping back from a raised fist. "Just... find Darla Foster, and that fuckwit Sergei Moscowitz. They'll corroborate every word in that report."

"Leave it, Marlowe." His voice was low. That of a parent no longer mad, simply disappointed.

"But there's proof! Proof of clear and present danger. Hell, the fucking *Genesis* is part of—"

"You listen to me, now, okay?" A fat finger poked into Marlowe's chest. The heart-attack red of Donahue's face a warning to shut up and do what he said. "Even if trillions of dollars and tens of thousands of lives hadn't just gone up in smoke, nobody's going to give a damn about the ravings of some Maelstrom meth-heads. No one's going to pay you a lick of attention either.

"But—"

"But nothing. You're a suspect, Marlowe. A prime fucking suspect to the worst thing to happen to this world in our lifetimes. If I hadn't put my neck on the line, they'd have hauled your ass off to solitary the second you showed your passport at Brezhnev-Carter."

"I want to help." The words came out as a whisper. Gentle, quiet, broken. "I need to help."

Donahue sniffed a deep, unsatisfying breath through his nostrils. They were talking past each other. As therapist after therapist had previously pointed out to Marlowe and Marlene. Both believed what they were saying to be of the utmost importance, the rest of the world be damned.

"Go home, Marlowe." Donahue slipped on a jacket, no longer looking at Marlowe, but at the door. The loud noise of a car speeding away cut across the ocean waves and stilted voices for just a moment. But Donahue wouldn't be waiting long for his own. He wasn't just an important cog in the system, he was the system. He kept disaffected voices quiet. He dampened expectations and silenced dissent. Marlowe could have thrown the bloody legs of Okechukwu and Bradley and all the others at Donahue's feet, and the reaction would have been the same. It was his job to keep the lines smooth. To keep the long peace by obfuscating the unalienable truth.

"What's going on up there? Huh? How many of these creatures are out there?"

"Go home, Marlowe."

But Marlowe would not relent. He'd come this far, and ended up this alone. What more was there to lose?

"You owe me some answers."

"And you owe me your fucking life, now I'm not saying it again." The jacket on, the doorway beckoned. The tears from Marlowe's eyes roundly ignored. "Go the fuck home. You're suspended. If I see you anywhere near UNSOC property again, I'll have you arrested and placed under Special Measures until you'll be begging for a winter holiday on Pluto. Now, please. Do us all a favor and go the fuck home."

In the minute after Donahue left, the outsiders began to take their first tentative steps back into the kitchen. Unpacking sodas and unwrapping half-bagel platters as if preparing for an onslaught of hungry mourners, instead of the dozen extended family members here out of obligation.

"I've called you a car," said an elderly man with a severe and untamed gray beard. He spoke from under a black hat and black suit of an Orthodox Jew. The women had not yet deigned to enter the sphere with Marlowe still around. "Thank you for coming to pay your respects to Charlie." He threw cellophane into the trash, then moved to unwrapping the next platter. "But please, don't come back."

CHAPTER 20: STRANDED WITHOUT AN EXIT VISA IN EAST BERLIN

Marlowe waited to pass through Checkpoint Charlie under a corrugated iron shack. Shuffling forward, stopping, shuffling forward. Today though, there was no rain on the roof to provide an incessant, untuned clanging. The Berlins were absent the usual awful symphony of snare drums played by rabid monkeys. The cities usually soaked in enough rain to drive the sanest man mad. No, today a cold sun sat high atop the East Berlin sky, as Soviet soldiers called each time traveler forward. Pointing in their faces a searchlight as deep as space and as cruel as time, beaming upon the guilty faces of the world.

On the metal table, Marlowe placed the few objects he had. The only ones he owned. A new vape pen. A satchel of some clothes and a facsimile copy of the apartment deeds he'd expensively managed to re-secure from the executor of his grandfather's estate. Spare keys would be in the good graces of an East German Housing Ministry functionary, who were of course notoriously happy to deal with private landlords grandfathered in from the days before communism. And for whom diplomatic immunity prevented their assets from being seized and redistributed. Marlowe was thankful he still had a blue UNSOC passport to show the guard. The severe-faced Russian inspected the pages. There was no heart to this one. No warmth or whiff of a hardening cock beneath his fatigues. The cute soldier he'd made so nervous on his last border crossing should be the last thing on Marlowe's mind. But when he had nothing else in his life to cling to, what was so wrong with engaging in fantasy?

"*Sleduyushchiy*," the Soviet guard called out, beckoning the next one forward while handing Marlowe back his passport. With that, it was all so easy. The border nothing more than a meaningless line in the sand. Compared to space, and the monsters lurking out there,

here the monsters were truly no more than shadows of history still haunting the present.

The anachronism of the border left behind, Marlowe squinted in the East German sun. This time there was no Stasi-provided car to whisk him down Karl Marx Allee. And he wasn't stupid enough to turn his phone on and hail a ride, although unlike in the West, ride-sharing here was free. The car's had a tendency to explode or break down on the Volksbahn, but still, it was free.

Instead, Marlowe walked, the Wall at his back, the vape happily working overtime between the lines of his mouth. The streets were quiet for any other afternoon. Just as the plane had been quiet, too. And the urinal at RFK.. There was barely a line for a coffee, either. The world was still asleep; still trapped in a disturbed haze at the nonstop images of horror broadcast round the clock from Florida. But people can only care about faraway tragedy for so long, until the joys and tragedies of their own lives fall back into the foreground.

No one really cared that Marlowe, by all accounts a suspect, if not an outright accessory to mass murder, could hop freely between continents while millions more remained trapped by events. Prisoners of borders, of walls, of worlds and circumstance. These were their own daily tragedies. He glanced up into the sky for a brief moment, and wondered when 'Dorvethan' might fall to Earth like the comet that wiped out the dinosaurs, and leave nothing left of humanity but traces of bone and blood on the frozen Lunar surface.

Marlowe walked quickly between grand buildings and bare streets. His breath mixing with the vape, puffing his engine towards the only place on this world he could just be. He came to a crosswalk bisecting a wide avenue named after some other gunslinging hero of a distant revolution. The six lanes in either direction devoid of life, but he waited for the jaunty green man anyway, watching the empty world while he too felt watched.

Neither person, nor dog, nor car waited nearby. No one looked out from the innumerable windows gazing down on him. It could be the buzz of a distant drone, or the arching scope of a satellite zooming in on the top of his head, but Marlowe's hackles were up. He sucked on the vape and took the chance to glance right, stretching as far as his neck would allow. No one. Not even litter flipping by on a bitter breeze. He looked left, along the trim of stone buildings fringing the highway, stretching from here to Moscow. There was nothing along these walls, nothing out of the ordinary except the absence of life. And a little puff of smoke.

It came from between two buildings. One Marlowe knew to be a Russian military intelligence office from previous sojourns in East Berlin. The smoke twisted in rounds that grew larger as they swirled into the air, suggesting it came from lungs, not a sewer grate. Mischief drew him forward. Mischief from a suggestive pinch between his legs. Mischief from the flash drive in his coat pocket. The story of the century detailed in a rejected report.

"Halo," Marlowe offered to a faceless soldier smoking against a dark alley wall. Quickly he stuffed away his vape. "Haben Sie eine Zigarette?"

The man drew his hand from the pocket of a Russian uniform, offering a soft packet of Soviet Laika's while he kept puffing on his own. But as Marlowe approached, the soldier threw his own finished away and slipped out a new one just as Marlowe took what was on offer. The Russian stood, one boot against brick, face almost covered by his cap. He lit the next one, then offered Marlowe a clip from the lighter. The face rose up. Smooth-cheeked and thin-lined. Almost recognizable. Like every Russian in this city.

"Do I know you?" The Russian soldier asked in thickly accented German. Marlowe lingered on his gaze as well, wondering the very same thing. Their cigarette smoke mingled in the bare few inches between them. His body smelled of brass and hard water. They were unseen by anyone. The soldier's skin under his stiff collar flushed as red as the badges on his lapel.

Why so nervous? Marlowe thought, then broke out into a grin. His memory piqued while the soldier's lips remained firmly shut, sealed, prickled with blueish stubble Marlowe had once imagined rubbing against his own skin. Barely a few weeks ago, when this same soldier had searched his bag and Marlowe had offered a casual smile to a man he was convinced wanted nothing more than his dick drained.

"Nice to see you again," Marlowe offered in Russian, with nothing to lose.

Was it him? Or just another smooth-skinned, dark eyed Slav with red stars on their lapels and the dead look of a conscript. It didn't really matter, as in another moment, the soldier's eyes lifted, his face bathed in the brilliant Berlin twilight. He didn't smile or nod but lifted an eyebrow just enough to acknowledge contact. They smoked in silence. It was a cheap Russian cigarette, so of course it lasted barely longer than four draws. With the lighted tip threatening Marlowe's fingers, he glanced back to the empty avenue, twisting in his head in an obvious motion. Confirming the fact they were indeed alone.

The Russian threw away his smoked butt. He bit his lower lip. Marlowe motioned forward, one foot between the soldier's legs. Their stance entwined. A stand-off. Who would move first? But Marlowe wanted only one thing. The soldier needn't worry. Without a sound or a fuss, and with no more effort than bending down to tie his shoelace, Marlowe crouched, his coat flapping over freezing cold stones like dry ice in the bone-dry sun.

Steam vibrated from the soldier's cock as it flopped out of his uniform. He looked down, not touching Marlowe nor showing any kindness. Marlowe sank his throat into the white-tasting dick as if it was his only purpose in life. The head smacked the back of his throat, the taste rolling around his tongue. Deep and deliberate, Marlowe worked his head back and forward as the soldier's hot, tobacco-flavored breath rose into the approaching twilight. The abandoned pink sky. They could have been the only two people on an entire planet, and they'd still not say a word after. Marlowe would perform the only form of love he'd ever known. As he sucked off the soldier, he grasped at a memory, as he always did. Not at the immediate pleasure of the moment, but the distance of a half-felt feeling, a long time ago.

Had Charlie ever cupped Marlowe's cheek? Running fingers along his face from the days before he shaved? Had Marlowe ever glanced up to see Charlie's wide-eyed smile, his partially curled lip, or listened to the bones of quiet moans delivered in a silent dorm room? Had they ever been anything more than body functions swapping body fluids? There was no one left to ask anymore.

And then, like the fleeting notes of a whispered dream, the feeling faded as the soldier's load flooded Marlowe's throat. The deed done, Marlowe gave one last loving lick, sending shivers along the man's shaft, holding on for a moment longer than the other man wanted. The soldier more forcibly withdrew, shaking off one last drop, stuffing himself away in his trousers. Marlowe's knees cracked as he stood. He waited for the soldier to push past him. To turn and leave as quick as their feet would take them, like all the others. But not like Charlie. He'd not left. He'd not faded. From the first teenage time they fumbled under a shared blanket, until the last days of Charlie's life, he'd never left him. Not really. Distance had come and gone. Marlene had come and gone. Marlowe didn't care about her anymore. He didn't care that now she knew. He didn't care now she would hate him forever. He only cared that he'd let her get in his way. He only cared that he'd let Charlie let Marlene get in his way. That he'd fallen for Charlie's Scorpio response to their predicament; to let Marlowe marry Marlene, to let him mortgage *his* life, so Charlie could avoid an uncomfortable conversation.

The soldier offered him another cigarette. He smiled like he wasn't planning to go anywhere.

"You liked?" Marlowe asked in uncomfortable Russian.

"*Da.*"

They smoked and shared a grin. Marlowe had to laugh at the oddness of not feeling any more shame. Perhaps that had been the half-remembered feeling he'd been chasing all these years. It wasn't the way Charlie cupped his cheek, or ran his fingers under a smooth chin, or grinned with his eyes, or curled his lip, or unleashed a quiet moan. It was simply that, for a time, like in early Eden, they had not encountered the concept of shame.

"From Russia?"

"*Du.*" Marlowe embraced the awkwardness, obviously looking across his body, around at his backside. If he'd been in a place he could turn on his phone, Marlowe would've offered him money to drop his pants and take pictures. The soldier looked like he'd be only too keen to accept. "I must return." He threw the quickly smoked cigarette to the ground. He was on the cusp of leaving. Marlowe slipped his free hand into his pocket, watching that feeling wander away. His fingers clasped around the half-remembered flash drive.

"Wait." The soldier stopped. He looked back, hopefully. Like Marlowe was ready to offer some money after all. "*Spasibo.*" The Russian's face fell, but only for a moment.

"It is I who should thank you."

"No, me," Marlowe insisted. "For the, um, cigarettes." What else could he say? Thanks for letting me suck your dick and not immediately disappearing as soon as your balls unclenched?

"Don't mention it."

"I have something for you." Marlowe spoke quickly. His Russian was fading the further on the conversation went. "It has much value." Marlowe unfurled the flash drive as the soldier's eyes widened. It might have a lot of value; be full of porn or state secrets, but what was a conscript without a personal computer to do with it? That's what his eyes seemed to communicate anyway, but Marlowe had quickly practiced what to say. "Find a journalist." He glanced at the street beyond. Shadows broadcast by the setting sun. Movement, perhaps, or the seditious whisper of the wind. The soldier noticed the drop in temperature, too. Marlowe thrust the flash drive into his cold hand and closed the man's fingers around it. "Give them this. It explains what happened in Florida. What happened to the *Genesis*... to Charlie Novikov." The soldier looked confused, but Marlowe didn't want to chance it by explaining things twice. "This is worth a lot of money. Sell it. Sell it to a Western journalist."

Marlowe didn't give him a chance to protest. His heart thumping harder than it had during their brief sexual encounter, Marlowe edged away. Without looking back, he walked briskly out of the alley, into the wide, deserted street. He crossed the highway without looking, unburdened by so many things. The weight of the world shifted, at least temporarily, to someone else's shoulders. Light-footed, Marlowe walked with the ease of a man who's only task left for the day is to go home.

The building's factor, Frau Kachkayev, grumpily let him back in to the apartment. She'd given herself away the moment Marlowe knocked on her ground floor door in the decrepit building; yelling from her kitchen table that he owed the DDR money before he had a chance to explain he'd simply misplaced his keys somewhere in The Maelstrom. Fifty U.S. dollars cheered her up though, and she left him with her spare set and the warm offer of dinner if he was ever hungry. Even if he was, the state of his grandfather's four rooms turned off his appetite. The place had somehow become worse since he'd last seen it a couple of weeks before. Or perhaps details like peeling floorboards, exposed wiring and brown liquid seeping from the radiators had faded fast from his mind, as does the pain of a torturer's interrogation.

There were no contractors in the German Democratic Republic, at least none that could be looked up in directory. After spending the rest of the evening until late into the night shifting all the leftover boxes of his grandfather's things into the smallest bedroom next to the barely functional kitchen, and taking down so many bags of trash he needed to ask Frau Kachkayev for more, he looked around the now empty rooms and the peeling wallpaper and thought, at least considered the thought, he could fix this place by himself.

What a great 'fuck you' that would be to Marlene.

Four days, four hundred black market dollars, and four and a half hours in the medical center for a cut to the head and what was probably a mild concussion from a falling set of kitchen cabinets later, Marlowe was quietly confident he had upgraded the apartment from 'hovel' to 'barely fit for human habitation.'

He'd given Frau Kachkayev carte blanche and another two hundred dollars for interior design, and as she peered over his shoulder from the entrance hall with a cup of Rondo coffee, she seemed more impressed at her furnishings than the result of Marlowe's non-stop renovations.

"The couch is not better against the other wall?" she asked, feeling more at home than Marlowe did. He'd even managed to get the fireplace going in the living room which the couch was right beside. "A spark from the fire might set the couch alight. I did just have it washed in bleach."

"So that's the smell. But no, there's a rather large hole in the wall back there from my brief experiment with wiring. And the plasterer can't come until next month."

"Very well." She fingered the blackout curtains which both kept out streetlight glare as they switched on in the early evening twilight, and the draught from the not-quite-fitting window panes. Marlowe walked behind her, willing the woman to leave after having spent the best part of a week with her forced hospitality, and quite wishing to just enjoy the fruits of his hard work.

She wandered into the kitchen. A lick of white paint on the walls and some metal countertops 'liberated' from an Albanian restaurant who's funding had been cut for political reasons gave the kitchen a brand-new look. Its functional brutalism would do very well in Bushwick.

"No gas?" She asked, fiddling with the cooker's nobs.

"Not until next week, but I don't mind. I don't really..." He trailed off as Frau Kachkayev stuck her head in the oven. A thought struck him. "You know," Marlowe said, loud enough for her to clearly hear him from inside the non-functioning oven, "I am so hungry after all this work. I barely ate all week."

"Say no more!" She inhabited the air of an excited puppy. "I have so many dumplings in the freezer. And soup! You need soup for this weather. I'll make you enough for the week." She patted him on the shoulder. "The beets are lovely this season. Pop down at nine, but not a minute before." Marlowe didn't need to hurry her out of the apartment, because she was already mounting the stairs.

"Thank you, Magda," he called out.

"I'll be using all my potatoes but give me your ration code and I'll take back from your next week!"

The front door firmly shut, and locked, Marlowe shuddered out a deep breath in a space finally his own. As he took a black beer from the fridge and sipped it in total silence, he wondered if he didn't prefer high ceilings over high-speed internet anyway. A warm fire he could stock himself, with his own wood, over gouging gas prices in the West. A decent ration code that kept him well-stocked with root vegetables, cheese, bread, beer and two servings of meat a week over a million choices from a thousand apps. Stories from the East so often focused on those who fled; their reasons why and tortured horrors from speaking out. But those were a trickle. What of the millions who stayed? Who wanted to listen to their stories?

Marlowe settled comfortably on the bleached couch, feet alarmingly warm and too close to the crackling fire. He peeled open the repurposed pad he'd clandestinely bought from the electronics store across the street from the Clara Zetkein People's Hotel. Surfing the rudimentary socialist internet was free, but Marlowe didn't much feel like reading extended essays on *Pravda* or trying to cruise guys through the cryptic messages left on community gardening forums. This close to West Berlin, he only had to fork over another ten dollars for a signal booster that let him connect to Radio Free Europe's powerful Wi-Fi network.

It had been five days since he'd handed the soldier a flash drive containing all of UNSOC's secrets. Five days that should have shook the world. East Berlin was a wonderful place to hide from Earth-shattering events, if one wanted. Often the last place to receive news from Moscow, nestled up against the Iron Curtain that meant one had to buy a repurposed pad and a signal booster with American cash to get access to the outside world.

Sucking down the beer so hard his throat hurt, Marlowe closed his eyes and opened up the *New York Times*.

He took everything in at once, quickly scanning the entirety of the page like the aftermath of a crime scene, trying to piece together the loose parts to make up the whole story.

Cleanup in Florida. More obituaries. Pictures of S-Nine in riot gear on Armstrong. Striking workers from Saturn waving red flags. Original red. Angry protestors with red MEGA flags camped outside UNSOC. News about Congress' backflipping positions on the *Genesis*. Pledges from the president to launch a second ship as soon as they could.

Lips pressed hard together, Marlowe flipped to English *Pravda*. The stories were not much different. Europe was standing firm on sending only one ambassador to deal with the dozens if not hundreds of newly declared independent states in The Maelstrom. The sale of oil drilling permits on Mars had been indefinitely suspended. Marlowe could only assume Marlene was behind that effort.

He clicked on another site. Still nothing. Not in the British press, not in the French, not trending on the social networks either. Only a very detailed search brought up a single story from *Der Spiegel*. A minor mention, almost tongue-in-cheek.

Rogue UNSOC agent alleges 'alien' involvement in Genesis *disaster.* Three paragraphs, that was all. He remained nameless but was described as *disgruntled* and *recently divorced*. The border guard had done his job; Marlowe couldn't fault him. He'd taken the story to a reputable news outlet who'd of course followed journalistic principles and contacted UNSOC for comment. They hardly needed to reveal their source. Marlowe was the only one who could have authored that report, and so the UNSOC PR team flushed into overdrive to paint him as nothing more than a nut who'd been *suspended pending a full investigation.*

And that was it. Marlowe's career was over. He'd been around long enough to know how these things worked at UNSOC. *Pending a full investigation* was code for they wanted rid of him but would play the paperwork game until he quit and they could dangle the severance package to make him sign an NDA.

He didn't know whether to smash the tablet in half or just sob into the bleach-stained couch. The urge for mischief bubbled up in his throat like bile. If he'd been in New York, or Paris, or Armstrong, or anywhere but East Berlin, he would have drowned these feelings in vodka, pills and dick. He had vodka, but it was never as fun without the promise of the other two to empty his mind and body of these pent-up feelings of utter uselessness.

Marlowe let the pad fall onto the hardwood floor of his apartment. This bizarre place he'd been gifted by his grandfather. His mind fluttered to the small room that should have been an office but was stuffed full of all Martin Reginald Marlowe's things. Boxes of books and newspapers. Diaries and postcards. Photo albums and manilla folders of ancient UNSOC paperwork. The one sliver of hope Marlowe was clinging to, that held him back from total despair, was the thought that just maybe, buried somewhere inside those dusty boxes, was a secret UNSOC would pay dear to keep hidden. But Marlowe had already busted their greatest cover-up, and nobody had cared. What were the odds of finding something *more* explosive than an extra-terrestrial being infecting the bodies of cosmonauts and causing tens of thousands of deaths?

Barefoot, Marlowe stepped across the floorboards, conscious of the loose nails he knew were still a threat on the newly repaired floorboards. Stepping quietly so as not to disturb the silence, he pickpocketed Russian vodka from the freezer but held open the door with a hurried breath. It sounded like alarms, perhaps fire or police, maybe coming towards him, to arrest an enemy of several states. But the noise that weaved in and out of the freezer engine didn't grow louder, it just maintained a heavy, steady thud and wail, like listening to a party though an air lock. Only through logical enquiry did Marlowe realize it was a Friday night, and the sounds were nothing more than the nighttime economy of West Berlin floating over the Spree. Marlowe was only a block from the river in Friedrichshain. In fact, as he closed the freezer and approached the thin kitchen window above the sink, standing on his tiptoes, the flashing blue and red lights were not the warnings of officialdom at all, but the sights and sounds of the lively West Berlin borough of Kreuzberg.

Over there was life. With all the pills and dick he could possibly want. He could cross the border at the Oberbaum Bridge in less than fifteen minutes and sink into a world that was open to stealing away his problems. It would always just be over there. He could never bring anyone back. He could never move forward, not in this apartment, he realized. There was no job he could do in East Berlin, no future he could see, nor any future he could imagine at all. Here he could just be. In an apartment that was his own. Surviving on rations and his meager suspension pay from UNSOC. He could just be, and perhaps for a while, that would be enough.

The weight of his grandfather's things was pushing against the kitchen wall. The unread, unsorted, unorganized papers. Procrastinating from opening even a single box of those had led him to this four-day orgy of home renovations. Kreuzberg was yet another procrastinator's paradise. It would always be. Now it was time to look at what had been and finally see if the past might hold any answers to the future. Not only of himself, but of the human race and its continued existence in a solar system whose defenses had long ago been breached.

Marlowe drank deeply from the bitter vodka. The ice cold sent him shivering into the pile of papers and books and diaries that had been deemed not worthy to make it into UNSOC history. Or too explosive to be let anywhere near official archives. He cracked open a box lid caked in dust and lifted the first book. A diary, much like the one he'd been given in Wiltshire, and had to leave behind on Delving Prime. Blowing off the caked-on dust, the date was handwritten on the cover: *December 1952.*

CHAPTER 21:
DISCUSSING THE
DORVETHAN PRINCIPLE
OVER DRINKS AT THE
RAINBOW ROOM

December 9, 1952
UNSOC Headquarters, New York
Population: 56,000 full time, 19,000 FTE, count-
less contractors (note to self: discuss with HR a
new employment status for space-based workers)

Four o'clock on a winter's afternoon was a perfect fucken' time for a shithead meeting. I could reasonably sit and sip on a double whiskey like I was waiting for Hope and Faith to arrive for their shift at a New Mexico stripper bar. The bright setting sun over Manhattan glimmered through my office's sky-high windows, blinding the poor bastards crowded around the couple of couches I had facing my desk, and facing the burning sun slowly sinking towards the California horizon. Of course, I saw things different these days. We were the ones spinning, not the sun. Pointing away from those disastrous missions to Venus, and towards the future. Luna, the space stations, even Mars.

"Director-General, the president is ready to sign the Mars Treaty," said shithead number one, his fat ass perched on *my* fucking couch. First to sit, last to get up. I should ask if there's a steel prod poking up his backside and that's why he's so in love with my fucking couch.

"The president-elect still has concerns," retorted shithead number two. A smart-ass with glasses who thought he was all that because he'd written some smart-alecy line *The Atlantic* said had won

Eisenhower the election. Something about trees on Mars. "The incoming Republican House leadership, too. Not to mention the Senate minority leader."

"And that's why he'll still be minority leader come January."

Shithead one had his ass parked on the couch to my right, stick up the proverbial, alongside three UNSOC guys I didn't know. There was a time I knew the shoe size of everyone I cut a check to. They were opposed by shithead two and his four (!) assholes from various branches of government I didn't care to know about. I sat like Sampson behind my desk, lifting my glass to just the right height to blind whatever bugger had the bad idea to open his trap and use up my oxygen, in my office.

"You gave Mars to the Soviets! The Treaty is a travesty of—"

"*President* Truman relied on his close personal relationship with Chairman Stalin—"

"Truman bent over and let Stalin rodger him up the beehive!"

I had to snort. Those Princeton and Yale eggheads might know a thing or two about what they think is important in life, but they sure couldn't shoot for shit.

"Director-General?" Shithead one asked me, but they all squinted my way. "Would you care to weigh in here?"

Care to? I downed the whiskey left over in my glass, wondering if it would be bad form to pour another. Papers and files covered my desk like I was house-breaking a loose-assed sausage dog. I'd have no hope catching up with whatever bullshit these boys were throwing at each other. So I used the one weapon I had left at my disposal; my giant, swaggering cock. I whistled—rudely—at shithead number two.

"Where'd you go to school, son?"

"Um… Harvard, sir."

"Harvard, eh? Did they teach you to walk on two feet at Harvard?"

"Well… sure."

"So waddle over here then, boy." Reddening under the collar, shithead two did as he was told. I handed him a framed photograph from my desk, but just before his tobacco-stained fingers took it, I held it back. "You got a grandmother, boy?"

"Of-of course, sir."

"She go to Harvard?"

"No, sir. She... passed away." He swallowed loudly, like he was ashamed to tell the Director-General of UNSOC about his poor dead grannie in case it might embarrass me. Dick head.

"Aw, well imagine speaking the next sentence about to come out of your pie hole to poor dead grandma Finklestein, or whatever the fuck your name is." I shoved the photograph frame into his hands. "Look at this and tell the class what you see." He stared at it, glasses slipping down his sweaty nose.

"Um..."

"Speak!"

"I see... I see President Truman and Chairman Stalin wearing space suits and shaking hands beside... beside a tree sapling."

"And *where* are Truman and Stalin? Not in a motherfucking forest?"

"No sir. On Mars."

"That's right! Gold star, Harvard boy." Now I stood up, because my hole was itchy and I looked like a prick scratching it from my chair. "Stalin and Truman planting a fucking tree on Mars, while Bess Truman is back on the ship baking fucking cookies or whatever the fuck she does. That's the Mars Treaty. A bilateral settlement to create a pristine planet some of those Congressman you're all so fond of sucking the dicks of wanted to open up to strip-mining. Fucking mining! Of course the Soviets would demand the right to unionize said miners."

"Is that such a bad thing?" Asked one of the cocksuckers from shithead two's group. Some smarmy young aide Eisenhower so loved to surround himself with.

"Jesus H. Christ," I said out loud, but to no one in particular. "Someone bring me that fucking whiskey over there." No one moved a muscle. "Now!" Three rushed for it, almost headbutting each other in the process. A large one was poured for me, and I sucked on the sweet elixir of life. "You Harvard boys really don't know shit about Marxist theory, do you?" They shook their heads, and I did mine. I sucked down a slurp of whiskey, and buzzed the intercom. "Dora, dear, make a note. Every new UNSOC employee needs a foundational certificate in Marxism-Leninism."

"Sure thing, director."

"She's a doll." I stood tall over the assembled pricks, the sun high at my back, blinding them like I was a one-man firing squad. "Two stage revolution theory, boys. First, a capitalist revolution creates a bourgeois paradise. Or hellscape, if you're a worker. Money and capital is poured into... let's say Mars. Resources are extracted, fat cats in Congress and Wall Street grow richer, and the Soviets quietly let all that happen. They'll pump in workers by the spaceship load, you'll see. They'll give us cheap labor, as cheap as chips. Hell, they'll even kick those workers in the teeth just to stir shit up." The Harvard set all looked at me like I was a drunken lunatic. What I might call the 'Bess Truman' face. One dumb ass piqued up.

"I thought the Soviets were generally pro-worker." He shuffled in his seat while everyone glared at him,

"Two. Stage. Revolution! Only when the workers have been so fucked over by capitalism will they then revolt, spurred on by a vanguard of guess the fuck who. Mars in the throws of a proletarian revolution. Luna, the mines in the Asteroid Belt, and wherever else humanity has decided to plant a flag and take a piss. System wide revolution. Galactic revolution. That's what the theorists in Moscow are planning for, do you understand that? They're playing the long game. And everything we want to give them, they'll swallow as gladly as your dearly departed grandmother did when courting your grandfather. That's the beauty of the Mars Treaty. Neither side gets what it wants. Mars remains off limits to settlement, mining, resource-stripping, and revolution. The parties are committed to the peaceful development of a habitable Martian atmosphere, and this new Eden is protected until at least the next century. I mean, how long is it supposed to take to terraform the place?" I said it to one of the eggheads, several checked their notes.

"Beyond the year 2000. Possibly the 2020s before Mars has close to a breathable atmosphere."

"Thank you and goodnight, boys. The 2020s. Hell, the Soviet Union could've collapsed by then. Or the US, who knows. But Mars, the biggest, baddest planet in our system, is protected. We'll have built a new Eden by then, and who'll want to destroy that? It's like... destroying the rainforest. Or mining in Antarctica. No, no. The Mars Treaty gives us another Earth, boys. And no politician on Earth, communist or capitalist, will win on a platform of destroying

Earth. That. That's what's worth saving. Worth sacrificing for. So, you go tell Dwight that when the Mars Treaty comes into effect, the Red planet falls under UNSOC custodianship, at least until it's no longer red. And if he has a problem with it, I'll set Bess Truman on his ass. Now, any serious business to discuss?"

The egg heads all looked at each other.

"Well… the Pope is complaining about the ban on churches in space."

"Again? Tell the Holy Father to fuck off. And I'm not interested in being bribed by his Nazi gold." The intercom cut through my burning desire to launch into an anti-clerical tirade.

"Sir, it's Doctor Johnson." I could hear the surprise in Dora's voice. Bless her fending off his self-righteous aristocratic sassiness. *"He's just telephoned from the airport and wants to meet. But your appointment with the Soviet ambassador is at six. Shall I cancel her?"*

"No, no. I'll meet him for a late drink at the Rainbow Room." No one else in the room suspected a thing. Dora was a master diplomat all in herself.

"Right you lot," I said, clapping my hands until they started to get up. "I've got real business to attend to."

They shuffled out and I poured myself another whiskey. I'd need it for the *appointment* with Svetlana. Our therapy sessions were not something I looked forward to. I'd never heard of such nonsense as *couples therapy* before Svetlana came up with the idea. Typical Marxists, always trying out new-fangled Freudian bullshit. At least the whiskey would soothe my tortured soul. Doc Johnson was not a man I wanted to antagonize. They say half the battle of managing any large group of people is letting the geniuses thrive. You point them in the right direction, decorate their office just so, and hope to hell they don't self-destruct before providing you with something useful. Doc Johnson was weeks away from a gravity expropriator which would exponentially increase our ability to create artificial gravity in the vacuum of space. We could finally build the kind of space stations the engineers had been dreaming up. Whole cities in space, drastically cutting the cost of space travel if we didn't have to spend a small fortune in rocket fuel every time we needed to send up an extra screwdriver.

The golden liquid ran through me like mercury dropping down

a thermometer. It lowered my hot temper. Svetlana always complained to the therapist I was hiding things from her. Gravity expropriators and the like. I said I was sick of our bedroom secrets making the Politburo's morning briefing. Irreconcilable differences is the phrase I'd been practicing. I drank as the sun went down. I had plenty of papers to get to the Doc, but it was safest to leave them here.

December 9, 1952
The Rockefeller Center

It was after ten PM when the elevator took me up to the sixty-fifth floor. A busty blonde on reception wanted my hat and coat, but I lit a cigarette instead.

"Marlowe." Was all I said. She nodded, her polite smile dropped and I watched the band jig up some jazzy nonsense while she desperately tried to wave over someone who knew more than she did. I'd said the magic words. "Franny!" I said, offering a hug to the older brunette who appeared out of nowhere.

"I'll take it from here," Fran said to the blonde, who was smart enough not to question goings on she didn't understand.

"How is he?" I asked Fran as we skirted the edge of the still-busy dance floor. Fran was all class. She waited until we'd mounted the staircase rising behind the bandstand before leaning back, neck exposed like she wanted to give me a vein.

"Very agitated."

"Fuck. You fed him?"

"Tried to. He wouldn't touch a thing." We stood at the top level, tables of well-dressed couples flickered through the well of smoke that rose upwards. White-coated waiters danced around. But our usual table had some other couple sitting there. It looked like the French ambassador and a woman too beautiful to be his wife. Fran was pointing to the veranda.

"He's outside?" I was glad I'd kept my coat.

"Insisted."

"Ah well... maybe all those months in New Mexico made him miss the cold. He is English, you know."

She smiled weakly. I could see these spy games we played in

her restaurant were wearing thin. I offered her a hundred. Not even with a handshake, just straight out.

"Thanks for taking care of him, Fran. I appreciate it." She took the hundred, but with a sigh. It went straight down the middle of her bosom, and an icy blast of winter air smacked me right in the face as she yanked the door open and practically booted me in the ass to get me out.

It was cold, but survivable. We were somewhat shielded from the worst of the wind, but the gargolic veranda was haunted by the shadow of bats in the night. The Doc was sitting with his back to a brick wall, table covered in full plates the waiters had clearly given up coming out to clear up. The Doc was smoking and sipping from a glass of red, but he was several bottles down.

"Brisk out, no?" I sat down. He didn't turn away from the view of downtown Manhattan, just kept on smoking and sipping. "Not nearly as cold as Pluto was, though. Man, I never want to go back there again." He might be looking the worse for wear, but his manners hadn't left him. He poured me a glass. "Weren't you the one who said chilling red wine is an act of barbarism?"

"It's a Lafleur from the late twenties," is all he said. "The barbarism has already occurred."

"You look like shit, doc." He crunched his neck, and I shivered at the bone-chilling clicks and the cold. He wasn't shivering, not at all. He wore a scarf, but a thin one. As if only to stop others from asking if he was cold. "What's that on your neck?"

"Nothing." He tightened the scarf, but the weird lump only rose up from his shirt collar.

"Cancer?" I asked, but it would be strange if it was. The bulbous chunk under his skin slivered away after I looked at it. Like some grand deception.

"I do not have cancer. At least that's what your doctors assure me, Martin."

"You've been spending too much time at Roswell. There's a reason it's off-limits these days. The radiation from the Messenger's ship is dangerous. You need to stay away." I drank deeply from the freezing wine, and watched the lights of New York flicker for a moment. A relatively cloudy sky blocked the twinkling lights of the *Roosevelt*, the first ship in permanent orbit. I thought of the cosmonauts up there, floating around, staring down at a cloudy Earth. "How's the—"

"I sent it down to Florida yesterday," Doc Johnson said, the normal English chill more clipped than usual.

"You didn't need to come all this way to tell me. But thank you. The gravity expropriator is a vital part of UNSOC expansion plans."

"Yes, I am aware of your testimony to the American Congress."

"Doc, you just shipped a fifty-million-dollar piece of revolutionary hybrid human-Messenger-tech. This is going to let us build space stations the size of cities. Colonize the moon, the Asteroid Belt. Hell, we can mine all that shit we found out on Io and Calypso and those places." I raised my glass against the cold. "Doc, take a fucking bow."

He returned a stare of such coldness that could turn this chilled red into a frozen Sangria. Bulbous pustules crawled up the sides of his neck, bubbling under his chin and around his ear as if his very body was under siege. I wanted to cut the tension with a joke. *What's got under your skin, doc?* But a different emotion eclipsed my normal good cheer. One I hadn't truly experienced since storming the beach at Normandy. Not even when the engine had failed that time trying to leave Pluto. Nor when I'd first set eyes on the Messenger. That tiny, shriveled gray body and those big eyes, as the life faded from a creature infinitely more intelligent than any of us. Not even when we translated his great warning. When Doc Scalzi showed us the final phrase, and we used his fancy reverse radio to beam the words back to the Messenger, and he responded in the affirmative.

I come to this place in peace, but with a dire/evil/terrifying warning. Your world/people/civilization is not alone. There are many, but there were many more before the great ending/closing/barrier. A terrible apocalypse/ ending is coming. You (plural) cannot stop it. You (plural) must only prepare for Dorvethan. Prepare for Dorvethan. You (plural) will only survive by defending yourselves. Defend your world/people/civilization. Dorvethan comes to all.

"You still have not responded to my report, Martin."

"Jeeze, not this Dorvethan conspiracy crap again, Doc. Is this why you came?"

"I do not believe there is anything more important in the universe right now, than this. You and your entire establishment are going the wrong way. Headlong in the wrong direction." His typical English stick-up-the-ass was sliding out. He leaned across the table, displacing all manner of frozen appetizers. His scarf slipped, the bulbous boils under his skin grew angrier in unison. "You are doing the wrong thing."

"Doc, we can't just—"

"Listen to me!" A half-full bottle of wine toppled from the table. He did not reach out to catch it, and neither did I. It fell on the table. White steam puffed from his furious nostrils like a steam train not slowing down, but speeding up. Wine stained the cloth and quickly froze, before the bottle rolled off the table and smashed on the ground. It was of no concern to Doc Johnson. In the five-something years we'd been working together, his face had aged a hundred. His eyes narrowed to alien slits. His lips recoiled across his mouth as if hiding his teeth was the most vital thing.

"I saw a great and terrible thing, Martin," he said to me, and not for the first time. But this time, I listened. "You did not look in the Messenger's eyes when we finally cracked the code. The fear, the terror of a creature with more power and knowledge than all of us on Earth. He was scared of it, Martin. Scared of Dorvethan. All of this. All of this terraforming Mars and coal mining on asteroids, it's wrong, Martin. Terribly, terribly wrong. It will only weaken our defenses when we should be strengthening them. You will all be distracted, and then there will be nothing to protect us from the collapse of space and time itself. From what is *Dorvethan*." I listened, for that's all I could do. He spoke cleanly, but with difficulty. It was hard, each word. "It's an old word," he continued, wine dribbling down his pustulated cheeks, "Dorvethan, I mean. Ancient. Before our time."

"Your time?" He ignored me. I wondered if he knew I was still here.

"We do not know what word means 'beginning.' None of their language survives. But it would certainly have been a damn site more dignified than the *Theory of the Big Bang*. Eugh." The wine continued to dribble as the man, if he was still a man, held back whatever bats of hell twisted and flapped under his pulsing skin. Get too close and one might get smacked in the face. "The truth of the matter is only this. The universe was born. The universe expanded, and now the universe is collapsing. We must either escape or hunker down. Or hunker down until we can escape. But it is coming, and it will come. Dorvethan is the end, my dear boy, and it is inevitable."

I watched the man I'd once idealized descend into nothing. A shell. Cancer-ridden perhaps. Infected with some alien virus maybe, but very much not himself. Marbles long, long gone. Yet I humored him, for what else was I to do?

"But this theory you have, when I read your memos before, it wasn't based on any kind of science, was it?" He sniffed, a wide-nostril sniff, and sat back against the stone wall. There was old wine in a glass. He gulped it down with such ferocity I feared he may eat the glass. "I mean, I recall what you wrote quite well. You said your-self there is no scientific evidence for what you called the Dorvethan Principle. In fact, there was only evidence to the contrary. That the universe is indeed expanding, not contracting. There is not a sign in the night sky of galaxies crashing into each other, or suns exploding with the force of a trillion A-bombs. There are no signatures in space for this Dorvethan apocalypse, where the supposed collapsing walls of space-time crush everything in their path until we are reduced back down to the singularity from which we came. Not a single spec of evidence to support constructing this *barrier* to cut the Earth off from, well, the entire universe… oh, and the sun. And from anyone who might be out there to help us."

"The absence of evidence does not equate to evidence of absence, Martin. Moreover…" he tightened his scarf, almost to the point of choking. "There is one very good reason we have found no other in-telligent life. For five years now, we've had access to the Messenger's maps, his radios, his communication devices, his… everything. We magnified it and built it and covered Arizona, Siberia and Western Australia in Messenger-tech radio telescopes. What have we found, Martin? Our technology could hear a pin drop fifty-hundred galax-ies away. What have we heard?"

"Like you said, it's only been five years. We'll find someone."

"No Martin," the Doc shook his head, almost violently. "We won't find anyone. There is no other intelligent life to find out there because all the intelligent ones have already closed themselves off behind their own barriers, or they've perfected the singularity transport theory we should be working on and taken their worlds through to the next universe over, the one that is not collapsing, Martin. Where we should be going. To escape the inevitable collapse of this universe. To escape Dorvethan, or at least, *at least*, to protect ourselves from it!"

"Frankly, Doc, I've heard more sense drinking schnapps with the Pope. It's not even theology, this. It's... crap, doctor. I don't know if Roswell fried your brain, or you've always been batshit crazy. But I've told you enough to stop this nonsense, and you refuse. Thank you for your work on the gravity expropriator, and on behalf of UN-SOC I truly appreciate your... Doc?"

His eyes rolled into the back of his head. I was about to launch up and run to get Fran. Foam at his mouth made it look like a seizure. "Doc? Doc, talk to me. Are you choking?" There was no time to run and get Fran. I reached out, ready to pull open his airwaves or give him mouth-to-mouth, but suddenly his lips split open and began to smile. And revealed something terrible in the process.

"Jesus Christ." I launched back in my chair, and it scraped over the ground, although not by enough. The Doc's jaw had quite literally detached with a python-sized grin. Instead of teeth he had a million needles. Each one sharp and evil. The pustules under his skin went berserk. They ran wild through his body, stretching out his skin and threatening to burst out of it. His eyes went red and reduced to the tiniest orbs.

As I had jumped from planet to planet in our solar system, from rock to rock and moon to moon, I wondered when I'd next encounter a creature not of this world, not of this species. I didn't expect it would be on the terrace of the Rainbow Room at Rockefeller Center.

"I came to protect you," the Doc said. But it wasn't the Doc. The cut-glass English had been replaced by a mangled, tortured sound like a gremlin had ripped out a set of vocal cords and was playing them like a guitar. All around his eyes, his cheek bones, his forehead, something not from here danced wild underneath a bag of skin that could barely contain it. "You turned your back on me."

"Doc, listen, I—"

"You condemn your world to death." The man that was once Doc Johnson vomited sounds more garbled than a Russian trying to recite Shakespeare. "Slow, agonizing, painful."

"Listen, you. Whatever you are. I'm the one in charge here. You come to this planet thinking you can tell us what to do?" That shut him up, for a second. *Oh shit,* I thought. He cocked his head like a wolf on the verge of ripping out my throat but was now taking another second to better plan his attack. He leaned his head to one side, so deep his ear was practically on his shoulder. A hundred clicks sounded like the vertebrae's snapping.

"Dorvethan. Comes. To. All."

"Get the hell out of here!" I shouted, kicking back the chair. On my feet, I snatched another bottle of red and smashed it on the wall behind him. Glass shattered near his beady red eyes, but he made no move. He wasn't coming towards me, at least not yet. But he grew. The bulbous beast inside him inflated. His scarf unraveled and fell. Tweed coat stitching stretched and frayed. I held the broken bottle up as my only weapon. The last defense of humanity. The creature inhabiting the Doc didn't react much but did seem to listen. He did seem to understand this was some kind of line in the sand. A wall down Berlin, of which he couldn't cross. Unlike the wall he wanted surrounding us in space, cutting off the Earth in a weird attempt to 'save' us from some universal cataclysmic collapse there was not one shred of evidence for.

"Get back! Get lost, go. Get out of here, whatever the fuck you are!" I shouted again, jabbing the sharp end of the broken bottle close to its neck. I guess he knew a slit throat would still bleed. He rose, if awkwardly. My heart thundered louder than D-Day, either D-Day. I was storming the beaches, but I was alone. With one broken bottle, running along the cold sands of Omaha. Facing a whole, angry universe of evil. "Go! Go back to wherever you came from. I mean it. Don't ever come back to this world, not while I'm alive, because I will fight back, and I will trap you in a cage so strong this universe really will be over by the time you get out. Now go, and don't ever come back."

The freezing air stung my desperate lungs. I sucked and sucked but couldn't get my fill of oxygen. Like a cracked porthole on a marooned ship. It got worse as the Doc stood. He did not look at me but past, back at the bustling restaurant sixty-five floors above ground. I moved back into his line of sight. He wasn't getting in there to cause chaos. But he didn't seem to want to. The thing turned away from me, then walked quickly across the terrace towards the

[263]

edge. I wanted to shout at him, as one does to anybody moving rapidly towards an abyss. But this was not an anybody. This was something wrong.

They had sometimes asked, the presidents, prime ministers, and chairmen I briefed, what exactly an alien invasion as prophesied by the Messenger would look like. Would it be fleets of space crafts, slipping past our heliopause like enemy ships penetrating airspace? Would it be stray asteroids, or weaponized planets, or lasers from deep in the galaxy?

No one knew, no one could say. My response though was always the same. Whatever it is, whatever the threat may look like, we need to be prepared. We need to prepare in a way that we'll never have to fight them here on Earth. Let's fight them by Neptune, in the Asteroid Belt, on Mars, on the moon if we have to. We'll defend Earth by spreading our colonies wide across the solar system, expanding out by multiple lines of defense to protect our inner core. To protect the Earth.

Yet the enemy was right here. Sipping Lafleur, nibbling pate, listening to the band play. Now he was walking away. Right to the edge.

"Don't come back!" I shook the broken bottle, but he couldn't see. No one could witness this invisible war. "Don't ever come back."

The man once known as Doctor Johnson, the preeminent physicist of his day, unsung hero of the Allied victory over evil, father of Messenger-tech and inventor of artificial gravity, stepped onto the walled edge. The city hung ahead of him. Lights and cloud. The wind whistled. The band played. The Earth spun. Then the body of the Doc was gone. Falling over the edge.

I waited, for more than five minutes. Panting and cold. Trying to steal back my breath, my sanity, turning through every question in my mind. Only after more minutes had passed, did I approach the edge to look down below. Nothing. The traffic on the city streets had not slowed into a snarl as if a dead body had fallen from the sky. There was no creature hanging off the edge, waiting to claw at my face and pull me down to hell with him. No sign at all anyone had ever been here.

I went back inside to where the couples danced to the music. I sat at the bar. I drank a whiskey, then another. I paid the tab, and then I left.

Three weeks later, I received a note across my desk. NYPD found something strange caught in the rafters of St. Patrick's Cathedral a block away. They thought it was some kind of weather balloon at first, or maybe a gag. They took it to the mortuary, but it wasn't a body. Just a bag of skin. Lifeless, boneless, innard-less, but otherwise rather identifiable by someone who read the papers and had seen Doc Johnson's picture in it a few months back announcing a breakthrough in artificial gravity research. Photographs of the 'body'-bag were sent to us and came across my desk.

"That's him," I said to Dora as I poured myself a whiskey at ten in the morning. I turned the photograph over. "Do me a favor, will you? If there's ever another case like this. A bag of skin turns up somewhere, just... don't tell me, all right? Better yet, burn those records on arrival."

"Like our unofficial policy of not hiring Catholics?"

"It's people of any strong religion, Dora. We don't discriminate."

"We just don't want to have to deal with God in space."

"Bingo. God lives in the sky, Dora, not in the cold blackness of endless space. The goddamn Pope told me as much, once I got him a little sozzled. We don't need a bunch of prophets and priests coming up there and poking their noses around for Christ on a cross. And we definitely don't need the headache of bags of skin floating around."

"You got it, boss."

"Thanks, Dora. Burn these files, will ya? And confirm my reservation with Madam Ambassador at the Rainbow Room tonight."

"Oh, I see this new-fangled couple's therapy seems to be working, then?"

I grinned. "Well Dora, something is."

CHAPTER 22: HISTORY ALWAYS REPEATS ITSELF, FIRST AS TRAGEDY, AND FOREVER AS FARCE

East Berlin, Deutsche Demokratische Republik
Population: 1,650,000
Ten months after the Genesis *disaster*

Marlowe was coming to appreciate Berlin in late summer, east or west. He'd woken that morning in Kreuzberg, in the West, to a warm September sun and lively birds chittering outside the bedroom window. He'd thrown it open to disturb the smell of sex in the room, while an accountant by the name of Anders who was originally from Hamburg but had come to the West to avoid the draft, and to have unlimited sex with men, made him coffee in the kitchen. Anders' standard office hours forced Marlowe to be gone by eight thirty in the morning. He appreciated that push to either go to the gym, go to the library, or go back home to the East. It gave his days regularity. Throughout the long German winter and into the spring, Marlowe had been spending a bit too much of his indefinite suspension salary on the boys and the bars of West Berlin. Now, with Anders in his life, he didn't need to spend quite so much to lie next to a warm body several nights a week.

After a curt German goodbye and the casual suggestion of a meeting later in the week, Marlowe wandered through the bright Kreuzberg morning, stopping in at the several English bookshops on his lazy way back home across the river. Browsing the newspaper headlines and the periodicals. It was strange just how easy it was to avoid any news about space when one wanted to. Apart from the occasional front-page headlines of the latest twists in system-wide politics; the coup on Armstrong, the endless revolutions on minor moons, and following whatever strongman had seized control of a clump of rocks in The Maelstrom, most of the time, there wasn't all that much interesting happening up there that was relevant for down here.

He did stop off at an ATM, just to double check his balance and that the latest payment had come in. It wasn't his pension, but the agreement he'd reached with UNSOC HR on indefinite suspension gave him eighty percent of his salary, plus benefits like global and inter-system travel (not that he had anywhere to go), and the usual exemption from all national taxes. UNSOC didn't have to give him a severance payment or rehoming and renationalization expenses, and Marlowe didn't have to do any work. UNSOC wouldn't investigate what Marlowe had done any more, as long as Marlowe stuck to his non-disclosure agreement. Both parties agreed to this for as long as the CCI had a budget to pay him. Indefinite, yes. Permanent, no.

It was a stalemate, much like Berlin. And much like Berlin, the stalemate would continue as long as both sides took care of their own affairs. The boat would remain unrocked. The report Marlowe wrote remained buried. The official line on the *Genesis* disaster— that it was an act of unconscionable terrorism by a deeply troubled individual—remained undisturbed by a single *Der Spiegel* story from an anonymous source. The article had since been taken down.

They didn't know of course about the typewriter Marlowe had at home. They didn't know he'd spent most days transcribing his grandfather's diaries, word for word. They didn't know he took pictures of each page with microfilm, and every time he was through in the West, Marlowe copied the images onto a computer. First at the library, then at Anders'. He logged into an anonymous email account, uploaded the images of the typed pages of the lost diaries, and saved the message unsent, as a draft, so no trail would be left online or offline. They didn't know all that, nor was Marlowe planning to tell them. That was the status quo. Just like Berlin, underneath it sat mutually assured destruction, but no one liked to think about that.

Marlowe preferred to take Checkpoint Charlie home, especially since he'd discovered the Russian soldiers' secret communication website. A simple message board that managed to jump on the back of a GPS signal to securely pinpoint a user's location to within a few feet of accuracy, yet stayed encrypted and anonymous. it was easy there to find soldiers looking to trade some drink, some drugs, or some dick.

But the Oberbaum Bridge was quicker, and more direct. Plus, Anders had provided Marlowe's fill of dick for at least a few days. He could go home and focus on his current project. The transcription of the diaries of 1962-63. The construction of the Khruschev-Kennedy space station was proving to be quite a wild story of bungled contracts and covered-up safety violations. Anders was unavailable for the next two evenings. Well, he was available, but at Green party meetings. Young, smooth-bummed Anders fancied himself the next West German chancellor. Marlowe had legitimately asked if a boyfriend from the East, or at least one who lived there and crossed the border almost daily, wouldn't be somewhat of a handicap in his quest for a seat on the local council. Far from it, Anders had said. The East was enjoying a resurgence in popularity among anti-capitalist and capitalist-neutral circles in the West. Marlowe however was a constant disappointment to Anders' friends when he couldn't regale them with tales of growing up in the DDR's Young Pioneers. Few were interested in any tales he might have of the Moscow UN-SOC Academy either. Up there held no more interest to them than the goings on in a UN-administered Antarctic research facility.

A brief wave of the pale blue UNSOC passport still in Marlowe's possession saw him across the bridge. It was the same passport which had been cut by the KGB on Brezhnev-Carter, so the chips and bugs inside it likely triggered an 'open' switch in the border guards' headsets anyway. In less than ten minutes, Marlowe was climbing the stairs of his apartment block, enjoying the wafting smell of bubbling beetroot soup from Frau Kachkayev's downstairs apartment. Marlowe unlocked his heavy door after nearly a day away from the place he'd vastly warmed to over the winter, subsidized heating bills notwithstanding. Bright summer light flooded the recently polished floorboards. A shaft of micro dust jumped up from the keys bowl as he threw his set in and hung up his coat on the hook.

An untrained man would have covered himself in steaming coffee at the shock of seeing that woman sitting patiently on his couch. But Marlowe's version of surprise was to give no reaction at all.

"Darla," he said, sipping the coffee just as he'd been planning to do. She sat like a guest of honor on his sofa, magazines disturbed on the coffee table. She'd kept on her gloves but loosened her coat. Marlowe estimated she'd been here for no more than half an hour, meaning she'd been alerted the moment he'd left Anders' apartment, meaning he was being followed and watched. Fair enough. He'd fair often suspected as much. "To what do I owe the pleasure?"

"Stop contacting me." She said it swiftly, like a fed-up ex-girlfriend. Marlowe shrugged my shoulders.

"Contacting you?" He said loud enough for all the listening devices to hear. Yet a faint buzz was coming from Darla's bag. She pulled out a small black device that looked like an old tape recorder.

"Enough with the *Genesis*, with the case files, with Dorvethan. All of it."

"You're being brave. Wouldn't it be easier just to have this chat at the KGB office?"

"No one but my department knows you exist. And I plan to keep it that way."

"Oh," Marlowe sat on the lone wooden chair on that side of the room. "You have a department now."

"Yes. Space security operations in the GRU."

"Ah, you've moved up in the world. Or at least Soviet military politics. I'm glad to have helped. And cheers to an operation well done." Marlowe lifted his cup in salute. Darla was not impressed.

"I was genuine, Marlowe."

"Oh, sure. As genuine as your hair color."

"If I wasn't, I wouldn't need this stolen equipment to come and talk to you now, would I?"

"I don't really know what it does."

"Blocks all digital interference so you can surf your gay porn websites in peace. And yes, I cracked the code to your pad."

Marlowe didn't react.

"I didn't even offer you coffee." Marlowe continued to sip his like he had no plans to actually offer her anything.

"No need. I'm not staying."

"Apart from telling me to stop contacting you."

"Yes. Stop. Stop with the emails you keep sending me, stop with the microfilm of these diaries. I delete everything you send, so stop with all of it. Not my jurisdiction, not my problem. If you want to stay here in East Berlin, that is. I have no problem with that. Better you're where I can see you. But whatever contact we did have was in a previous life, do you understand?" He shrugged in response.

"Pass on my best to our mutual friend."

"I won't, but I will leave this as a gift… and…" she pulled a file from her bag marked *classified* in Russian and handed it to Marlowe. Instantly he recognized the picture. And the Russian was coming easier to him these days. He read the single page file three times over before sitting back with a soft smile he couldn't contain. Whatever Darla's motive for coming to see him, she didn't need to provide this.

"Are you surprised?" She asked.

"That Donahue has been in the pay of S-Nine for all this time? Not really. More surprised he kept it secret. Half of the Pentagon puts it on their resumes."

"And the other half are double-dipping," she added, then stood up, tightening her jacket. "Don't be disheartened, Marlowe. It's one big game, and we're all playing it. We take Phobos, so they take Calypso. So we take over Armstrong, so they fund an insurgency in Vietnam. So what."

"So what except I lost," Marlowe said. She shrugged. "You didn't lose though, did you Darla? With your new job and your department. Tell me one thing though, one thing I've been wondering for months now."

She waved her hand to stop him.

"I promise you, we only knew of Dorvethan since after the *Pegasus* incident in 2016."

"What do you mean?"

"I mean no one in the highest echelons of the Soviet or American governments knew about the creature, or beast, or condition called Dorvethan before the *Pegasus* incident, I promise you that." Marlowe studied her face; tired, but not overly. Smooth and perky. She was pretty, Marlowe had to give her that, and she wasn't lying. She knew nothing about her own ignorance. She knew nothing of the stories he'd been sending her, either. She didn't know the truth of Dorvethan, even as it stared at her straight in the face. Even as his apartment was full of diaries, ones he'd diligently transcribed and tried to entice her to read.

Or was it all a fantasy? A strange little sci-fi detective novel written in the spare time of his grandfather, who'd seen it all. And made up some stories. Marlowe felt like the apartment's gravity expropriator had just been switched off.

Darla sighed. She was about to say something but went to the door instead.

"Piece of advice, Marlowe. Don't waste your time chasing ghosts. Even the ones who seem real."

Marlowe felt a tear threaten his cheek. The wave of Charlie-related sadness he'd tried so hard to let wash over him crashed against the rocks of his shore. And Sergei, and all the deaths that had been and would be. And the crumbs of reality he barely had left to cling to. What had that old man put him through? Marlowe shook his head at himself and nodded a knowing smile. It really was all a game, and he didn't know the first thing about playing it.

She waited. He opened his mouth, as if to speak, but he said nothing. She finished it off, though.

"Like I said, don't contact me anymore. I know everything I need to about this Dorvethan creature." Marlowe blinked, ingraining the reality that Darla Foster knew nothing of Dorvethan at all. The murderous alien probably still sucking human insides out in space and leaving their floppy bags of skin to float around the newly independent states of the solar system was not what they should be worried about. His grandfather had spelled it out so clearly and chosen consciously to ignore it. Doc Johnson's warning that Earth should be fortifying itself inwards, protecting the world and its people until a solution to the true meaning of Dorvethan could be found was sealed up in these diaries, in this East Berlin apartment. Unread by her. Unknown to the world. Perhaps death by alien was preferable to the unknowable horrors of the end of space-time. Perhaps this creature was the Messenger's own warning to seal Earth off before it was too late. Marlowe wiped away helpless tears.

The spray of sadness washed up against her, too. He wondered if Sergei was dead, but it didn't seem right to ask.

"Don't worry, Marlowe. We're tracking Dorvethan. We know

where the creature is and we've got it contained. I'm in the right place now in the hierarchy to keep an eye on things. We have all our resources ready if the creature ever tries something again. You… you did well. You did your job."

"Dorvethan comes to us all."

"What?"

"Nothing. Nothing at all, Darla. Did you know my grandparents saw a marriage counselor in the fifties?"

"Did I… what?"

"Oh yeah. The Director-General and the first Soviet ambassador to UNSOC had some trouble in paradise back in the day.

"They seemed to get over it."

"They did."

"I met your grandmother once, just before she passed away."

"I didn't think you were that old," Marlowe said, unkindly. She let it slide. She was about to leave, after all. "He knew she was passing intelligence to the Kremlin." Darla stopped, but only for a moment. The door beckoned, an ending. Two other spies might have parted ways with a last fuck. But they weren't spies, nor were they each other's type. "Just be mindful of what assumptions you are basing your decisions on, Darla."

"I'll bear that in mind, Marlowe."

"Good day, Darla."

"Good day, Vladimir."

The door shut, with Darla on the other side of it. Marlowe sat on his chair and stared out of the window, up into the sky, for a long time. Until the Earth had turned away from the sun, and the nighttime lights of the ships, the stations, the bases and asteroids beamed down onto East Berlin itself, the divided city, and Marlowe's face was lit by infinite stars.

CHAPTER 23: AN INVESTIGATION INTO AN ANOMALY BY THE PEOPLE'S COMMISSARIAT OF MARS

Novi Siberia District, Martian Republic
Population: 8,105
Five years later

"Giddy up!" Marlowe smacked the horse and it began to gallop through the tall Martian grasslands of Novi Siberia. It was called that way because the sea of crabtree fibers flowering atop the sword-size blades of grass made it look like a snowy wasteland. A hundred miles to the east on the shore of Isidis Bay was the fishing village of Fortschritt, where they farmed salmon three feet long and weaved these crabtree fibers into fishing nets for themselves as well as fish net stockings to send to the brothels in Western Xanthe. To reach the city, they had to sail by sea across the northern reaches of the Boreal Ocean, since the rebels now held all of Eastern Xanthe. But still, Marlene Marlowe (despite the divorce, she'd dropped the Novikov because of Charlie and paid Marlowe a handsome sum to use the name) wouldn't allow a single thing on Mars that was not grown, made nor mined right here. Fishnet stockings and all.

He'd come from Fortschritt several days before. He still called it by its proper German name, meaning progress, but there weren't many Germans left there anymore. The distant location and promise of manual labor, either wrestling giant salmon or giant leaves, meant the village was populated almost exclusively now by hand-boys. Former hand-boys, Marlowe should say. Vietnamese and Thai, mainly. They called it Fort Shit, and they didn't much like Marlowe hanging around there. A detective employed by the Martian Republic wasn't too popular in many places these days. Fortschritt wasn't much of a target for the Soviet-backed rebels, though. Their stronghold had always been the worker towns and factory barracks either side of the Chrysian Gulf and into the Meridian Plain. Some of the larger towns of Sabea as well, but they weren't as strong in the spread-out agricultural regions where Chinese and Indian workers proliferated, and particularly not somewhere as boring and uneducated in the ways of Galactic Marxism as Fortschritt. Marlene could be thankful for Soviet prejudices about which color of worker counted as a proletarian for their revolutionary purposes.

The horse kept neighing and sneezing as they cleared their own pathway through the tall grasses leaning heavily down with their crabtree fibers. The sun was an hour or so away from setting, and he hoped to make it to the spot crossed on the map under his saddle before freezing nightfall. The place was barely an outpost, unmarked. Marlene herself had helped him plot the coordinates with a compass. And she never liked to help him with anything. But the distress call had been urgent, then violently ended. Marlowe hadn't heard it himself as he'd been chasing a renegade Black Mooner through the brothel lane along the underside of the Wall that divided east and west Xanthe. But Suella Montclaire, the city commander, said she'd never heard something so blood curling as the screaming coming through the radio from some unplotted outpost on the wild edge of Novi Siberia.

It had been quickly established this wasn't a rebel attack. First of all, there was nothing of value in the thousands of square miles of crabtree fiber plains. Secondly, it was the rebels who'd been desperate for a ceasefire when Moscow's blank checkbook slammed shut last year. It was an open question whether or not there would still be a Soviet Union to even send them guns and bullets by the end of this year, and there certainly wouldn't be much of a rebellion without them. Finally, they'd confirmed through some back channels that the rebels had not been responsible, and in fact they had received their own distress call, from the exact same coordinates.

The sun was setting over the rusted hills in the western horizon. The edge of this world always felt that bit closer than on Earth, like he could almost reach out and touch the horizon line. The horse nuzzled the ground for some shoots to chomp on, and Marlowe un-hooked his hip flask and sucked down several gulps of good whis-key he'd helped himself too from Marlene's office. Even as Chancel-lor of the Martian Republic, her office was a corrugated metal shack with a mud-and-wattle floor, but at least her whiskey was good. She liked to pretend to be neutral, but she still took the American's guns and booze.

Marlowe's narrow eyes under the brim of his unironic cowboy hat as he scanned the horizon and sucked on his vape. The outpost should be somewhere along the edge of the crabtree fields, just be-fore the tree line of the great redwood forest. There was a shallow ravine that ran north-south from here all the way to the ocean. An old riverbed that hadn't yet been restarted, where the deep ground still gave out iron-rich rust-red soil.

A flock of bats scoured the darkening sky, haunting the plains and threatening to feast on those who dared stop for too long. A flut-ter lifted in his stomach as their echo-screaming pinged on a high register, but Marlowe waited for the horse to finish taking a dump. The bats flew away, but another layered thumping caught his atten-tion. The sound of galloping; hooves kicking up solid ground. Mar-lowe reached for his antique six-shooter, hardly a practical weapon, but a frontline detective wasn't a high priority for the precious few shipments of arms that came in. He didn't unholster, though. There was only a single horse with a single rider coming towards him, weaving through the man-high grass path he'd already forged. Hardly worth wasting a warning shot on.

He vaped as he watched the figure, sending slight puffs of fruit-flavored electronic smoke into the atmosphere. Marlene would have his balls if he did such a thing in Xanthe. There might not be much dick to be had out in the wilds of western Mars, but at least he could vape in peace.

"*Dobriy vecher,*" Marlowe called out *good evening* in Russian. The strange horse began to slow. The man on it was wrapped in thick wools from his mouth down, a rumpled Stetson on his brow. Clearly a lonely, solo traveler. Marlowe was dressed the same.

The man yelled back in Russian, but Marlowe couldn't quite hear. It was hard to know if the words were aggressive or not, it was Russian after all. He pulled his horse a little closer as the new arrival slowed to a cantor.

"Respublika or Narodnaya?" The man was saying. Marlowe pursed his lips at the forthright question. No chatting up, no hello. Just are you with the Republic or the *people*? It was times like these Marlowe missed UNSOC and that pale blue passport's diplomatic immunity. He went for a different tack as the man and his horse grew ever closer.

"I'm out here investigating an accident," Marlowe said in plain English, his voice carrying over a newly brutish sunset wind. Despite seventy odd years of terraforming, the air still had that otherworldly scent of magnesium and rust. "Over by the tree line," Marlowe pointed to the forest due north of where they were with the hand not holding the reins, just to show he wasn't actively armed. "There was a distress call, I came to see what happened, to see if I can help."

The man was barely ten feet away, his own horse now gnawing at whatever Marlowe's hadn't managed to chow down. He wondered how the horses were communicating, he knew they did. The stranger's one was an all-black beast, and a male. Marlowe felt his own tremble slightly.

"There was an accident," the stranger spoke in English, with an accent. Not asking, just repeating the facts under his wrapped-up face. His gloved hands reached up, also unarmed, and began to unravel the layers of knitted scarves wrapping up his sallow, windswept skin. Face pockmarked with exhaustion and stubble. Marlowe's pounding chest knew his identity before his mind caught up to the reality staring at him in the face.

"Sergei!" He didn't want to sound shocked, or upset, or happy or anxious, but all came out at once. The Russian stared back, smiling slightly, as if he'd followed Marlowe all this way and knew exactly what he was doing. "Man, you look like shit."

"I look five years older."

"That's being generous. Did you come from Fortschritt?"

"Yes, from there. They said you left two days ago."

"I did."

"Ah. I thought you would have been to the site and back again already."

"Well, it's nice to see you, too, Sergei. Can I ask what the fuck you're doing out here?"

"Same thing. Investigating the accident."

"For fun, or…"

"For the People's Commissariat of Mars."

"We're always on the wrong side to each other, aren't we?" Marlowe gave a disarming smile, Sergei returned it. It did make Marlowe feel slightly less apprehensive about the ability of the rebels if Sergei was the best they had to offer. Although they'd both been sent to the middle of nowhere to investigate something nobody knew anything about, so perhaps it didn't say much about either of them.

"Shall we?" Marlowe said, getting the horse moving northward.

"It is this way." Sergei was pointing out to the west, closer to the hills. Marlowe found himself biting his tongue.

"Fine, you lead the way."

Surprisingly, they had quite a bit to talk about. The years of absence had deadened whatever anger they both might have had for each other. Marlowe for feeling set up and then betrayed, Sergei for… well, Marlowe couldn't imagine what his problem would be, but they let it be anyway. Marlowe shared his whiskey, and Sergei shared the latest from the supposedly crumbling Communist Bloc. According to his version of events, the riots from Budapest to Helsinki were nothing but the fault of agitators and crisis actors. An excuse for the West to leave Russia out of the *Genesis II* mission, so no Russians would be on the next shot to Alpha Centauri.

"They just don't want Russians," Sergei said the conspiracy out loud. "And blame us for what Charlie Novikov did."

"Yeah," Marlowe agreed, "that is unfair."

"We know it's not true."

Marlowe chewed on his lip as the heavy leaves whacked against their thighs and the horses' asses in the dark. There was a lot he would like to say to that. Where was that certainty five years ago, when Marlowe had lost everything for telling the truth. Where was the support from him, or his boss? Darla had completely gone off the grid, Marlowe had never seen her since that one afternoon in his apartment in East Berlin. The emails he tried a few more times to send Martin's diaries bounced back. She had followed through her promise and cut off communications and wanted no part in the knowledge that the universe would one day collapse in on itself, and all life would cease to exist. That Dorvethan would come to them all.

"Yeah," Marlowe finally said, slowly and shrugging. "What you gonna do?" He channeled his best Donahue for that one.

They rode in silence through the Martian night, sharing whiskey under the bright light of satellites and space stations, the republics and kingdoms and socialist collectives of the solar system. As the tall grasses subsided, they turned on the torches mounted on the horses' heads. The ground was open until the edge of the forest further on, bumpy with rocks and moss from the long dead riverbed.

"There's the outpost," Sergei said as they turned toward a bend of the tree line. A watchtower in the distance had a spotlight hanging loosely from it. A few huts were scattered around. A waystation of no more than two dozen loggers most likely, ever more encroaching on the tree line.

"Are they all asleep?" Marlowe said without thinking as they approached the quiet camp. There were no fires to fight off the cold. No smoke. The searchlight wasn't even following their approach. "What did your distress call say?"

"Not much. Some kind of trouble. They were not clear."

Marlowe nodded, but listened to the sick feeling swirling in the pit of his stomach. One didn't spend their life as a detective and not learn to trust gut feeling.

"They're all gone," Marlowe eventually said, and with some certainty. Then added: "they must've fled."

Sergei said nothing as they rode into the small camp. The horses were getting scared, or were scaring each other, because they kept neighing loudly every time they caught sight of the other one.

"C'mon, girl," Marlowe said. His voice echoed in the darkness between the watchtower and the wooden huts where no one seemed to live. "There's footprints over here." They led to the forest line. Sergei trotted over, pointing a handheld torch to the ground.

"These people tried for a quick escape."

"So they did," Marlowe agreed. The prints were rushed, dragging the ground in some places, or with wide strides between others. Some had run, some had scurried. Some had fallen and crawled. "If they ran into the forest they'll be long gone." Marlowe stared into the wall of trees a skyscraper high, wondering if it was even possible to go through there on a horse. Suddenly there was a cold wind on his back. "Sergei?"

He caught sight of Sergei's horse just beyond a hut, but with no Sergei on it. The animal was standing, not moving, not so much as chewing the ground. It was like he was surrounded by the sorts of things only beasts can see. "C'mon, girl," Marlowe said to his own horse. With a bit of digging his heels into her side, she did eventually turn and walk, very reluctantly, towards her cousin. Marlowe dismounted.

"Sergei?"

There was a light coming through one of the thatched huts. Broken and slanted, breaking the silence with the shivering of horses in the stillness and cold of the Martian outlands. They used to compare the sensation to that of the first pilgrims, setting up at Roanoke. So far from civilization they might as well be stranded. Sleeping on a new land, under new stars, alone on an empty continent. Of course, that wasn't true then. On Earth there were indigenous civilizations, and people. Hundreds of millions. Mars was a different kind of loneliness. Normally, space was cramped. Small stations, squished living quarters on an asteroid or moon base. But Mars was something else. A couple of hundred thousand souls running around what was essentially an empty, unspoiled Earth. One hoped that one was alone. One hoped that one was the first to walk these parts. The only one.

"Sergei?" He asked again, approaching the hut torch first, ready to knock back the woven grass curtain. A branch snapped behind him. He spun around, torch flying over the crabtree grass blowing in the distant wind. "Where are you?"

"Over here," came the muted reply, not from the nearest hut, but another one. Marlowe kicked up soft, loose ground as he turned. The soil out here was not quite fertilized. Too far from the coast for much rain. They needed to flood this riverbed. Perhaps the crabtree grass field should be at the bottom of an inland lake. Marlowe saw the light poking through the thatch. He trudged around to the entrance, but the horses neighed with agitation at being left alone.

"Sergei, what are you doing…" Marlowe's words failed him as soon as he peeled back the grass curtain of this hut. He swallowed, or tried to, but his throat had no more moisture. Sergei was standing amongst it all, torch pointed downwards, then left and right and three hundred and sixty degrees all around. All around. "Is it the same over there?" Marlowe's voice was already hoarse. He couldn't swallow. He could barely breathe in here. Nor did he need to wait for an answer. He knew it to be true.

Sergei began to retch among the rotting corpses. Dozens of them, covering the ground like a mulch. No, not corpses. Legs only. Bloody stumps of feet and thighs, the dark skin of Vietnamese and Indians, bottom halves scattered like a graveyard turned upside down.

And, as if to cement the reality of what they were seeing, hanging up in the corner, over a slatted beam, was a bag of skin. Loose, with nothing inside it. Marlowe shone his torch, his feet knocking through stumps of thighs and loose kneecaps. Sergei was being openly sick now. Unlike in space, these bodies were decomposing. But Marlowe had to see. He had to see what was under the bag of skin. The scratchings, the markings.

"It..." Sergei tried to say, still coughing up vomit. "It was done by Dorvethan?"

Marlowe slid away the bag that was once a body, the scratched symbols underneath in an alien language immediately familiar to him. They were burned in his brain. "It says Dorvethan, yeah, but that's not what did all this... that's not what that word means."

"W-what?" Sergei threw up again. "So what did all this?"

He felt the symbols carved into the wood with his own fingers, following the marks, the indents and grooves of the warning. A warning Marlowe was starting to sense was only meant for him. All of this, to get to him. The warning of the end of galaxies. The end of time. What was hundreds of lives for billions upon billions. Or not. Perhaps the demon had no other agenda than its own demonic existence. Everything else was lies and falsehoods. The beast had only to feast, it would eat whomever, whatever. What was true. What was fake. What was conspiracy. What, in actual fact, was Dorvethan?

Marlowe had splinters in his fingers from tracing the scorched black letters.

"Marlowe?" Sergei wanted to leave the hut of death. "What did all this?"

"Something much worse," he said, with barely a whisper. Something else had caught his attention on the ground. Sticks... or bones. He shone the torch down to where bloodied clothes covered up something. A message left by whatever had done this. Holding his breath and biting his tongue to keep from vomiting himself, he carefully lifted the clothes with the toe of his boot. Before he could react, his eyes read the letters. The single word spelled out in stick and bone like runes on a mountain side. Spelled perfectly.

M A R L O W E

Sergei was back outside and throwing up. Bats screamed into the night as the stench of rotting flesh scattered around the hut burned in his nostrils. Here, Marlowe stood alone in the Martian outlands, under a threatening night sky of terrifying stars where infinite death hid, watching only him.

EPILOGUE: AN AUDIENCE WITH HER MAJESTY, QUEEN OF THE MAELSTROM

"I'm looking for someone," Darla Foster said to the serving woman. She returned an unimpressed look in her tight and colorful head wrap. Darla was drawn to her bare arms jiggling as the woman spit-polished a magnetic goblet, and Darla made her eyes obvious as she watched the woman work. The Lighthouse Bar on Trenchfall was filling up fast with knuckle-dragging meathead mine workers once exiled to The Maelstrom, who now made their home among the violent libertarian frontier of the asteroid belt. Darla held the package tightly under her arm, letting its awkward shape push her body outwards, towards the serving wench staring at her dead in the eye as her entire body wiggled from the neck down.

Darla winked, the woman cracked a smile.

"You got money?"

"Of course." Darla's heart fluttered a little, both from the woman she wanted nothing more than to be suffocated by, and the open question of just how far her last remaining notes would take her. The wench shook her head, the twisting moves snaking down her bosom. She glanced back to a sign and smacked it with pudgy fingers. *No rubles* it said in several languages.

"How's Lunan lira?" Darla pulled out some crumpled plastic notes from inside her low-cut top, as slowly as she could. She just hoped not to have to count them out. Fortunately, the wench enjoyed the move, and the clear suggestion of more to come.

"On the house, love."

Darla put away her last remaining lira and watched the far end of the bar where the stage was set and ready for the performance. Rowdy miners pushed forward, their skin sparkling with star dust.

She heard more Russian than ever before. She thought she saw an ex-colleague suspiciously sharing a vape in a dark corner at the far side, his face gaunt as they all became from too long working in the asteroid belt. This was the direct result of chaos at home. The USSR limped on, the power structures in Russia lingered because there was nothing left for it to collapse onto, and few left to challenge it. Everyone with an ounce of sense wanted out. They couldn't go West, but they could go up. And up they had come.

Darla drank bad beer quietly, her back against the bar as the wench dealt with the rowdy crowd. She held tight the bag under her arm, silk covering a padded envelope wrapped in duct tape to disguise its true value. Darla kept a wide stance, doing her best to not be knocked and jostled. The men, seemingly unused to a woman in their lair, kept a respectful distance. Or perhaps they could tell from her unsparkling skin and functional coat she was KGB.

"Looking for someone?" A man wearing damp, heavy coats and frayed, thinning dreadlocks slid patchy elbows onto the bar, wet from the spilled drinks. Darla glanced him up and down, he wasn't looking directly at her, but suspiciously away, nervously watching the men watching the stage. He had a metallic peg leg angled too close to her feet for comfort.

"That depends," Darla said, keeping her voice low but flirty. "Is there anyone interesting I should know?"

"That depends… How much cash you got?"

Darla shifted the package away from the stranger. She didn't know quite what to expect from the Queen of The Maelstrom's pimp, but someone with sticky fingers and layers to hide liberated goods in did fit the bill.

"What I have is far better than cash."

"Than rubles? That's for sure." The man grinned a smile of yellow teeth and gnawed stumps. "And unless you got a dick in that handbag of yours, I don't know what you want to be spendin' your cash on my boy for."

The lights lowered in the bar and the crowd *oohed* in anticipation. A silence sloshed over the audience as they burped and shoved forward, wave by wave. Darla made no move, and the man noticed. A spotlight shone onto the stage, exciting the burly, sweat-stained miners and their ale cups, and soon they were the only two figures left at the bar-end. On stage, two long, bare legs wearing a pair of shimmering glass shoes with eight-inch heels began to dance sensuously on the stage, their owner still obscured by the half-darkness.

"I'd like to have an audience with Her Majesty," Darla said. She couldn't hear the man's reaction because just then, the crowd erupted in a chomping, furious delight. Dazzled by the spotlight flipping around the oily muscles and dirty white vests, the workers became enraged by the figure emerging fully on the stage. Their skin was the color of a sunset, and most was visible under the shimmering gown cut to the navel, then from hip bone to the floor. They dazzled with inviting softness as a golden wig flipped across their bare back.

"Hello, boys. Did you miss me?"

Darla received a nose full of damp, dreadlocked beard that stank like an ashtray. The man was right in her face, leaning in not to whisper but to shout over the noise right in her ear.

"That's the queen!" He yelled. "You wanna meet him?"

"Absolutely," Darla replied, shouting loudly over the pounding techno beat the supposed Queen of The Maelstrom was now dancing around the pole to. "I'm about to make you both very rich," she said. "Why don't you buy me a drink?"

The man grinned wide enough to reveal a couple of gold teeth back there, presumably the ones not knocked out in a fight or pawned for rocket fuel.

"Potato Vodka?"

"Is there any other kind?"

The man grinned. Darla knew the answer in a place like this. 'Potato,' i.e. *real* vodka was more than premium. She nodded vigorously as their *queen* started to strip for the boisterous miners.

"*Da. Spasibo.*"

Franx sat on the edge of the booth, wrapped in silks so rich they could have been a bedspread in the Czar's Winter Palace. The Queen of The Maelstrom sipped on a thick, blood-red drink served in a tall martini glass. Darla wasn't so sure it *wasn't* human blood, given the residue it left on the glass. Franx's dreadlocked enforcer Abraxes stood as an honor guard right beside, never taking off a single layer of the heavy, fousty clothes that made him look like one of the newly homeless living in the Moscow subway.

"Is it they, them?" Darla ventured, her throat now dry. One drink at the bar was the limit of Abraxes' hospitality, and she was fully prepared to be billed for that after. "He? She?" Franx raised a manicured eyebrow as varnished fingernails rimmed the sharp edge of the glass. "I would like to be respectful."

"Show me the gift you brought, and you can call me whatever the fuck you like, darlin'." Franx apparated a real cigarette from the bosom of his wrap and placed it between full lips stained red from the drink. Abraxes leaned down, ignited the cigarette with a metal lighter and passed an unheard word to Franx which made him grin, but unkindly so.

The package Darla had liberated from the depths of a Moscow bunker sat between them on the table. She stared at it more than Franx, as enchanting as this Maelstrom drag act was. The brown paper tied with string and tape stared back. The bloodshed, the bullet that had grazed her knee, the three good men who'd perished so she could bring this one offering to one person. She was the Humbert Humbert attempting to pry away the precious Lolita, who had one hand wrapped around a nasty cocktail while precious lips sucked on a Marlboro.

"Can I open my present now?"

The petulant voice broke Darla's concentration. She looked up at him, the uncaring, pinched face. The body she'd heard had never been kissed by natural sunlight, raised like a cockroach behind dumpsters and in drainpipes. The unassuming yet undisputed leader of half the asteroid belt; their collective GDP about to outpace that of the Soviet Union, or what was left of it. Franx had no need for bodyguards. For they were deep on Trenchfall, and Trenchfall was but his winter palace.

"I represent a consortium," Darla began, her voice more broken than she'd expected. Franx barely looked interested. Abraxes less so. "A consortium of true socialists. Generals, politburo members, former UNSOC officials. Those of us who still believe better worlds are possible. The last Galactic Marxists, you might say."

Franx rolled his eyes.

"Meaning there's no cash in that package, *you might say.*"

"Please, let me finish," she said, exasperated. It piqued Abraxes' interest. Franx flicked ash on the floor and raised an annoyed eyebrow.

"So what, you want to Make Russia Great Again, or something of the sort?

"Something of the sort."

"Hmm." Franx took a last drag from the finished cigarette and dropped it on the ground. Abraxes immediately crushed it with his boot. "This sounds like a *you* problem, Darla Foster." He made a move to get up.

"For now, yes. For now it is my problem. Soon it will be yours, Your Majesty."

Franx clasped the drink with both hands instead, as if he'd never intended to do anything more than recross his legs.

"The impending collapse of the Soviet Union? Not so much, We welcome immigration to The Maelstrom. As you might have gathered, our natural birth rate is somewhat lacking. We try, of course, but somehow I still remain childless." Franx rubbed his thin stomach. Abraxes snickered.

"The universe exists in a balance," Darla said, echoing words she'd spoken again and again; from bunkers to board rooms. "Night and day, sea and land, man and…"

"Indeed."

"What I'm trying to say, is that what happens when that balance is upset? When UNSOC all but collapsed in the months after Open Space, the sturdy trifecta lost a precious leg. But we still had two superpowers left, to keep the other in check. To stop our worst excesses bleeding out and staining the Earth."

"I don't live on Earth. In fact, I've never been. Never cared to visit."

"When Russia falls, Franx, America will come for you." He stared back with hate in his eyes. Disgust, contempt, but something else, too. Acknowledgement. Understanding. "Look what the Americans are doing now, supplying weapons to the Martian Republic so Marlene Marlowe can crush her own people who dare to ask for a better wage and a day off. Propping up those criminal gangs who operate from the dark side of Luna just to stick it to the workers and scientist's collective governing Armstrong. You're a fool if you don't think the CIA have agents stationed all across this asteroid archipelago, just waiting for the time to strike. And what's more, you're sitting on the gold. The silver. The neodymium, the terbium, the europium, the galinium. They're coming for you, Franx. For you and your queendom."

The silence between them filled with smoke from another cigarette Franx had lit somewhere in the endless stretch of time she had been speaking. Summing up the weight of an unseen future. Not unseen, undiscovered. But the map pointed one way. One way that would make her life, and the lives of the millions, billions of socialists throughout history worthless.

"You came from nothing, Franx." The desperation was evident in the echo of every word, but she didn't care. This was their last hope. "So did I. So did we all. We were the workers and soldiers. We fought the bourgeoisie and the capitalist slave owners and the Czar and the Nazis, and we built something. One side of one world where people thought about something more than money, Franx. Where every person could know they would never go hungry, never go unsheltered, never uncared for, never be useless."

"How'd that go for you?"

"How's the alternative going for the rest of us?" She shot back. Her last shot. Franx threw down the end of the cigarette. Abraxes crushed it underboot once again. "There's not a single Russian on the new *Genesis* crew, did you know that?"

"Again, that seems like a *you*—"

"They think they've won!" The table shook as her fists smacked it. Spit flew from the violent corners of her mouth. Franx was taken aback, Abraxes reached for his weapon. "They think they've won the space race." She sat back down, her heart still aflame. "They think they've defeated UNSOC, think they've won the Cold War and now won space, too. They think everywhere from Luna to Trenchfall to Alpha-fucking-Centauri belongs to them. President Landers will send off that colonizing ship with a big fat American flag they'll plan in the soil of another solar system and claim it for themselves. And you, Franx, you're nothing but their backyard. They did it to the indigenous populations, to the Pacific islanders, to the South Americas. If it wasn't for Roswell and D-Day, when would they have stopped?"

"Never." It was Abraxes who spoke. Both Franx and Darla stared at the man who so far had been strong and silent. "They would never have stopped. There is nothing more terrifying in this universe than the flesh-eating virus of slave-capitalism."

Darla felt a pang of pride that her beliefs were still worth something. She nodded with intent, glaring at Franx to acknowledge the counsel of his closest advisor. Like any good queen though, Franx gave utterly nothing away. He sipped his drink and pointed to the package.

"Gimme."

Abraxes may have been on her side for a moment, but now he was back to Franx. Leaning on his metal peg leg, he swept the package toward Franx who tore it open with gusto. Darla quietly held her breath. Impressive, it was. But enough?

"Wow! Is this...?"

"Yes," Darla proudly said. Franx handled the pearl and diamond diadem with the utmost care. "A favorite of Alexandra Feodorovna, the last empress of Russia. And now it belongs to you. From one dynasty to the next."

"You're pawning off Romanov treasures to ferment a socialist revolution?" Franx asked with a wry smile.

"Do you know of a better way to pay for such a thing?" She returned the look. Franx slid the tiara into place on his head. Abraxes held up a silver cigarette holder as a mirror.

"Touché, madame."

He looked as proud as could be in the crown. Many of the Consortium had been skeptical of Darla's plan. They did not believe any ally worth having could be won over by trinkets stored away in Kremlin archives.

"I have a whole vault in Moscow of treasures," she said, gazing as if admiring the crown. In honesty, it suited a figure such as Franx. "The greatest rulers should have treasures to match. Yes, your men could make you these jewels, but where's the history? Where's the specialness? No, you're building a great nation, Franx, and every nation needs a storied history on which to build their golden age."

"Abraxes, if you wouldn't mind bringing my new ally a glass?"

He hobbled across the room to a cabinet melded together with scraps of iron and driftwood. The door screamed open, and he brought over three champagne flutes in one hand, and a dusty bottle in the other. Franx popped the cork without a second thought, and poured for each of them until the glasses were overflowing. Not until both he and Abraxes had one in hand did Darla reach over to take her own, still with some reluctance. But with the Pearl Drop Tiara firmly on the head of Franx, such fears were fading fast.

"First things first," Franx said, "we'll stop this second *Genesis*." Darla stifled a grin of getting exactly what she had wanted. "Abraxes, find out how they blew up the first one. Let's see if they're available again." Franx raised his glass, and Darla followed. "To the final victory of Galactic socialism." They reached across the table and clinked champagne glasses. Abraxes had already drunk his and was pouring another. "Workers of the solar system, it's high time for us to unite!"

"I'll drink to that."

The End.

www.ingramcontent.com/pod-product-compliance
Lightning Source LLC
Chambersburg PA
CBHW030648020726
47493CB00006B/1931